Calculus of Death

Joel Spring

ISBN: 0692790047

ISBN 13: 9780692790045

Library of Congress Control Number: 2016959906

Phoenix Books, Mt. Vernon, NEW YORK

Chapter One

It's 2002 and I'm in my new college office, staring at a 1946 photo of me outside Kenny's, the foster home where I was raped. It is in a shoe box of photos in one of the cartons I'm unpacking. I wonder what was going through my six-year-old mind. Outside, students play Frisbee on the campus mall. Next to the office window is a table covered with academic awards.

In the photo, my hands are shoved into pockets of suspender-supported checkered pants. I stand next to Grandma. She's wearing a straw hat with a black bow sticking up on one side and an unflattering flower-print dress. One of her many husbands—I don't remember all of them—holds up a limp hand as if waving at the camera. He's in a light-colored suit and is making an effort to smile. Smirking, Grandma stands with clenched fists. My hair is neatly combed. I'm looking down at the ground. Other photos show wisps of rumpled brown hair sticking out from the top and sides of my head.

In another photo, I'm resting in Grandma's lap as she sits on a swing and grasps the ropes hanging from an oak tree outside the front door of Kenny's adobe house. The brown-clay building is nestled in a grove of oak trees down a dirt road from the two-lane highway running from San Diego to Alpine, California. In those days, it would take my mother an hour or two to make the trip in her clunky green Hudson, up winding roads filled with lumber trucks. Now it takes thirty-six minutes traveling twenty-nine miles on Interstate 8. Another photo shows me trying to smile while I am posed on the front seat, clasping the steering wheel of a topless truck. The swing and Kenny's house are in the background.

For my mother, World War II was party time, free from my father, Billy Durant. I'm Billy Durant Jr. There is a wartime photo showing Toots—we called our mother Toots—drunk and riding in a large laundry cart through the Crown Room of San Diego's Del Coronado Hotel. Her head is sticking up with her legs and arms draped over the side. She is being pushed by rowdy-looking naval officers, who, I assume given the photo's 1944 date, were in training to kill the Japanese.

There is a partial view of the Crown room's thirty-three-foot-high ceiling paneled in Oregon sugar pine and a chandelier designed by *Wizard of Oz* author L. Frank Baum. He wrote the *Wizard of Oz* there during a vacation. My mother and the fighter pilots appeared to want the wizard's magic as protection from death and, in my mother's case, from the boredom of the typing pool at the US Naval Supply Depot.

My father, after running away from his Choctaw home in Oklahoma, joined the navy medical corps and spent the wartime patching together sailors in ship sick bays. Later, he told me about an unexploded bomb missing him in the USS *Saratoga*'s operating room during the 1941 Wake Island battle. My mother always referred to him as "that old son of a bitch" and after the divorce cut his head out of all family photos. Later, I found out that he was descended from and named after Choctaw Indian chief Billy Durant.

When Dad went to sea, Toots put me in day care while my brother Jimmy attended school. On party nights, she turned babysitting me over to him. After the 1944 divorce, while my father prepared for the invasion of Okinawa, she decided to be free of childcare and dumped us in a foster home in Alpine with ten other boys. Toots found office work and got child-support payments from the navy. The final papers required the navy to deduct payments from Dad's check and send them directly to Toots; there would be no "deadbeat" ex-husband. I heard Toots telling a friend that foster homes cost less than Dad's child support.

We called our first foster home the "Old Lady's." It was there that I started referring to my brother as Sonny. He was eleven and I was four when Toots delivered us to the Old Lady's and quickly returned to San Diego.

I remember sitting at a long table with the other boys while slices of white Wonder Bread flew through the air. You raised your hand when you wanted a slice, and the Old Lady sent it spinning to you. The prints in the butter, Sonny told me, were from rats in the cooler. Every night a sticky, sweet, cold rice pudding was served as dessert.

When we complained, Toots moved us a quarter mile up the dirt road toward the main highway to Marge Kenny's adobe house, my second foster home.

Marge's father, Carl Kenny, escaped World War I by disappearing with his wife and adolescent daughter into the forest near Alpine. Carl mixed adobe clay with straw and water and poured the mixture into brick molds. He built a substantial one-room cabin with the dried bricks using clay mortar to seal joints.

Over the years, Carl, with help from Marge's future husband, Frank, added new rooms. When I moved in, there were three bedrooms, a combination living and dining room, and a small wood-burning kitchen. Marge added a brick bathroom during World War II and paid for a toilet to be installed with a septic tank. We used an outdoor shower with a wooden water tank suspended by a rope from an oak tree. The showers were cold and brief.

In the early thirties, Marge's father was bitten by rattlesnakes after slipping and falling down a hill into their nest.

It was whispered that Marge's husband, Frank, was killed in a 1935 gun battle after he slept with a neighbor's wife. Marge was left with two teenage children. She claimed that the killing resulted from a property-line dispute and not her husband's infidelity.

In 1944, I was the youngest of the boys, ranging from four to thirteen, at the Old Lady's. We were all crowded into a wooden bunk room, where in the evenings naked boys grabbed and fondled each other. Later, at another foster home, I introduced neighborhood boys to this play. Their parents quickly learned of it, and I was ordered to stay away from them.

Sonny carried his anger about his parental abandonment into Alpine's pristine woods by hunting, trapping, and stuffing animals. I remember sitting next to him as he cleaned a trapped skunk, nicking its scent bag and sending its spray into the air.

He started collecting old taxidermy magazines and convinced Toots to buy him a four-ten shotgun, which he could easily hold at age eleven. This launched Sonny on a life of gun collecting. After retirement, he hung on the wall above his favorite chair a framed lifetime-membership certificate from the National Rifle Association. Toots packed a small twenty-two pistol in her purse and would occasionally unload it so that I could play at shooting trees and animals.

After moving to Kenny's, I would wander along a clear stream at the bottom of the dirt road below the Old Lady's. I spent time looking at tadpoles and small fish among the rocks and watching coiled rattlesnakes basking in afternoon sunshine. California wild roses bloomed near the stream, and groves of manzanitas, oaks, and pines could be seen as I walked along the water's narrow path through changing terrains.

I'd strip and play in the pools of crystalline water. The air was crisp and clean. This was the reason why Benjamin Arnold had founded Alpine in 1887 to improve his asthma. The US government recognized the air's healthy quality, and Alpine's slogan became "The cleanest air in the USA by government report." Now Alpine's Chamber of Commerce boasts that its Viejas Casino and Factory Outlet employs thousands of workers. The Golden Acorn Casino is only a short distance east along the freeway.

The Alpine school bus stopped on the main highway at the top of the dirt road leading from Kenny's. I remember little of these trips to Alpine or my kindergarten and first grade. Abandonment and rape clouded my world.

I can't remember any school friends. I have one memory of taking a Halloween pumpkin with a cutout face to kindergarten. Older bullies pulverized it in the playground.

Living with us was Kenny's nail-biting twenty-two-year-old daughter, Alice. She lived a reclusive life in her bedroom. Occasionally she changed from soft, cotton nightgowns into jeans and plaid shirts and would go to the swing and spend hours whistling and rocking back and forth.

My brother and I slept in another bedroom. Marge Kenny occupied the third. Marge's son, Alex, who had recently returned from the army and

North Africa with a stomach condition causing frequent and bloody bowel movements, slept on the living-room couch close to the bathroom.

At night, I often felt a warm dampness spread over my pajamas. I would run to Marge's bedroom, where she would order me to strip off my urine-soaked pajamas, would dry me, and would have me climb naked into bed. I would cuddle my body against her as she lifted her nightgown so that our bodies touched.

One night I awakened. Feeling the pressure of a full bladder and fearing another bed-wetting accident, I hurried to the bathroom. The door was open. Alex was sitting on the toilet, grunting, and farting. He told me to come closer.

As he reached out to touch me, I couldn't control my bladder. He helped me pull down my wet pajama pants and stroked me. I still remember the pain as he forcefully bent me over the toilet.

Chapter Two

"Hallelujah, I saw Christ in the bus window comin' here!" From a back pew, a voice rang out from a sad sack of a bald man who looked fifty, dressed in baggy khaki pants and plaid shirt, and waved his arms in the air.

"Jesus, hear his voice! We can all meet him. I feel Christ's love moving through my veins," testified a blond-haired, overweight woman in the first pew; she sported a large, black hat with a red rose and wore a loose, plain, black dress. "When I see Jesus, I can see my dead dad in the background waiting for me in the promised land."

I was squeezed into the middle of the third pew between Sonny and Helen Anderson, my fourth and last foster mother. Next to Helen sat her son, Tim, and her bus-driver husband, Eddy, along with two other foster boys, Phil and Mark.

I had heard Toots and Marge Kenny fighting over money before I was moved to the Finches', my third foster home. Sonny was sent to a small farm. Both foster homes were in El Cajon, then a semirural San Diego suburb. It was the first time we were apart.

"At least I'll not have to take that mountain road; El Cajon is closer," was my mother's comment as she bundled us into the Hudson with our clothing bags. "She wants too much, and her kids are crazy—Alice swinging all the time babbling to herself—and I don't trust Alex. He creeps around. Saw him going through our car. The war messed him up. Good riddance to Alpine. Bunch of white trash!"

I lasted only a month with my third foster parents, Casper and Judy Finch, before Toots moved me to the Andersons' house. At the Finches', neighborhood parents complained about me molesting their kids.

The Finches would lock me in the house and tell me not to leave. One time, trying to escape through a window, I knocked over a tank of expensive tropical fish. I remember running around with tears streaming down my face in a useless effort to save the fish that were flopping around and leaving a trail of water, excrement, and aquatic plant life on the Finches' expensive oriental carpet.

After the Finches, I was labeled a "problem child," which sent my mother searching for foster homes that could handle me. This led to the doorstep of Helen Anderson, who was featured in local newspapers and *Look* magazine for working magic with kids like me.

Toots cut a deal for the two of us. Sonny was acting out on the farm. He shot a couple chickens with his four-ten shotgun. They took away his gun. He ransacked his bedroom and scribbled hate messages on the wall.

The Anderson's three-bedroom ranch house was on a grassy knoll and looked down on a paved road. In back was a terraced yard with one section devoted to vegetables and a small area for play.

A dirt road ran alongside the yard and led to the Four Square Tabernacle and Horace Mann Elementary School. Every Sunday we would troop down to the Tabernacle with their son, Tim, hurrying ahead.

When Tim graduated from high school, he was given a special award for having never missed a day of school. I remember him sick and vomiting but insisting on going to school. After high school, he became an evangelical minister and saved souls throughout California.

Helen's food rules were strict as she was managing four foster children and one son. The refrigerator was off-limits to kids. We could have syrup or margarine on our hot cakes but not both. Only four glasses of milk a day. No extra helpings. I never felt hunger, but I did feel deprived by not being allowed to open the refrigerator at any time for a quick snack or drink.

At fourteen, Sonny got a newspaper route that sent him bicycling down dirt roads and stopping at the local grocery store to use his earnings for junk food. He started picking on me, and reports of fights came from his junior high.

Sometimes in the bedroom we shared with the other foster boys, Sonny would lean down from his bunk and pinch me for no reason. He'd send me into a crying jag at the dining table by belching into his hand and holding it over my glass of milk. He took out his anger by torturing me.

I can't remember learning anything Horace Mann Elementary School except to hate school. I was traumatized when a teacher leaped up from his desk, grabbed my hand, and twisted my pencil out of it. He placed my fingers around the pencil into what was considered a proper position for writing. It hurt, and I continued writing with the same poor penmanship.

Things were stable at Helen's. Toots and she became fast friends. In later years, when Helen's husband, Eddy, died of cancer and I was at college, Toots and Helen would play in Las Vegas.

Toots transformed Helen from a model foster parent to a gambling fanatic and what people of the time might call a loose woman. Toots showed that evil could triumph over good.

It was the Tabernacle I loved; it was filled with shouts of joy and redemption. Displayed on the wall behind the lectern were the words "Jesus Christ the same, yesterday and today and forever." On a sidewall was a painting of Aimee Semple McPherson, founder of the Four Square Church and evangelical media celebrity up to her death in 1944. She pioneered the use of radio evangelism to call people to God.

"I came to the sweet spirit of Jesus," Helen told Sonny and me on our way to our first tabernacle service, "hearing Aimee on the radio. I listened to every broadcast in the thirties. I fell on my knees in front of the radio every time she said, 'Lift up your heads, ye people; lift up your faces, too; open your mouths to sing his praise; and the rain will fall on you.'"

In later years, I read that Charlie Chaplin told Aimee, "Whether you like it or not, you're an actress."

Below McPherson's painting in the Tabernacle was her evangelical exhortation:

> And my task, as I see it, is to interest you folks to help me
> to help them to join the line right around the whole world!
> Not only to help the heathen abroad but to help the hea-
> then in Los Angeles.

It was magical—the rapture, the joy, and testimonies of redemption and finding signs of Jesus in every nook and cranny of life. To parishioners, Jesus appeared in mirrors, windows, coffee cups, supermarket displays, cracks in sidewalks, and buildings and dreams. One parishioner claimed to have seen Jesus when he ended a week of constipation.

I read over and over again another McPherson quote on the church's wall: "O Hope! Dazzling, radiant hope! What a change thou bringest to the hopeless, brightening the darkened paths and cheering the lonely way."

I hoped that Jesus would fill my soul and make me forget. One weekend Toots decided to treat us to a trip to Knott's Berry Farm. We stayed overnight in a run-down Anaheim motel. I don't remember the rides and games. I do remember the chapel by the lake with its glow-in-the-dark Jesus. In the light, it was a simple portrait. In the dark, Jesus glowed, and his eyes opened.

I still have the card Toots bought me, but Jesus no longer glows. The card has folding cardboard doors on the front. Opening it in the dark reveals a bright-eyed, glow-in-the-dark Jesus. I placed the card next to my bed and opened the doors every night in the hope that Jesus would handle my pain.

In the end, the evangelical messages had more effect on Sonny and Helen's son, Tim. Since Jesus never answered my prayers, I gave him up.

Sonny was born again in his twenties and in retirement attended the Calvary Church, where his son led a Christian band. The Calvary Church was a 1965 breakaway from the Four Square churches. By the mid-1960s, it focused on the Jesus movement and served hippies and surfers with a literal interpretation of the Bible and a Calvinist belief in predestination.

Guns and Christ became my brother's belief.

I was ten when Toots decided to move us to LA. As we rode to LA, Sonny whispered to me that Toots had a new boyfriend living there.

We moved into a small, white house in Culver City, near one of America's earliest automobile racetracks, the Culver City Speedway, which opened in 1920. The speedway attracted teenage car addicts like seventeen-year-old Sonny. He and other "hoody" friends met at the track;

they wore their Levi's jeans low with cigarette packs rolled up to their shoulders in the short sleeves of white T-shirts.

Sonny enrolled in Venice High School with its famous 1922 statue of *Spiritual* modeled after actress Myrna Loy. Toots stuck me in the fifth grade of some elementary school that I don't remember except that I hated it.

We settled down in our little, white house with Sonny and me sharing a bedroom. Toots's new boyfriend, Dave, would visit and even took me to see—the occasion is clear in my memory—the minor-league Los Angeles Angels play baseball against the San Diego Padres.

It was difficult to adjust to Toots after six years in foster homes. Sometimes flying into fits of rage, she would blame me for all her problems and would say, "I wish you'd never been born."

Chapter Three

I've tried to piece together sources of my mother's rage. Toots seldom talked about her past. She was born in Marion, Utah, to Charles McDonough,
who worked as a Union Pacific stationmaster, and Shirley McDonough,
whose mother drifted from Ohio to California and was somehow related
to President Rutherford B. Hayes.

In passing, Toots mentioned living in a Catholic orphanage in Reno, at
a farm in Oregon, and with her best friend in San Francisco while in high
school. Imagine my surprise when I discovered that I had one uncle and
two aunts, while I was examining a shoe box of photos, newspaper clip-
pings, and Toots's passport. It was sent to me after her death from heart
failure in 1986. Her first heart attack occurred at a 1969 Roller Derby in
LA. Her 1960 passport shows a birthdate of January 19, 1912, something
I didn't know because she hid her age as I grew up, and it described her
as five foot two with blond hair and hazel eyes.

There were detailed references to her grandmother Flora Combs,
whom Toots admired, maybe because they shared a similar spirit. Flora
ran brothels in San Francisco, made a fortune renting beds during the
1906 earthquake, and then invested in developing Berkeley and the area
around LA's public market and Angels Flight.

That old son of a bitch (meaning my father), Toots claimed, lost Flora's
fortune when he tried to con money from her by having Sonny baptized
Catholic to show family allegiance to the Church. Also Toots's mother
Shirley claimed that Flora died on a trip to Rome to get a papal dispensa-
tion for a seventh divorce. Flora gave up on the family and left her brothel-
earned money to Catholic charities.

Toots loved to talk about Flora. At twenty, in 1885, Flora entered
the oldest profession after marrying and moving from Cincinnati to San

Francisco. She was quickly separated from her abusive new husband, Ben Casse. Ben took employment on a Japan-bound freighter and left Flora penniless and hospitalized from his severe beating.

Released from the hospital and not knowing that he'd left town, she went searching for Ben. Hungry as she looked for Ben around the shipping docks in Buena Vista Cove at the east end of Pacific Street in San Francisco's infamous Barbary Coast, Flora accepted a sailor's offer of a meal.

After the meal, the sailor took her to one of the many seedy hotels squeezed between the Barbary Coast's bars and dance halls. Called Pacific Paradise, the hotel was a brothel. Happy to be fed and enjoying the time with the sailor, Flora was stopped by the brothel's madam at the front desk on her way out. The madam asked if she'd like to work.

After several years of whoring with drunken sailors, Flora, an enterprising woman, concluded that she wanted to manage and not practice the trade. Toots said that there were many stories about Flora taking over the Pacific Paradise Hotel.

In one story, she killed the madam, stole her funds, and paid a sleazy lawyer to put her name on the brothel's deed. In another story, the madam fell in love with Flora and bequeathed to Flora her money and Pacific Paradise. In another version, the entire crew of a Russian ship took turns with Flora, guzzling vodka. In the early morning hours, they broke into song and declared Flora the best on the Barbary Coast.

A riot broke out when the madam ordered her thugs to clear the Russians from the premises. The Russians won and left several thugs paralyzed. The madam was left on Pacific Street, naked and babbling incoherently from a brain trauma caused by vodka bottles crushed on her head. In this version, Flora convinced a lawyer to get the brain-damaged madam to sign the deed over to her.

By the 1906 earthquake, Flora owned not only the Pacific Paradise Hotel but also seven other establishments, making her the so-called Queen of the Barbary Coast. Included in Flora's collection were famous whorehouses, such as Sailors' Dream and Climax and Creamed. She expanded out of the Barbary Coast to serve elite clientele and opened a discrete boutique brothel near Nob Hill named Pleasure.

In an early photo taken at a farm in Corvallis, Oregon, Toots looks between six and eight years old. She is sitting outside a wood-framed house and clutching a doll next to her older sister, Alice—I learned my aunts and uncle's names and locations by the notations made on the photos' backs. Behind Toots is her younger sister, Lucile.

Next to Lucile are Toots's mom, Shirley, and my uncle Marion. A V-shaped scissor cut removed the head but not the body of Toots's father, who is sitting behind Lucile. In a fit of anger, someone, Toots or Grandma, cut out my maternal grandfather's head.

Other photos at the farm show Toots barefoot and wearing a dress made from a flour sack.

In a photo labeled "Reno," she looks about ten and is surrounded by nuns in a Catholic orphanage. There is no record of who put her there or why.

Apparently cutting spouses' heads out of photos became a family tradition. Toots cut my father completely out of a 1941 photo taken by a house photographer at the Club Cinderella in New York City. He was stationed at Brooklyn Naval Yard, posted on destroyers that protected freighters headed to England. Placed in an official club folder, the photo originally showed them dancing together.

In the photo, Toots looks as if she is deeply in love with my father. After the divorce, she cut the photo in half, removing my father completely. In the photo, Toots looks happy and smiles dreamily with love into the face of her vanished partner.

A 1943 photo labeled "Clinton, Oklahoma," when Father was stationed at a newly opened naval air station, shows a group of men and women sprawled around someone's living room on a couch and the floor. A V-shaped scissor cut has removed a head, obviously my father's, from the figure Toots is smiling at.

A 1935 landing card and photos taken on the SS *Virginia* are reminders of Toots's trip to meet up with my father when he was stationed at a naval hospital in Panama. She was twenty-three, and Sonny was two.

Toots later told me that in Panama, "I realized the old son of a bitch was a drunk and gambler who would come home late at night and line up his winnings on the bedroom dresser. I'd brush the money onto the floor in the morning." Between being homebound with a two year old and the heat, humidity (pre–air conditioning), lizards, and fighting with Dad, Toots started thinking about leaving him.

A San Francisco background appears in her teenage photos. She mentioned to me that she lived with a friend while in high school. These photos hint of her life and interests. On the back of one, from when Toots was eighteen, is written, "Lucile and Alice on the fleet with some sailor boys—taken 1930." Another 1931 photo labeled "Russian River" shows Toots and Alice wearing bell-bottom pants and hugging, their hands rakishly holding cigarettes.

In 1932, Toots killed her boyfriend in an auto accident while driving wildly back from a party. Toots never told me the details, but she did talk about her friends surrounding her hospital bed, singing, and putting get-well banners on the wall behind her.

Headlines of a newspaper article in the shoe box read, "Girl Driver Wrecks Car Dodging Peril: Peninsula Party Ends in Death of One, Broken Bones for Others." Toots is described as an insurance-office worker and, under the newspaper's headline of "The Injured," as "Hazel McDonough, twenty, 525 Stockton Street, driver of the car, deep cuts, broken shoulder, and shock."

Her boyfriend, Steven Gough, twenty-one, died from a broken rib that punctured his heart. The newspaper reported that Toots and Steven were riding in the rumble seat when around midnight she got cold and they moved to the front seat. According to the two other passengers, Toots took over driving and immediately sped up, passing cars. The car skidded off the road when she braked to avoid an oncoming car.

One year later in 1933, she married Dad, a very handsome sailor. She would never answer my questions about how they met and why they married except to say, "At a dance."

Sonny was born on November 7, 1933, which leads me to suspect that she was pregnant when they married. Conception must have occurred in late 1932, a short time after Toots killed her boyfriend.

Toots didn't waste much time.

Chapter Four

Things got tighter when Sonny was thrown out of Venice High School and joined the air force. Toots stopped receiving his child support. He'd been getting into trouble with the "wrong" group shortly after we arrived in LA and settled into a small house in Culver City. I remember Muscle Beach near the Santa Monica pier. Sonny took me there with his Culver City racetrack friends. Now the barbells and weight benches are caged along the Venice boardwalk. Then they were open, and heavy lifting and curls were done standing in the sand.

With greasy hair formed into ducktails and wearing the standard uniform of jeans and white T-shirts, Sonny and his friends would pile into hot rods, sometimes leaving me to cry on an empty street not knowing when or if they would return.

Sonny always came back, dangling a cigarette from his mouth and using a comb to smooth out his ducktail. They all liked whisky.

"Sonny is enlisting in the air force, and we've got to move," announced Toots one morning at the breakfast table where my brother was sporting a black eye, swollen lips, a bruised cheek, and black and blue marks running down his arm. I was eleven, in fifth grade, and planning to go to the local junior high school in a couple years.

"I want to stay here and go to junior high," I blurted out, secretly dreaming of attending Venice High and repeating Sonny's glamorous life of fast cars and drinking.

"We've got to find a cheaper place." Toots stared at Sonny as if she were ready to slap him. "Sonny got in a gang fight in the school bathroom. He hurt a lot of people. They threw him out of school."

"Air force. You'll see Dave," I suggested.

I looked enviously at Sonny and asked, "Who's gonna look after me? Maybe you should marry Dave, with Sonny going to be in the air force with him."

Looking sullenly down at his cereal, my brother mumbled, "Shut up. I won't see Dave. Toots won't see him, either. He gave up on her."

Seeing Toots wince, I asked, "He won't come over anymore? He's OK. I like him. He doesn't love you?"

Bursting out in tears, Toots leaped up and ran from the kitchen.

"See what you did?" my brother hissed. "Get real. No man is going to stick with her. She'll climb in any bed. Dave got tired of it."

"What'd you mean 'climb in any bed'?"

"You're too young—bet you don't know about the birds and bees."

This was the '50s, and I lived in a world of sexual ignorance. But I didn't want him to know. I changed the subject. "Gonna fly fighters?"

Sonny shoved back his chair so hard that the top splintered against the counter. "Shit, I don't know what I'll do. The judge said a delinquent home or the air force. Not much choice."

"Judge? Were you in court? Is that where you guys were last night?"

In a week, Sonny disappeared into the air force. As a school dropout, he was destined for the enlisted ranks, which ended all hopes of flying fighters.

Without Sonny's child support and with Toots working sporadically, we survived in LA by selling furniture and statues that Toots had bought in Panama and Dad had brought back from a navy cruise around Africa. I remember a teak table with ivory inlay on the top and along the legs. Its sale paid for several months' rent. A large ebony table with legs sculpted like an elephant's head and trunk with real ivory tusks and a top with inlaid ivory in diamond patterns paid a year's rent. I still have some of these pieces—teak gods, jade ashtrays, and two ebony statues.

The statues now reside in a collection I call the Garden of Love that sits on top of a living-room bookcase with various pre-Colombian erotic pieces from Costa Rica. The larger thirteen-inch statue depicting a figure seated on a stool, I call "Toots." The smaller nine-inch statue of a man standing clutching a walking stick, I call "The Old Man."

In between husbands, Grandma Shirley appeared after Toots sought her help.

"She'll buy us a house if I pay for the furniture," explained Toots. "I can get the stuff on credit."

The two of us moved with Grandma into a three-bedroom house in LA's Westchester neighborhood. Grandma thought that it was safer than Culver City and Venice.

"Just beach bums, drunks, and scumbags living there," was Grandma's judgment about our former hangouts.

The move was immediately conflictual. Grandma believed that the living room—she called it the parlor—was off-limits to children, meaning me, and should only be used when entertaining. This meant that we could only enter the house through the door to the kitchen, where we spent most of our time, or in our bedrooms.

Shortly after moving in, Toots announced that we were leaving after she came home one night to find me crying and sitting on the front lawn. Grandma had banned me from the house for wearing muddy shoes in the kitchen. After a shouting match in which Grandma insisted that kids should learn to clean their feet before entering a house, Toots said that it really wasn't a home with being banned from the living room. Toots packed.

It wasn't easy. Toots was still making payments on the furniture, which she packed into a rented trailer that she hitched to our black 1949 Chevrolet coupe that replaced the Hudson. With little money, she hoped to find a government job in San Diego that paid more than temporary office work in LA.

She sat me down as if I were an adult and not a child of twelve and laid out our family budget. On the plus side were her last paycheck and my child support, and on the deficit side were furniture payments, the cost of gas to San Diego, and money for shelter.

I sat in the front seat as Toots raced down the two-lane Highway 101 and raged about the "Old Man," her mother, and me, the curve ball in her life. "I could just flop someplace. Now I have to worry about you.

"The Old Man couldn't keep it in his pants. I told him no. But the captain was there. I got tipsy, and he pushed me into a back room. I couldn't scream with the captain and all the others at the Christmas party. Nine months later you were dumped into my life."

This is how I learned that I was a Christmas party accident or, in more graphic words, the result of marital rape. I was born nine months after the party.

We moved into a dilapidated beach motel with warped floorboards, a pull-chain toilet that seldom worked, and a shower with cold rusty water. Living next to a drive-in, we lived on hamburgers. Our motel window looked out on the ocean from the cliffs in San Diego's Pacific Beach neighborhood.

Toots left me at the motel while she searched for work. Left alone, I wandered the beach, inspected local stores, and read. Toots was an avid reader of romantic historical fiction. There were always paperbacks around, even in the motel room. She read herself to sleep.

So at twelve, in 1952, I became a reader of historical romances. My favorites were Frank Yerby's *Foxes of Harrow* and *The Vixens*, with their unveiling of Southern sexuality—something I didn't fully understand until I took sixth-grade sex-ed class. I read the sexy passages over and over again and tried to understand the references.

In later years, I discovered that Yerby was black, something hidden by his publisher. I had a good laugh because Toots was a racist and didn't realize that her favorite author—she read all of his books—was an African American.

She got a job in security at the Naval Electronics Laboratory on Point Loma at the tip of San Diego Harbor. We remained in Pacific Beach and moved into a tiny one-bedroom beach house. Toots took the couch in the front room, and I slept in the bedroom so that I won't be disturbed by her late-night outings.

She decided that I didn't need a babysitter and would leave in the evenings with the warnings "Don't answer the door"; "Don't let anyone in"; and "If I bring anyone home, stay in your bedroom."

Now forty Toots was worried about finding a man because of her age and having a kid. It was in Pacific Beach that she gave me the task of using tweezers to remove the gray hair from her head.

"Don't tell anyone my age" and "Don't tell any guy you're my son," she warned me. When men came in the evening, Toots hurried me to the bedroom, out of sight of her dates. Sometimes she entertained at home with me hiding in the bedroom.

The suicide attempts began after I finished elementary school and we moved closer to her job. She rented a two-bedroom ground-floor duplex in Point Loma and signed me into Point Loma Junior High School. I spent my time alone that summer. Toots bought a parakeet that we named Princess to keep me company.

When I entered junior high in September, it was difficult for me to make friends. I'd had several in Pacific Beach. But at Point Loma Junior High, cliques were already formed from elementary school and neighborhoods.

At thirteen, my mind was gripped by sexual imagery. The sex-ed course in sixth grade occurred just as I experienced my first wet dream. Masturbation came easily. I kept trying to push my mother out of my pubescent fantasies.

"I'm going to take a bath," announced Toots one evening. Earlier she had said that she didn't feel well and had retreated to her bedroom.

I sat on the couch and read with Princess on my shoulder. Toots walked back and forth to the bathroom. She'd been crying earlier and took notepaper and a pen into the bedroom. I heard the bathroom lock click.

"Are you OK?" I called, knocking on the bathroom door.

"Just leave me alone!"

Sensing something wrong, I tried the knob and then started slamming my body against the flimsy door until the latch snapped out of the striking plate.

I stumbled in to see my mother lying in a bathtub of blood.

Chapter Five

I tried not to look directly at Toots, who was naked and slumped down in the tub with bloody water up to her breasts. Blood flowed from her right wrist. A red-tinged razor blade rested on the bathtub's side.

Crying, I looked in the medicine cabinet for Band-Aids and gauze. Not letting my eyes rest on her nude body, I grabbed Toots's arm and tried to staunch the blood by wrapping gauze around her wrist. She was breathing but barely.

Sobbing, I wondered whom to call. We had no friends. In our personal phone book, she'd written Faye Keaton's name and work number.

"We work together," Toots had said at the time. "If you can't reach me in an emergency, call Faye." Using Faye's last name, I hurriedly looked for her home number in the city phone book.

"I'll be there, but gotta bring my kid. Have to wake him." Faye didn't sound pleased to hear my voice or about the situation.

I slowed the bleeding and, in a display of modesty, tried to cover my mother's body with towels. The doorbell rang. There stood Faye, her hair in rollers, wearing a nightgown, with her sleepy-eyed six-year-old son in pajamas.

"What's happening?" snapped Fay. I directed her to bathroom.

"Jesus Christ!" she screamed, running out of the bathroom and calling the police for an ambulance.

The police and ambulance arrived. Faye quickly bundled her kid back in her car and went home. In a whirl of activity, Toots was rushed into the ambulance. The police asked a few questions, gave me the hospital's name, and left.

An eerie silence filled the apartment; it was broken by the sound of the parakeet chewing on a cuttlebone. I was alone. In later years, the police would have called social services, but this was the early 1950s.

Alone, not knowing what to do, I went to bed for a troubled night of sleep. I got up the next day, dressed, made my breakfast, and went to school. I couldn't focus on schoolwork.

At lunch and recess, I isolated myself and watched the other kids play. I envied their happiness. No teacher asked me if anything was wrong.

I walked home from school and made dinner, a chore I'd been given back in Pacific Beach.

"I told them at work she had the flu," Faye said when she called to say that she'd checked with the hospital and Toots was doing OK. "I won't be calling again. You can check with the hospital."

I ate and wandered into Toots's bedroom.

"Tell Ben I love him," a note on her pillow read. "I'm so tired and lonely. I have nothing. I tried to go on. This is the way out of my misery."

Looking around the room, I fantasized about Toots's naked body.

After reading and playing with the bird and climbing into bed, I tossed and turned, torn between fears of Toots's death, of my future, and of images of her body. I tried not to masturbate.

"She'll be home tomorrow," a kind voice told me after I called the hospital and was shuttled from department to department.

I stayed home from school, cleaned the apartment, and made sandwiches for Toots's arrival. I strung a welcome-home sign between the birdcage and floor lamp. The ambulance arrived shortly before noon. An attendant brought her through the door in a wheelchair with a bandaged arm across her lap.

"She can walk," the attendant gruffly informed me. "She has instructions on what to do." He handed me a pill bottle. "These'll help her sleep."

"Why didn't you let me die? Stupid kid. I'll never forgive you." Oblivious to the welcome-home sign and sandwiches, Toots stood angrily in the middle of the living room. Snatching the pill bottle from my hand, she hurried, cursing, to her bedroom.

We settled into a routine of school and work. We didn't talk much. She scowled at me when I served dinner. I started going to bed early to escape into my thirteen-year-old sex fantasies.

Two weeks later her trip between bedroom and bathroom began again. Only this time she was dressed in a newly bought blue nightgown with puff sleeves and embroidery around the neckline and bottom. Her hair was curly after a beauty-parlor trip. She made frequent stops in the kitchen to fill a glass from a newly purchased whisky bottle.

I sat silently on the couch and suspiciously watched her comings and goings.

"Why didn't you let me die?" she berated me from the hallway.

She started to stagger. Finally she fell and passed out in front of the bathroom door. I tried to rouse her. In her bedroom were another suicide note, a pill bottle, and half a glass of whiskey.

"My mom tried to kill herself and is passed out on the floor." I'd learned how to call the police.

Putting her on a stretcher, the ambulance medics checked the pill bottle and mumbled about sleeping pills and getting her stomach pumped out. Looking at me and knowing that this was her second attempt, the police asked for the name of my closest relative.

I gave them Sonny's name and an address at an air force base in South Carolina. After Toots was admitted, the hospital called. They were keeping her under observation until the police talked to my brother.

My lonely trips to school started again. Two days later my brother appeared, having driven across country.

"I'm not staying here," said Sonny as he opened the car's glove compartment to show me a pint of whiskey.

"Got some girls to see up in LA." He quickly wrote down a phone number and handed it to me. "Call me when Toots gets home. I'll have to go back then. Don't worry; she'll get over it. Just another busted love affair. I'll talk to the police."

He left.

"Why didn't you let me die?" yelled Toots after coming home.

Resuming our school and work routine, Toots came home in January and announced that we were driving to Alaska.

"We're going to Florida. I'll get a job at the Pensacola naval air station," she said the next day after someone told her that January was cold and snowy along the Alaskan Highway.

Withdrawing her government retirement money, we packed the car and, in early January, drove from San Diego to Pensacola. This was 1953, before interstate highways. Most roads were two-lane and often passed through town centers.

Princess rode on the steering wheel and hopped with each turn. Toots made me the navigator. This meant reading maps and making sure that we didn't get lost. The worst time was going through cities, where Toots expected me to have the route memorized.

"Why didn't you let me die?" and "You've ruined my life!" and "Wish you'd never been born," she would yell when we got tangled in city streets. "Can't you read a map? What good are you?"

I remember long stretches of Texas's roads disappearing into the distant horizon. With few cars on the road, Toots put her foot on the dashboard and read romance novels as Princess hopped around. We went through Austin to Beaufort, Texas, and then on to New Orleans.

Toots had a Friday-night-cowboy attitude about life—spend it while you can. With her retirement money, we hit most of New Orleans's fancy restaurants. She bought me "proper" clothes for these splurges. We ate at Delmonico's. I remember the oysters Rockefeller she ordered for me. There is a photo of me sitting on a stool at the Court of the Two Sisters. We stayed at the St. Charles just off Canal Street and took a paddle wheel up and down the river. For one week, I was her day and night companion, but her sadness continued.

We arrived exhausted after driving straight from New Orleans through Mobile, Alabama, to Pensacola. We'd blown a lot of money, and Toots searched for a cheap motel.

On Pensacola's outskirts, a flashing neon sign announced, "Dreamland Motel: Rooms and Kitchenettes—Weekly Rates."

Flypaper hung from a naked lightbulb in the tiny kitchen. The bathroom was an outhouse, and a common shower room was covered with mold. There was one bedroom and a foldout in the front room. The windows were stuck shut. The only ventilation came through a screen door, and air was circulated by a fan on the dresser.

We'd picked up some bread, mayonnaise, and a tube of liverwurst for dinner. I still love these sandwiches, particularly with Wonder Bread. Toots claimed that they were God's food as they provided a complete meal. "It's as good as Spam," she said, spreading a glob of mayonnaise on the white bread. This would be our diet, liverwurst and Spam, until she got a paycheck.

The next day Toots headed to the naval air station and left me to fend for myself. The motel was just off the main highway from New Orleans, and in back was a reddish dirt road leading away from the highway.

As she left, I complained about having nothing to do.

In a hurry, Toots fumbled through her purse for the pistol. She handed it to me and put a box of shells from her suitcase on the kitchen table.

"I see a lot of trees on that back road that you can use for target practice. That'll keep you busy."

After she left, I started reading one of her novels and, after finding the right passage, masturbated.

I shoved the gun in my Windbreaker—it was a little chilly at that time of the year—and started walking down the dusty dirt road.

I'd never seen Southern poverty. This was the 1950s. As I walked, I encountered lean-to shanties with black families sitting in front. Old rusted cars and farm tools surrounded outhouses in back.

I'd walked about half a mile looking for a spot to target practice. Turning a bend, I saw an open stretch of road without any shanties along the side. Concluding that it would be a good place to target practice, I took out the twenty-two pistol, opened the cylinder, and loaded it with shells I'd stuffed in my pocket. Seeing a big cypress tree, I decided to make it my target.

I'd just started to aim when an older black man stumbled out of the bushes and wove a path toward me.

I didn't think. I just reacted and started firing.

Three red stains spread across the man's shirt. He fell. I ran up and looked at the blood coming from his mouth. Panicked, I hurried back to the motel.

Chapter Six

Images of blood in the man's mouth and bathtub crowded my mind as I ran back to the motel. It was still early afternoon, and Toots won't be back until late—maybe the next day if she found a man. As she'd left, she'd told me to make some sandwiches for dinner.

I kept rehearsing the scene trying to change its outcome—maybe shooting at another target, waiting and not shooting, or just leaving the gun in the motel room. My brain kept racing through all the "should haves."

Trying not to cry, I put the gun on the kitchenette table's red-checkered oilcloth and rummaged through Toots's bags for her cleaning kit. I found the cleaning swab, brush, and rod. Removing the cylinder, I put cleaner on the brush, shoved it into the pistol's short barrel, and stroked, back and forth.

Suddenly I felt sick. I never made it to the sink. I sprayed vomit over the pistol, table, and floor. Gagging from the rancid smell, I grabbed a kitchen towel and tossed it over the pistol as I ran out the screen door. I couldn't fight back the breakfast rising in my throat. Leaving a yellow trail, I ran to the outhouse. Afterward I sat on the room's stoop with stinging snot running from my nose and mixing with tears.

"Why was I ever born?" I called out. I was greeted in the kitchenette by flies buzzing around the table and sticking to the flypaper hanging from the ceiling light fixture.

Fighting back tears, I wiped the pistol, and using the only two towels provided by the motel, I cleaned the table and floor, rinsing out the chunks of breakfast. I felt a strange quietness in my body. I finished cleaning the pistol.

I neatly repacked the cleaning kit and emptying the pistol's cylinder. I thought that Toots would be suspicious if only three bullets were used.

I put the spent casings and unused bullets in my pocket. Walking back down the road, I randomly tossed them into the woods.

By early evening, Toots hadn't returned. I spent the afternoon agonizing over what had happened. I wondered if the man was dead. I was tempted to walk back to check, but I feared getting caught.

My fantasies were populated with prison scenes from Hollywood movies, which tempted me to go to the motel owner and confess my sin. At least in prison, I would be surrounded by men who would fill my loneliness.

Around six, according to the yellowed, plastic wall clock over the stove, I decided to make dinner. My choices were liverwurst or Spam. Princess rested on my shoulder as I read and munched on my sandwich. Drained, I went to bed early after deciding Toots wouldn't be back that night. I hoped to escape into masturbation and sleep, but I tossed and turned with dreams of blood, Toots's body, and the black man lying in the woods.

As the sun peeked through the window, I could hear a banging and moaning from the front room. Words were whispered, and the screen door banged shut. I got up and slowly opened the door to see Toots sprawled naked under a sheet on the foldout bed. A nauseating smell of cigarettes and whisky filled the room. I was relieved to see the pistol untouched.

Headlights pierced the early morning dawn as I heard a car start up outside the room. On seeing a police officer come through the screen door, I quickly closed the door. *Oh God,* I thought, *he wants me.*

"What's happening?" I heard Toots's startled voice awakened by the banging door and sound of shoes.

"Just forgot my hat. What about a little more?" I could hear a male voice.

"Enough," pleaded Toots.

The sound of a hard slap sent me running from the bedroom. Toots's lip bled as a white policeman dangled handcuffs in front of her with one hand while with the other hand started unzipping his pants. The policeman was startled when I charged him diving and biting his leg. Toots screamed.

"Shit," yelled the policeman, knocking me off his leg. "You whore, you didn't say there was a kid here. You fuckin' around at a bar with a kid by himself. I should have taken you in."

I could see the black and blue marks on Toots's shoulders and arms as she sat up.

"You bastard, get out of here," she screamed.

Picking up his hat from the floor, he looked at me and said, "Kid, keep your mother from hustling at bars. Not the best way to get money. Next time she'll be in jail. I gave her a break. You should thank me. Just a little rough sex—feels good. You'll know someday."

"You fuckin' shit," cried Toots. "I should report you."

He hurried out slamming the screen door. You could hear the tires spinning in the gravel as he gunned the police cruiser.

"Are you OK? What happened to your arms? Need something for your lip?" I said and ran to Toots.

Putting on her slip, she got up and rinsed her mouth at the sink. "Some guys are rough. Don't you be like that. Couldn't do anything; he'd put me in jail. Just a cracker cop thinking he's big shit."

I didn't want to hear anymore. I glanced at the gun.

"Had fun shooting; got the target every time." I tried to sound proud.

"Good for you." She tried to smile as more blood seeped from her lip. "Stay out of trouble. I am going to bed; need more sleep. Make your breakfast." Without any further words, she shut the bedroom door.

Obediently I spread mayonnaise on a piece of white bread and cut some Spam. I looked out the screen door as the road in front came alive with work-bound cars. I fed Princess and freed her to fly around the room. She landed on my shoulder. The Spam left a salty taste, which I washed away with milk.

Maybe, I thought, *I didn't really hurt anyone. No one's coming for me. The guy probably got up.*

Tempted to check on the body, still in my pajamas, I stepped outdoors. At that moment, the white motel manager came out of the office.

"Be careful," he called over to me. "The radio said someone was killed on the back road. Tell your mom. Probably nothing; these niggers shoot each other all the time."

I hastily stepped back inside. I sat on the couch with Princess and waited for the sirens and flashing red lights. But nothing happened. Needing to go to the outhouse, I pushed open the bedroom door and gathered my clothes as Toots snored away.

"Your mom OK?" the tall red-haired manager asked as I hurried from the outhouse to escape its smell. "I saw a cop car in front this morning."

"Car problems," I hastily replied, realizing that lying was now part of my life. "He helped her back. Nice cop. She'd spent the day looking for work."

"Pretty early in the morning." The man sounded unconvinced. "White women shouldn't be out all night."

"Had to take the car to a shop; wouldn't start." Lying, I pointed at our car. "They left it in front of the shop after it was fixed. Cop helped her get it and followed her home to keep her safe. I guess he heard about the killing."

I could tell he didn't believe me.

"Well," he laughed, "we get all types here. You're mom up? Tell her about the shooting when she's awake. Those niggers might kill her."

Relieved that they thought it was black people killing each other, I went back into the kitchenette, picked up the gun, and fondled its barrel.

"I got the job," Toots announced, emerging from the bedroom around noon. "Just out celebrating a little afterward. We needed some extra money before my first paycheck. Got to get you in school."

She washed her face and brushed her teeth in the sink and started heating water for coffee.

"These schools are segregated," she explained. "I'm putting you in the white school. Don't tell anyone about your son-of-a-bitch father being Indian. They might put you in the black school. Just be quiet when we go to register you."

"Segregated?" I questioned.

"Crazy laws here. Blacks in back of the bus and segregated schools. Don't know what they'd do with your son-of-a-bitch father."

"A colored body was found on Cutler Road on the outskirts of town," announced the car radio on the way to school registration.

"Identified as fifty-two-year-old Ben Carson of fifty-two Cutler Road. An autopsy revealed a high percentage of alcohol in his blood. Colored neighbors said that Ben was frequently drunk. Police said he'd been shot three times in the chest by a small-caliber gun. One bullet pierced his heart. A police official said they were focusing on a local dispute, because of frequent reports of shootings between neighbors on Cutler Road."

Once I was registered for the white school, Toots asked the motel manager where I should get the bus. The next day we stood on the main road until an old city bus pulled up and opened its doors. The first thing to catch my eye was a sign in the bus's back reading, "This part of bus for colored race." Hoping that no one knew about my Indian father, I sat in the white section.

I was locked in a fantasy world as I looked from the bus's window, vaguely aware of the passing landscape. There was a kaleidoscope of images—shooting and seeing the black man fall with blood coming from his mouth, Toots bathing in blood and falling in the hallway, her nude body, and the policeman beating her. I imagined lifting her nightgown as she lay comatose in the hallway to find out what women looked like. Sexual imagery merged with violence.

Looking out the bus window, I imagined pointing the pistol and shooting people in cars and on sidewalks. I made a car in front blow up as I threw a bomb at it.

I noticed kids in the back of the bus getting up as we pulled in front of a gray, clapboard building with no landscaping and a dirt playground. The edifice indicated it was the Booker T. Washington Colored Junior High School. A chattering group of black students moved to the front and clambered down exit steps as the bus's doors opened. I imagined shooting at them.

Next the bus pulled in front of a brick building landscaped with flowers, bushes, grass, and a paved playground filled with equipment. A carved wooden sign with gold lettering hung in front: "Robert E. Lee

Junior High School." I hurried into the building with the other white students and asked a teacher where I could find 201, my assigned seventh-grade homeroom.

"We have a new student," announced Miss Graystone, a pleasant-looking, elderly woman with bouffant hairdo and a plain, black dress and shoes. "Billy Durant from California," she said pointing at a desk in the back. "You can sit there."

"Seen any movie stars?" whispered kids. "Let's hear your Yankee talk. Do you surf? Are you a beach boy? How do you keep your niggers in line?"

"Quiet in back," shouted Miss Graystone. "Since you're new, Billy, we'll give you the honor of doing the daily Bible reading and prayer." Picking up a Bible from her desk, she waved me to the front telling me to, "Read John chapter fifteen, verses twelve and thirteen to the class."

I remembered at the Four Square Tabernacle looking at a Bible that I was too young to read. I didn't know what she meant. Seeing my confusion, Miss Graystone took the Bible, opened it to the passage, handed it back, and pointed at the section.

The class laughed at my accent as I read,

> My command is this: Love each other as I have loved you.
> Greater love has no one than this: to lay down one's life
> for one's friends.

I wondered if the passage had been selected by God because I had no friends.

Maybe Jesus, I thought, *whispered in Miss Graystone's ear to give me this passage to read.*

"Listen to that Yankee talk," a muscular-looking boy sitting in front called out to a giggling class. "We should have won the war."

"Quiet!" shrieked Miss Graystone. "People have different ways of talking. Billy, give us a prayer."

"Oh, God, save me," I shouted, remembering prayers from the Tabernacle. "I have sinned! I saw Jesus standing at the bus stop, and

I threw myself on his mercy. Ring the bells of heaven so I can enter the pearly gates."

"Hallelujah," one kid called out. Miss Graystone looked startled. Maybe it was my shouting the prayer or the prayer itself,

Another student stood up. "Bathe me in the sweet blood of Jesus."

"Billy, please take your seat," Miss Graystone whispered to me. "This isn't a camp meeting. Tone it down next time. But it was lively."

Embarrassed by the ordeal and student responses, I sat down. I couldn't pay attention to the lessons, despite Miss Graystone's nagging me, "Do your work. Stop daydreaming."

I was lost in a fantasy of pointing a gun at the class, shooting the boy who had made fun of me, undressing Miss Graystone, and killing the black man.

Chapter Seven

For two weeks, we settled into a routine of work and school. The Dreamland Motel became home. Toots planned to look for an apartment after her first paycheck. Sometimes she was at the motel at night but seldom on weekends. She left the gun in her suitcase—she couldn't take it to work at the naval air station—with the understanding that I could use it anytime.

Gradually the segregated bus gave me a sense of power. While I worried about being an imposter sitting in the front seats, I enjoyed the privilege. I liked watching black people being forced to the back.

On one trip to school, all the seats were filled when a fat white man got on.

"You there," bellowed the dumpy, white bus driver pointing at a seat where an elderly black woman sat, "get up."

The white man waddled to the vacated seat as a black student stood up and offered his seat to the elderly woman.

My feeling of privilege dissolved as I was confronted by the situation's injustice and the compassion of the black student.

"That's not fair," I called out.

"Boy," roared the bus driver, "you shut up. This is white man's law."

Scrunching down, I tried to avoid the glares of other white passengers.

Arriving, I looked forward to the religious part of homeroom. Despite some giggles about my accent, I volunteered to lead class prayers. I drew on memories of the Four Square Tabernacle to bring evangelical students to their feet as I shouted out my belief in the "sweet blood of the lamb." Ms. Graystone began to enjoy the revival quality I brought to morning exercises. She told the class that I was a model of how to pledge allegiance to the flag.

"You should stand tall like Billy," ordered Ms. Graystone, "and clearly say the words. God and country are most important. Prayer and the pledge make America great."

Kids, wanting to know about California life and intrigued by my accent, approached me during recess and lunch. "I hear niggers can ride anyplace on a bus," snickered Charley, the muscular kid who made fun of my accent as I chewed my sandwich. "You Yankees should keep them in their place. We don't want any of those ideas down here—they'll bother white women, and they smell. Can't imagine sitting next to one on a bus."

"What about Indians?" I asked. "Do they have to sit in back?"

"Indians are colored, so I guess they sit in back," answered Charley.

After that, when I rode the bus, I was bothered by my racial lie. One morning I decided to live up to my father's heritage and calmly took a seat in back next to a black kid. Bedlam erupted.

Black kids shouted, "White boy, sit up front. This is ours."

Always an enforcer of racial rules, the white bus driver stood up and literally screamed, "Boy, come up here! Ain't you got no sense?"

Other white and black riders bombarded me with insults and commands. I finally moved up front. In class, I could hear kids who had been on the bus whispering about the incident. At lunch, Charley reminded them, "He's a Yankee; got weird ideas about niggers."

I didn't tell them about Dad. I was tempted to prove my racial worth by bragging about killing a black man. I bit my tongue.

Hours alone at night, I stroked the unloaded pistol and played at shooting imaginary foes. I was afraid to take it outside for target practice. Apparitions from foster homes became my targets. Over and over again, I shot Alex Kenny, the Old Lady and the Finches. I liked shooting at Alex, aiming for his crotch.

At night I found it difficult to sleep without first imagining myself a Nazi general invading France. World War II movies provided the images.

"Take this town." Dressed in a Nazi uniform, I pointed at a wall map as others took notes. "If you follow this route, you can kill many of those French pigs. Take their women."

"Rip her shirt and skirt off; let's see what these French bitches have," I ordered, after my army destroyed the town's buildings and women and girls were lined up against a wall. I fell asleep as the women were tortured. I started needing more and more violent fantasies to sleep.

After two weeks of work, Toots announced that we were going back to California. She complained about her navy officer boss. "Fat bastard is always trying to grab me." She didn't like Florida and missed San Francisco.

"As soon as I get paid," she told me, "we're out of here. We can stay in Frisco with my high school girlfriend, Sue, until we get a place."

We raced back across country with Princess hopping up and down on the steering wheel. Escaping murder ran through my mind. Maybe, I wondered, it was because he was black. When road conditions allowed it, my mother read historical romances with her foot on the dashboard. Thinking back, I wonder why we didn't die in an accident.

"I'll look for a job there." Crossing the Bay Bridge, Toots pointed down at Treasure Island, an artificial island used as a naval station. "Wish it'd been around when Sis and I were chasing sailors."

Exiting the bridge, she drove to Van Ness and Pine, where her high school friend, Sue Welsh, lived in a run-down, corner apartment building.

Clambering up to the second-floor apartment, Sue greeted Toots with a hug and said I was handsome. I was overwhelmed by the smell of her dozen cats. The carpet was torn by cat claws, as were the edges of the furniture. Cat urine reeked throughout the apartment with urine stains decorating the carpets, including the small one in the reeking bathroom. Sam, her lover, was sprawled on a threadbare couch in an alcoholic stupor.

"Don't mind him," said Sue, helping us with our luggage. "You should get everything out of the car. We're on the edge of the Tenderloin; can't be too careful. You guys can sleep in here."

"My son use to sleep here until he went to jail." Sue took us into a room inhabited by cats, a stained blanket lay across the bed.

"He only took some cigarettes from the corner store, and the owner went apeshit. He'd be out by now, but he beat up a guard. You two can share the bed, or we got a cot."

"What about Princess?" I whispered to Toots.

"We've got a parakeet in the car," explained Toots as she looked around the room staring at the two cats on the dresser and another sharpening its claws on the drapes.

"No problem," said Sue. "I'll get the cats out of here and move the litter box into the bathroom. Bird'll be OK if we keep the door shut."

As I brought the cage into the apartment, Princess panicked and started squawking and flying from side to side. I put the cage on the dresser of the bedroom as Sue shooed the cats out and used her foot to push the litter box into the bathroom.

Toots and Sue settled into the kitchen and caught up on old times.

"Can I go out?" I asked, wanting to escape the smell and cat hair.

"Be careful around here," advised Sue. "Stay on Van Ness. Gay guys in the Tenderloin want good-looking kids like you."

"Where's Van Ness?" I really wanted to ask what she meant by "gay guys." I'd never heard the term.

"The big boulevard in front. Make a left onto Pine, and some guy'll get your butt."

"Sue!" exclaimed Toots. "He doesn't understand. Do you, Billy?"

"How old is he? Looks big enough to get into trouble."

"Thirteen, and a good kid. Still wet behind the ears. Do you know where to go, Billy?"

"Don't make a left onto Pine; stick to Van Ness," I repeated, wondering what a gay guy was.

Stepping out of the building, I looked up and down Van Ness and saw mostly car dealers and business buildings on each side. There were only a handful of people.

Looking up Pine Street with its crowded sidewalks, I saw seedy bars, dirty windows of small grocery stores, a couple diners, and several hotels with signs reading "Rooms by the hour."

I hesitated. Should I follow Sue's advice? Van Ness looked dull. Emboldened with the thought of being an escaped killer, I dismissed concerns about safety. I started walking on Pine away from Van Ness toward the heart of the Tenderloin.

Nothing happened as I passed crowded bars and women hanging around the entrances to hourly rate hotels. Some of the women kidded with me. "You want a little? Bet your prick ain't big enough yet. Come back in a couple years."

In front of a bar at Hyde and Pine, a man stumbled out the door, looked at me, and said, "You're a cute kid. I got some candy cane for you." He laughed and reached over to pat my butt.

I hurried across the street and continued on Pine until the bars disappeared and the neighborhood changed into expensive apartment buildings. Up ahead, I heard the pinging of what turned out to be a cable-car bell.

Looking up Mason Street, I could see the tower of the Mark Hopkins Hotel. I continued along Pine to Powell Street with its cable-car tracks, upscale restaurants, and hotels. Looking toward Market Street, I could see the front of Union Square and decided to take a look.

Walking down Powell toward Market, I went into the St. Francis Hotel, stared at the marble pillars, ornate chandeliers, and plush carpeting, and wondered who could afford to stay here.

I left the hotel, crossed Powell, and found an empty bench in Union Square. I felt hungry and wished I'd asked Toots for money.

I decided to rest and watch people and passing cable cars.

A well-dressed man sat down on the other end of the bench. He smiled at me. "Beautiful day, isn't it?"

I nodded and looked away.

The man moved closer. "Shouldn't you be in school?"

I hadn't thought of school. I realized that I was truant. *Is this guy,* I wondered, *a cop?*

"Just got here from Florida; Mom's taking me to school tomorrow," I hastily replied, worried about being arrested.

"Big trip from Florida. You take the train or drive?"

"Mom drove; she's here for work."

The man moved closer.

"You're a good-looking kid. Got any girlfriends? Any back in Florida?"

"No," I replied. This was the first time I'd been asked about girlfriends.

"Handsome boy like you should have them crawling all over you. Do you like girls?"

"I never had a girlfriend."

The man put his hand on my knee. "Any boyfriends?"

Confused, I felt myself swelling, finding the man attractive. "Knew some boys back in Florida and before in San Diego."

"You hungry? I got some doughnuts and sweets in my room."

His hand started moving up my leg. I felt a wave of desire. I looked down and could see a stain appearing near my fly. He also noticed and put a hand on my shoulder.

I bolted and hurried back to the apartment.

Chapter Eight

I returned to Sue's apartment just as Sam, wakened by the chatter of Sue and Toots, stumbled off the couch and headed for the bathroom. "Jesus Christ," he yelled stepping into the cat litter. "Why's this here?"

Sue and Toots came running. "We moved it for the parakeet," Sue explained, turning on the tub's faucet. "Stick your feet under the water. It should take the crap off."

"Parakeet," Sam repeated. "Don't we have enough pets with all the fuckin' cats?"

Wearing only a yellowed pair of formerly white underpants and a T-shirt reading "I drink wine because I don't like to keep my problems bottled up," Sam balanced on one foot. He put the other foot with clumps of brown and litter under the faucet.

"Shit, this is cold. Sue, get me a towel," Sam barked. "Who's she?" He nodded at Toots.

"School friend staying with her son till they get an apartment. I gave them the kid's room."

Unsteady, trying to shake his foot dry, Sam fell backward, hit his head on the sink, and fell face first into the litter.

I rushed over to assist Sam to his feet. There was a slight gash on his forehead, and used litter clung to his cheeks. Smeared cat shit covered his T-shirt leaving visible the words "I drink wine."

"He's filthy. Can't put him on the couch in this condition; he's gotta shower and change," Sue said.

"Put him on a kitchen chair," Toots suggested. "Billy, you hold him so he doesn't fall off."

"I don't know if we can get him under the water." Sue turned on the shower. "He's got no clean clothes. Never does his laundry."

"Billy, keep holding him while I get his underwear off." Toots grabbed the bottom of his shirt and lifted it over his head, avoiding the litter on his cheeks and chin.

"Put your arms around him and the chair while I get the underpants off."

"Well, look at that." Sue gestured at his erect penis. "He's always ready. Only thing he's good at when sober."

Turning away, I blushed. I'd seen nude boys with developing organs and remembered my rapist. It looked enormous.

I couldn't hold on. My heart was still pounding after hurrying from the man in Union Square. My mind tried to control my desires, which it didn't fully understand. As Sam slipped back onto the bathroom floor, I left and joined Princess in our room.

Coming out again, I saw Toots gently slapping Sam's face as Sue poured water on it, soaking the floor and sending a stream into the living room.

"Wake up, you son of a bitch," Sue ordered, pinching his cheeks. "Stay away from that muscatel—you'll end up a wino."

They got him to his feet and started drying him with dirty towels. I found the whole scene disgusting. I didn't want to stay with Sue. I helped take him into their bedroom, sneaking quick peeks as he went flaccid.

Before sleeping, I was on the cot, and Toots had the bed. She agreed to leave as soon as possible. "I had no idea," Toots sighed.

We left after a week. A woman at Toots's new job on Treasure Island was desperate for a roommate to share expenses. Before moving, I spent the time keeping the cats away from Princess, helping move Sam from wine bottle to couch to bedroom, and worrying about cat piss getting in our luggage.

It didn't take long to pack and get out of the apartment. Sue and Toots hugged and vowed a lifelong friendship.

The three-bedroom apartment was on Clay Street in Nob Hill. Today I couldn't afford an apartment in this area. Jennie Taylor, our roommate, was friendly, clean, and very neat, the ideal person to share an apartment with. I heard Toots tell Jennie that my child support paid our share of the rent.

I loved it. I had my own bedroom. A block away I caught the Powell Street cable car to Fisherman's Wharf. From there, I took a bus to my new junior high school in the Marina District. My third school in the seventh grade.

I even had friends. Two white girls in my class joined me every morning for the trip to school. June Pendleton—I'll never forget her—was the first girl I'd ever kissed. She lived with her working mother in a first-floor corner apartment over a deli at the cable-car stop. You could look out her bay window and see my apartment on Clay and up and down Taylor Street.

"They do it like this," June said, putting her lips on mine as we stood in her apartment one day after school. It tasted so sweet. It was my first kiss. I can still walk under the bay window and remember the sweetness of those kisses. They were innocent kisses. We'd heard of French kisses but weren't sure what they were.

At school I met Jerry Janko, who lived with his father in a single room of a sleazy residential hotel on Jones Street. His mother had died in a car accident. His father seldom left the room. They lived, according to Jerry, on his mom's insurance money and his dad's disability payments.

"Dad drinks," Jerry informed me during one lunch hour as we hung out along the wall separating the school from Chestnut Street. "We some-times drive down the Peninsula to visit the spot where we crashed. I was in back. Nothing happened to me. Dad still has problems walking; spends most of his time in bed or at the bar downstairs."

One Saturday Jerry said that his father wanted to take us on a drive. It was the weekend, and Toots reluctantly agreed.

"I gotta piss." Jerry's father frequently pulled off the road to take a nip of wine and walk around to the passenger side to unzip his pants.

"Let's go back," Jerry finally ordered as his father got drunker. "You're gonna kill us."

Relieved that we made it back alive, I headed back to our apartment to find Toots huddled in bed.

"You never think of me," she said. "Left me alone on a weekend. What was I supposed to do? You only worry about yourself, selfish—why'd I have you? Out with friends all the time."

I went to bed loathing myself. Jerry and I had made plans to meet the next day. But now I worried about Toots. I felt bad that she was lonely.

The next day I said to Toots, "I'll stay. I was supposed to meet Jerry, but I can call it off."

"I got plans," Toots said. "I don't know about you going out. You might get in trouble. Your old son-of-a-bitch father is looking for an excuse to end child support. Stay here."

"But I've got nothing to do," I pleaded. "Jennie is away; I'll be alone."

"Good," Toots said, grabbing her purse as she left. "Now you'll know how I felt."

Ignoring Toots, I met Jerry in front of his hotel, where he was trying to juggle three oranges that kept landing on the sidewalk, splitting, and leaking juice.

"Can't do this," Jerry said, wiping the juice on his jeans. He tried throwing them into a city waste container about ten feet away. Two went in, and the other splattered on the pavement.

"You stink," I kidded. "Bet I can."

"Oh yeah? Try it."

"Where'd you get the oranges?"

"Lifted from the market." Jerry pointed at a small corner store. "Ever pocket store stuff?"

"You mean shoplift?"

"I'll show you. We'll go in, and you ask the guy for something. I'll grab stuff to juggle."

"I don't know what to ask."

"Ask for a pack of cigarettes. Say they're for your mom."

"I can't buy cigarettes!"

"It doesn't matter. It'll keep 'em busy telling you."

I met Jerry outside the store. He'd taken more oranges.

"Here, catch," he said, tossing one to me as we moved away from the store.

We started tossing them back and forth to each other. Jerry crossed the street. We played catch, throwing them over cars. He started moving down the sidewalk as I followed on the opposite sidewalk. We became more and more excited as we threw the oranges higher and higher. We ran around people to make our catches.

One of my oranges didn't make it and splattered on a car's hood. I threw the next one harder, only it was too hard and high. It smashed into a neon bar sign above Jimmy's head and sprayed glass shards onto the sidewalk.

Jimmy took off running. I froze.

"You bastard kid, come back!" A man shouted, rushing out of the bar seeing Jimmy hightailing it away.

"I broke it," I called from the other side of the street. I don't know why I didn't follow Jerry's example and escape. Dodging traffic, I crossed the street.

"You're an honest one." The man's anger disappeared as he looked me up and down. Waving me into the bar, which he owned, he said, "Honest or not, you're going to have to pay. I'll call your parents. What's your name?"

"Billy Durant. Mom may be out. I live with her." I wrote down the home phone number.

Toots was there. Her date hadn't worked out.

The owner smiled at me and gave me a glass of Coke as I waited on a barstool. "You look like a good kid."

Toots showed up about a half hour later. I could see she was furious. My stomach tightened as I anticipated her screaming at me. Her expression changed as the owner praised me.

"You should be proud," said the owner. "You've got a truthful kid. The other one ran away. It was an accident. They were just playing."

He handed Toots a bill for seventy-five dollars. "These signs aren't cheap. I think it's important for him to pay. Kids need to learn responsibility."

"He doesn't have this kind of money." Toots glared at me. "I can't afford this."

"He should pay. I can get him work." The man smiled warmly at me. "It's a good lesson. You should be proud of him, not like the others. Kids today don't know responsibility. Billy crossed the street and confessed. Not many will do that."

"He can't work. He's only thirteen."

"Not in this bar. He can deliver papers. I know someone at the *Call-Bulletin*. He can make weekly payments."

The owner wrote out a contract with an agreement for me to make weekly payments. "I don't know how much you'll make. We can decide later on weekly amounts, Billy. Just sign here."

"He can't sign." Toots looked quizzically at him. "He's underage."

"He'll learn responsibility. I trust him." He pushed the handwritten contract and a pen across the bar. "Billy, just sign."

"Be proud of him," he told Toots as we left. "This is a generation of losers. The war messed up families. Billy, come by tomorrow, and I'll get you the route."

As we started walking to the apartment, Toots was clearly confused. Her anger was tempered by the man's words.

"Maybe you'll turn out to be more than a burden. I never thought of you delivering newspapers."

By Wednesday, I was delivering to the Fairmount and Mark Hopkins hotels and to apartments along California Street. It was easy. I learned how to take advantage of appearing honest.

Chapter Nine

I'd wait for my newspapers on the corner of Mason and California across from the Fairmont Hotel and on the side of the Pacific Union Club. I put the newspapers in a carrier bag. Slinging it over my shoulder, I crossed the street into the ornate Fairmont lobby. Shortly after I started the route, the headline for March 5, 1953 was "Stalin Dies."

"Give me the papers. I'll take care of them. We don't want newsboys wandering the corridors," the bell captain, Charley Krupp, a thin sandy-haired forty year old with a slight foreign accent, told me.

"You're a good-looking lad." Charley said the next day as he stood proudly greeting guests in a gold-trimmed green uniform and top hat. He protected the entrance from people he thought didn't belong.

I received the same treatment across the street at the Mark Hopkins. At the apartment buildings along California, the superintendents ordered me to leave the papers with them. They didn't want me strolling around their buildings. Delivering papers in piles reduced the route's time to thirty minutes.

"How do I get my money?" I asked Charley. I was scheduled for news-paper collections every two weeks.

"Can't handle money; you've got to go to each room. There are some long-term guests. The penthouse is tough; they're really cheap. McCormick family has been here for five years, which may be the last time they tipped."

"Will they be there?"

"Best to collect in the early evening after work and before dinner; more likely to be in."

"And if they aren't?"

"Leave a bill at the front desk. They'll help you with the paper work. But you'll be less likely to get a tip. They're more likely if they see your face. Look sad; it usually works."

I got a similar story at the Mark Hopkins. At the apartment buildings, the supers said they'd let me in to collect. They didn't handle money.

At thirteen, it was a big adventure to knock on the Fairmont's penthouse door. Charley drew a hotel road map leading to the rooms receiving papers. The penthouse covered the hotel's entire eighth floor.

"Maybe you can get a foot in the door," Charley told me. "The penthouse is pretty impressive, done in the twenties. The map on the entrance ceiling shows sky and stars. Big place. McCormick's stinking rich. They pay a fortune."

I knocked softly. Nothing happened. I knocked harder, and the door flew open. "Who's there?" A woman dressed in a maid's uniform with a little white apron stared at me.

"Here to collect for the *Call-Bulletin*. Two bucks plus tip." Charley warned me to always mention a tip.

"I'll get Mr. McCormick. I can't handle money. Come in and wait."

I walked in as she shut the door. Remembering Charley's advice, I looked up at a sapphire-blue rotunda with the gold stars.

"Nice looking," said a man walking into the foyer and noticing me looking at the ceiling. Dressed in a maroon smoking jacket with black pants and patent leather shoes, he looked like a movie star. "Designed by art historian Arthur Pope," he explained, "back when the rich knew how to live. I'm Frank McCormick, and you must be the newsboy. You got a name?"

"Billy Durant," I gulped. "Here for the *Call-Bulletin*. Two weeks, two dollars plus tip."

"Billy, you're good-looking. Want to come in and look around?"

"Thank you. I need to collect for the paper."

He handed me a five-dollar bill with a softly whispered invitation. "Come back, and I'll show you the whole place. You're really cute. Leave enough time for some treats the cook can whip up. Keep the change. Hope to see you soon."

Frank touched my shoulder as he opened the door to let me out.

Three-dollar tip, I thought. *Wait till I tell Charley.*

Not everyone was home. I left some bills at the Fairmont and Mark Hopkins's front desks, and the supers said they'd let me back in to collect.

There was enough for my first payment to the bar owner. The owner patted me on the head and called me "a good kid."

I stopped by Jerry's hotel and found him sitting in the lobby talking to a man wearing makeup.

"Billy, this is Marvin. He makes movies up in his room. He'll pay us."

"Movies. Is this place big enough for all the cameras and stuff?" I wondered.

"Just a small camera," Marvin smiled, looking at me intently. "I sell through the mail. You and Jerry make a good-looking couple. How about both of you at once?"

"How much?" Jerry asked.

"I'll give you guys a tenner. You can split it."

"Ten bucks," Jerry gasped. "When?"

"Not today. I've got to go out. How about tomorrow? Can you be here, Billy?" Marvin ran his hand down my back. "It'll be hot. See you." He waved as he left the hotel.

"Let's go out," I said to Jerry. "I've got stuff to tell."

We walked down to Hyde Street as I told Jerry about my newspaper collections.

"You think we can get into that penthouse?" Jerry asked.

"Might be able to; the man was nice. I won't be back there for two weeks; that's the collection schedule. Hotels' front desks are collecting the other money. But I still have to go back to the apartments. Supers will let me in."

"Can you get me in?"

"Super at one buzzes me in. I've never seen him. We could go in together."

The next day after I finished my route, we stood in an apartment-building vestibule as I pressed the super's bell. "Billy Durant, collecting for the *Call-Bulletin*," I said into the speaker after the super answered. The door buzzed, and we hurried in.

After taking the elevator up and down and roaming corridors and testing doorknobs to see if any were unlocked, Jerry suggested that we try the basement.

"Last year," Jerry explained, "we stayed in a place where people stored stuff in basement lockers."

Stepping out of the elevator, we saw tall metal cages lining one wall. Another passageway led to a room filled with pipes and a boiler.

"Look in there." Jerry pointed into a cage. "Bet some interesting stuff in those suitcases."

He fiddled with the combination lock. "We can come back with a hammer and break these."

"Super will know it's me. I'm the only one he lets in."

"Come back tomorrow," Jerry planned. "I'll come in with you and stay after you leave. You can buzz the super that you're finished. I'll let you back in later."

"What about meeting Marvin tomorrow. We promised. Plus it's ten bucks."

"He can wait; just a queer."

"Queer?"

"He wants to take nude movies of us. Did you think it was a cowboy and Indian flick?"

"Nude?"

"Sells them through the mail. Last month I saw him take a pile of film to the post office."

The next day I left Jerry in the apartment building. As I exited, I buzzed the super. "Finished. I'll be back in two weeks. Thanks!"

I waited about an hour. We'd tried to time it, but neither of us had watches. I walked down California past the building. I couldn't see any sign of Jerry. I made the trip several times before I saw him. Checking that no one was around, he let me in. We hurried into the elevator and down to the basement.

Jerry had busted a half-dozen locks. He'd already opened boxes in the first locker. Shredded pages and photos from a baby book were on the floor.

"Let's open more," laughed Jerry. "We can have fun. Maybe find something valuable."

Pointing at the ripped pages, I wondered, "Shouldn't we put them back in the box? Anyone coming down can see the mess."

"Good thinking," replied Jerry. "It'll take them longer to discover. The more time, the less likely they'll think of you."

We systematically went through the contents of several lockers, ripping and destroying family mementos, particularly baby books, wedding albums, and photos. It felt good imaging the hurt faces looking at our vandalism. In one trunk full of family photos, we took turns pissing.

About the fifth locker, we got nervous. We started putting things back and hooking the locks on the doors. We didn't find anything of value, only old clothes and shoes along with family mementos. There were some baby carriages. Bicycles were the only things of value, but we worried about being seen taking them out.

We left empty-handed but ran up the street laughing. I still worried about getting caught since the super knew I had been in the building.

When I went back the next day for a delivery, the super simply took the newspapers. Two days later no one responded to the super's bell. Not knowing what to do, I simply left the papers by the mailboxes. The next day someone at the mailboxes told me that the super had been fired. "He was always drunk. Never paid attention to who was in the building. He let the lockers be vandalized. The owner fired him. Hopefully there will be a new one soon.

"Think I can go with you to that penthouse?" asked Jerry before my next collection.

"What'd you have in mind?"

"I don't know. Maybe get in the place and look around and see what we can do. You said he was friendly. Maybe queer."

"What's a queer?" I wanted to ask this after he had called Marvin a queer.

"You don't know what a queer is? It's a guy who likes other guys, like a guy liking a girl. They play with each other. That's what Marvin wants to make a movie of—you and me."

I felt a wave of revulsion at the idea and angrily responded, "We did that at a foster home. I got kicked out of another for messing around."

"We won't do any of the queer stuff." Jerry looked questioningly at me. "You never told me this stuff. Marvin tried that on me. That's why I didn't want to jump into making a movie. We're supposed to get nude."

Two weeks later Jerry and I stood in the penthouse's door as the maid informed us, "Mr. McCormick wants you to come in. Those were the instructions he gave me after you left last time."

She leaned down and whispered, "Be careful. He's weird."

"Billy," McCormick smiled, greeting us, "good to see you again. Who's your friend?"

"This is Jerry. He just wanted to come with me."

"You two want some ice cream? Let's go to the kitchen. I'll get rid of the maid. Just the three of us."

I looked at Jerry, who smiled at McCormick. Jerry said, "Sure, I'll take some ice cream. Got chocolate? Any fudge? Billy, you want some, don't you?"

McCormick led us into the largest kitchen I'd ever been in.

"Billy, what flavor?" he asked, opening a freezer.

"Strawberry."

"Strawberry and chocolate coming up." He opened a cabinet near the sink and took out ice-cream dishes and a scoop. From a drawer, he gave us spoons.

We perched on stools at the kitchen counter and ate away. I noticed Jerry looking into other rooms. I wondered what he was planning.

McCormick came over and put his hands on both of our shoulders. He ran his hand down my back and then softly wrapped it around my stomach.

"You two are cute. Want to have some fun?"

I noticed his hand sliding down to Jerry's crouch.

Nervous, I jumped off the stool. McCormick's hand moved around to my behind. He started rubbing and pressing his body against me. "We can have some fun. I'll pay to see your cute little butt."

Memories energized my growing panic. A magnetic strip next to the stove held a collection of large chef's knives. Rage and fear gripped me. I remembered the pain. I grabbed a carving knife and shoved it into his leg. Blood pulsed out as he went to his knees.

Chapter Ten

"You fuckin' kids!" yelled McCormick, slowly rising as blood flowed down his pants leg.

I stood stunned, holding the knife. Jerry started moving toward the door. Realizing that running would not protect us, Jerry barked, "You queer. Trying to get in boys' pants; you're the fucker."

"Hand me one of those towels," moaned McCormick, pointing at a rack near the sink.

Dropping the knife on the floor, I hurried over with a towel as he removed his pants.

"Not that bad." McCormick grimaced dabbing the wound. "Not deep. On the side. You're lucky I don't call the police. I will if you ever talk about this. You can help with some bandages."

"Let's get out of here," Jerry urged.

I followed McCormick as he limped down a hall to a medicine closet. Taking out gauze, he handed me the roll. "Wrap it around the wound," he calmly ordered. His shock at me stabbing him was being replaced with worries about police and bad publicity.

"Ouch, careful." He looked down in pain as I fumbled with the gauze.

Shaking and starting to cry, I blurted out, "I'm sorry. Don't know why I did it."

"Keep your mouth shut." He reached into a pocket of his smoking jacket and threw a roll of money at me. "Take this. I was going to give it to you anyway."

As the bleeding stopped, McCormick decided that there was no permanent leg damage. Still feeling pain, he shrieked, "Both of you get out!"

I scooped up the cash. Jerry was waiting by the entrance door. I showed him the money roll.

"Looks like a lot," Jerry grinned.

We started counting when we were alone in the elevator.

"Fifty bucks," Jerry gasped. "I wonder what he wanted for this type of money."

"I don't know, but I'm scared. I can't believe I stabbed him. The police'll get me."

"Don't worry," Jerry told me as we stepped out of the elevator into the gilded hotel lobby. "He'll be in big trouble if the police found out what he wanted from us."

I worried about myself. I'd killed one man and stabbed another. "Should we make up a story?"

"You said you knew that guy over there." Jerry pointed at the bell stand. "We could give him a story to cover our tracks."

We went over to the bell stand where Charley stood looking resplendent in his hotel uniform.

Jerry and I explained what happened without mentioning the stabbing.

"He started rubbing my butt," I told Charley. "That's when we got out of there."

"Should've warned you; all sorts of rumors about him and little kids. He comes on to our bellboys."

"Will he pay me for the papers next time?"

"He'll pay. Don't worry. He runs a big insurance firm. The publicity would kill him. Probably increase your tips."

We split the fifty dollars. I took my share to the bar owner.

"You're really a responsible boy," the bar owner said, noting my payment in a ledger. "You'll get this paid off soon."

He followed me outside and shook my hand. "Boys like you are the only hope of keeping America great. Honest and trustworthy. I wish more kids of your generation were like you."

Walking back to Clay Street, I wondered about my violence. I couldn't figure out why I had gone for the knife. Was I a born killer? But everyone said I was good."

The next day my math teacher, Miss Schilling, asked me to stop by after school. "Nothing bad," she assured me. "Just want to talk."

I sat across the desk from Miss Schilling, a warm-looking woman loved by her students.

"I want to be frank," she smiled. "I didn't like you when you first came into my room. There was something strange about how you talked and acted."

I gulped, uncertain how to respond. Did she know? Maybe in my actions, she recognized a killer.

"Then I realized," she continued, "you just act old for your age. Almost like an adult. You're a good kid. Would you like to be class monitor? I need someone I can count on."

"What?" I blurted out, clearly confused.

"Class monitor. Hope you'll do it. Good students need to be pushed."

"OK," I said. My mind kept rehearsing events in the penthouse.

"I see from your records you live with your mother."

"Yes, divorced in the war."

"A lot of problems with war babies like you. You're an exception and should be a model for others your age."

"Thank you." I didn't know what else to say.

The next day I took on monitorial chores of emptying the pencil sharpener, passing out paper, and carrying the attendance report to the main office. The principal, Mr. Walker, was standing outside his office when I brought the attendance report.

"Are you Billy Durant?"

I nodded yes.

"Miss Schilling says good things about you—smart and conscientious. I'll put you in with the advanced group next year. You'll like these students. Our best."

At lunchtime the next day, I cut into the cafeteria line when a girl who'd been eying me waved me in. The next thing I knew I was lying semiconscious on the floor. A large black boy had decked me, saying, "Boy, you don't cut in front of me." Rubbing my jaw, I picked myself up and sheepishly moved to the end of the line.

"I got a call at work from your principal," Toots told me that evening. "He wants to see me. What kind of trouble are you in? I told you to be careful. That old son of a bitch will use anything to cut your child support."

"I didn't do anything," I pleaded, worried that Toots would go into a screaming fit.

The next day Toots and I sat across the desk from Principal Walker.

"I want to thank you for coming, Mrs. Durant." Walker beamed. "It's a pleasure to have your son. All his teachers report him as polite, honest, and smart."

Toots looked quizzically at me. I wondered if, after that compliment, she was ruminating over constantly telling me, "I wish you'd never been born."

"I asked you to come in," he continued, "because of yesterday's incident. I'm sure Billy told you."

"No," Toots replied. "We never talk about school. I do tell him to be good because his father wants to take him away from me."

"Your son was knocked out at lunchtime yesterday by one of those bullies coming into our school."

"But I cut in line," I reacted. "I did the wrong thing."

"Knocked out!" Toots suddenly acted maternally. "Why wasn't I told? When I send Billy to school, I count on you protecting him. What bully? I'll sue!

Ignoring Toots's threat, the principal stood up and went over to a school-district map on the wall. He pointed at the demarcation of the neighborhoods served by the school.

"The blue line was our old district. Last year they moved the line to include the Fillmore neighborhood. That brought in these troublemakers and bullies."

"Fillmore!" exclaimed my mother. "Isn't that a colored area?"

"Precisely. They came as war workers." Walker sat down. "They brought nothing but problems. Parents are complaining, and our teachers say that they are ruining classes. We created special classes for them. They were dragging everyone else down."

"I caused the problem by cutting in," I repeated.

"You don't have to protect him." Walker smiled at me. "I know you're afraid he'll get you again. He's been kicked out of school. If I had my way, they'd all be kicked out. Good riddance to a bad bunch."

"I'll make sure Billy doesn't cause any more problems," said Toots, ignoring the racial implications of the principal's remarks.

"Billy is not the problem. The teachers love him. We'll do the right thing by him. What we are doing to protect quality kids like him is getting these Fillmore students kicked out."

As we left the school office, Toots looked confused. She had come prepared to give me hell for being a school troublemaker; she hadn't expected me to be praised.

"But I cut in line," I told Toots, getting into our car. "I'm the problem, not the other kid. I don't even know his name."

"That's life," commented Toots. "Some get punished; others go free. Be thankful the principal doesn't like coloreds."

"Does Dad really want me?" I asked with too much hope in my voice.

"You never appreciate anything I do for you," shouted Toots as she started the car. "The old son of a bitch doesn't want you. He's too busy with his girlfriends. You're my cross. He just wants to cut support. You'd better be good, or we don't eat or pay rent."

Chapter Eleven

In Miss Schilling's class, my love affair with math started. While others worked simple problems, she'd sit me next to her desk to learn algebra.

"You've got a natural math talent. You're one of the best students I've ever had," she praised me. "I asked Mr. Walker to put you in my advanced eighth-grade class next year."

Jerry took less demanding classes, so the only times we were together were lunch and gym. PE included exercising, playing games like kickball, and running around a small track. Every Monday the coaches inspected our shorts and gray T-shirts for cleanliness. Girls wore blue single-piece uniforms with elastic at the top of the thighs and at the upper part of the chest. Gym period ended with a communal shower. I tried not to stare.

Jerry and I started goofing around during a kickball game, maliciously kicking it at others.

Mr. Cleaver, the gym coach, saw what we were doing and ordered us to stay after school. We'd heard he liked to dress boys in girl's gym outfits. He'd pull them down and paddle with a small, wooden board drilled with holes. Burned into the wood were the words "The Board of Education."

"He better not try that stuff on me," whispered Jerry as we entered the coach's office. Lying on the coach's desk was the much-feared "Board of Education."

"Billy, Jerry," barked Mr. Cleaver. "You're troublemakers. I saw what you were doing. You know what this is?" He picked up the paddle and waved it. "You'll get five swats, more next time."

He reached into a desk drawer and pulled out two girls' gym outfits. "Go put these on and come back."

We went to our lockers, undressed, and pulled on the uniforms. "Look at this," Jerry said, snapping the elastic band around the chest. "I might grow boobs to fit."

"Do you think he's really going to ask us to pull these down?" I felt a stirring of rage.

"He'll pay if he does."

Back in his office, Mr. Cleaver smiled. "You two look good in those. Act up again, and I'll make you wear them every gym period. You guys know what you did and why you're being punished."

I nodded yes. Jerry just glared.

"Wipe that look off your face," Mr. Cleaver said to Jerry, "or I'll give you ten paddles."

He got up from his desk and swung the paddle in front of us. "Turn around, pull the uniform down, and bend over," he commanded.

Afterward Jerry and I vowed revenge. Jerry was outraged, and I felt the pain of my past.

"I'll get his address from the phone book," Jerry planned. "We'll go trash his place. I'm gonna tell the principal. Pervert. I'll get him fired."

Coach Cleaver lived near the school in a second-floor apartment on Lombard Street. We walked over and checked his apartment number on the mailbox. It was a corner apartment with a bay window facing Lombard.

"There's a light on," pointed Jerry as we stood on the sidewalk outside the building. "We should come back when he's gone."

"How'll we get into the building?"

"Ring an apartment on the top floor and hope they buzz us in," answered Jerry, looking thoughtfully at the coach's bay window. "My old man got some tools to pry open a door lock. He sometimes takes stuff from apartments when we ran short of cash."

In the coach's large living room was a flowery, upholstered couch with matching chairs. The arms were draped with crocheted lace doilies. We spied a target for our revenge on a large corner table covered with athletic trophies. Above the table was a framed NCAA award for "Best All-Round Athlete, NCAA Track and Field Championship, University of Minnesota, June 1938."

I grabbed the framed award and shattered its glass with a statue of a baseball player inscribed "All-League Baseball Champions, Balboa High School, 1934."

Jerry grabbed the frame from me and said, "I wanna tear this up. That bastard, he can't do that to me and get away with it." Jerry tore the award into small pieces and tossed the pieces into the air. We smashed the trophies and scattered them across the rug.

Jerry went into the kitchen for a knife and began cutting up the couch and chair cushions. I took another knife to the doilies and then threw porcelain animals displayed in a carved, wooden breakfront at the wall.

Laughing with glee, we smeared ketchup and mayonnaise on the walls and used their containers to shatter the glass on the breakfront. We stood and admired our destruction.

"Let's check the bedroom," suggested Jerry.

We ran into the bedroom, waving our knives and cutting any cloth we encountered: bedspread, sheets, clothes, and more doilies.

"Look at this," I exclaimed, opening the drawer of a bedside nightstand. The drawer was filled with photos and drawings of nude boys in a variety of sexual poses.

"Wow," said Jerry. "I knew he was a pervert."

We spread the photos on the bed.

"Look what these queers do." Jerry held up a photo of two boys about our age giving each other blow jobs.

"Do they do this?" Though horrified, I was getting a real sex education.

"I guess so," replied Jerry, pausing at a photo of a naked Mr. Cleaver fondling a boy. "I think I can get the bastard fired with this one and that one over there." He reached across the bed to retrieve a photo of the coach having anal intercourse.

The photo sent me into a rage. I sliced my knife into the mattress and hurled a bedside lamp against the dresser. Jerry pocketed the two photos. We ripped up the others and made a pile of the pieces on the bed.

"Go to the living room," Jerry ordered. "I'm going take a crap on the photos and bed."

Miss Schilling was very nice the next morning. "Billy, you're my smartest student. I'm nominating you for the Good Citizen Award. It will be given at the awards ceremony at the end of the year. I'm writing a strong letter of recommendation about your good character."

After lunch, rumors of Cleaver's firing swept through the hallways.

"When no one was looking, I left the photo of the coach sticking it in that boy on the office counter," explained Jerry. "No one could miss it. I'm wondering what the secretary thought when she saw it. I stuck the other photo on the bulletin board at the school entrance."

Then Jerry disappeared. It was two weeks before the end of the school year when I couldn't find Jerry at lunch. After my newspaper route, I went searching for him.

"The police arrested his old man," the hotel clerk told me. "He was caught burglarizing an apartment."

"Jerry?"

"Child services took him away—probably a foster home, I imagine."

Jerry was the best friend and maybe the only friend I'd ever had. As I walked back to my apartment, my loneliness mixed with sadness. I fought back an uncontrollable rage bubbling to the surface.

We moved that summer to an apartment in the Marina District a few blocks from school. I was able to get the newspaper route in the area. The most exciting thing was delivering to Joe DiMaggio and Marilyn Monroe's house. I'll always remember the number: 2150 Beach Street. I never saw them. The housekeeper paid.

I started binge eating to fill the loneliness. Toots bought me a bike for the newspaper route. I often stopped at an Italian Deli on Lombard Street to buy rolls, cheeses, and salami. Being thirteen going on fourteen, along with bicycling, kept the weight off.

When eighth grade began, I was feeling good about my Citizenship Award at the seventh-grade graduation ceremony and my placement in Miss Schilling's advanced math class.

Then Toots sent my world spinning with the announcement that we were moving to Hawaii. After being in three different schools in the seventh grade, I wondered if my eighth-grade experience would be similar.

"The whole office is going," Toots said, obviously excited about the transfer. "The navy is moving us to the headquarters in Pearl Harbor. They're shipping us and our stuff for free."

I must have looked upset. I don't think she understood my pain at being moving again.

"Don't look at me like that," she snapped. "Why don't you appreciate anything I do for you? You'll be able to surf and ride outriggers. They say it's beautiful."

I stood on the deck of a navy supply ship and sadly waved good-bye to the Marina District as we headed for the Golden Gate Bridge and open ocean.

As soon as my belly felt the ocean swells, I was sick. I spent the first days in my bunk taking Dramamine. Finally we decide it was making me even sicker. Five days later we saw Diamond Head and were greeted at a Pearl Harbor dock by lei-covered hula dancers singing "Sweet Leilani."

Toots found an apartment in a four flat in Waikiki near the Ala Wai Canal and Fort DeRussy. This was 1954, before airlines unleashed floods of tourists. Rents were cheap, and Waikiki had only a handful of hotels, like the Royal Hawaiian and Moana Surfrider. With my navy dependent's card, thanks to my father, I had easy access to Fort DeRussy's mostly empty beach and floating swim platform. Later Fort DeRussy served as military R and R during the Vietnam War.

Unlike my segregated experience in Pensacola, I was greeted by students of many races when Toots enrolled me in eighth grade at Robert Louis Stevenson Junior High. At fourteen, my hormones were on the move, excited by young Hawaiian and mixed-race girls. My first love and date was Betty Mae Nakashima.

I complained of back pains. Toots sent me to see an orthopedic doctor. He recommended weight lifting and sent me to a gym in downtown Honolulu operated by Rex Revel, a body-building champion with muscles popping out all over his body.

"Shit, bunch of muscle-bound freaks," said Toots after seeing Rex's gym. "Go ahead; probably good for you. I'll send the old man a bill."

After a couple trips to the gym, I became friendly with Jack Lister who could bench-press three hundred pounds.

"Ever swum off Diamond Head?" asked Lister as we both stood under adjacent showers. "Lot of small, salt tidal pools to soak in."

After my next gym visit, I got in Lister's car, and we headed out to Diamond Head. He parked on a pull off overlooking the ocean.

We climbed down the rocks, passing several men stretched nude on towels and enjoying the sun. Lister said hello and pointed to a secluded place between two boulders to lay out our towels on. Then he stripped and stood naked.

"You can take everything off here," urged Jack. "Skinny-dipping is the practice here."

Apprehensive, I stuttered, "Not for me." I was wearing my bathing suit under my pants. I'd wondered where I would change. So I slipped off my pants.

"Come on," he chided. "That's the fun here."

Jack reached over, grabbed the top of my bathing suit, and started pulling it down.

I was blinded by rage, and a fist-sized rock found its way into my hand. Out of control, I started hitting Jack in the face. Blood flowed from the gashes. In a fury, I leaped on him.

Several of his friends ran over and pulled me off. Realizing what I'd done, I pulled on my pants, raced to the road, and started walking toward Waikiki. I looked back and could see others attending to Jack's wounds. An argument broke out. The final words I heard were, "You can't call the cops. He's underage. You'd go to jail for molesting him."

Chapter Twelve

After school hours, Betty Mae and I would dance in our socks on the teak floor of her living room. In San Francisco, Toots had sent me to Arthur Murray to learn ballroom dancing. She always emphasized two things: treat women politely and be a good dancer.

"Walk on the outside near the road." Toots stated her rules for respecting women. "You protect women from splashes. Always help with a chair, open the door, put your napkin on your lap, hold your fork and knife properly, help remove and put on coats, let the lady order first, and never, ever be rough."

Interspersed between "I wish you'd never been born"; "You're my cross"; and "Why didn't you let me die," Toots took me to operas, Geary Theater productions, and the library. Later when she was chasing a much-younger man in Thailand, she wrote me, "He's just like you." I was groomed to please women.

"You want to do the tango for the eighth-grade talent show?" asked Betty Mae during school lunch hour.

"You're gonna dance?" Toots was excited at the idea but didn't like Betty Mae. "You doing it with that Jap girl?"

"Yeah." I grimaced, aware of Toots's ongoing racism.

Toots bought me a beret and allowed me to use an ivory-inlaid ebony cane from my father's African trips. To "Hernando's Hideaway" and applause, we glided over the lunchroom floor dipping and twirling.

Afterward Betty Mae invited me to dinner. "Good Japanese meal. Don't pay any attention to my parents; they don't like me with a white boy."

One day in math class, Alan Chang offered to show me how to spearfish.

"Sneak me into DeRussy. They've got a good reef," he said. "Get some surgical rubber tubing at the pharmacy and a wooden block. I've got some extra spears."

He took me to his house to make a Hawaiian sling by drilling a hole in the wooden block and attaching the surgical rubber. After the spear was put through the hole, the rubber was stretched back and released.

On our first hunt along the reef off DeRussy, I speared a blowfish. I watched in terror as it expanded.

"He acts queer," said Toots after Alan left one evening. "Pretty girly. Look out!"

Surprised by Toots using "queer," I mumbled, "I don't think so. He acts like other Chinese boys at school—they're nice."

Bette Mae asked me one day after school, "Wanna go swimming up in the valley?"

"I don't have any trunks. I'd have to go back to the apartment to get them."

"You can wear your pants. They'll dry on the way back. Lots of kids just jump in."

I followed Betty Mae up a narrow path in the Moanalua Valley surrounded by lush vegetation. At the end was a waterfall cascading into a shallow pool surrounded by rocks and orchids growing on trees.

By February, Betty Mae and I started kissing and stroking each other on our swimming trips.

In March, with no hint of why, she dumped me. Maybe I should have been bolder.

One day just before I graduated from the eighth grade, the principal, Mr. Kahiau, called me to the office.

"We're putting you into the advanced ninth-grade group. You've got passable language skills, but you excel in math."

"Language skills, me?" I questioned. "How's that? I can't write very good."

"You passed the Standard English test. Do you realize that Hawaiian schools are separated into Standard English and Pidgin English? Most Hawaiians and Filipinos go to the other schools. They're not very good."

"You'll do well in this ninth-grade class," continued the principal, "and go on to Roosevelt High School. Honolulu's best!"

Alan and I continued hanging out and doing homework together. Betty Mae avoided me in the school's corridors. I hung out with other girls, but nothing happened.

During the summer of 1954, before I entered high school, Rex Revel invited me to perform in his body-building review. Jack Lister never returned to the gym. In the gym, men no longer approached me after the Diamond Head incident. Jack Lister must have told his buddies I was jailbait.

"I don't have muscles for a body-building show," I said, surprised that Rex even asked me.

"You won't do the body-building stuff. Just hula on stage with the others. Wear a bathing suit and shirt. You got a uke?"

"Can't play."

"Act like you're playing. If you don't know the words, lip-synch. Just follow others when we hula."

Dancing next to me in Rex's chorus line, a man wearing a flowered, green swimsuit and matching shirt asked, "Know the song 'He's a Mahu from Waipahu'?"

"No," I answered, trying to look like I was singing and doing a proper hula. I'd never seen him before—he probably went to the gym on different days.

"I'm Billy Durant," I whispered. "I can't do the hula."

"You look good." Our hips touched as I tried to keep up with the words "Lovely hula hands, graceful as the birds in motion..."

"I'm Craig Kaiko. Haven't seen you around."

Finally the performance ended. We made room for the body builders. The audience applauded and shouted as the real draw of the night performed thigh and abdominal poses and popular chest and bicep positions.

"You wanna go outside for air?" Craig asked as we stood in the wings. "I'll teach you the Mahu song. We're gonna do it next."

I recoiled at Craig's suggestion. Looking at him, I could see the same inviting smile that Jack Lister had worn.

"No," I responded apprehensively. "I'll stay here and watch the body builders."

Later I found out that "Mahu" referred to "gay." The opening lyrics were "He's a Mahu from Waipahu, and he gives all the boys a thrill." The Mahu song was not in Rex's review.

Rex Revel's review was the highlighted of a summer of swimming and spear fishing before I entered tenth grade at Roosevelt High. It was 1955, and I was fifteen or, as my teachers often, said, "You're fifteen going on fifty."

At Roosevelt kids were starting to drive.

"Want to go to a drive-in movie with my cousin?" asked Charley Saunders during chemistry class. "They're showing *Blackboard Jungle*. Supposed to be pretty hot."

We piled into Charley's car. I sat next to his cousin Suzy Chandler, who was visiting from a sugar plantation on the Big Island. Except for the opening song, "Rock Around the Clock," I remember little of the movie as Suzy taught me French kissing and put my hands up her skirt.

"Want to visit Hawaii?" asked Suzy, licking my ear. "My parents don't care. They think I'm too alone on the plantation."

I was surprised that Toots agreed to the plane fare. I suspected that she wanted time with a new boyfriend. In those days, they weighed you before getting on the small prop plane serving Hilo.

Suzy greeted me at the Hilo airport. She was sixteen and old enough to drive us back to a sprawling plantation house surrounded by sugar cane a short distance from Naalehu. Her parents paid little attention to me or our comings and goings.

"They fight all time," said Suzy, taking my small bag into a bedroom next to hers. "I hate it here. I only see cane rows and hear them argue. Hard to have friends." She kissed me, pressing her body against mine.

That afternoon we toured black-sand beaches and a hot lava flow from the Kilauea volcano. We returned at dinnertime. Sitting around a polished Koa dining table served by plantation staff, Suzy's parents grunted at each other while we touched under the table.

Afterward we went to Suzy's bedroom. I sat on the bed as she removed her clothes. I'd only seen my mother naked. I was worried about coming as I stared. I stripped. I'd never been naked before a girl, and she guided me into bed. I lost my virginity in a plantation house as I listened to the calls of tree frogs.

Returning three days later, I took the airport bus to Waikiki and walked to our apartment. It was late afternoon. I called Toots to let her know that I was back.

"I got something exciting to tell you tonight. You'll love it," Toots said. I was instantly apprehensive. These announcements often released some new peril in my life. "There're some minute steaks in the fridge," she continued, "and salad makings. I'll be home early."

Humming along to Hawaiian songs on a local radio station, I coated the minute steaks with Worcestershire sauce to Toots's liking. Timed for Toots's arrival, I heated the broiler, tossed the salad, and cut pineapple rings for dessert. Always conscious of her figure, we ate low-calorie dinners.

While I was whistling "Aloha Oe" and excitedly thinking of Suzy's invitation to see her again, Toots burst through the door.

"We're going back!" she shouted gleefully. "Got a transfer to CINCPAC offices in San Diego. Nothing here but palm trees. This place is too small."

After Toots left for a night of celebrating our return to San Diego, I went out around midnight to Kalakaua Boulevard carrying a small hammer from the tool kit under the kitchen sink.

Strolling past parked cars, I looked around for witnesses as I broke windshields and side mirrors. Thinking about Suzy, moving, and attending another school, I stopped next to an expensive new Lincoln Capri convertible. I pounded the hammer against the passenger door, leaving a line of dents. Then I broke the side mirror and passenger window.

Still checking for witnesses, I spied a baby-blue Cadillac El Dorado parked on a dark side street. After breaking into the car, I destroyed the dashboard and broke the steering wheel. Using the hammer's claws, I tore the leather upholstery. Relieved, I headed back to the apartment.

A week later, adorned with orchid leis given at a dockside ceremony, we boarded a supply ship headed to San Diego. Standing at the rail as Diamond Head passed from view, I tossed my leis into the ocean, which, according to legend, guaranteed my return. As I walked the deck weepy eyed, my mind was flooded with images of Suzy, spearfishing, and orchid-covered pools. Hawaii was the happiest place I'd been.

Chapter Thirteen

We moved in with Toot's friend from Oklahoma, Christine McCarty. Christine and Toots were close pals when Dad was stationed in Oklahoma. Christine married an MD who was a US Navy captain. Toots called her before leaving Hawaii.

"Buster," answered Christine, referring to her husband, "is gonna be on sea duty for six months. We can have fun; plenty of space for you and Billy." On the navy transport to San Diego, Toots warned me, "Don't tell anyone this, but it was rumored that Christine was a prostitute before marrying Buster. He was a big catch."

Christine's ranch home was in Clairemont, a small San Diego community in the hills overlooking Mission Bay and Pacific Beach. I was given a room connected by a door to the garage. Christine's eight-year-old son, Michael, had the bedroom next to mine. Unknown to me, Toots and Christine agreed I would babysit Michael on their nights out. Toots occupied another bedroom in the four-bedroom ranch house.

Enrolled in the tenth grade at Mission Bay High in 1955, I found a job selling ice cream at a Frosty Freeze in a nearby mall.

Christine's house was near Balboa Avenue, where I caught the bus down to Mission Bay High.

"You a new student?" asked a cute brunette dressed in tight sweater as we waited for the bus on my first morning going to school.

"Just moved from Hawaii."

"I'm Wendy Kelly." She politely offered her hand.

"Billy Durant."

We sat next to each other on the bus and chattered away. We were in the same grade.

After a week of talking at school and on the bus, she invited me to dinner.

Joel Spring

"Good evening," said Wendy's father as I walked into a living room filled with bookcases with other books stacked on every available space. Beethoven's Third Symphony played on their hi-fi. Wendy's mother, Margaret, sat reading in a rocking chair.

"Dad's a scientist at Scripps; Mom reads a lot," explained Wendy, waving at the books.

The dinner-table conversation was lively, unlike my experience at Suzy's. Both parents asked about my background. I learned that they were living in Clairemont because of Margaret's asthma. Regrettably they'd had to move from the intellectual community near Scripps to the Clairemont hills.

"Mom was selected at Stanford," whispered Wendy to me as we went to her room after dinner, "to be part of Lewis Terman's longitudinal genius study."

Before I could ask about the study, Wendy started kissing me and putting my hand on her breast. Her parents didn't seem to care about us being alone in her bedroom.

I was often left to care for Michael. Toots and Christine sometimes disappeared for several days. At least I knew how to cook, feed the kid, and hustle him off to school.

I lived in a swirl of sexual activity. One early morning I heard noise in the garage. Opening the door from my room, I saw Christine naked, sprawled across the hood of her car, being screwed by a stranger. After a weekend in Ensenada, a Mexican town south of San Diego, Toots laughed, telling me, "I said his butt was too big. He said you couldn't drive a spike with a tack hammer."

One evening I visited Wendy, bringing a recording of a Mozart piano concerto I'd bought with my Frosty Freeze earnings.

"I brought this over to hear." I showed her father the record.

"Put it on," he said, barely looking up from his book. He was a stereotype of a pipe-smoking academic with elbow patches on his jacket. Born in Boston, he had a Harvard PhD in marine biology.

"Hoped you'd like hearing it," I said, trying to impress him. The music played in the background as we ate.

As we retreated to Wendy's bedroom, she asked, "Want to go with us to Zion National Park? It'd be during the Easter holiday."

On the trip, I slept on an inflatable mattress in shared motel rooms. It was a first for me, traveling with a regular family. At the park, I was in a separate tent, which didn't keep me from sneaking away with Wendy. Nothing dramatic happened on the trip, which was an unusual experience for me.

When we returned to San Diego, Wendy looked sadly at me and said, "Dad and Mom think we're spending too much time together. I've got to go meet other boys at our Unitarian Church."

"They don't like me," I said. I imagined their feelings about my divorced, typist mother, a father who never graduated from elementary school, my Choctaw Indian background, and, of course, my mother's family. As they steered Wendy away from me to other boys, we would occasionally date throughout high school, including me taking her to the senior prom.

During the summer, Buster returned from sea duty, and we had to move. I'd got a summer job at a pet clinic near Clairemont. Dr. Wilson, the vet, owned a house next to the clinic. He needed a night attendant. He offered the house rent-free for my evening work. At night I'd answer a buzzer to take in sick and injured dogs and cats.

"Let's have a party." I invited classmates to the pet clinic at the beginning of my junior year. I was sixteen.

"Get me some booze," I told the man who cleaned the kennels handing him money, "and I'll clean for you on Sunday."

Gloria, a large-busted girl, stood at the pet clinic's surgical table and selected from the whiskey and vodka I'd laid out. "I guess more vodka," she slurred, already drunk. I thought of all the animals cut open on the table. Six other students poured more for themselves.

"What's in these cabinets?" asked Gloria, randomly opening doors.

"Animal drugs." I retrieved bottles of tranquilizer and sodium pentothal. Holding up the sodium pentothal, I said, "Anyone want to try truth serum?"

"Sure," said Gloria. "I'm into the truth. Do I drink it?"

"I need to inject it. Anyone else want to try? Only a little bit, or you'll go to sleep."

I took hypodermic needles out of a drawer as everyone gathered. Only Gloria was willing to experiment.

I put the needle in Gloria's vein. She began to wobble as the serum coursed through her body. We disappeared into an adjacent examining room, closing the door as others continued drinking.

"Take me like a dog," Gloria said. In a hypnotic state, she lifted her skirt and struggled out of her panties. She almost collapsed getting on her hands and knees. It was my first time having sex on the floor of the pet clinic.

Things got weird with the animals. One night a German shepherd was brought for boarding. The dog nuzzled my crotch as dogs frequently do. I reached down and started masturbating him. I tried bestiality, but the dog bit. After that, I would wander by the cages and select an animal to torture using any method that didn't leave permanent marks. Sometimes Dr. Wilson commented on the dogs snarling at me when the kennel man brought them through the office.

I got carried away with a tan Chihuahua, strapped it to a table, and experimented with different drugs and surgical clamps. When it died, I carried the dog back to its cage. No one knew I had done it. The owners sued.

"What a good student!" declared my teachers. "You're so polite! I wish others were like you."

My social studies teacher, a former marine, said, "We need boys like you to stop the commie menace." He put me in charge of the movie projector. I showed right-wing movies about communist takeovers and fighting collectivist thinking for individualism. I secretly sided with the communists and dreamed of dropping nuclear bombs on San Diego.

"Student Wins Math Contest!" My photo and a short article appeared in the *San Diego Herald* in my senior year. It was 1958. As the West was plunged into worries about the Soviet Union launching the first space capsule, suddenly my mind was valued for its possible contribution to winning the Cold War.

Math and girls were my passions. Toots had trained me well. The phone frequently rang with girls asking me out. They often had cars. They liked my dancing and manners.

"I wish other boys were like you," they'd whisper in my ear.

I still pined for Wendy and kept modeling myself after her father. I started smoking a pipe. My collection of classical records expanded. A therapist later told me, "Wendy's father was your male role model."

Dr. Wilson praised my work at the clinic. Teachers and counselors pushed me to apply for scholarships and colleges. Whenever I felt angry, there were always the animals.

It was a pleasant surprise when Wendy sat down next to me in the school lunchroom and said, "I convinced my parents to take you to our church."

"I'll come if you go to the prom with me." The "yes" came unexpectedly fast.

The Unitarian Church surprised me when a congregant demanded during the service's discussion time that "Jesus's name should be taken out of our songs." No Four Square Holy Rollers at this church.

After the service, Wendy handed me a pamphlet and explained, "We do not tell you what you must believe. Instead we invite you to join in a conversation with us about the meaning of life, love, and service."

Attending Wendy's church renewed our relationship. I think her parents were impressed with my many scholarship offers.

I had to make a decision about which one to accept. Toots didn't know anything about colleges but persuaded me to take a four-year navy scholarship emphasizing that "Officers are gentlemen by an act of Congress."

After Toots's dating experiences, I should have known better. The navy scholarship was generous: room and board, books, tuition, and fifty dollars a month of spending money. From a list of schools provided by the navy, I chose Brown University's math program for my navy scholarship. Images of shooting down planes flooded my mind when I received a Congressional appointment to the Air Force Academy.

Toots drove me to Vandenberg Air Force Base for the academy interview. I was housed in the base's Bachelor Officer Quarters.

"Have a drink, kid." I was handed a glass of whiskey after I found Vandenberg's Officers' Club. A drinking contest was going on. Staggering back to my room, I spent the night retching.

"Time for your physical; be at the gym by zero eight hundred," a voice ordered through the door. My head pounded. Stumbling out of bed, I hurriedly dressed, asked for directions at the reception desk, and slowly made it to the gym.

I was ordered into a pair of official air force shorts and a T-shirt. I was timed on hurdles, measured on how far I threw a basketball, and counted on the number of chin-ups I could do. As I left the gym, I knew that my air force appointment was doomed.

The next day another air force candidate offered to drive me to my Brown interview at the Los Angeles Harvard Club. I packed my clothes, some smelling of vomit and alcohol.

Dressed in a wrinkled Hawaiian sport shirt and dirty khakis, I pressed the Harvard Club buzzer. A butler-like figure looked me up and down as he let me into the club. From the foyer, I could see a formal dining room with a large group of men and boys dressed in suits talking and eating.

"I'm here for a Brown interview," I told the doorman. Grunting, he pointed at the dining room and said, "Go in there; they'll set you up."

"Gotta call my brother first; he's picking me up. Can I use a phone?"

Sonny, who was out of the air force and living in LA, told me he'd be right over. I gave him the address.

"I can't stay long," I told the man at the dining-room reception desk. "My brother's picking me up soon."

Looking disdainful, the man reminded me that it was an interview.

I said, "I thought I'd meet someone and talk. I didn't know it was a dinner." Looking around the room, I mentioned, "I don't own a suit and tie."

My brother arrived in low-slung Levi's and T-shirt with a cigarette dangling from his mouth. "What kind of place is this?" he asked, looking around in wonderment. "Pretty fancy."

We hurried out.

Chapter Fourteen

"We wish you the best in your future academic pursuits," concluded the rejection letter from Brown University.

"Your low physical aptitude score disqualifies you from admission to the Air Force Academy," explained the air force letter.

"We're pleased to inform you that you will be stationed at Naval Reserve Officer Training Corps at the Illinois Institute of Technology located in Chicago, Illinois. Sign and return the enclosed acceptance form," read the navy letter.

I boarded a bus in San Diego for Chicago as my dry-eyed mother hurried back to her car. Dad promised to send me the child-support money. I was able to save money between the navy covering costs and giving me expense money along with my dad's monthly checks.

As we entered Chicago, a siren pulled the bus over to the curb. I watched the driver step off the bus, reach for his wallet, and give the cop a ten-dollar bill. This was crime-riddled Chicago.

After arriving at the Chicago bus terminal, I loaded my luggage into a cab and was taken to a steel and glass Ludwig Mies van der Rohe–designed dorm near Thirty-First and State Street. I checked in with the housemother.

"Don't walk off campus," she said, "and don't do to the El at night. This is a bad neighborhood."

Heading to the cafeteria, I looked across State Street at small red-brick apartment buildings where black men and women could be seen hurrying in and out. It was in sharp contrast to the mainly white campus.

"Stay away from the houses across State Street," an orientation counselor warned the entering class.

"I hear they're whorehouses," whispered a student next to me.

"Don't walk off campus at night," continued the counselor.

Drunk that night at the dorm party for entering students, I yelled across the rowdy crowd, "Let's go check out the whores."

Five of us crossed State and were greeted by a well-dressed black man with a clipboard.

"What kind you fellows want? I got 'em all—fat, skinny, beautiful, suckers, and some that take it in the ass."

"I got five bucks," I said. "What can I get?"

I left the others bartering with the pimp as I was led by another man into a building and upstairs to a room with a heavy black woman lying naked on a grimy bed.

As she started slipping a condom on me, there was a pounding on the door and yells of "Police!" The whore jumped up and raced out of the room with me following. This was Chicago.

The next day I attended my first navy drill. At the conclusion of the senseless marching and after learning the correct parade rest and attention postures, I lit a cigarette.

"Don't smoke until you are dismissed," commanded an officer, grabbing my arm.

Fuck, I thought to myself, *Toots never said anything about this side of navy life.*

A required navy course on fire power, which I mistakenly thought was about putting out ship fires, awakened me to the fact that I was being trained to kill. The instructor started talking about trajectories, gun calibers, and famous sea battles. I liked thinking about guns but not being required to jump to attention when the instructor or an officer entered the room.

Classes were another matter. I loved and excelled at math. Chemistry was a bummer with the professor talking the whole time with his back to the class. He opened the semester with the words, "If you have ovaries, you shouldn't be taking chemistry." Toots would've slapped him.

In my English class, I instinctively reacted against the corporate conformity described in the required reading of William Whyte's *The*

Organization Man and C. Wright Mills's *White Collar*. Any possible pleasure thinking about the navy's giving me the right to kill was negated by taking orders, wearing a uniform, and fitting in.

In the 1959 spring semester, I escaped. I closed my savings account and packed my clothes in small gym bag. I bought a one-way bus ticket to Mexico City. I boarded cursing, "Fuck the navy,"

I sat next to a girl, Nancy Selena. We made out with all the way to Mexico City. Between pleasuring each other, I stared at the passing scenery and wondered where I fit in after Wendy's Unitarian youth group, my Brown rejection, and now the navy.

Nancy was met by relatives as we stepped off the bus in Mexico City. She slipped an address to me as she whispered in my ear, "That was fun. Go here, and they'll set you up."

Using broken Spanish learned in San Diego, I exchanged money and took a cab to Zona Rosa. A flight of stairs led to an apartment with mounds of peyote buttons along the living-room wall.

"You here to buy?" asked a long-haired, bearded Anglo pointing at the peyote.

"Nancy Selena gave me your address. Said you'd set me up. What's that stuff?"

"Peyote. Ever try it? You can drop some for five pesos. Good for dreaming."

"Need a place to stay; just in from Chicago."

"Serapes in the next room. Bed down on the floor. Ten pesos for floor and peyote."

"What'll it do?"

"You'll get sick, and then you'll love the colors."

"Sick?"

"Only some vomiting. It's worth it."

Fuck, I thought, *why not?*

It tasted like soap. Forty-five minutes later, I was vomiting into a filthy toilet and watching my food particles change colors. I stumbled back to my floor space and wrapped the serape around me as a kaleidoscope of colors painted the ceiling. I awakened the next morning with a headache and a desire to do more.

"Take the bus to Acapulco and then to Puerto Escondido," advised the long-haired man. "American artist colony is there with plenty of drugs. They'll take you in."

Late at night I arrived in Acapulco and selected a cheap hotel from a guidebook. When I pounded on the door, windows flew open with women waving me in.

"Fifty pesos for special tricks," a whore yelled down.

Frightened, wondering if I'd be robbed, I walked down a ramp to the beach. Using my gym bag as a pillow, I watched shadowy figures moving crablike over the sand and stealing purses and clothing from unsuspecting couples embracing under the moonlight.

Headachy from lack of sleep, I chewed a mushroom my host had given me in Mexico City with the warning, "Stronger and different from peyote; be careful. Could lose control. Some don't remember what they did. At least it doesn't make you sick."

Slinking figures, lovers, ocean, and stars melded into a ballet of lights dancing across the sand. I followed an apparition of the black man I had murdered down the beach.

When I awoke, my bloody hand held a knife. Looking around in the early morning light, I saw few people on the beach. I buried the knife and washed my hands in the salt water. The blood mixing with water reminded me of Toots. My gym bag was gone, but my wallet was still in my pocket.

In a distant corner of the beach, I could see rotating red beacons of police cars. A cluster of uniforms surrounded an object on the sand. I mounted the break wall and walked in the direction of the uniforms.

Reaching the police, I looked down and saw a badly mutilated naked man with gashes across his face and body. One police officer was scooping the lifeless man's genitals into a bag.

Frightened, I wanted to hurry to Puerto Escondido. Stumbling through my broken Spanish at the ticket office, I was told to change buses at a crossroad near Terjoruco, where I jumped off the bus in front of a cantina.

Drunken Mexicans and loud ranchera music blasting from a jukebox greeted me as I headed to the bar for cerveza. A drunken man emerged from the crowd showing me his police badge and announcing to all I was a *"malo Norte Americano."*

As best as I could understand, he was offering his daughter in marriage or jail time. Confused, I ran out and jumped on a bus just stopping in front. It took me back to Acapulco. Not wanting to be there, I took a bus back to Mexico City.

My savings were dwindling, and my bag of clothes had been stolen on the beach. Luckily an outdoor market offered cheap pants and shirts.

What to do next? I found the train station and looked at the list of departures. In two hours, one was leaving for New York City. I had a few dollars left after buying a ticket for the Aztec Eagle.

Exhausted, I fell asleep as the train pulled out of the station. I awakened to a panorama of cactus, rosette scrub, sagebrush, and arid mountains. An older man with a European accent sat down next to me and struck up a conversation.

"Where you headed?" he asked in halting English.

"New York. And you?"

"Paris. I'm getting a boat in New York."

"Long trip," I commented.

"Friends in New York. Difficult to get from Mexico to Europe. This is the easiest way. Want a drink? I got tequila in my compartment."

I followed him back to his first-class compartment. After several shots of tequila, his hand rested on my knee.

I succumbed to enjoying the sensations.

We were not disturbed until Laredo, Texas, where the crew and engine were changed, extra passenger cars added, and the name changed to the Texas Eagle. We were headed for Penn Station, New York City.

The rest of my trip was spent in the first-class dining room, the bar car with its beautiful Southwest murals, and the man's compartment. Arriving in the spectacular Beaux arts Penn station, he handed me a hundred bucks, kissed me on the cheek, and wished me well.

At the information booth, the woman on duty said, "The cleanest and cheapest place is the YMCA a few blocks away."

I checked into the Y. I saved money by eating in my room and exploring the city by foot.

Then I got bored and called a student friend, who told me that navy officers had come and taken all my personal stuff from the dorm. They had left a message for me to contact them if I appeared.

I took the train back to Chicago. I was broke and worried about the navy. Would they throw me in the brig?

I went from the Chicago train station to the Great Lakes Naval Training Center.

The sailor at the gate looked puzzled when I announced, "I'm turning myself in. I'm AWOL from an NROTC scholarship."

The sailor spoke into a phone, and a lieutenant hurried over from a nearby building.

"You left a navy scholarship program without telling anyone?"

"Yes." I could feel a cold sweat damping my shirt. "Went to Mexico. I was at the Illinois Institute of Technology."

"Why would you throw away money?"

"Don't know." I suppressed a desire to tell him that the navy sucked.

"We've never had a case like this. Do you have contact info? I'll need to contact JAG."

"JAG?"

"US Navy Judge Advocate General. They'll contact you."

Confused by not being thrown in a brig, I supplied the phone number of the IIT dorm where my friend Larry Folsom had agreed to let me sleep on an unused bed.

"Is that all?" I was still bewildered by the navy's reaction.

"Never heard of a case like this." The lieutenant looked sourly at me. "I still wonder why."

I took the bus back to Chicago. Ten years later I received an honorable discharge in the mail with a blank service record. Thankfully the navy's bureaucracy never sent me to the brig.

A friend of Larry's, Beryl Bellows, invited me to join him and Jay Reiner to drive a pickup truck for a company to Fresno, California. I'd been back ten days and was hooked up with a nursing student, Veronica Perry. The truck cab only held two.

We threw a mattress into the back for Veronica and me. Beryl and Jay expressed envy across the country as we bounced around in back. At one point a Greyhound pulled alongside on a four-lane highway going into Kansas City. I'd just started going down on Veronica. Glancing up at the stares, I flipped back our blanket for a full view of our bodies. What a trip!

Veronica didn't want to leave me. But after five days, I felt uncomfortable around her. It wasn't dislike but, as I realized later, a fear of intimacy. I couldn't emotionally bond.

After getting Veronica on a bus back to Chicago, I hitchhiked to San Diego to see Toots.

I stayed with Toots, getting a job as a dishwasher. The job lasted only two days when the owner decided he didn't like my attitude.

The California State Employment Bureau sent me to an interview for counseling kids at Camp Jeffery near Alpine. Hired, I supervised wards of the court. These were my types—foster and delinquent kids. It was hard. I drank a bottle of wine under a tree after the first group left. I shared a tent with a flamboyant gay guy.

I saved my earnings, since the job provided free food and a tent. Toots, always restless, asked if I would like to go to school in Europe. She said, "I can get a job at any US base in Europe. I like the navy air station in Spain."

I immediately thought of Wendy, who was going to school in London. Her father had transferred to England to do oceanic research. I got a passport and ticket on the French liner *Liberté* for Plymouth, England. Toots was to meet me in England a month later, after she resigned.

Boarding the ship in New York City, I found my two roommates to be gay Stanford art professors. After rejecting their attention for a female student I met at the ship's bar, I worried that I would attack my roommates. I had a reoccurring nightmare of cutting the dick off the man who befriended me on the train.

Chapter Fifteen

The British stamped my passport, "November 10, 1960—Ninety days: No Employment." A lighter transported passengers from the ship to a Plymouth dock near the train to London. I'd written Wendy, who'd sent an inviting and romantic letter along with her address in a London suburb.

Buildings and sky looked gray and bleak as I crossed England. Arriving in Paddington Station without a place to stay, I asked at an information desk. Like in New York City, they recommended the YMCA. The cab ride took me past bombed World War II ruins. I was surprised to find the country still recovering. The Y was in a Georgian building in central London on Tottenham Court Road. It was dirty and the rooms small. I asked for a bath and was sent to a room with a monstrous tub.

The next morning I felt slightly ill as I looked at a plate with kippered herring, stewed tomatoes, an egg, and a rasher of bacon. I heard what sounded like lips smacking together. Looking up, I saw a man across the table give me a seductive smile and make kissing motions. I almost slugged him.

I hurried to the Y's main office, where a bulletin board listed rentals. A boardinghouse near Hampstead Heath offered a shared room that I could afford.

"How do I get here?" I showed the address to the clerk at the front desk.

"Easy enough," he replied. "Take the Underground to Hampstead and follow this route." He quickly drew a map.

The boardinghouse was only a short distance from the Underground station. Following the hand-drawn map, I was led to a grimy-looking brick four story. Along the way, two British girls, thinking my clothes looked odd, asked me where I was from. When I replied, "America," they chattered about movies and dating all the way to the boardinghouse door.

Mrs. Cameron, a middle-aged war widow wearing a threadbare flowery dress, greeted me.

"You'll be sharing a room with a lawyer from Singapore. Breakfast is between seven and nine in the morning. Try to be quiet at night; my young one is studying for his eleven-plus exam. It'll determine the rest of his life."

I moved my luggage from the Y to my new room. It was still early in the day, and I hadn't met my roommate. I was confused by the water system in the shared bathroom. Above the sink and bath were hot water heaters, which didn't seem to be operating. I checked with Mrs. Cameron.

"You mean you don't have anything like this back home."

"No, we just turn on the hot water."

She showed me where to insert pennies to ignite the burner. "Just wait; it'll get hot."

I left and wandered down to a restaurant claiming to serve Italian food. The restaurant, like the boardinghouse, was bone-chillingly cold. I ordered spaghetti and received a tasteless dish of tomato sauce on overcooked noodles with bread and margarine.

I took the underground to Piccadilly Circus and hunted for a tourist office to get directions to Wendy's house in Merton Park. Returning to the boardinghouse, I found my new roommate, Lee Loong, dressed in a wool overcoat, wrapped in a blanket, shivering in a gray, wingback armchair, and reading a thick book. He looked about thirty.

"I'm Billy Durant," I introduced myself. "It's cold in here."

"I don't know how they live like this," grimaced Lee, pulling his blanket tighter. "I've been freezing since Singapore."

"It's cold," I agreed. "I'm from California. Can we put pennies in that gas space heater?" I pointed at one in the room's fireplace.

"I can't afford to," Lee replied. "Tight budget. Here to finish my law degree."

"Where're you going to school?"

"No school. I'm to take dinners at the Inns of Court before a getting a license in Singapore."

"You just eat?"

"That's about it—British imperialism—must meet law association members."

"What's Singapore like?"

"Hot, lots of turmoil. Some want independence. Many Chinese killed by Japanese. There are still racial tensions between Chinese, Malaysians, and Indians."

Ignorant of the British Empire and Singapore, I commented, "Your English is very good. You've got a British accent."

"I went to English schools. Raffles did a good job building up this part of the empire."

"Why English?" I wondered what I'd learned in school. I don't remember encountering anything on the British Empire.

"Those Brits knew how to rule. You know, 'The sun never sets on the British Empire.' We now say, 'The sun never sets on the English language.'"

"What?" I wondered, exposing my ignorance of the world.

"I heard Americans are parochial. Technically, according to English parlance, America is a settler colony that got away. Brits made a fortune shipping slaves to your country."

Again I'd never heard the term "settler colony" nor thought of the British promoting slavery.

I started feeling chilly and put some pennies in the gas space heater.

Thanking me, Lee offered to go downstairs to get tea and returned with a teapot covered with a cozy with two cups and saucers. We sat back and looked at each other. I was still trying to get used to the sight of a Chinese man huddled in clothes and blankets and speaking with a British accent. I was dressed in a flashy, green, sport shirt, black sweater, and Levi's.

"You look so American," commented Lee. "I've seen many American movies."

"Could you tell I was American if you saw me walking down the street?" I remembered the girls who had followed me to the boardinghouse door.

"Probably," Lee replied, sipping his tea. "Your walk, clothes, and speech are so American. Not a bad thing; you got rid of the Japs."

"My dad was in the navy in the South Pacific fighting Japs."

"Good for him. He was protecting the British Empire."

"What? We were protecting America."

"Besides Pearl Harbor, Japanese invaded British strongholds all over Asia, including Singapore, Malaysia, and Burma. Of course Brits are in Africa. Look what they did to India; it took Gandhi to get them out. Terrible rulers; just took our money. We'll get independence soon."

Lee's conversation was an eye-opener. As I waited for a train to take me to Wendy in Merton Park, I thought about how little I knew of the world. I had been surprised when Lee had told me that most of the English estates were built on wealth from the slave trade and colonies.

Still thinking about Lee, I rang the buzzer of a tidy two-story brick house. Again "tidy" was the best description for this bland suburb forty minutes from Piccadilly Circus. I worried about my lack of worldliness in front of Wendy's parents.

Surprisingly Wendy greeted me with a warm kiss and ushered me inside, saying, "Thank God you're here. You have no idea how stuffy and awful these English guys are."

She opened the hallway's first door leading into a parlor, where her parents, now looking very British, were sipping tea and reading. They didn't act happy to see me as they grunted a welcome.

Wendy hurried me out of the room to her bedroom, where we kissed and rubbed our bodies against each other. We still hadn't made love.

"I'm going to Grenoble to study French. We could meet," whispered Wendy, panting into my ear. "My parents won't be there."

"Grenoble?"

"Grenoble University, near the French Alps."

"Toots is coming in a couple weeks. She wants to go to Paris. There's a US military base near there. I could see about getting to Grenoble."

"You can take a train from Gare de Lyon. I'm taking the boat train to Paris next week and then to Grenoble."

Wendy was rubbing against me so hard that I thought I would explode. I backed away, thinking her parent wouldn't want to see a stain on my pants. She gave me her address in Grenoble and suggested I send a telegram giving my arrival time.

I took the train back to London, excited at the prospect of lovemaking near the Alps.

Getting off the train, I went to the American Express office near Piccadilly Circus where Toots had said she would mail me. The office was packed with Americans exchanging money, accessing wired money, buying train and channel tickets, and getting mail. In 1960, American Express was the home away from home for Americans.

After I waited thirty minutes in the mail line, there was Toots's letter saying she would arrive next week in Southampton and I should find a London hotel for a couple days. The letter contained an American Express money order, which I used, according to the letter's instructions, to buy boat and train tickets to Paris.

I promptly got in another line to cash the money order and then another line to buy the tickets. Two hours later I left the babble of American accents and returned to the boardinghouse. Mrs. Cameron told me how to get to Southampton and expressed regret that I'd be moving out the following week.

"Good to see your mum," she said. "Lee's also leaving. Taking his last dinner tonight."

Taking the train to Southampton, I waited at the immigration station at the dock's entrance and watched the SS *United States* being pulled by tugs into its berth.

As the ship unloaded, I could see Toots in the distance surround by three or four men. They clustered around her while standing in the passport line.

Thinking that she wouldn't want them to know about me, I moved to a back wall. I was right. She embraced each man and ignored me until they left.

"Fun guys," she said, not even giving me a hug or kiss on the cheek. "I'm meeting one of them in London."

"I got us tickets from here to London and for the Paris trip. Booked a London hotel, but," I said angrily, "I guess you won't need it with all those guys to fuck." I'd never spoken to her like this before.

"Billy, watch your language. It's only one guy."

After two nights in a London hotel, we took the train, ferry, and another train to the Gare du Nord. Using an American Express guide, I located a hotel near the train station. The American Express office was minutes from the hotel, where Toots checked on transportation to the Orly US Air Force base nine miles outside Paris.

I waited in the hotel lobby and was immediately approached by a girl about my age.

"You American?" she asked with a heavy French accent. Wearing a green dress and a pair of sad-looking brown shoes, she sat down next to me. I was immediately attracted.

"I'm Alice Bellamy. I know the clerk," she pointed at the front desk. "You staying here?"

"With my mother. She's looking for work."

"I like Americans. Plus I can practice English I'm learning at the Alliance Française and from watching American movies."

"I'd like to learn French."

"You can. I could take you to the school. My apartment is near there."

Chapter Sixteen

It didn't take long for Toots to hook up with air force major Jim Curly while applying for jobs at Orly. She moved to a hotel near Orly, leaving me alone in Paris. This left me time to explore with Alice. She took me to her school on Boulevard Raspail near the Luxembourg Gardens. Her sparsely furnished one-room apartment was a couple blocks away on Rue Sainte-Beuve.

Courses were cheap in US dollars. Everything was cheap for Americans in 1960. I paid for a basic French course and sat for my student photo as Alice fussed with my hair, putting little spit curls across my forehead. There were several firsts at the school—my first taste of yogurt and use of unisex toilets with mixed gender lines.

With great anticipation, I followed Alice to her apartment, stopping at a horsemeat butcher.

"I've never had horsemeat," I commented, wondering about the tacos I had eaten in Tijuana as a kid.

"Oh, you want other meat?"

"No, I like new things."

She cooked with a French flare, mixing vegetables with hunks of meat on a two-burner gas hot plate. Of course the meal was served with wine. My first French love affair was on a narrow, single bed below Monet prints.

After a week learning French and exploring Paris with Alice, I found Toots at our hotel.

"You OK?" asked Toots. "Jim's showing me the city. Not much chance of a job here. We should go to Spain."

"Is it OK for me to visit Wendy in Grenoble?" I asked.

"That's why I wanted to see you. Jim wants me to go to Cannes for a week. Do you mind? You could see Wendy."

I was growing uncomfortable with Alice, who talked seriously about going back to the United States with me.

The night before, lying squeezed together in her narrow bed, she'd whispered, "I've waited for a man like you. I'd like to see America."

I escaped from Alice the next morning. Toots gave me money for Grenoble as we checked out of our hotel. I avoided a departing conversation with Alice and hurried to the Gare de Lyon for the first train to Grenoble.

Wendy was all over me on my arrival and whisked me away to her campus apartment. We walked along the Isère River and kissed against a background of snowcapped Alps.

"It's been hard waiting," she said between kisses and unbuttoning my shirt. "I always wanted this. My parents warned me against you—said you're from a family of losers. They want a Stanford or Harvard man for me."

I unsnapped her bra as she unbuckled my pants and pulled me onto her bed.

"I wanted you all through high school. They were mad when you showed up in England. We're free of them."

As I started stroking her body, I got more and more excited.

"You feel so good. You're my man. I dream of us marrying."

I went limp.

"What happened? Did I do something? I don't have much experience."

"I need some water," I said and slowly got up from the bed. I didn't understand my panic. "It never did this before." I looked down at my deflated penis. "Maybe we should have tea or something stronger."

She pulled the sheet up over her breasts and stared at me. I looked out the window at the mountain snow. Slipping on my clothes, I told her I was going for wine.

Once on the sidewalk, I didn't stop running until I got to the train station. The next Paris departure was in two hours. I crossed the street to a café, chose a table in the back shadows, and ordered brandy. By the fourth drink, I relaxed.

I was happy to get back to Paris. Many years later I received an e-mail from Wendy about our high school reunion. I didn't attend. We never mentioned Grenoble.

Wendy died in her forties of blood cancer. Her husband sent me ripped pages from her diary with a note calling me a "scumbag." I read several pages before tossing them in the trash. They were filled with grief and self-doubt about what had gone wrong in Grenoble and why and how I had disappeared. She had contacted police to find out if I'd been hurt. One sentence claimed I was the only person she had ever loved.

Back in Paris, there were four days before Toots's return. We had agreed to meet at our original hotel. Worried about my manhood, I headed to Montmartre and sampled sex shows and women. No problem getting it up.

I found a little club on Rue Drevet marked with a sign showing whips and chains and the name "Se Torturer." I paid a small cover to enter. On stage a nude woman was kneeling wearing a leather neck collar. A chain ran from the collar to an eyebolt embedded in a post in the middle of the stage.

A man wearing only a leather mask was whipping her. Blood trickled down her sides. The man mounted her and bit into her shoulder, drawing blood. In the room's dim light, I could see other shadowy figures embracing. I'd never felt this excited.

"Want to see more?" asked an English-speaking thirtyish-looking man in a dark suit who sat down at my table.

He slid a card across to me. "I noticed you when you came in. You're a good-looking kid. They'd like you. Go to this address on Rue Androuet." He quickly left.

I could barely make out the address. There were pictographs of torture instruments. After searching around the street, I found the address.

I rang the bell for apartment 3A. I couldn't understand the French response, but I was buzzed in when I gave the club's name, "Se Torturer."

Candles lined the room illuminating a young man and woman hanging from ropes attached to a ceiling beam. Men and women wearing only animal masks formed a circle around the couple, chanted, and swung cat-o'-nine-tails. Below the couple was a large metal pan to collect their blood and waste. The stench of the couples' involuntarily released feces mixed with clouds of incense.

As I entered, a woman wearing a cat mask gave me a hand cultivator with three sharp prongs. She whispered something in French, stroked my groin, and pointed at a clothes rack in the corner. Seeing my quizzical look, she asked in English, stroking me harder, "You Brit?"

"American," I gasped as she squeezed me harder. I stared at her nipples, pierced with small ivory tusks.

"Always like Americans. They know how to play. Hang your clothes on that rack; you're just in time."

"Time for what?"

She handed me a dog-face mask. "The killing."

"Killing?" I wondered.

"Remember your little rake," she called after me as I went to the clothing rack, stripped, and donned my dog mask.

I joined a chanting group surrounding the hanging couple. Screams pierced the air as hand cultivators stripped away skin.

I could feel the skin peeling away as I raked the woman's thighs.

Leaving in a daze in the early morning hours, I stumbled to the hotel where I was to meet Toots.

Toots got back the next day in a foul mood with a bruised cheek. "Fuckin' men. I thought the bastard was OK."

Never explaining what happened in Cannes, Toots and I packed and bought train tickets at the Gare de Lyon to Madrid. Another train would take us to Seville.

Armed men wearing shiny three-cornered hats with the rear part folded upward carried machine guns as they patrolled buses and trains. Franco was dictator.

We stayed in a cheap hotel near Seville's main cathedral.

"You never know who I'll meet," said Toots as she left for the US naval station at Rota.

I kept a busy tourist schedule and even saw a bullfight. Toots returned two days later with no job but enough money to get us back to the States.

"Go see what we can take back to the United States," she ordered, sending me to the American Express office.

There were berths on a passenger-carrying freighter traveling down the Guadalquivir River from Seville to New Orleans leaving in two days. We booked tickets.

In the stateroom's enclosed bookcase, I found a variety of books from small guides to Burma to one showing a kneeling man supporting the world on his shoulders. Intrigued by the cover, I took Ayn Rand's *Atlas Shrugged*, published in 1957, from the case, I didn't know when opening its pages that it would become my Bible and its main character, John Galt, my model for living.

Why does this story speak to me? I wondered as I consumed the tale of struggle between individualism and conformity.

I thought, *John Galt's like me. Never willing to give in.*

Rand's description of Galt's war against groupthink and government controls reminded me of my feelings about the navy—everyone marching in step to the same tune.

I started dreaming about Rand. As the freighter rolled in an Atlantic storm, I awoke shaking from a nightmare of naked women ravaging my body with bites, scratches, and hand rakes as I lay tied to a table. A figure, looking vaguely like the photo of Ayn Rand on the book, cut my bonds, setting me free.

The next morning I quickly fingered my way through the book's pages and found the passage, "Every man is free to rise as far as he's able or willing, but it's only the degree to which he thinks that determines the degree to which he'll rise." *I'm smart*, I thought, *I should be able to do anything*.

I felt good thinking of being right in fighting the crowd and attempts by women like Wendy to use sex to tie me down.

Plagued by guilt at being born and killing others, I was set free by Rand. For Rand, morality was an intrusion in a free market of individuals making self-interested choices.

Galt relieved my soul with the words "By the grace of reality and the nature of life, man—every man—is an end in himself, he exists for his own sake, and the achievement of his own happiness is his highest moral purpose."

Just before landing in New Orleans, I asked Toots for money to buy a bus ticket to Chicago and a couple meals. Inspired by Rand, I wanted to return and "shrug" my way to the top, free of morality and guilt.

Chapter Seventeen

I arrived in Chicago free to do what I wanted. Ayn Rand was my prophet. Toots paid for a phone call from New Orleans to Chicago. Larry Folsom had moved from the dorms to an apartment on South Wells Street near the White Sox's Comiskey Park. He left a key under the doormat. With a few dollars and one light suitcase, I took a State Street Bus to Thirty-First Street and walked over to Wells.

I found the key but knocked first before going in. To my surprise, Jay Reiner, whom I'd traveled with to California, opened the door.

"Billy, Larry said you would be coming. Navy looked hard for you. I guess they gave up."

I hugged Jay and dropped my suitcase in the living room of the two-bedroom basement dwelling. The place smelled musty. The used furniture was dirty and ripped. Dishes were piled in the sink. Through the bedroom doors, I could see clothes strewn around unmade beds.

"You're staying here?" I asked.

"We're sharing the rent. Larry's in class now. You can sleep on the couch. Any plans?"

"I need a job." I didn't feel like explaining Ayn Rand's inspiration.

"Could get you on the railroad. Any interest?"

"You're still a train nut, sleeping in the yards watching box cars?"

"I've been spending time at the IC yards. I've got all their yard maps and schedules."

"IC?"

"Illinois Central. I can get you work at the La Salle Street Station moving freight. I'll check with friends about the IC."

Two days later I was moving freight around on the La Salle Station docks. The following week, I was interviewed by the IC for a flagman's job. The next day I was collecting tickets on IC commuter trains running from their Michigan and Randolph Station to Chicago's southern suburbs. I bought a trainman's watch, which was checked monthly by the railroad's timekeeper. The railroad supplied a trainman's uniform and conductor's hat. My girlfriends said that the hat looked sexy.

When I started in January 1961, railroad wages were high because of the union contract with the Brotherhood of Railroad Trainmen. Free medical care was provided by a railroad hospital. I earned $7.40 per trip—a lot of money in 1961--which could last from a half hour to an hour, depending on the route. I was on the extra board and filled in for sick or vacationing trainmen who had regular assignments. For morning rush-hour trips, when they most needed extra workers, I received an early morning phone call offering a particular trip. Everything was based on seniority.

During the day, I'd hang out at the Randolph Street train room with its bunk room of leather mattresses. When a job was available, the telegrapher would announce it, and extra board workers would bid. Those with the most seniority won. You could literally work all day and into the night. This meant fat paychecks.

I moved from Larry's into a single hotel room with a Murphy bed located on Fifty-Third Street in Hyde Park near the IC station. My major concern was a functioning telephone for those early morning calls. I hated waking the girls who occasionally stayed overnight.

Motivated by John Galt's call for individualism and success, I focused on making as much money as possible.

Picking up girls in coffeehouses was easy. This was the beatnik era. I read Jack Kerouac's *On the Road* and realized that I'd been on my own road. I later learned that many Beats were gay. On my off-duty hours, I started wearing black turtlenecks and a beret.

The Green Door Coffeehouse on Fifty-Seventh Street near the University of Chicago was my favorite. There were nightly poetry readings, newspaper racks, chessboards, and a lending library of radical books. The wood-paneled interior was thick with pipe and cigarette smoke as groups debated politics and economics while others read or played chess.

I found a wild-eyed group espousing Ayn Rand's freedom. The girls were particularly interesting. Freedom was morphing in sexual freedom. In the Green Door's back corner, a rack displayed Ayn Rand's books.

One evening while debating the idea of selfishness and happiness as the highest moral purpose, I met Carla.

"Hello," she said, sitting down next to me. "Seen you here before. I'm Carla Brieder."

"Billy Durant. You a Rand fan?"

"Love her. Makes me feel free."

Wearing a beret held in place by bobby pins in her thick blond hair, she was thin, full busted, and looked about my height. I loved her cute little nose and full lips.

"And you?" she asked.

"Read her on a freighter from Spain. She spoke to my soul."

"Sounds romantic. You in school?"

"No, conductor on the IC. Maybe I took your ticket when you rode."

I followed her when she got up to leave.

"Want to come to my place? I've got a room on Fifty-Third."

"Sure, what's freedom for? But I've got to be back at the dorm by eleven."

"How old are you?" I asked, worried suddenly about statutory rape.

"Nineteen. Dorm hours are strict. I can get someone to forge a note to stay over a weekend. Otherwise I've got to sign in and out." This was 1961, before colleges loosened up on their parental role.

Afterward I was happy that she couldn't stay overnight. I won't have to see her in the morning.

I hurried her back to the dorm, and with a swift kiss, she ran in, just making the eleven o'clock sign in.

At the end of the 1961 summer as my savings grew, I decided to try college again with an Ayn Randian desire for achievement. The railroad schedule was flexible, except for the morning and evening rush hours. During the day, I could leave the train room for classes.

I enrolled at Roosevelt University near the IC's Van Buren Street Station. Opened in 1945 as a YMCA college, it was named after Eleanor Roosevelt. My goal was twofold: find out about myself and make money.

"Why do you think the way you do?" Professor Loren Baritz opened his course on American intellectual history.

Shit, I thought. None of my courses in sociology and psych asked that question.

I followed Professor Baritz to his office.

"Your opening question got me," I said as he invited me in.

"Why?"

"Trying to figure out my life."

"This isn't a psych course. We're dealing with thinking."

"Does being a Choctaw mean anything?"

"You're an Indian?" Baritz reached up on his bookshelf and retrieved a book on the Trail of Tears. "Ever read about this? Might explain some of your thinking. Choctaws forced to march across the country. Many were killed. US Army did a lot of raping."

"I wonder about my father," I mumbled.

"How's that?"

"He was an Indian, alcoholic, and gambler, according to Mom."

"Government did awful things to Indians." He handed me the book. "Read this, and you might understand your father."

Still thinking about my father and violence against the tribe, I went to the Green Door after my last train trip.

"We can only be happy if there are free markets," Carla was arguing as I sat down.

"Schools control our ideas," I interjected, thinking of Professor Baritz's lecture on how nineteenth-century school people tried to control the public mind. "We can't be free if our minds are shackled."

"Rand contends," asserted Phil Anderson, a bearded student in full beatnik garb of beret and turtleneck, "we must see reality objectively. Then we can pursue rational self-interest."

"What about emotions?" I didn't want to admit to my uncontrolled anger that had dotted my life.

Sipping his cappuccino, Phil retorted, "That's why we must ensure that our perceptions are real. Only a free market will let us allow self-interest to lead to happiness."

Cappuccino was a new experience requiring, by my taste, plenty of sugar. I asked, "Wouldn't free markets result in more violence? What about emotions and control of ideas by the powerful?"

I walked Carla back to Blackstone Hall and continued the discussion on freedom and happiness. After a long kiss and a promise to meet in my room next afternoon, I walked up Blackstone toward my room on Fifty-Third Street.

Just before Fifty-Fifth, a large black dog ran out of the bushes snarling and trying to bite my leg. It was late with only me on the sidewalk. After my high school pet-clinic experience, I knew to kick the dog in the throat. The snarling ended with the dog gasping for breath. I then kicked it hard in the stomach and balls. I couldn't stop. I left a dead dog with broken legs and brains leaking from its smashed head on the sidewalk as I hurried on.

That night I kept waking from nightmares about vicious attacks on women.

"Do you think free markets can end violence?" I asked the next afternoon as Carla and I relaxed from lovemaking.

"I guess," she replied innocent of my personal worries. "If all people were selfish, they would avoid hurting others to protect themselves."

"That doesn't make sense." I sat up and leaned over to kiss her. "Selfish people kill if they don't think there'll be consequences."

"You should ask Phil; he knows this stuff." She snuggled closer.

"Do you think I should grow a beard?" I was thinking of looking Beat.

"Ugh, I hate beards. I know it's big among Beat men, but it's hard to kiss. Some of those bearded guys are phonies trying to look hip. I love you the way you are."

The word "love" panicked me. I leaped up, wiped myself off, and started donning my uniform.

"Like to go to Valois for a bite?"

"OK," replied Carla, startled by my abrupt dressing. "I'll need to wash first."

Valois was near the Fifty-Third Street IC station. You could watch your food being prepared and cooked. I ordered my usual coffee and Denver omelet always cooked in butter. Carla asked for a hamburger and Coke. We took a table near the window and watched passersby.

"Aren't you worried about me getting pregnant?" Carla put ketchup on her burger and French fries.

Jesus, I thought. I hadn't considered this possibility as I always used condoms. Suddenly feeling sick, I pushed the omelet away from me.

"You're pregnant?"

"No, silly. Just raising the issue. You know, last year they came out with a pill."

"Pill?"

"Birth control pill. Lot of girls taking it. Feels better than a rubber."

"Sounds good. At least you're not pregnant." I was feeling anxious about the direction of the conversation—love, having a kid.

"You want kids, a family?" Carla looked sweetly at me.

"No, I want to be free, free to be me."

"Me, too." Carla's reply surprised me. Worried about where the conversation was going, I was about to run for a train.

"The pill makes me free," she continued. "Girls at Blackstone are talking about sexual freedom. They gave me pills at the school's clinic. I started yesterday. You can stop buying those things."

Relieved that she wasn't trying to tie me down, I needed to get the next train downtown to work the five-ten rush-hour train to Blue Island.

We kissed on the sidewalk and agreed to meet that night at the Green Door.

I sat down on the IC's wicker seats and waved at the trainmen working the trip. Staring out the window at Lake Michigan in the distance, I tried to piece together the meanings of freedom—to be selfish, promiscuous, and, this was my problem, mean and hurtful.

Chapter Eighteen

Through the thick smoke, I could see Phil and Carla clustered with others around a large table next to Ayn Rand's bookstand. I ordered a large cappuccino and took it to the table. Sitting next to Carla, who was focused on Phil's argument on morality, I took out my tobacco pouch and filled my pipe. On the wall were new posters of the Cuban Revolution and Mao.

"If I sleep with Billy," asked Carla putting her hand on my knee, "is that immoral? I know my parents would say it is."

"That's religious stuff," replied Phil. "That kind of morality only exists in religion. Do you think you'll burn in hell?"

"Without religion," responded Sarah Strom, another economics undergraduate, "wouldn't people just kill each other in a free market? Shouldn't humans be guided by some rules?"

"Whose rules?" Carla rubbed her hand on my thigh.

"As individuals," answered Phil, "we follow our own rules. In a free market, individual rules will create a morality of the marketplace."

"But what happens," I asked, "if an individual likes violence?"

"A free market wouldn't foster violence," snorted Phil, lighting his pipe. "The lesson of the market is that self-interest negates violence. The free market teaches 'Do unto others as you would have them do unto you.'"

I hit the sack late, tired from the long day and emotionally drained from coffeehouse debates about violence and free markets. The phone rang around four in the morning with the telegrapher assigning me to the six ten out of Flossmoor. I hurried to catch a train to Flossmoor for the trip. Throwing on my clothes, I stumbled out the door and headed down Fifty-Third to the IC station.

Groggy and cold—a November chill was in the air—I stood shivering on the train platform. At the far end of the platform, a couple was yelling at each other. Their voices got louder and louder, making my headache worse.

He shoved her against a trash can, scattering garbage across the platform.

"You fuckin' bitch," I could hear the man say. "I wish you'd never been born. Get out of my sight. We're finished."

Sobbing, the woman ran down the platform stairs. The man stood, lit a cigarette, and leaned his head back to blow smoke into the early morning sky.

I don't know why, but I started moving toward him. Through the dim platform lights, I saw that we were alone. At that time of the morning, few people traveled to Flossmoor. My head pounded. I could feel the words "I wish you'd never been born."

As I got closer, I saw the train lights approaching. The man looked questioningly at me and said, "You work these trains? They're fuckin' crappy. Those wicker seats leave prints on my butt. Why don't you get something soft?"

The trained slowed as it entered the station. Just as the head car of the braking train passed, I shoved the man. Looking down, I could see a dark image spin around the train wheels. The doors opened, and I shouted a hello to the conductor.

That afternoon everyone in the train room was discussing the mysterious death and the trail of body parts from Fifty-Third Street.

I asked trainmaster Paul Shafer about it.

"Police don't know. Any ID was destroyed by the train wheels and later trains. Probably a suicide. It happens all the time. Maybe a woman. Never discovered it until the sun was up. Given the train traffic, they'll never find all the body parts."

I left for class.

"Human society has always consisted of masters and slaves, and the slaves have always been and are today the foundation stones of the social fabric." Professor Baritz was quoting nineteenth-century socialist Eugene Debs when I sat down in a vacant chair in back of the room.

My hand shot up. Baritz nodded my way.

"Wouldn't free markets end masters and slaves?"

Sneering, Baritz answered, "Capitalism always has masters and slaves."

"I mean a real free market—like Ayn Rand talks about."

"Let's stick to the nineteenth and early twentieth century. Rand is a kook."

Returning to his notes, Baritz described Debs as the last hope for the United States.

"After Debs," he continued, "there was nothing to stop capitalist masters from taking over. They controlled the schools and engines of ideas, blinding workers to the truth."

Looking irritated, Baritz again recognized my waving hand.

"Didn't Debs cause violence? What about the Pullman strike? Doesn't socialism cause bloody riots?"

"It's not socialism but people struggling against armed capitalists. The capitalist starts the violence. Please let me just finish," responded Baritz with an edge in his tone.

I waited until after class and then followed Baritz to his office.

"Didn't Debs want war—class war? Isn't that violent? Didn't he make violence a religion?"

I looked at my notes from the library and quoted Debs on Christ: "I did not believe Christ was meek and lowly but a real, living, vital agitator who went into the temple with a lash and whipped the oppressors of the poor, routed them out of the doors, and spilled their blood."

Dismissing me with a wave of his hand, Baritz said, "Yes, it's capitalism. Do away with capitalism, and everyone will live happily together."

"Doesn't government wage wars?"

"Capitalists own the government," he barked, slamming the door.

After two train trips, I met Carla at Valois, where she was already eating fish sticks and a garden salad. Kissing her on the cheek, I got in line and wondered what to eat. I found Chicago food dull after California and Hawaii. Deciding on corn beef and cabbage, I took my tray over to Carla.

"How's school?" I set my tray down.

"Good economics course this afternoon. Visitor from England talking about Adam Smith's failure to understand that society needs real free markets. And you?"

"I love the history course even though the guy's some kind of communist. He says free markets cause war and mayhem. But I'm learning a lot about American ideas. We talked about socialist Debs—you know, the labor organizer."

"They ruin free markets."

"What ruins free markets?"

"Labor unions!" Carla raised her fist in the air, looking like the poster of Rosa Luxemburg at the Green Door. "Down with unions and collectivism and up with individualism."

People turned around to look.

"Some in here could be labor people, like me," I said.

"I thought you were the rugged individualist with all your spouting of Ayn Rand."

"I'm in the Brotherhood of Railroad Trainmen. Good pay."

"You just joined?"

"Had to for the job. I didn't give up who I am."

"You don't have principles," Carla abruptly stood up. "I can't love a man without principles. I'm going back to the dorm. You can finish these; they're greasy and awful. I'll never have fish sticks again."

She shoved her plate toward me, turned, and started crying.

"Christ," I said. "How does discussing unions lead to tears?"

Looking back at me, she whispered, "The pills didn't work."

Leaving my barely eaten food, I followed her out of the restaurant.

Standing in front of Valois, she wept, "You don't love me."

"What's that got to do with the baby?"

"You were supposed to say that you love me and we should get married."

"Well, I didn't and won't. How do you get rid of the kid—is that possible? Maybe you should think of adoption or leave it in a church."

"Me! Why not us? It's your baby."

"I don't give a fuck. I'm not gonna be tied down. I'll leave the country—get rid of it!"

Crying and shrieking in the middle of the sidewalk with passersby looking at me as if I'd hit her, Carla sobbed out, "You're leaving me."

"You're responsible." Anger welled up in me. "You wanted those pills rather than rubbers. You tricked me into marrying you. I wouldn't marry you if a gun was put to my head."

"What?" She slapped me.

"This guy bothering you?" a burly looking man asked, stopping and looking angrily into my face.

"Mister," I replied. "You should stay out of this. I haven't touched her. She's angry because I won't marry her."

Carla waved him away. The man left.

By this time Carla was choking and gagging from all the shouting and crying. "You just led me on."

"Get real," I said. "You're not the best cunt I've ever had. I can get plenty more and better than you. Don't bother me anymore and don't call." I turned and headed for my room.

"You won't get away with this," she shouted after me.

"Fuck off. Find some other sucker."

"I'll make you pay," screamed Carla.

"You screwed everyone. Remember, free love. How do I know it's my kid?"

"You were the only one. You think I slept around? It's your bastard."

I turned my head laughing at her as I crossed the street.

Later in life, thinking about Carla, I was grateful they didn't have DNA testing back then.

I waited a week before returning to the Green Door. I stood in the entrance scanning the room for Carla. Not seeing her, I bought a cappuccino and sat down next to Phil who was discoursing on happiness and rational thought.

"Haven't seen you for a while," commented Sarah Strom smiling across the table.

"Been working hard," I replied. Turning to Phil, I responded, "I can be happy as long as I'm free. I don't know about the rational part."

"I agree," Phil replied. "Reason and individualism is the path to happiness. Rand is right."

Sarah came around the table moving a chair next to mine. "You know Carla left?"

"No!" I said softly, not wanting this to be a group conversation. "We broke up. She said she was tired of me."

"She dropped out of school and went home. Never told anyone why. Did you know?"

"She said she was tired of Chicago and me. Slapped me. I never felt so rejected. I loved her."

"She slapped you? Thought she might be a mean type. Are you OK?"

"Besides a broken heart, no physical damage."

Sarah took my hand and whispered into my ear, "Do you want to talk about it? She really is a bitch leaving you like that."

"We could go outside and talk. This is too personal for here," I said. Sarah motioned with her hand toward the door.

"You poor thing," she said, hugging me once we were outside. "It's too cold to stand here and talk. We could go to the lounge at Blackstone."

"I'd feel sad, knowing Carla lived there. I miss her. We could try my room."

Lying back after lovemaking, I told Sarah, "That was great. Carla was terrible in bed. You're the best I've ever been with."

"I always envied Carla being with you. She is a bitch for leaving you. You know how to treat women. Her loss is my gain."

Chapter Nineteen

"You're smart," Professor Gary Feller complemented me as we emerged from Roosevelt into the noise of Michigan Avenue. "You're good applying math to economic problems. Would you like some extra work?"

"I've got plenty of work. The railroad pays well."

"I'm not thinking of the money part."

He was tall and long limbed, and it was hard to keep pace with him. Professor Feller and I often spent hours after class discussing free-market theory. He looked like a college professor. His tweed suit matched his sandy hair.

In his thirties, he worked at the Chicago Economic Institute on the campus of the University of Chicago. It was a hotbed of free-market theory. Feller made a little on the side teaching courses at Roosevelt. He confided in me a need for the extra money to support his mother who was sinking into the abyss of Alzheimer's.

"I like you. You seem honest, good work habits. Would you like to help develop economic models to measure growth and profit and loss?"

"Thanks, but school and work take up most of my time."

"It's not about money. You could have one foot in the door for a University of Chicago PhD. They'd never admit a graduate of Roosevelt."

"Hadn't thought of a PhD. I'm still in my undergraduate program."

When we reached Randolph Street, I planned to head to the train room to see if I could bid on a trip. Feller insisted we go for coffee in a nearby Pixley and Ehlers.

"I know Hayek wants someone to use math to explain his free-market theories. There's a rumor he's planning to leave next year for the University of Freiburg, big loss for Chicago."

Hearing Hayek's name, I became more interested. "I read the *The Road to Serfdom*. Close to Ayn Rand's ideas. But he's leaving. How'd that help me?"

"With Hayek comes Milton Friedman; they hold seminars together. Students complain about Friedman's teaching, but there's no greater advocate of free markets."

Back in my room after lovemaking, I asked Sarah about Hayek and Friedman.

"Hayek's great," she said, kissing me. "Hard for undergraduates to get close to him."

"Do you think I should do it? I make more on the railroad."

"We could see more of each other." She snuggled closer. "I could get my parents to sign a waiver for me to leave the dorm. We could share a place together."

Shit, I thought, *she's getting demanding.*

"We could save money cooking at home."

"That won't work; I like living alone. My train hours would drive you nuts. I don't think you'd like waking at four in the morning."

"I'd love to be with you." She started climbing on top of me. I angrily pushed her out of bed.

"Time to go. I'll walk you back to Blackstone."

I've got to get out of here, I thought after leaving Sarah at Blackstone Hall. I wanted a girl who just liked sex and didn't want a relationship.

I avoided Sarah and at the Green Door ignored her attempts to talk. Two nights after I shunned her, she followed me out of the coffeehouse.

"Why won't you talk to me?" She attempted to grab my hand.

"You're OK, but between work and school, I don't have time. I'm not the type you want to get involved with. Let's be friends."

Shocked, verging on tears, Sarah tried to grab my arm. I pulled back and started walking toward Fifty-Third Street.

"I thought we had something. Didn't you like loving me?"

"It was OK. Friendship is best."

"Aren't you inviting me to your room?"

"Get lost! Plenty of women around."

"You're a shit!" she yelled. "Now I know why Carla left you. I'll fix you. I'll tell girls what you're like. I'll call at all hours. You've got to answer. You won't know if it's the railroad."

The following day Professor Feller came to my rescue. After class, he excitedly told me, "Something's come up that would pave your way into the university. Plus you can make some money."

"It's a little strange," he continued. "The Chicago Economic Institute signed a contract with the state of Alaska to do economic impact studies. But no one at the institute wants to go to Alaska, particularly in January. I need the money. We could do this together. I'd like you to handle the statistics."

"I'd quit my job to winter in Alaska, I don't think so."

"They'll pay you four hundred dollars a month plus travel, hotel, food, and gear."

"That's less than I make on the railroad. Plus it's colder there than Chicago, which is cold enough."

"I looked into that. The first place we'll be is Sitka, on an island off the coast. It's warmer there in January because of the ocean currents. Just heavy rainfall."

"How long? What happens to me afterward?" I was intrigued with the idea of Alaska. "I can't just come back to my IC job. I'd lose my seniority."

"They say one or two months for Sitka. You'd still be under contract when you return. The institute will keep you busy finishing the contract, and there'll be other opportunities. You can finish undergrad work at the University of Chicago with the institute covering your tuition."

"What'll happen in Sitka?"

"They need to figure out the economics of building a Japanese pulp mill. There are issues of taxes, housing new workers, and paying for new roads. What you think?"

"I've gotta look at a map and read up on Sitka."

Feller's offer was a potential game changer. An Alaskan adventure and an elite college degree were tempting.

It was an hour before I reported for the rush-hour trains. I dashed into Chicago's Central Library located at the train station's entrance. I was shocked to find that the average Sitka January temperature was forty degrees. It had been the capital of Russian America. The local totem carving tribe was Tlingit.

"What do you think?" Feller asked after the next class.

"It's warmer and sounds interesting."

I decided to go after receiving phone calls from Carla who was home in Iowa planning to have her kid. I screamed into the phone, "It's not mine, you whore!" That didn't keep her from calling back. I was planning to change my phone number but worried she'd appear big bellied at my doorstep.

"You'll never get anywhere," pointed out Feller, "on the railroad. It's a dead-end job. This is your chance."

On January 3, 1962, I flew to Seattle. There Feller and I boarded the Alaskan ferry *Malaspina*. Sitka didn't have an airport. Small floatplanes landed in the harbor.

Docking in Sitka, we discovered that the terminal was several miles out of town along Halibut Point Road. We'd received instructions to check in at the Sitka Hotel, but no one told us how to get there.

We started hitching up a windy road hugging the shoreline. It was an unusually clear day, according to locals. A first for both of us was seeing bald eagles resting on hemlock and spruce branches while others swooped down and pulled fish from the water. In the distance, we could see a snowcapped volcanic island. The water was dotted with heavily wooded little islands. Between the trees there were glimpses of a sea-lion pod herding schools of herring toward the shore for easy eating.

Finally a rusty pickup appeared going in the opposite direction toward the ferry dock. Fuller waved and the truck pulled over to our side of the road.

"Want a ride?" The red-bearded occupant rolled down his window.

"We're trying to get to the Sitka Hotel," answered Feller.

"Long walk; hop in back. I'm checking some crab pots near the ferry dock. Only take a minute."

Feller threw his bags into the truck's bed and climbed over the tail-gate. The back smelled of fish. I climbed in, almost stepping in a bucket with fishhooks hanging down from its rim. There were several coiled ropes and a couple crab pots. We tried to keep our bags out of the damp fish slime coating the floor.

Stopping at the terminal, the red-haired man introduced himself as Walter Becker. Black suspenders held up his jeans, which were tucked into red, rubber boots—in Sitka, these were called Halibut boots. Becker looked out from the dock at some flags floating in the water.

"Just checking to see if they were still there; someone's been stealing crab pots. My boat engine's being repaired; had to drive out to check."

Bouncing along in back, we passed trailers and houses resting on hard rock. Many had rusty cars and old boats in their yards. We left Halibut Point Road at Katlian Street, which took us through a Tlingit village of weathered shacks to the town center. We were greeted by a tall totem pole with a naked white man on top.

"That's Baranof," said Becker, pointing at the naked man after we arrived at the Sitka Hotel next to the post office. "Supposedly Tlingits carved it as a joke."

We struggled to get the bags out of the back. They smelled fishy.

"Try the Pioneer Bar. It's down Katlian Street, a couple blocks from here; some tough chicks in there. You here for long?"

"A couple months," I replied.

"I don't think you'll want to stay at the hotel long. Loggers use it for R and R—some big fights. They've been known to run their chainsaws early in the morning."

"Where else is there?" asked Feller.

"I could put you up on an island. You'd have to row a short distance to shore."

"Sounds crazy." I picked up my bag and pushed open the hotel door.

"Not so crazy when you hear the loggers. My boat is in Thompson Harbor. Walk up Katlian, and you'll see a bunch of fishing boats. Mine's the *Taku*, a trawler. Just ask anyone on the dock. They'll tell you where the boat is."

"Thanks," Feller said and shook Becker's hand. "State is giving us an office. The hotel will be OK for sleep."

"Are you working for the state?"

"We're studying the economic impact of locating a pulp mill here," answered Feller, picking up his suitcases to follow me to the hotel's front desk.

"Economic impact!" Becker suddenly looked angry. "You watch it. That pulp mill could kill fishing around here—filthy, spewing all sorts of crap into the water."

After checking into our small rooms with cigarette holes in the blanket and a green mold in the bathroom, we asked at the desk where we could get work gear.

We were directed to Russell's Clothing, a short distance from the hotel on Lincoln Street. I was startled to see in the middle of Lincoln Street a nineteenth-century Russian Orthodox cathedral.

"You'll need Halibut boots," Jim Miller, the clerk, told us.

"We're not wading." I scanned a boot rack. "What about hiking boots?"

"That's what you wear hiking here. Forest floor is damp. They're comfortable and won't slip on wet rocks. We've got socks for them."

"What else?" Feller asked. "This is being paid for by the state."

"You'll need rain gear and gloves. Are you planning on fishing?"

"No, just studying a possible pulp mill," I replied, looking at the racks of fishing lures, poles, and reels.

Miller's face turned red. "I hope you're not working for the fishermen. We need that pulp mill. This town is dying. They want to stop it—claim that it'll kill the fishing. Bunch of nonsense. There's a whole ocean out there."

We carried our gear back to the hotel. We asked about food, and the hotel clerk directed us to the Dock Shack on Katlian. "Always fresh fish," he said. "Then try the Pioneer just down the street. Best bar in town."

After a delicious hunk of halibut, Gary and I walked into the smoke-filled Pioneer Bar. Some at the bar were passed out, heads resting in their arms. A group of young women wearing fishhook earrings was playing pool. Tables of fishermen were talking about their latest catches. A ship's bell hung over the bar with a sign, "Ring this bell to celebrate big money catches. You will be buying drinks for the house."

When the fishermen found out we were studying the pulp mill's potential impact, free drinks began appearing. Crowding around our barstools, the fishermen bombarded us with warnings about dead fish.

A dishwater-blond woman, looking thirty, leaned against my stool. Pinned to her jean jacket were dozens of colorful fish lures. "Want to see my boat?" she asked.

"I'm pretty tired," I said. I found her attractive even though she was older than me. "I'm Billy Durant," I said loudly through the din of voices.

"Shirley Strauss." She squeezed my shoulder. "They call me Big Fish."

"Big Fish?"

"That's because I was fishing off Solcum Arm and hooked a four-hundred-pound halibut. Biggest fish anyone had seen around here. After hoisting it up on the dock for pictures, they named me Big Fish."

"Jesus, a four-hundred-pound fish. Can't imagine. Do you have any of those photos?"

"In my cabin. Boat's named *Chisholm*. Stop by tomorrow when you're rested. I'll take you out trolling."

Drunk and tired from traveling, we stumbled back to our rooms. I was awakened around two in the morning by pounding on the wall in the room next to mine. I put a pillow over my head to block the sound. Then someone shouted, "Louie, I'm going kill you!" The loud noise of a chainsaw started, and the banging got louder.

I went down to the front desk, where the clerk was sleeping in a chair under a blanket.

"Loggers from Kruzof," he informed me. "Nothing I can do with drunken loggers. They might saw up some furniture with the chainsaw. They always pay. It's their big night on the town."

Chapter Twenty

At breakfast Professor Feller said he'd got a call from the local state agent working on the pulp mill project. Their office won't be ready for a couple days. He'd checked at the hotel desk about hiking. The clerk recommended the four and one-half mile Indian River Trail leading to the Three Sisters Mountains. Along the way, the clerk explained, were easy pickings from thimbleberry, blueberry, and salmonberry bushes.

"I'm going to the *Chisholm*. She offered to take me out." I said, not wanting to accompany him on the hike.

Feller said, "Beautiful level trail, the clerk said. I'll be able to try my gear. Put on my Halibut boots this morning." Feller lifted his leg for me to see.

I looked out the hotel café's window at light rain. "I'll be doing the same."

Feller took off for his hike, while I went to my room to put on my boots and rain gear.

As I walked to Thompson Harbor, the name "Big Fish" made me giggle. After I passed the Alaskan Native Brotherhood Hall, the rain ended, leaving an overcast sky of silver gray and white clouds. I could see the fishing boats tied up in Thompson. The area around the harbor entrance was filled with yellow cedars. At the head of the dock, I asked a tall guy carrying jerry jugs of gasoline where I could find the *Chisholm*.

Putting the jugs down, he laughed, introduced himself as Max Steuben, and said, "You mean Big Fish."

"That's right," I said, realizing that I was entering a close-knit fishing community.

"She's tied up at the end of the second slip." He pointed up the dock. "I don't know how she does it. Always a highliner."

"Highliner?"

"She's got the biggest catches."

Following his directions, I walked passed ravens and gulls fighting over fish scraps. A sea lion was snorting and diving. The air smelled fresh, a mixture of salt water and cedar. Big Fish was sitting on the dock's ledge next to her boat with a cigarette and coffee cup.

"Wondered if you'd make it." She stood up, pushing back her rain hood and exposing surprisingly delicate features. A scar, which I hadn't seen in the dim light of the Pioneer Bar, ran from her right cheekbone down to her lower jar. I thought it looked sexy.

"Wouldn't miss it." I stared at the tall poles sticking up from the *Chisholm*'s deck.

"She's thirty-six feet and wooden. I love her. Been fishing before?"

"Never. Don't know anything about it." There were wire lines running from the poles to a hand crank. Flashers, plugs, hooks, and cannonball weights were set out. In the stern was a cleaning table.

"You look like a real Cheechako—clean boots and gear, not a scratch or scuff mark."

"Cheechako?"

"Alaskan newcomer. Wanna come on board?" she asked as she nimbly stepped on the dock's ledge and over the boat's railing. Offering her hand, she pulled me on board.

"Let's go inside. I'll get you some coffee."

Entering the cabin, I saw a small sink and propane burner. Food and storage cabinets pasted with photos of her prize halibut lined the wall. In front were the boat's controls. Looking toward the stern, I saw a small ladder lead down to a room with two bunks.

We sat in the wheelhouse sipping coffee as the diesel engine warmed up.

"We'll take a short trip up to Katlian Bay and troll a little for salmon. Probably not catch much, but you'll learn what it's about."

"I'm not good in rough seas."

"Inside all the way, Katlian is like a pond. Tlingits have a little spot there."

We headed north to Mosquito Cove and turned into Katlian Bay. Throttling down, Big Fish gave me the wheel and pointed at a distant mountain.

"Keep the boat pointed in that direction while I drop the line. We'll use an orange flasher and herring plug."

I continued steering toward the snowcapped mountain, pulling a line held down by a cannonball weight. Eagles soared overhead, and I spotted a brown bear hurrying into the woods at the boat's sound.

Suddenly a small bell tingled at the end of the trolling pole.

"We got something big," she yelled, turning the winch to bring it on board. "It's probably a king."

I felt sick imagining the fish being dragged to death. What would Big Fish feel being pulled with a hook piercing her mouth? I couldn't look at the beautiful fish as Big Fish sliced into its gut using a salmon knife with a blade at one end and a spoon at the other. Big Fish used the spoon end to scoop out the innards and back blood and then tossed them into the bay.

"About fifty pounds," she said, coming back into the cabin with a little fish blood on her sleeve. "Worth good money."

Pointing at a clear area near the head of the bay, Big Fish ordered me to steer in that direction.

"No more fishing. We'll anchor off that Dolly Varden stream."

"Dolly Varden?"

"Sea run trout."

We dropped anchor about one thousand yards from the stream, and Big Fish motioned me below.

"You're a sexy-looking guy," she said, shoving her hand down my pants. "Feels good and big. Let's get naked."

Pushing me down on a narrow leather mattress, she climbed on top.

"This feels good," Big Fish said, bouncing up and down.

I felt nausea from the boat rocking in rhythm to her bounces. Just as she screamed a climax, I threw up my breakfast on our stomachs. A yellow slime trickled down her belly onto mine.

"Shit," she yelled, jumping up, gaging at the smell, and running naked onto the deck to vomit over the rail.

"I warned you about my seasickness," I called out, trying to find something to clean up with.

Big Fish motioned me to come outside, pulled up a bucket of salt water, splashed my breakfast off her belly, and then threw the rest over me.

"Never came like that before," she said, handing me the towel.

Back at Thompson, Big Fish gave no indication of wanting another romp in the hay. That night I dreamed of hooking and dragging her and then using a salmon knife.

I avoided Thompson and the Pioneer Bar as we settled into our office in the Cathedral Apartments across from the Russian Orthodox church.

We were greeted in our new offices by the state agent, Max Steuben, whom I had met going to see Big Fish. He supplemented his income, like many in town, with weekend commercial fishing.

"Let me explain what's happening," Max began. "We have data on potential earnings by pulp mill workers, the numbers of people who might be attracted to work here, the cost of building a road to the site, and the amount of the pulp mill's tax breaks. We're waiting for the waste study."

I stood, looked through the data, and planned ways to weight the figures for determining the economic impact. Before the age of desktop computers, a calculating machine sat on my assigned desk. At the institute, data would later be put on IBM punch cards for further analysis.

"What waste study?" asked Professor Feller. "There was nothing about one in the packet sent to us."

"Local concern is that the plant's waste will pollute the area. Tomorrow we're floating oil barrels from the plant's location to see where they go. Prediction is that they will go directly to sea."

"And if they don't?" I asked, organizing the data folders.

"Pulp waste is toxic. If it spreads around, it could keep the herring away. No herring, then no salmon, whale, or sea lions."

"How is this being measured?" As a budding economist, I was only interested in numerical data.

"The distance the barrels travel from the opening of Deep Inlet, which is on the opposite shore from Sitka. The closer to Deep Inlet indicates that barrels are headed directly to sea."

"What distance do the barrels have to be to indicate the pulp mill will pollute of Sitka Sound? Is there data on the economic impact of pollution if the barrels don't go out to sea?" Feller asked.

"No distance from Deep Inlet has been determined and there is no data. You'll have to figure it out."

"Billy, can you do that?" Feller came over to my desk and began looking through the folders.

"I'll work it out. We have figures on income from fishing, and I will determine the geographical area affected by any pollution. I'll get a dollar figure."

"There is worry about the social impact," explained Max. "People live here for its beauty, clean ocean, whale watching, birds, and recreation."

"Qualitative issues can't be measured. I only work with numbers. They tell the truth," I replied.

I spent several days tallying up the numbers. Despite the tax breaks for the mill, the numbers showed a positive economic impact on Sitka.

I spent some time thinking about how to measure the impact of pollution. I worked out a cost-benefit formula for the distance of the barrels from Deep Inlet as they headed out to sea. This cost-benefit formula was combined with the other data.

The night before receiving the report on the drifting barrels, I fantasized about Big Fish lying naked on a cleaning table. My bloody salmon knife lay next to her. I saw dark water with fish floating on top. Rolling Big Fish off the table into the black water, I watched as an octopus tentacle pulled her under.

The report described the barrels meandering through the tiny islands just off Sitka before slowly going to sea. This suggested major pollution for waters south of Sitka.

Using my cost-benefit formula, I balanced the pollution cost with the other economic benefits. The result was a big reduction in positive economic impact.

I sat back in my chair haunted by a dream. I could legally kill and ruin people's lives. A rage slowly percolated through my system. Big Fish hung from a dockside scale. From the black water came hundreds of crabs that slowly climbed on her and ripped off her flesh.

Trying to shake away the fantasy, I sat up, adjusted my pollution formula, tweaked the numbers, and signed a report containing no mention of pollution—only economic prosperity. I gave it to Professor Feller. He signed.

Sleeping that night, I dreamed of economists descending from the sky wrapped in black capes lettered with "Give Me Free Markets or Give Me Death." The economists stood around the fish scale as crabs finished snacking on Big Fish's body.

Chapter Twenty-One

A year later I was doing quite well. Institute economists loved my work. Give me a data set, and I can make up any truth. Professor Feller didn't want to return to Sitka to measure the pulp mill's recent economic impact, so they sent me.

Excited about returning to Alaska, I called Toots about my good fortune. I had avoided contacting her after coming to Chicago. I tried to keep her out of my mind. But my Alaskan adventure reminded me of the many things we had done together. I don't know why I felt guilty, since she'd made no effort to reach me. I wanted her to love me.

"Toots, Billy," I spoke into the phone in my room. "Calling to see how it's going."

"OK, back working at the supply depot; got an apartment near Mission Bay. What's up with you?" Her tone was not inviting; in fact, she sounded irritated that I had phoned.

I gave a brief account of train work and college. "The big thing is my work in Alaska. Headed back there; it reminds me of our trips."

"How so?" she asked curtly. "We never made it there. Remember, we went to Florida."

"Maybe after Alaska, I could visit you; haven't been to San Diego in a while."

"Don't expect to stay with me. I've only a studio," she snapped and hung up.

I sat on the edge of my Murphy bed and stared at the receiver. I should have known better than to call her. I felt like shit.

Traveling back to Sitka took my mind off the rage I felt toward Toots. The town was booming from pulp mill income. Standing on the rocks behind the Alaskan Centennial Building, I looked down into the murky dark water. The limpets, chitons, and rock plants had disappeared, leaving a slippery slime hard to walk on.

The price, I thought, *of economic growth.*

At the Pioneer Bar, I was surprised to see Big Fish on her usual barstool downing whisky shots.

"Thought you'd be out," I said, sliding onto the next stool. "Silvers are running."

"Fuck, if it isn't Billy," she slobbered, with touches of spit on the sides of her mouth. She leaned over, hugged me, and kissed my cheek. "This calls for a celebration."

She got off her stool and moved in a drunken stupor to the bell hanging over the bar. Slurring, she announced, "For the only guy who puked on me when I came."

With cheers from all, she rang the bell. Bartenders hurried around giving free drinks as she wove her way back to me.

"This is my week in town," she explained, downing another shot. "Fuckin' pulp mill ruined Sitka Sound. Gotta go around Chichagof and Admiralty islands to get any fish. I'm out three or four weeks. I might move to Hoonah, but I'd lose my money for the Thompson berth. Gotta piss."

I watched her stumble to the bathroom with her large halibut-shaped earrings swinging.

When she returned, I noticed wet spots around her crotch. "Splash yourself washing?" I pointed at her jeans.

"Couldn't get 'em down fast enough." She was barely able to climb on the stool, and her hand landed on my pants. Squeezing my leg, she whispered with a whisky and cigarette breath, "You staying someplace?"

"Sitka Hotel."

"No seasickness there. I liked it with you. Take me with you. I'm tired of the boat."

"There are loggers, fights, and chainsaws at all hours," Billy warned, "but no waves."

I steadied her as we lurched to the hotel. I almost lost her when she decided to walk on the seawall behind the totem. Finally in my room, she stripped, lost bladder control, and fell in bed fast asleep. I cleaned the floor and stared at her body. I fell asleep rubbing against her.

In the morning, she got up to pee and called from the bathroom, "Can I use your toothpaste?"

"Sure, but not my brush."

"Only use my finger; easier on the boat."

Excited by watching her body return to bed, I was immediately shut down by the foul odors of alcohol and bile coming from her mouth.

"Wanna go for breakfast?" I offered.

A blast of putrid breath answered me as she climbed on top wearing only her halibut earrings.

"Don't you wanna fuck?" she called out just as a chainsaw started in a distant room.

"Can't focus with a chainsaw going."

"I'll help focus you," she yelled, bouncing up and down.

At breakfast I smelled a faint aroma of urine as she ate a logger's breakfast of eggs, hash browns, pancakes, and a rare steak.

"Has the water got bad? I couldn't see any life on the rocks behind the Centennial Building. The water was black," I said.

Shaking her halibut earrings, she told me, "Week after the mill opened, the water color in Sitka Sound became brown and then black. No herring, no fish. Small run of pink salmon in a stream near the mill. That's all."

"University gave me some funds. Can I hire you to take me out in the sound? I want to see what's happened."

"Sitka Sound, you'll get sick. Some swell and often high seas."

"I'll hold a bucket. I wanna to see the damage."

Sure enough, I began filling the bucket as the Chisholm cut through three-foot seas. The blackened water started turning turquoise as we neared Kruzof Island about fourteen miles from Sitka.

"Isn't this a bitch," Big Fish grimaced, looking at the water. "We're this far out, and it's still killing. I'd like to gut the person responsible for this."

I felt a slight pang of guilt.

"I need to get back," I whimpered, retching into the bucket.

"It might be a while," Big Fish looked at an angry cloud coming from the southeast. "I know a cove we can duck into. It looks like a big blow."

"Shit," I said, "I'll be throwing up all over the cove."

"Got an inflatable on board. Pump it up, and we can camp on shore. I got large plastic sheets to tie between trees as cover and put on the ground. Blankets, a fire, and fuckin' will keep us warm."

She sat in the inflatable as I passed her a roll of plastic, blankets, food, some dishes, spoons, and a rifle.

"What do we need the gun for?" I asked, almost dropping it in the water.

"Brown bear," she answered from the dinghy. "Can't trust them. They might attack for any reason. Know how to shoot? Or is it like your fishing?"

"I can shoot," I answered, passing down a basket of food. "Learned as a kid in the California mountains, and my mother let me do target practice with her pistol."

I watched her row to shore and carry the provisions above the tide line. Returning, she climbed back on board, checked the anchor, and handed me the end of lines attached to the bow and the two corners of the stern.

"Hold these lines; we'll secure the boat. I don't want some big wind moving it while we're ashore. Get in." She climbed into the dinghy.

I awkwardly got in. Landing on the pebble beach, I jumped out, protected from the water by my Halibut boots. After she got out, I pulled the inflatable above the tide line. Big Fish walked around the cove tying the three lines to different hemlock trees and creating a triangle to keep the boat from moving too far in any direction.

"That should keep her." She looked around for a level spot to sleep on and with trees to spread the plastic between. Taking marbles from her pocket, she shoved one into a corner of the plastic, looped a line around it, and tied it to a tree.

"One time used rocks, but they cut the plastic when tied. Smooth marbles are best." She proceeded to tie and stretch the plastic to protect us from the rain.

On the ground, she placed another plastic sheet and put our blankets and provisions on it. Underneath the plastic was a thick carpet of moss and spruce and hemlock needles.

She took a small shovel and dug a shallow fire pit protected from the rain by the overhang of the plastic canopy. We filled it with dry kindling, which in a rain forest is hard to find, and gathered some larger dry branches. Using a blowtorch, she started the fire.

"Here it comes," she called out, ducking under the plastic as the sky unleashed a torrent of rain and the wind howled. We watched the boat pull on its three lines.

As we sat on the ground plastic, the rain pounded down above us. Big Fish put her arm around me and reached into my pants. I tried to back away from her urine smell and bad breath.

"Christ," she exclaimed, letting me go, bending forward, and clutching her stomach. "I gotta take a shit."

Grabbing toilet paper from our provision bag, she ran up the hill behind us and looked for a sheltered spot. Finding one under a hemlock, she squatted.

"Help!" I heard her shout over the roar of a brown bear.

Jumping out from under the canopy, I could see a large bear, later estimated by Fish and Game as weighing eight hundred pounds, moving toward her.

"Get the gun!" she yelled, pulling up her pants and waving to scare it away.

I grabbed the gun, released the safety, and aimed.

"Shoot!" she yelled.

For no explainable reason, I didn't immediately shoot. A ghostly image of Toots pointing a pistol at me blocked my view of the bear. I cowered as Toots's spirit approached me. I saw her finger squeeze the trigger.

I froze. At that moment, the bear charged Big Fish.

Its claws ripped off the front of her face. Fascinated, I watched the bear bite her shoulder and tear open her stomach. Dead, she lay in a pile of her own innards.

When the bear started toward me, I fired, grazing its side. I'd never used a bear gun before and was unprepared for the powerful recoil that moved me back a couple feet.

The wounded bear continued toward me. I carefully aimed, hitting it in the front leg and shattering its bone. Roaring, it limped closer. This time I crushed the front of its skull.

I hurried past the dead bear to the pile of what had been Big Fish. I stood fascinated by the heap of flesh and the blood soaking the moss around the hemlock.

Sheltered from the rain, I sat on the plastic and wondered what I would do. I didn't know how to run the fishing boat. There was a radio on board. I'd asked her about using it the first time we went to Katlian Bay. She'd shown me how to turn it on and send out a Mayday.

Worried about rescuers asking why I hadn't shot in time to save Big Fish, I concocted a story about the difficulty of finding the rifle and then figuring out how to shoot it.

The wind and rain lasted through the night with me wrapped in blankets under the plastic canopy. Nightmares of the bear attack alternated between it ripping apart Toots and Big Fish.

Around noon the next day, the sky brightened, and the fishing boat settled into calm waters. I rowed the inflatable out to the boat and sent a Mayday. A voice responded, wanting to know the conditions and location. I explained the bear killing and gave a rough location—I wasn't sure where we were exactly but knew it was the east side of Kruzof.

A couple hours later, I heard a helicopter with pontoons buzzing along the shore. Spotting the *Chisholm*, it carefully landed in the water, avoiding the security lines running from the boat to shore.

I rowed the inflatable over to it as a man wearing an Alaskan Fish and Game uniform and a woman with a camera stepped onto the floats.

"Where are the bear and victim?" asked Kale Robinson of the Alaskan Fish and Game. "This is Nancy Tarbell from the *Sitka Sentinel*."

I ferried them one at a time to shore.

"What a mess," Robinson said, looking at Big Fish's remains.

Finding Big Fish's remains too gruesome for the camera, the reporter took photos of the bear from every angle. Then she asked me to hold the rifle for more photos.

After telling my story, I asked about the boat. "I can't run it. How'll I get it back?"

"We're sending out a boat," Robinson explained, "with medical people for the body and crew to remove the bear. Someone will be able to take the boat back to Sitka. It looks pretty secure with all those lines. You can ride back with us."

The next day I was greeted with admiring stares and handshakes as I entered the hotel café for breakfast. Someone handed me the *Sitka Sentinel* with several photos of the bear and me holding the rifle. The headline read, "Cheechako Kills Monster Bear, Loses Girlfriend."

Wherever I went in town, I was congratulated for the big bear kill and given expressions of sympathy for the loss of Big Fish. That night a special memorial was held at the Pioneer Bar. It ended with fishermen swinging gaff hooks at each other, sending six to the hospital and me staggering back to the hotel cursing my mother.

Chapter Twenty-Two

The *Sitka Sentinel* faxed the story and photos to the Chicago Institute of Economics and followed up with a phone call to ask about my work. Another *Sentinel* story appeared on June 13, 1964, under the headline "Economist Bear Killer Tries Saving Girlfriend." The article embellished my story saying that I charged the bear to save Big Fish. "Worried a shot might hit his girlfriend, he hesitated before firing. Finally, realizing his girlfriend was doomed, he aimed and fired, hitting the bear three times before it fell."

On the third day, a photo showed me standing next to the pulp mill manager receiving a citizenship award: "Economist Billy Durant Honored for Heroism." The article explained my role in the mill's economic-impact study. "Only through his brilliant mathematical work did Sitka's economy boom."

The university's newspaper, the *Chicago Maroon*, filled its front page with the *Sitka Sentinel's* photos and bear stories: "Institute Bear Killer Cites Randian Inspiration." I don't remember mentioning Ayn Rand to the Sitka reporter. It turned out that the *Maroon* reporter went to the Green Door and interviewed Phil Anderson and others in the Ayn Rand group.

"He was always a rugged individualist," the reporter quoted Phil as saying. "True follower of Rand. I can imagine him standing up to anyone, even a bear."

Confusing "bear killer" with "bear markets," the institute's president Barry Peek welcomed me back with, "I hope you didn't lose too much. Market downturns occur. I keep everything in Panamanian banks. Stock market is casino gambling."

"I killed a bear; no money to invest in markets. Just back with the final economic-impact statement for Sitka," I explained.

Gray bearded and close to ninety, Barry Peek, an economic guru decades ago, held his position as an honor that no one else wanted. Sometimes details slipped his mind.

At the institute's next meeting, I was awarded a Free Market four-year scholarship.

"This special award," President Peek told me, "is for promising students in economics. It was created in 1959 by the Free Market Austrian Fund. You will receive free tuition and an annual five-thousand-dollar stipend. As a condition of acceptance, you must agree at the conclusion of your undergraduate program to write an essay on the value of free markets for human happiness."

I left Peek's office starry-eyed at my future prospects. Office secretaries congratulated me on my Alaskan venture. Miriam Wilson, Peek's secretary, gave me her sympathies about the death of Big Fish. "I lost my husband. I know how hard it is to suffer the passing of a loved one." A work-study student wanted to know if the name was really Big Fish.

Feller was the first institute member I encountered after leaving Peek's office. He hugged me. "God, I can still remember her; must have been hard. The articles on the bear kill and the mill got the department to award you the scholarship."

Wanting to savor the moment over coffee surrounded by Ayn Rand's books, I hurried out of the institute's building to the Green Door. I'd already completed the required math and liberal arts courses at Roosevelt. I only needed the scholarship for my final two years.

Walking, I thought of my love of math. Here was the perfect program— number-driven economics. People could be hidden behind numbers. My festering rage could use numerals to bring destruction.

Images of numbers cascading from the sky and burying humanity alive filled my head when I was in classes on micro- and macroeconomics. Sometimes it was hard to focus. Courses on economic analysis painted visions of poverty and destruction safely and legally hidden behind numbers.

I saw Sarah, Phil, and others sitting in the back as I ordered a cappuccino.

"Bear killer," Phil greeted me, putting down a ragged copy of *The Fountainhead*. "Your newspaper articles drove me back to the source." He laughed. "Randian individualist rises from the ocean."

Ignoring his sarcasm, I sat down, asking, "Can I do anything in a free market, kill animals and humans?"

"You know how to hurt," Sarah shot back, getting up and storming out of the coffeehouse.

"What was that about?" Ben Carson, a gifted philosophy student wearing a black turtleneck, watched her leave. "Of course shooting a bear to save yourself is a rational choice in a free market."

"You're crazy. I don't even know why you're asking," smirked Phil.

"What about shooting humans? I guess you could argue that if it's defensive, it's a rational choice. Couldn't you always claim you were acting in defense? Kill at will?"

Puffing on his pipe, Phil offered, "Killing in defense is rational, but it doesn't lead to a moral code. You have to see your action according to general personal utility. In the long run, does killing increase your lifetime satisfaction? It does if it saves you."

"War may lead to personal destruction and have marginal utility," suggested Ben. "The more you kill, the less satisfaction and personal safety."

"When you killed the bear," continued Phil, "weren't you trying to save that woman? She was important to you. Rational choice says that killing might increase your sexual pleasure. Killing, in this case, has a great deal of utility."

Back in my room, I lay awake and wrestled with my anger, guilt and lies. The scholarship brightened my future.

The next day Feller called me into his office.

"Before the summer ends and you begin fall courses, we have another project."

I sat down, leery of taking on something else with my psyche still disturbed by letting Big Fish die and haunted by my lies.

"You're the institute's hero. The president wants to make the most of your ability. We've been given a contract by Danbury, Illinois to do an economic analysis of their water system."

"Water system? I don't know anything about that."

"We don't have staff to do this contract," explained Feller. "The institute is getting contracts from all over the country. The Danbury one is minor. You don't need to know the details of a water system. Just juggle the figures."

"What's the issue?

"The town is expanding, and there are problems at the sewage-treatment plant. Some existing pipes date back to its founding in the 1850s. They need to be replaced. The town relies on a questionable source, the Illinois River."

"Would I be doing this alone? I don't think I can."

"The town is providing an office and will put you up in a boarding-house in the river district. It's a short trip on the IC. I'll come down once a week."

"What are they paying?" I felt like a true economist asking this question.

"One hundred weekly, plus expenses. You can start next Monday."

"I've gotta clean up from Sitka. Is there money in the budget for clothes? I don't know if I can do such a quick turnaround."

"We can call it 'supplies.' Any good economist knows how to work a budget. Just buy what you need when you get there."

"Is there anything to do there? I just can't work all day. Small-town Midwest doesn't sound appealing."

"I hear the City Tavern is fun. Maybe, and I hope it doesn't have another bad ending, you can meet another Big Fish."

Danbury City Hall was bustling with planning for the area's most important event, the Danbury County Fair.

"At least," I thought while being escorted to my small office by the city's clerk, Karl Sharper, "I can get up to Chicago on weekends."

Karl, a tall, lanky man looking a little like Abraham Lincoln, pointed to a desk piled with folders and diagrams of the Danbury water system. "You'll find everything you need in that stack. We want the cost of expansion to match the amount allocated in the city budget."

Karl picked up a folder and pulled out a sheet with the city budget. "Also you need to include increased water usage in the costs of the sewage-treatment plant."

I inwardly groaned as I looked at the folders.

"I know nothing about water or sewage systems. I only deal with numbers. Are there any cost figures for this project?"

Karl picked up four folders marked "Water Pipe Expansion," "Old Pipes," "Water Treatment," and "Sewage Treatment." He said, "These contain the potential costs. They can be modified as you work on the numbers."

"Why did you contract with the institute to do this?

"The local developer, Winthrop Swift, insisted that we use you. He loves Austrian economics, whatever that is. He runs the local John Birch Society—richest man in town."

"Swift has power over this project?"

"Swift and Mayor Chance are close friends. They often meet for dinner, and he gives money to the mayor's campaigns. Both belong to the Birch Society."

"John Birch Society?"

"Fighting the commie civil rights movement. Local chapter is big with connections across the country. It's trying to save America from Soviet provocateurs spreading ideas of equality."

"Sounds interesting. I've never heard of the Birch Society." I wondered why they were never mentioned during discussions at the Green Door.

"You'll find out; the mayor has invited you this evening. They're meeting at eight. Here's the address."

Karl handed me the address printed on a card with an American flag and the words "Stop one world socialism—Get the United States out of the United Nations."

"I better check into my boardinghouse and grab some dinner if I'm making the meeting. Can I get a cab?"

"I've got a taxi card here. I knew you'd need it to get around town. This is our recommended company; they're loyal to America. I'll have the secretary call one for you."

He handed me a card: "Loyalty Taxi—Keep Commies Out of Our Town."

Chapter Twenty-Three

After grabbing a catfish sandwich at the River Café, I called Liberty Taxi. The driver rattled on about local politics. "You're goin' to the only place trying to stop this communist civil rights movement. We got a lot of coloreds here. They're getting too pushy. They need to be kept in their place."

The cab stopped in front of a small two-story, redbrick building on Oak Street. Red, white, and blue bunting was draped over the front door. A smiling, white-haired Winthrop Swift opened the door. Dressed in pants and a shirt decorated with golf clubs and balls, he clasped my hand, "You must be Billy Durant; been waiting to meet you. Got good recommendations from the citadel of free trade. We're always fighting collectivism."

"Citadel of free trade?" I wondered out loud as I was ushered into the main room.

"Chicago Institute of Economics. They're our only hope to stop those commies."

Projected on the screen in front of the room was a map labeled "Black America: The Communist Plan."

"That's what the commie civil rights movement wants. Turn those states into black enclaves and drive out all the God-fearing whites."

Along the right wall were carved wooden plagues depicting crosses wrapped in American flags.

Seeing me look at them, Swift explained, "Those were modeled on that great magazine, *the Cross and the Flag*. Its founder, Gerald L. K. Smith, knew back in the 1930s that commies were the real threat. He organized the Silver Shirts to stop them."

Along the left wall, under a sign reading "Great Americans," were portraits and photos of patriotic leaders. There were two I couldn't identify.

Smiling, Swift said, "The photo with the sign 'Save our Republic: Impeach Earl Warren' is our founder, John Birch. The one with the saying, 'Under Every Dashboard Is a Communist,' is our major funder, Fred Koch. He realized the dangers of communism while developing Stalin's oil fields."

After singing the "Star Spangled Banner" and saying the pledge, I was introduced to a group of ten middle-aged white men, some in suits and ties and others dressed in leisure suits.

"Billy's here to help expand our great city. Using the principles of freedom, he'll make sure development is fiscally sound."

A fortyish-looking man with blond hair and an unwrinkled face raised his hand and told me, "I'm Warren Williams. Own a local construction company. These niggers are causing trouble. They want me to hire them. You know they can't work like a white man. Less work at the same pay as whites will drive up costs. Can you stop this?"

Other heads in the group nodded in agreement. A fat man dressed in tight pants and jacket called out, "I run the biggest hardware store around these places. I've got niggers that clean, but now they demand jobs in sales. No customer goin' trust a nigger. How do we stop these commies? They're even demanding equal pay. Talk about communism!"

Another man in a business suit puffing on a cigar responded, "Equal pay. Those niggers wouldn't know what to do with extra money. Have you seen how they live? I'll drive you through the nigger neighborhood."

After the discussion concluded on themes of Christ, atheistic communism, and the civil rights movement as a communist plot, Swift stood up, announcing, "Good news; we've entered the popular media."

"About time," someone called out.

"It's supposed to be critical, but the song 'John Birch Society' by this group the Chad Mitchel Trio is recruiting. The national group is getting daily letters asking to join, citing the song. Many say they didn't know that our God-fearing anticommunist group existed."

"Listen carefully," said Swift, walking over to a phonograph. "You'll see why patriotic whites are running to our organization."

Oh, we're the John Birch Society, the John Birch Society,
Here to save our country from a communistic plot.
Join the John Birch Society, help us fill the ranks.
To get this movement started, we need lots of tools and cranks.
Now there's no one that we're certain the Kremlin doesn't touch.
Oh, we're the John Birch Society.

Everyone applauded at the end, spontaneously stood, and chanted, "Oh, we're the John Birch Society, here to save our country from a communistic plot."

Liberty Taxi took me back to my boardinghouse on Kennedy Drive, where my room overlooking the Illinois River was decorated with wallpaper depicting plows and barns. A sleigh-shaped bed was covered with a blue, quilted spread. There were a mahogany writing desk and two chairs upholstered in brown leather. A print of Jesus Christ hung over the bed.

Though tired from the long day, I had trouble falling asleep as images of Christ and communism floated through my head.

At the Green Door Coffeehouse, I had admired many posters of the civil rights movement and had been tempted to join the struggle. There was a striking one of a black woman asking for "Power and Equality." Another showed black and white hands shaking with the declaration "United We Shall Overcome." All the Ayn Rand fans agreed there could only be a free market if all were equal to compete.

The next morning city clerk Karl Sharper asked how the meeting had gone as I was walking down the hallway to my office.

"OK," I mumbled, trying to avoid discussing communism and civil rights.

"I couldn't make it last night," Karl said. "We've had some great meetings. Two weeks ago there were two guys from the Minutemen."

"Minutemen. Who are they?" I asked.

"These guys believe any organization over four will be infiltrated by the FBI and communists. They'd just come back from the Soviet Union with tales about communist control using chemicals."

"Sounds paranoid. It would mean the John Birch Society was infiltrated."

"You should know their story before determining the cost of the water-treatment plant."

These continuing weird stories were starting to make me question my acceptance of this job.

"They visited a prison camp," continued Karl, ignoring my remark about infiltration of the Birch Society, "where only a few guards were needed for thousands of prisoners. They asked the guards how they were able to do it."

"Is this a true story? Can you trust people who call themselves Minutemen?"

"These are true Americans. They know we're about to be taken over by communists. They're stockpiling weapons in their small cells to combat the coming terror."

"What's this got to do with the water-treatment plant?"

"The guards wouldn't tell them how they controlled so many prisoners. They didn't find out until they talked to a friend in Moscow. They put fluoride in the prisoner's drinking water."

"I thought fluoride prevented cavities," I responded, walking into my office with Karl following.

"Fluoride breaks your will. It's part of a communist plot to get all US water systems to add the chemical."

"I don't understand." I sat down at the desk and began to look through the files.

"It will make the commie takeover possible. Numb people's minds with fluorides, and they won't resist."

Opening the water-treatment-plant folder, I noted "fluorides" as a cost item.

"But the budget shows fluorides. Do you want me to remove it?"

"That's only in the nigger neighborhood. Water going there will be treated."

Looking up from the folder, I wondered, "You want communists to control the black community?"

"No, fluorides will calm 'em down. Stop all this protest stuff. Last week they marched around Scully's Diner demanding service. Can you imagine? They got their own eating shacks."

After Karl left, I phoned Professor Feller.

"It's crazy down here. All they talk about is commies in the civil rights movement. Now they want me to budget the system to hurt black people."

"You've only been down there a day." I could hear him sigh. "What happened?"

"I went to a John Birch meeting last night with the town's bigwigs."

"They're funded by Fred Koch, a great fighter for free markets."

"I know. Saw his photo at the meeting. But these guys sound like kooks."

"The institute would be very upset if you raised a fuss. Just go along with them."

"But I support civil rights as necessary for a free market."

"Just don't say anything about it," Feller said emphatically. "Sometimes there are strange bedfellows as we work for freedom."

Agreeing to be quiet, I hung up and began looking through the folders. There were some funny-looking costs. There were costs for replacing old pipes leaching lead into the water system. What was strange was that not all the old pipes were being replaced.

I went looking for Fred to discuss this seeming anomaly. He was in Mayor Chance's office talking about policing the county fair. For twenty years, Mayor Chance, with his powerful friends, had had tight control of the city.

"How'd you like the meeting?" asked the mayor as I entered his office.

"Very interesting. Learned a lot about politics. I have a question about water-pipe replacement."

"Yes," replied the mayor.

"Why are only some being replaced? Lead is dangerous; it affects kids."

Fred went over to a zoning map on the mayor's wall. "We're replacing the pipes in these districts." He pointed to two zones marked four and five. "These areas pay the higher property taxes, so we're focusing on them."

"They're also white districts," interjected the mayor. "Don't say anything to those civil rights commies."

Mayor Chance got up from his desk and pointed at zones seven and eight. "These people don't pay much in taxes. City can't afford to change all the old pipes. New pipes should go to those who pay more."

I noticed that someone had written across zones seven and eight "Coloreds."

"So you're not replacing pipes in black districts?"

"Most of their kids are retarded anyway. A little lead won't hurt them."

Chapter Twenty-Four

It'd been years since I'd dreamed of the black man stumbling toward me with three red stains flowering across his chest. I awakened, hysterical about what I'd done. Brushing my teeth, I stared in the mirror and searched my face for signs of a murderer. Was there such a thing as sin?

I arrived before others crowded the corridors of city hall. It was June 3, 1964, and the sticky southern Illinois summer weather was arriving.

In my office, the first thing I looked at was the cost of replacing old pipes and adding fluoride. Using the price per foot for new pipes, I estimated the amount for replacing all lead pipes. The total exceeded the entire project budget. I recalculated without including new pipes for the black section of Danbury. The result fitted the budget. The cost of fluorides was minor. The major expense was for equipment to add fluorides to the water system.

Going over to the table where Fred had piled the water-system diagrams, I remembered the zoning maps in the mayor's office. The high price for replacing pipes in the black community—it was the largest and oldest part of Danbury.

An interesting cost was for equipment to separate the water treated with fluorides from the untreated to ensure white neighborhoods didn't receive any of the supposedly mind-numbing chemical. I thought there was a certain irony that the paranoid fear of fluorides as a communist plot would result in fewer cavities in black neighborhoods.

Calling down to the mayor's office, I made an appointment to see him at eleven that morning. It was now nine, which gave me time to do another estimate using figures for treatment of lead poisoning. I called the University of Chicago Medical Center and asked for their poison control center. They supplied the cost of diagnosing lead poisoning and estimates on treatment.

Using these costs and the number of citizens affected by not removing the pipes, I concluded that medical costs for not removing the pipes far exceeded the cost of replacing the pipes in black neighborhoods.

Glancing at the clock, I had five minutes to put my work in a folder for the mayor.

Mayor Chance and Winthrop Swift were in an animated conversation about banks and Jews when I poked my head through the mayor's open door.

"Come in, Billy." The mayor waved me to an empty chair. "We're talking about big bankers preying on communities like ours. That's why we need to stick to the budget. Don't want those Wall Street shysters getting their hands in our cookie jar. Bonds and loans that's what they want."

"Tell me, Billy," Swift said and looked at me. "How do they teach banking at the University of Chicago? Are bankers considered a hindrance to free markets?"

"Borrowing money is part of the free market," I answered. "Interest rates follow the supply and demand of cash."

"What if international kike bankers control the money?" Almost whispering the question, the mayor leaned forward. "They could break nations and our little community."

"We've got evidence," added Swift, "of a Jewish conspiracy to weaken nations for communist takeover. Debts from high interest rates and manipulation of currency values are key to promoting communism."

"I want to point to some problems in the budget." I tried steering the conversation to my concerns.

"Budget," Swift responded. "We need to cut the budget and taxes to stop communism. Any red in the budget will lead to Reds taking over. Red in the budget means Jewish bankers loaning money or issuing municipal bonds."

"Look at these numbers," I said, handing the mayor a sheet with my calculations. "Not replacing pipes in the black neighborhoods will result in future higher costs for treating lead poisoning."

"That's future costs," Swift snapped. "We're concerned about the imminent communist takeover. We need a balanced city budget and low taxes."

"Otherwise Jewish bankers will take over," the mayor agreed. "Communism is an international Jewish conspiracy."

That night the dead man I shot appeared again in my dream. He rose from the position where he had fallen. He advanced toward me. As he got closer, the blood spurted out from his wounds and covered my hands and the gun. I tried to run. His hand reached out and grabbed my shoulder.

I heard a pounding at the door. "Who's there?"

"You OK?" It was the landlady's voice.

"Why?"

"Your screaming woke everyone up—must have had a nightmare."

I opened the door and apologized profusely, "Sorry, bad dream."

When I returned to bed, the dream appeared again with me drenched in his blood. The murdered man's hand was pulling me into the dirt road as I dropped Toots's gun and tried to run away. I couldn't resist.

He pointed down the road, where a large group of emaciated black people was writhing on the dusty ground.

The next day I skipped my office for the library. I wanted to do research on the effects of lead poisoning and fluorides. I found only positive reports on fluorides and cavities. There were newspaper articles about fringe groups linking fluorides to a communist takeover.

I made a list of medical problems associated with lead poisoning to determine if these existed in Danbury neighborhoods with old pipes.

For adults, the easiest thing to check was the number of miscarriages or premature births in contrast to symptoms difficult to find data on, such as high blood pressure and reduced sperm count. For children, there were developmental delay and learning problems.

I asked the librarian if there were numbers on miscarriages and premature births for Danbury. She suggested I check local hospital records.

Regarding children, she presented me with the local school report containing the number of students in special-education courses. The numbers were higher in neighborhood schools serving districts with older water pipes. Especially high was the number of special education students in black neighborhood schools.

I called Liberty Taxi to take me to the Danbury Hospital. On the way, the driver complained about draftees not wanting to go to Vietnam. "It's fuckin' Joan Baez's commie music. We must serve our country. Communist takeover of Vietnam means communism will win here. We've gotta stop it. They should shoot anyone not going."

At the hospital's administrative center, I explained my purpose in studying the effect of lead seeping into the water system.

A helpful clerk, Shanna Kimberly, gave me the numbers on Danbury miscarriages.

"I can't break this down by neighborhoods. Can I ask you about lead poisoning?" I said.

"Sure."

"It causes miscarriages?"

"Yes. I've had two miscarriages," Shanna said; she looked sad. She was in her twenties with light-blond hair and an attractive face. "My husband and I want children."

"Where do you live?"

She named a neighborhood served by old pipes.

"It could be the water," I suggested. "But there are other reasons for birth problems."

From the hospital, I headed to the River Café for biscuits and ham. I sat with lists of schools and special-education classes. As I looked at the zoning map I brought from the office, it was clear to me that the highest numbers were occurring in areas with older pipes.

I wrote the number of special-education students in each school district on the zoning map. Then I compiled a list of lead poisoning symptoms with special attention to miscarriages.

I tossed and turned that night. My nameless victim appeared again, pulling me through the dust of shaking bodies. Some bodies shouted out, "I can't remember my name. I hurt all over." On the roadside, fetuses were piling up as women smeared in their own blood wept for their losses.

The ghostly figure turned to me and pointed at the carnage. Echoing through my mind was the statement, "You did this."

I awakened in a cold sweat, feeling guilt and remorse about my first murder and the crimes I was about to commit.

The next day I went immediately to the mayor's office with my findings. He quickly dismissed the idea of lead causing increased numbers of special education students.

"Zones four and five are poor white trash. You could predict they'd have more. White trash do a lot of inbreeding. They pay more taxes than the niggers; that's why we're replacing their pipes."

"But," I protested, "there is a direct relationship between lead poisoning and mental impairment."

"Lead or no lead," the mayor laughed, "white trash and niggers always retarded. Only good thing about zones four and five is their high Klan membership."

"You mean the Klu Klux Klan?" I was horrified.

"They march in their white sheets to get me elected. They're friends of this office."

"What about the miscarriages?"

"We just hired you to work on making a good budget," said the mayor angrily. "Are you a commie?"

Worried about the institute's reaction, I decided not to pursue the discussion. I backed out of the office and took my maps and budget tallies to my desk.

I phoned Professor Feller to complain that I was being made responsible for racial discrimination and harming black children.

"They're a bunch of kooks claiming to be fighting an international Jewish banker conspiracy to spread communism by balancing the city budget on the backs of black people."

"Don't say anything," warned Feller. "The institute gets upset if we lose contracts. Just do the budget the way they want."

"But it's criminal!" I almost shouted into the phone. "The mayor just said he wanted to keep the support of the Klu Klux Klan."

"Billy, you're losing your way," Feller responded. "We're not judging values. A free market means free ideas."

"But this free market of ideas is leading to miscarriages, developmental delays, high blood pressure, and other medical issues. How can I in good conscience do this?"

"I understand." Feller suddenly sounded sympathetic. "Freedom can lead people down a crooked path. I'm coming down next Monday. That'll be June eighth. Let's try to finish this work up so you can get out of there. I don't want to leave you there for the entire summer."

That night my childhood murder victim was standing in the road surrounded by dead and crippled black people, some of them trying to crawl away from a water bottle engraved with a skull and crossbones. I could hear a voice urging me to redeem myself for murdering an innocent black man: "Kill those who harm us."

Wet sheets clung to me when I awoke, my heart racing from feelings of shame and sin. I glanced at the clock. It was three in the morning. I got up to pee and returned to a restless sleep.

Again the figure appeared, but this time he pointed Toots's pistol over the black bodies strewn across the road. He aimed at shadowy images of the Mayor Chance and Winthrop Swift. "It's time for redemption," the voice told me. Toots appeared as big as life and said, "I wish you'd never been born." I awoke shaking with rage.

Chapter Twenty-Five

Despite the harm I was committing, I went to my office to complete a budget to be certified by the institute and given to Mayor Chance. The certification would protect the mayor from any future incrimination for poisoning the black Danbury population.

I'm just doing my job, I thought to myself, trying to shut out images of the mayor and Winthrop Swift lying in the road with dead black people. Holding Toots's pistol, my hand was forced to point at the mayor and Swift.

The mayor stopped by and offered to take me to the evening's Birch Society meeting.

"I think you'll understand the importance of balancing the budget to stop Jewish communism after this meeting," he told me. "We've got more proof on the importance of cutting taxes and good budgets."

I sat silently through the evening's meeting. There were presentations and discussions on how balanced budgets and low taxes were the best resistance to communism.

I was distraught when the mayor dropped me off at my boardinghouse. I called Liberty Taxi, which promptly carried me to the City Tavern in an old nineteenth-century wood-frame building. I was greeted by the smell of cigarette smoke and whisky and sounds of country and western music coming from a jukebox. Old plows and farm tools decorated the walls. It was a large room with a long, oak bar and scattered tables and chairs.

"You got an ID?" I was asked as I ordered a shot of whiskey with a beer chaser.

"He looks old enough to fuck; just serve him," a blond-haired woman called down the bar.

I produced my old US Navy card with my photo and birthdate.

"What about a driver's license?" the bartender asked, squinting at the navy card.

"I don't drive. The navy card is valid," I insisted.

"Let 'em drink," the woman called again and moved to the stool next to me. In the dim light, she looked pretty in a red- and white-checkered gingham blouse and matching skirt. I guessed she was ten years older than me.

Handing back my ID card, the bartender poured me a shot and set down a glass of draft beer.

"How old are you, honey?" the woman asked. "My name's Crystal Ball—don't laugh; my mom was inventive."

"Twenty-four." I tossed back the whiskey followed by a gulp of beer. "I'm Billy Durant."

"You're cute. You drink like an old factory worker but look like you've never worked in your life. You new around here?"

I quickly explained why I was in town and ordered another shot. She looked impressed that I was working for the mayor's office.

"I see you wanna get drunk. Lose your girlfriend?"

"No girlfriends. I just don't like what they're asking me to do."

"Those big shots run the town. At school their kids called me white trash. They and the fuckin' Klan ruined my life."

"How?" I was suddenly interested and waved for another refill.

"I loved this black boy, Herman Jones. He invited me to the high school prom. They lynched him from a tree surrounded by burning crosses. After all these years, I still haven't got over it. Buy me a drink?"

"Sure." I nodded at the bartender to fill her glass after mine. "They're racist." I threw back another shot. She looked more and more attractive as the alcohol worked its way through my system.

"I joined the local civil rights group," she slurred. "I still want revenge. Like to string the mayor and that shit Winthrop Swift from a tree. Can you imagine what it's like to see your teenage lover hung in front of you?"

"What'd you do?"

"Couldn't do anything. Guys in white sheets held me and forced me to look. They cut a Klan symbol into my arm."

Pulling up her sleeve, she showed me a scar depicting a cross in a circle. The cross contained another scar.

Pointing at it, she explained, "That's supposed to be the mystic Klan symbol. The little scar in the cross is blood—called a Blood Drop Cross. Fuckers said it'd be a reminder to stay away from black boys. I'd like to cut their pricks off and shove them down their throats."

I ordered both of us another round.

"You wanna dance?" asked Crystal, grabbing my hand and pulling me onto the dance floor.

My legs wobbled as we danced to a slow lament to lost love. She pressed against me, putting her head on my shoulder.

"You want to get them?" I whispered, kissing her ear.

"Love to."

"Any thoughts?"

She put both arms around me and pulled me tight. "There's a tree near the Danbury dam. I spent hours looking, imagining them hanging from it."

The music switched to a fast tune and sent us back to our barstools holding hands and kissing.

"You wanna come with me for the night?" She waved for another refill.

"How do we get them up in the tree?" Now thoroughly drunk, I knocked back another shot. "Don't know if I can do much in bed," I slurred.

"We can get you up while we're talking about getting them up." Crystal giggled.

It's hard to remember getting from the City Tavern to her room a couple blocks away. I awakened next to her in a room decorate in cats—photos, statues, real cats, cats on cups, and the smell of kitty litter.

"Fun," she whispered, rolling on top of me. "You're good!"

"I can't remember anything," I moaned with a drunken headache.

"Just remember the bass contest. Get in the mayor's boat. I put the pills in your pants pocket."

I downed aspirin and several cups of coffee before going to city hall. I remembered the posters for the Danbury Bass Tournament on several walls. Seeing the mayor's door open, I poked my head in and asked, "Going to the Bass Tournament on Saturday?"

"Wouldn't miss it." The mayor pointed at a stuffed bass on his wall. "Seven pounds. Won the tournament that year. You fish?"

"Did some salmon fishing in Alaska."

"That's big stuff. I am goin' out with Swift on Saturday. Wanna join? You won't catch anything the size of salmon. It'll be fun. You could teach us some Alaskan tricks."

After work, I went to the City Tavern to meet Crystal.

"The mayor invited me to go on his bass boat along with Winthrop Swift. You sure we can do this? Swift is a little heavy to pull up a tree.

"I know someone who'll use his pickup with a power winch. No problem!"

"Won't he know what we're doing? Shouldn't we keep this secret?"

"Don't worry. He's the brother of my lynched boyfriend. He says he'll do the cutting."

Only a little drunk that night, I enjoyed my romp with Crystal and quickly fell asleep. My nightmare returned with the man again pointing over the black bodies strewn across the road at faintly outlined images of the mayor and Swift with bloodstained pants ripped open in front.

"Beautiful day," the mayor greeted me, handing me a pole after I stepped into the boat. Swift was attaching his favorite bass plug.

"I put a Rebel on your line," the mayor said. "It's a lure that's always worked for me."

"Hope you don't mind staying out late?" Swift asked. "We use light so we can fish until the tournament ends at midnight."

"If lights don't work, we'll try dynamite. Always brings a big catch to the surface." The mayor laughed.

They started drinking as soon as we left the dock. Wanting to be in control, I only sipped on a beer.

It was boring floating around and listening to them getting drunker and drunker as they complained about civil rights, Jews, fluorides, and communism. We'd stop occasionally along the shore to piss. Swift opened a hamper and passed out sandwiches of bologna, white bread, and mayonnaise sandwiches.

We didn't catch much. Swift pulled in a one-pounder, and the mayor's were too small to keep.

As it grew dark, I suggested we float near the dam. "In Alaska," I concocted, "fish like to be near dams at night."

While they cast, I slipped Crystal's pills into their beer bottles. Resting between casts, Swift announced he was taking a little nap. "Quick power nap, and I'll bring in the biggest bass ever caught in a tournament." Soon the mayor joined him, snoring loudly.

I glanced at my watch. It was nine thirty, the time we had agreed to meet. I saw Crystal standing on the bank near the tree. With her was a black man. Next to the tree was a pickup with ropes attached to a winch.

Televisions and newspapers the next day were filled with our ghastly deed. Pictures were blurred around the two men's midsections as they dangled naked from the tree. One photo showed a Star of David cut into their chests. A news story hinted at perverse mutilation to the bodies and mouths.

The Danbury police issued an official statement that they could find no motive for the brutal murders and no evidence.

"The murder site," the statement said, "had no footprints or tire marks. Stakes with unknown symbols were planted in a circle around the tree. Experts are being brought in to identify them."

"Rabbi Menahem Schneersohn Identifies Symbols as Those of the Kabbalah," headlined the next day's article.

"The Star of David and Kabbalah symbols," interpreting the news article, city clerk, Karl Sharper commented to those in his office, "indicate the murders were carried out by a secret cell of the Jewish international communist conspiracy. Both victims were targets because of their work with the John Birch Society to maintain Christian American values."

The police briefly interviewed me, focusing on my knowledge Jewish mysticism and communism.

Caught up in the town paranoia that the deaths were a conspiracy, they readily accepted my alibi that around five that afternoon, the mayor had let me out of the boat near the road from town to meet Crystal who had driven me back to her place.

She vouched that we had spent the evening in bed.

Gossip up and down the corridors of city hall focused on a plot by international Jewish bankers in league with the Soviet Union.

"I just saw it on TV," Professor Feller phoned the boardinghouse. "Can't do anything since it's Sunday. I'll be down tomorrow. I'll notify the institute that we're finished. There'll be chaos with police and FBI. Just organize everything and put it in folders. We'll take them with us and send Danbury a bill."

The dead man smiled at me that night. He took my hand and waved it over the supine black people in the road. They rose. I thought he kissed me, but they were Crystal's lips.

Chapter Twenty-Six

Beginning fall classes, I headed to the University of Chicago Bookstore on Fifty-Eighth Street where a large group of students was waving signs that said, "We Won't Fight Another Rich Man's War"; "Resist the Draft. Don't Register"; "Bring the Troops Home"; and "End the War in Vietnam." Some had Mao's *Little Red Book*. I took a copy of the Students for a Democratic Society's *Port Huron Statement* from a table at the store's entrance.

I'd started having war fantasies. I could only fall asleep by imagining myself a general planning the invasion of Vietnam. When newspaper photos appeared of napalm burning villages and people, they were added to my fantasy. I had to decide if battle casualties were worth the effort.

Leaning over a map, I envisioned myself putting stars next to some Vietnam villages using a cost-benefit analysis. Starred villages indicated that American troop losses were worth the village. I marked the map "Calculus of Death."

With my credits accepted from Roosevelt, I was beginning my junior year. My first class was Professor Gunther Grass's Advanced Macroeconomics.

A large crowd was massed outside the classroom door. Pushing my way through a sea of antiwar signs, I entered a classroom with walls covered in black and red paint declaring, "Professor Grass, Pentagon Stooge" and "Grass Causes War Casualties."

Humorously someone had added a drawing of a marijuana leaf next to his name.

Standing straight in a tweed suit and bold, blue tie, Professor Grass looked from the front of the class at the twenty or so desks filled with protestors and registered students. On the chalkboard behind him, Grass had written, "Macroeconomics: Understanding the source of the world's problems."

"Quiet!" Professor Grass tried to silence the unruly mob. "I've called campus security. Everyone but students registered for the course, out."

"You're a Pentagon pig!" someone yelled from the back, pointing a "Get Out of Vietnam Now" sign at Professor Grass.

"How many babies have you killed?" screamed an undergraduate blond female in jeans and black turtleneck waving a sign of "Dow Napalm Kills Children."

Professor Grass held up his textbook, *Macroeconomics: The Nation State, Globalization, and Free Markets*, and pleaded, "I'm saving people from starvation, not killing children. Free markets feed the world; communism starves it."

The mob pushed back the arriving campus police. Unable to control the crowd, the police cancelled the class and formed a ring around Professor Grass to escort him threw a jeering crowd. Spittle dribbled down Grass's face and clothing.

Outside, the San Francisco Mime Group was doing an antiwar skit. I watched and followed the group into the administration building. Down a long corridor from the entrance, I could see students blocking the office where they were hiring for Dow Chemical.

I remained at the entrance and watched the Dow protestors. To my right near a staircase, Young Americans for Freedom were chanting, "Get those commies."

A frightened young woman clutching textbooks entered. She wanted to get to the registrar's office. She asked me if it was safe.

At that moment, the Chicago Police appeared at the entrance. I could see them through the glass doors clutching batons and looking frightened.

"You're safe," I assured her. "The Chicago Police are here."

Suddenly, apparently unaware that the doors were unlocked, the police started breaking the glass door panes. They came streaming in, swinging batons and first beating the Young Americans for Freedom. Several fell screaming down the stairwell.

They dragged the woman next to me out the door and beat her. I followed as one blow split her lip and another broke her nose.

I stood outside the entrance amid a chaos of squad cars, bloody students, and faculty helping to carry the wounded to waiting ambulances.

Hurrying away, I went to find out about Professor Grass and the macroeconomics course. He was in a deep discussion with Professor Feller.

"Billy." Feller motioned for me to join the discussion. "Do you think we're in danger?"

"Haven't heard students wanting to hurt anyone," I answered. "I did see police beating people."

"They should all be beaten," barked Grass. "This is a university. We're in a quest for truth."

"Why our class?" I wondered.

Answering for Grass, Feller suggested, "It might be our military contracts. Professor Grass's Pentagon work is doing a cost-benefit analysis on napalm use. We all have military contracts."

"I got a prize for it at last year's economic meeting," boasted Grass. "My mathematical model was the first to combine chemical burning with losses of US troops. It clearly showed that napalm saved American lives and was cost effective."

"Students were probably inflamed by TV news showing burning villagers running down a road," I suggested.

"Communist propaganda," retorted Grass angrily. "TV should show American troops being saved by burning the village. My model clearly shows the benefits of napalm bombings. They protect and grow the economy."

"This is a very patriotic department," added Professor Feller, almost putting his hand over his heart. "President Peek wants us to get government contracts. He's got the biggest contract for a cost-benefit estimate on using nuclear weapons in Vietnam."

"His isn't as big as the one awarded to the psychology department to develop torture techniques that respect American values and don't physically harm," claimed Professor Grass. "I've been asked to develop a macroeconomic model for measuring the value of psychological torture for strengthening our nation and economy."

My mind boggled at the idea. "How do you measure that? What do you use in the model?" My thoughts raced across all the possibilities.

"Good question," Grass complimented me. "We'll work on the problem in class, if the class ever gets going. The model will include the cost of torture, benefits to governments, the effect on economies, and the protection and development of free markets. Very complicated. Feller says you can do the math for this type of model!"

"Yes!" I was excited at the prospect. "I'd love to see your model on napalm benefits. Do you use IBM punch cards for calculations?"

"My model was developed for the IBM 650 computer. A representative told me the more advanced IBM System 360 Model 20 will be out this year. He said that magnetic tape will replace punch cards."

A student ran up to Grass with a message.

"They're moving our class," Grass told me, "and secretly calling students about its new location. The provost advised keeping the location confidential."

"How did this happen?" Grass asked me. "I thought the admissions office screened out commies."

"They're not communist," I replied, handing Professor Grass the *Port Huron Statement*. "They call themselves the Students for a Democratic Society, or SDS, and consider communists to be reactionary old-school radicals. It's a big conversation at the Green Door."

"Why?" Grass said. "For the thirty years I've been here, this campus has been a bastion of Americanism."

"Maybe," I suggested, "the problem is the draft. Few want to fight in jungles. What's the point?"

I left and hurried over to the Green Door to hear more about the demonstrations. The Ayn Rand group was sitting at the usual table. The antiwar movement had taken over most of the space with banners and SDS pamphlets. Polaroid photos of police beating students decorated the walls.

"It's the government suppressing the people," argued Phil as I sat down. "They draft people to fight. Militarism kills individualism. I'd support the SDS, but they're like European socialists."

There was a new girl at the table. I was attracted. She'd substituted the beatnik uniform of all black for a brightly colored T-shirt with flower designs. She apparently wasn't wearing a bra. When she gestured while talking, I could see pink nipples pushing against the cotton. Her dark-olive complexion contrasted sharply with her intense green eyes. She was about my height and wore an interesting pair of jeans that flared out at the bottom.

"I'm Billy Durant," I said, moving to a chair next to her. "I haven't seen you around before.

"Alice, Alice Conklin. Just started school. I'm from LA. I was thrilled to hear there was an Ayn Rand group. Any dope around here?"

A hush fell over the table. This was the Midwest. For all their talk about freedom, few students here had used drugs.

"What kind of dope? I loved the peyote I took in Mexico." I moved my chair closer.

"I'd like to score some LSD or pot," Alice said, smiling into my face. "I don't know if you can get this stuff out here in the sticks."

"Sticks?" Phil sat up. "This is Chicago, the Second City, not small-town Midwest."

"I can get us some pot," I offered. "We could smoke in my room."

"You're fast," she said. "I thought you farmers were hung up on sin."

"We believe in free love," I said, standing up. "Seems to be part of this movement."

"Ayn Rand was hot." Alice indicated she wanted to leave with me. "Her message of freedom was about free love. Life is about pleasure—individual pleasure."

I bought a bottle of tequila on the way to my room. A fellow conductor had told me that I could get pot from an apartment near the lake. We stopped, and I bought a lid. Alice carried a pipe in her pants pocket.

"How old are you?" I asked, opening the door to my room.

"Eighteen. And you?"

"Twenty-four, six years older. I guess I'm the older generation." I pulled down the Murphy bed and hoped the sheets were clean. She slipped off her T-shirt, revealing nicely molded breasts. I felt obligated to remove my shirt.

We lay on top of the spread, smoking and drinking.

"I must confess," said Alice, taking a hit from the pipe and a long pull from the bottle, "I've not been with many guys. We did nude swimming and all that."

"You a virgin?" I felt myself getting wasted. I wasn't use to pot and was worried about the paranoia starting to grip me.

"One guy. Boy, am I drunk." She stroked my chest. "He didn't know much. Still feel like I'd never given it up." She took another toke and yawned.

"You want to sleep first?" The ceiling was spinning when I looked up.

"Christ, I don't think Ayn Rand would fall asleep. She'd seize the moment." Alice looked drowsy. "Maybe a little nap."

I slipped into sleep and a fantasy. A large IBM data processor sat on the floor next to me, and a Vietnam map hung on the wall. Under the machine's pulsating IBM symbol was a drawing of Professor Grass's napalm model. I was wearing a freshly ironed general's uniform.

Through the room's window, I could see children playing among banana trees and thatch huts. I picked up a phone and could hear myself saying, "Start bombing; we'll save men and money."

I could feel Alice nestle against my chest as horrific scenes of burning children, mothers, grandparents, and animals filled my head.

Chapter Twenty-Seven

Alice woke up an hour later and ran to the bathroom to relieve herself of the alcoholic poisons swirling in her stomach. Her movement woke me up. When she didn't return, I got up and found her on the bathroom floor curled up in a towel and the bath mat. I helped her up and guided her to the bed, where she promptly fell back asleep.

The empty quart of tequila stood on the nightstand. Glancing at it, I wondered how we could have consumed so much.

We both awakened around ten with Alice moaning and holding her head. She looked embarrassed as she hurriedly put on her dirty flowered T-shirt. She tried straightening her hair with my comb.

"I missed my first class," she worried. "Do you have aspirin? I gotta change for my afternoon classes. This is not the way for me to begin school. Plus I was supposed to be back in the dorm last night by eleven."

"Don't worry; not much happens the first day. Contact your prof or his secretary, tell 'em you were sick, get the syllabus, and find someone to tell you what happened in class."

"I've only got to worry about this morning's class. Shit, I look awful." She stood in front of the bathroom mirror. "You got an extra toothbrush? My roommate promised to sign me in if I was late. I hope so."

"Use your finger. An old Alaskan trick."

"Did anything happen last night?" She sounded panicky. "I don't want a baby."

"Don't worry; nothing happened. I was too drunk. I like you, but you may be too young for me. Let's get some breakfast."

We sat in Valois, downed coffee, and hoped that buttered toast would settle our stomachs.

"Where'd you grow up in LA? I lived in Culver City and Venice as a kid."

"Outside of LA in Pasadena. Wish I'd been in Venice. More fun."

"I lived in foster homes and then with my mother. She moved around a lot."

"We never moved or did anything. Dad's a lawyer, and Mom is always busy with her garden or knitting group. Dad always said, 'Why go any-where when you live in the land of milk and honey?' We never even went to the beach."

"How'd you start reading Ayn Rand?" I asked as I got up and brought back more coffee. I ordered two Denver omelets and assured her that they were the best in Chicago.

"Friends at my high school started reading her. We'd meet at my house. My dad's a libertarian, so he'd join us."

"What made you come all the way out here?"

"Had to get away. Pasadena's dull, my family's boring, and I wanted to see the world."

"Chicago is hardly the world."

"It's far enough. Plus I want to experience winter and all the seasons. Even the weather is dull back home."

"What about the drugs? Did you do antiwar stuff?"

"There was a small group of us—about six people—who smoked weed and talked about *Atlas Shrugged* and American imperialism. Pasadena High School is overrun with conservative kids and parents."

"You said something about nude parties. I've never done that." I got up to retrieve our omelets.

Looking hesitantly at the mixture of ham, peppers, mushrooms, and eggs, she brought a forkful to her mouth. "This is delicious, but I won-der—" She started choking. "If I can keep it down."

"You'll be OK," I assured her. "Good to eat something. You don't have to eat it all. What about the nude parties?"

She looked down and mumbled, "Never really happened; we talked about it. I was trying to impress people."

"Then you're a virgin."

"Yes."

"Thank God, nothing happened last night. I'd feel terrible. Drunk is not the way for your first time. How about the antiwar stuff?" I glanced at my watch. "We should get you to class. I'll walk you. I've got to stop by the institute. Where's your one o'clock class?"

"Wieboldt Hall. It's an intro philosophy course, supposedly based on the Great Books idea. How do I look? Should I change?"

We both stared at the assorted stains around the flowers on her T-shirt. Stopping back at my hotel, I ran up and got a long-sleeve shirt for Alice to cover her dirty shirt.

"Now I'll see you again when you return the shirt." I smiled, wondering if I should pursue her, given her age and innocence.

Reaching Wieboldt Hall, Alice gave me a quick kiss on the cheek and whispered in my ear, "Tonight at the coffeehouse around eight. I'll have your shirt."

Walking through the campus's main quadrangle, I was amazed at the number of antiwar banners and posters. Speakers were trying to be heard over chants of "Ho, Ho, Ho Chi Minh! The NLF is goin' ta win."

An excited Professor Grass was the first person I encountered near the institute's offices.

"I've been looking for you. I got the torture contract. Psychologists will be helping, but I need your genius to create an analytical model. Feller and Peek claim you're the new wunderkind. You did great work in Alaska and Danbury. You've shot a bear; now you can shoot some Vietcong."

"I've got classes," I protested. "I want to graduate! I'm getting old. I'm twenty-four and need to get on with my life."

"President Peek talked to Mihaly Csikszentmihalyi in psych," explained Grass. "He's the big flow theorist, and they've worked out a way for you to get credit for the project. In fact Peek thinks you'll get enough to graduate. Plus you'll be learning a hell of a lot about economics, psychology, and politics."

"I wonder if I can combine economics with psychological theory; seems to fit discussions on market behaviors."

"Vietnam will be a great training ground for you," said Grass excitedly. "You could be a pioneer in behavioral economics. This contract is so big that Peek will work out anything with you. Come to my office; I'll show you the paper work."

I followed Grass to his office, which was decorated with drawings and photos of Adam Smith, David Ricardo, Von Hayek, and a host of other economists. Along his bookshelves were academic awards, many from European universities. A painting of Ayn Rand hung above a bookcase devoted to her writings.

Sitting down at his desk, Grass gestured for me to sit in a chair alongside him. Rummaging around in a drawer, he pulled out a folder marked "Government Torture Study" and passed me a government employment form.

"Jesus," I said, looking at the sheet, "eight thousand a year plus expenses."

"It also covers overhead, so you'll have an office. We need you badly. I don't want to give you a big ego, but many around here think you're smart enough to win a Nobel Prize. When we're through, you'll have a degree and be launched on a career. You can probably use the study in grad school for a quick PhD."

It was hard to believe that I was being offered this much money. A quick mental calculation told me that I would be able to move from my Murphy-bed hotel room to an apartment overlooking the lake.

"We'll go to Vietnam as a team—you, me, and B. F. Tanner from psych. He's the best behaviorist in the world. Reward and punishment is key to get people to talk."

"When does this start?"

"We'll arrange everything by December. You'll be on the payroll next month. We should be headed to Vietnam in January. You'll get credit for spring 1965 courses with your work on the project. Sign!" He indicated the employment sheet I was holding.

Grass saw me staring out his office window at what seemed like an endless stream of antiwar signs marching to the administration building.

"I know what you're thinking," said Grass, leaning back in his chair. "Those protestors have got to you. But remember they're worried about the draft. Most never heard of Vietnam or knew where it was a couple years ago. You'll be a hero by shortening the war."

"Shortening the war," I repeated, staring at the employment form.

"Those Reds melt easily. They'll give us all the info we need. They're only fighting because they're ordered to. You think they believe that Marxist crap? Most remember the freedoms brought by the French. Western colonialism has a bad rep. It helped save the Orient."

"I know this sounds cowardly" I asked, "Will I be in danger in Vietnam?"

"No, all our work will be at the command center. We can stay at the Hotel Continental in Saigon. From what I understand, great French Vietnamese food, oldest Western hotel there. You can even get a girl." Grass smiled. "I hear they're cheap; they keep GIs happy."

I was having a hard time making a decision. Something didn't sound right. Great food, great hotel, a bad war, and torture didn't seem to make sense. But there was something in my mind urging me to go.

Still wondering what I should do, I put the paper on Grass's desk. He handed me a pen. My hand trembled as scenes of torture filled my mind. I knew I wanted to hurt. But something nagged at me. Was there a wisp of morality in my mind? I signed.

Alice was already with the Ayn Rand group as I grabbed a cappuccino. She was now wearing a blouse with bamboo and elephant designs and a clean pair of what she called bell-bottom jeans.

I sat down next to her as Phil started a monologue on Ho Chi Minh's writings. "He introduced the idea of racism to the International, which is a plus. He is fighting against the horrors of French colonialism—and the French were terrible. But he is communist! He could have done the same thing by declaring his free individualism."

Leaning over, I softly touched Alice's arm and said, "Want to go with me tonight?"

She nodded yes.

"Then you support the war since it's against communism?" I asked Phil.

"No, we can't win, and I'm not going."

"You're eligible for the draft?"

"Yes." Phil was suddenly shouting. "Those fuckers aren't going to get me in a jungle to be killed. Did you hear how those Vietcong torture? They run little bamboo splints up your prick."

All heads in the Green Door turned to look at Phil as he climbed on a table, raised his fist in the air, and yelled, "Resist! Resist the government stooges!"

Phil pulled out his wallet and proceeded to slowly tear up his draft card and fling the pieces around the room. "Take that, you fuckin' govern-ment. I'm goin' to Canada."

Others joined him, creating a confetti of draft cards drifting around the room. Some ran outside, burned their cards, and sang "Give Peace a Chance."

I took Alice's hand and led her back to my room. That night she lost her virginity.

Chapter Twenty-Eight

In October, I started meeting with Tanner and Grass about Vietnam. By November I'd moved into a one bedroom on Fifty-Fifth and South Shore Drive with a stunning view of Lake Michigan. My relationship with Alice was ideal, because she had to go back to her dorm every night.

Some weekends her friends forged notes allowing her to stay overnight. Otherwise I felt like I had a sex partner with no commitment. I enjoyed going to sleep and waking up alone. I did worry that Alice might become too attached.

"We don't want to physically damage them," Grass emphasized. "The military doesn't want the world to think we torture. We must psychologically break them."

"We could begin with a variety of methods to find which is effective," suggested psychologist Tanner. "I've looked through the psychology literature, and there is no clear guide to torture. We should begin by making them feel helpless and then try other methods."

"What I'll do," I said, "is start making a mathematical model with different methods of torture; of course this will change as we go along. I'll call your first torture stage 'learned helplessness.'"

"The cost-effectiveness of learned helplessness will be calculated by the value of the information." Grass sounded joyful. "Such as the amount of US military lives saved, the economic value of those lives, savings on war material, and shortening the war."

"Any costs?" I wondered.

"Our personal expenses and the interrogation rooms and equipment. Then there is the value of the enemy killed and the cost to US international reputation for torturing. This gets a little complicated, because our global image is tied to trade deals. We don't want to look as bad as the communists."

"You'll have to add the cost of the deprivation rooms I'm design-ing. They include special sound machines and revolving floors and ceil-ings," added Tanner. "There will be special plumbing. I was reading up on Chinese torture methods. *Lingchi*, or death by a thousand cuts can work, but too many scars. Water methods are better."

"Water is cheap," smiled Professor Grass. "This might be our most cost-effective method."

"I've got some descriptions on using water," Professor Tanner con-tinued. "These two came from an old 1920s British journal on controlling colonials. Victims are strapped down, and cold or warm water is dripped slowly on their forehead."

"It'll be cheaper to use cold water. Heating a lot of water can get ex-pensive," suggested Grass.

"How does that get them to talk?" I asked.

"Victims can see each drop before it lands. Since the forehead is sensitive, they eventually go crazy, feeling like a hollow is forming in the center of their brains."

"This is great—water torture combined with starvation will really cut costs. The food bill will be greatly reduced, and we can use any kind of water, even polluted." Professor Grass hurriedly wrote in his notebook.

"Another method recommended for British Malaysian subjects is strapping the victim down on a board with their heads slightly reclining and slowly pouring water on a cloth covering the face." Professor Tanner rummaged through his notes.

"What happens?" I was curious.

"I found it." Tanner held up a page of notes. "British Army officials liked it because its effects lasts for months and the psychological effects for years. All they had to do was mention it to previous victims, and they immediately became compliant. Rated as the best method for controlling colonial populations."

"Wow!" exclaimed Professor Grass. "Low-cost water, years of obedi-ence, and no signs of physical harm. This is great."

"Not quite. It sometimes damages the lungs and brains from oxygen deprivation. The British did report broken bones from victims fighting against restraints; we can design soft ones to avoid injuries," suggested Professor Tanner.

Lying in bed and looking at the lake after walking Alice back to her dorm, I played with ideas about what Professor Grass was calling "humane torture." I thought of showing captives manipulated photos of their wives or children dead or mutilated. Remembering the famous 1860 photo of Abraham Lincoln's head on John Calhoun's body, I knew you could easily edit and distort photos. I fell asleep imagining colored photos showing open stomachs of beloved ones.

January arrived and we were excited at the prospect of tropical heat in the midst of Chicago's freezing winter. The military arranged for us to fly to Osan Air Base in South Korea and from there to Da Nang, a former French air base. We would be taken from there to our quarters at Saigon's Hotel Continental.

Alice got a pass for the weekend, and we hunkered down and watched snowstorms whip up waves in the lake.

"Will you miss me?" worried Alice. "There are stories about the women over there."

"They're gooks." I kissed her. "At the military briefing, we were warned about incurable forms of gonorrhea. Gooks can't make love like good American women. I promise I won't get a disease."

She started kissing my face and whispered, "I don't know what I'll do if you get hurt. I love you so much."

Alarmed by Alice's affection, I knew it was time to get rid of her. She was becoming too close.

"I'll be gone a month or two." I got out bed and went into the kitchen for water and called back, "You should look for someone. You'll need a guy while I'm gone."

Alice came running into kitchen. "Are you trying to get rid of me? You think I can fuck any guy?"

"How does my military work fit with your antiwar protests? I don't think this'll work."

"How can you say that?" Alice started crying.

Seeing her standing nude and crying got me excited. Floating through my brain was an image of her nude body strapped to a board as I poured water. I needed to hurt her.

Hoping to calm down, I grabbed some pot. I didn't want to let that part of me be exposed. We lay in bed and took tokes as I ran my fingers through her hair.

"Can you call?" Alice asked.

"Expensive, unless I can use a military line. I'll write. Do you have a photo I can take?"

"Yes, and I want one of you."

I had trouble sleeping as scenes of torture mixed with images of Alice.

The next day we flew to San Francisco and from there to Osan. We were put up in base housing until space was available on a flight to Da Nang.

Four days later a small Vietnamese man dressed in a French bell-boy's uniform took me to my room. We passed through the hotel's inner courtyard with its beautiful tiled floor and flowering frangipani, which the bellboy said in broken English had been planted in the 1890s. I'd never experienced a luxury hotel. The room was spacious, with a couch and chair near glass doors that opened onto a balcony overlooking the opera house. Copies of French impressionist painters decorated the wall, and the dark, wooden floor was partially covered in oriental rugs.

That evening we shared a table in the hotel's Le Bourgeois Restaurant and sipped onion soup before our *steak frites*.

"I thought there'd be Vietnamese food here. It's all European," I commented, enjoying the soup.

"I thought so, too," replied Professor Grass. "These colonialists took their food and culture with them. I thought I was in Paris when I saw my room."

The next morning a military car transported us to an old rice ware-house along the Saigon River. An army guard stood in front of a steel door.

"This is where they're keeping the important Vietcong prisoners," the driver explained, stopping in front of the guard.

After we showed our identifications, Major Virgil Abel met us inside.

"We've just about completed your special rooms following the specs you sent. As you can see, the warehouse has been converted into a prison."

We followed him past a row of cells. Through the bars, we could see Vietnamese men wearing only shorts sitting on bunks or the floor with a toilet hole in the corner. Each cell held one prisoner. There was constant surveillance to stop communication between prisoners.

At the end of the row, soldiers were working on four large rooms with wires running out to a variety of equipment, power sources, and plumbing.

"The toughest problem was getting the floors and ceilings to revolve," explained the major. "At first they went too fast or too slow. We put in better controls for speed. Venting in food smells was difficult. We ran a thousand feet of tubing from one of our mess-hall kitchens into an air compressor that will blow into each room."

"Why food smells?" I asked.

"We're putting them on a starvation diet." Professor Tanner went over and opened the heavy steel door to one of the rooms. "Food smells will make them feel helpless."

"I never understood the moving floors and ceilings," wondered Professor Grass.

"A moving floor will cause disequilibrium, and a spinning ceiling will create vertigo," Tanner explained, "which will make them feel nauseated and headachy and will cause a ringing in their ears."

"Certainly humane torture," commented Grass. "Billy, you'll have to include the costs for operating all this equipment."

We followed Tanner into the room.

"I hope we got this right," the major said. "You can see that the table can be slanted up or down. We decided to use rubber for the restraints to reduce broken bones. The ceiling was painted with the swirling design you sent."

"How are you going to keep prisoners from tampering with this stuff?" I asked.

"The prisoners will be chained to those eyebolts in the corner near the crap hole," the major pointed. "The short chains will keep them from reaching the equipment."

Professor Tanner walked over to the table and looked at a complicated mechanism hanging over it. He noted the speakers mounted in the corners of the ceiling. Sound was an important part of his methods.

"That was hard to make," said the major, noticing Tanner's curiosity. "According to the specs, the drip from the water tank should have a regulator to control speed and size."

"Yes." Tanner was elated. "An article said it was more effective if you confused the victim with different types of drops landing on the forehead. If it's steady, they have certainty about when each drop will arrive and how it will feel. Without that certainty, they become highly anxious. The article claimed it only took a day to break one prisoner."

"Cheap and humane," smiled Grass.

There was a sink in the corner opposite to where the prisoner would be chained. Over the sink hanging on a wire line were cloths made of a variety of different materials. As Tanner explained, different fabrics affected the prisoner's feeling of drowning.

"This will be up and running by tomorrow," assured the major. "General McCarty has selected four prisoners for you to begin with. Two are Vietcong generals. One is a Russian political aid, and the other is a priest."

"Priest!" we exclaimed in unison.

"The French built churches in major villages with priests acting as spies for the colonial government. Father Edmond Auger became a traitor helping the Vietcong. Claimed it was God's work. He knows a great deal. General McCarty is particularly interested in getting him to talk."

"I came to extract information from Vietnamese, not French priests." Grass looked upset. "It's one thing to torture Orientals but quite another to do it to white Europeans."

I was startled by the comment. It smacked of the racism I had heard in Danbury. "Even a priest can be an enemy," I said as I glared at Grass.

"Suppose so," he sighed.

"Start limiting the diet of these four prisoners," directed Tanner. "Twelve hundred calories is the minimum for an average adult male. I'd like it to be half of that."

They'll feel deprived with the food smells, I thought.

"Remove their shorts. We want these four naked; it makes them feel more vulnerable," continued Tanner.

"Yes, sir," answered the major. "When you arrive tomorrow, the four prisoners will be chained naked and will have a limited diet of six hundred calories."

"Also," ordered Tanner, "start the ceilings slowly spinning. This will create some disorientation before we begin."

"What about the sound? The amplifier will play at varying volumes. A song will start off softly and then quickly turn to ear-shattering and then back to soft. A three-minute song will go through twenty cycles of volume changes."

"What song?" I asked.

"We polled our enlisted staff for what they thought was the worst song of the year," smiled the major. "It was 'Do Wah Diddy Diddy'."

"What kind of song is that?" Tanner reacted. "Never hear of it."

"By Manfred Mann. The opening is 'Now we're together nearly every single day, singin' Do wah diddy diddy dum diddy do'."

"That'll drive them crazy hearing it constantly at fluctuating volumes. I'd say anything to turn it off." I grimaced, feeling pleasure at the pain they'd experience.

Chapter Twenty-Nine

We sat, drank Vietnamese coffee thickened with condensed milk, ate croissants, and planned the day's activities.

"Jesus," complained Professor Grass, "this coffee is awful. Can't we get a real breakfast?"

"We're supposed to get there at nine. You know the military likes promptness." Professor Tanner looked visibly excited by the day's prospects. "I hope they cut back on the calories and chained them in the deprivation rooms. If the ceilings are moving and music playing, they should already be disoriented."

In the military car headed to the prison, Tanner speculated that it would only take one or two days to break the prisoners.

"Do we know what information the military wants?" I asked. "How will I give economic value to info?"

"We'll have to coordinate this with military operations," indicated Grass. "If the info leads to an enemy defeat in battle, then the military will have to help determine the economic value of the victory."

"Why don't we start with the priest? Westerners will be more difficult to break than Orientals," Tanner suggested.

I gagged from the food and toilet smells as we entered the room. The squatting naked priest was chained in the corner. The ceiling was slowly spinning which, combined with the smells, made me nauseated. Near the table were a Vietnamese interpreter and an army captain holding a binder.

"I'm Captain George McCracken, and this is Lou, our interpreter. Father Edmond Auger was arrested for giving information on our troop movements to the Vietcong. Records on him were kept by the French, because he helped Ho Chi Minh when Ho was a student protesting French rule. We want to know the priest's Vietcong contacts."

"Put him on the table," ordered Tanner.

The captain called out in hallway for help. Two privates appeared as the captain removed the chains from the eyebolt. They dragged the priest to the table and held him down as the restraining straps were tightened.

Tanner ordered the spinning ceiling to stop. I suspect it was making him as sick as me.

I stared at the naked priest's filthy body as Tanner ordered the table to be reclined so that water would run into victim's nose. He went over, selected a silk cloth, and wet it in the sink. He then filled a water pitcher.

"Does he speak Vietnamese or French?" asked Tanner the captain.

"Both, but the interpreter only speaks Vietnamese," replied the captain. "I'll ask the questions as we go along." He took a list out his binder and began the interrogation.

"Name your Vietcong contacts."

When the priest heard the question from the interpreter, he spat at the captain.

"Now we'll see how this works." Tanner placed the cloth over the priest's face and began pouring water on it.

The priest started gagging and fighting for air. His body arched and pulled against the restraints. We backed away as he sprayed urine.

"I can see how this makes them feel helpless," I said, avoiding the urine.

Tanner poured more water, causing the same reaction, but this time the priest's bowels opened and added more aroma to the air. He lifted the cloth off the priest's face and asked the captain to repeat the question.

The priest let out a torrent of French words that none of us could understand. The interpreter ordered the priest to reply in Vietnamese. Switching languages, the priest said something. The interpreter said he was too embarrassed to repeat it and simply indicated that the priest would not cooperate.

"Chain him up," ordered Tanner. "Turn the lights up, start the ceiling revolving, and begin playing 'Do Wah Diddy Diddy.' He'll talk in the morning. Let's see one of the generals."

The captain led them into the next room, where a chained Vietnamese man was squatting in the corner. "This is General Hoàng Minh Thảo, a key military planner. We would like info on any future Vietcong operations."

Tanner indicated to the two privates who had followed us into the room to put the naked general in restraints on the table. The table was moved so that water would drip on his forehead. The captain started the machine and checked to see that there would be variation in speed and size of the drops. The general stared blankly at the ceiling.

"Bring in a map or a list of military targets tomorrow. I am sure that by tomorrow the general will talk."

Tanner checked the straps around the general's wrists to see if they were secure.

"Turn off the lights," instructed Tanner. "Start the music and the floor rotating. This, along with water torture, will soften him up for tomorrow. Do the same for the other general."

"What's the Russian's background? Is he a spy?" asked Grass, writing down extensive notes on the cost of the operation. "I'm calculating the cost of electricity. Having the lights out will save some money."

"And drive them crazy," I almost shouted. "After a night of water torture, moving floor, and 'Do Wah Diddy Diddy,' they may be too upset to say anything. Is there a limit?"

"Billy, you're too soft," smiled Grass. "It looks cost effective."

"The Russian is a military and political consultant. He only speaks Russian and Vietnamese. Central Command requested a Russian translator to ensure accuracy in the translation. She should be here next week."

"She?" I was surprised that a woman would be joining us.

"A KGB defector named Anna Amasova," the captain explained. "The Pentagon wants to use her knowledge of Russian spying for the interrogation. His name is Major Arkady Ourumov, a specialist in undercover warfare."

"Fuckin' communist," Grass angrily said. "It'll do my heart good to break him. Maybe do something extra before the Russian translator arrives."

"Extra?" I was aghast at the vehemence in Grass's comments.

"We can constantly change temperatures in the room from extreme heat to cold," suggested the captain. "Darkness, variable drips and music volume, starvation, smells, and a rotating table for a week should weaken him."

That night we dined on tasty European food. Even Professor Grass with his midwestern taste appreciated the bruschetta with sun-dried tomatoes followed by a creamy tomato soup with lobster salad. There was a French-wine pairing with each course. The next course was local grilled fish served on basmati rice with avocado mousseline and followed by duck à l'orange with garlic and rosemary dumplings. For dessert was crème brûlée and Italian ices washed down with cognac. We were stuffed and exhausted from the interrogations. Drunk, I stumbled back to my room.

Professor Grass had complained to the hotel about the breakfast menu, so the next morning we sat down to plates of pancakes, bacon, ham, eggs, pork sausages, hash browns, and toast.

"This is more like it," exclaimed a delighted Grass. "Get this in my stomach, and I'll have energy for the day."

"I wonder how the prisoners spent the night?" I was still bloated from last night's dinner and only poked at my eggs.

"We'll get them to talk today," mumbled Tanner, his mouth full of pancakes. Wiping off the syrup running down his chin, he said, "I looked closely at articles on teaching helplessness before bed last night. We're doing the right thing."

A waiter appeared with a telephone and plugged it into a socket under the table. "Professor Grass, a phone call."

Grass listened intently, occasionally grimacing. Putting down the phone, he told us, "We've got some problems with the priest. Father Edmond Auger is a hero among the antiwar protestors back in the states. Leftists in the Catholic Church see him as protecting the Vietnamese from the French and Americans. Signs bearing his portrait and name are being carried through streets in San Francisco and New York."

"What does that mean for us?" asked Tanner, pouring French tomato sauce on his hash browns and eggs.

"I was told to go easy on him," related Grass, "and have the guards clean him up for a public appearance. Some of the demonstration signs, particularly those carried by leftist priests in Chicago, claim that he's being tortured. A Los Angeles parish just announced that it was releasing doves as a gesture of support for the priest."

Remembering the demonstrations at the university and conversations at the Green Door, I warned, "This could be a public-relations disaster for the military. I know students will jump on this as an example of American brutality and exploitation."

"How do you think he survived the night?" Grass looked worried as he took another mouthful of eggs.

"He was pretty tough when we talked to him yesterday," Tanner uncertainly responded. "Most likely OK, but he will need a shower after soiling himself. When do they want him for a public appearance?"

"Today. They've arranged a noon press conference. They want photos of him looking alive and well sent to stateside newspapers." Grass stood up, indicating that we needed to get started. "The military is mounting a public-relations offensive against the antiwar movement."

Captain McCracken switched off the music before opening the door to Father Auger's room. The priest was leaning against the wall; he was missing large parts of his hair. Pieces of hair and scalp littered the floor. Blood was seeping from his scalp face where he had ripped out his hair. His body was covered with bleeding scratches from either his fingernails or the chains. Vomit was caked on his breast. His eyes had a maniacal look of a man who'd lost his senses.

"Well, that was effective," I sarcastically commented, thinking of what the students back in the Green Door would think of his condition. "It shows what a night of 'Do Wah Diddy Diddy,' a spinning ceiling, and bright lights will do. He looks crazy. Shouldn't we feed him?"

Grass ordered the captain to unchain the priest, bring him some food, put him in a shower, and find some clothes that fit him.

"Look at his arm," the captain said. "He took bites out of his forearms and legs. Do you think he was eating himself?"

The priest started whimpering as the guards removed the chains. He couldn't stand up. As the guards lifted him, he screamed and started foaming at the mouth. Babbling incoherently, the priest made no effort to resist. Wanting to avoid touching his filth, the guards attached a hose to the sink and washed him down.

"We've got to be kinder," urged Grass. "He will be on international television. Get a doctor in here to treat his wounds."

The translator, Lou, tried to talk to the priest but received nonsense responses followed by wild shrieks. Lou shrugged his shoulders, saying the priest had gone crazy.

Things started happening quickly. A doctor appeared and tried to bandage the wounds while the priest kept hitting him. A guard came rushing in with clothes that looked like they might fit. They tried to clean and dress the priest. He would go limp, making it difficult to even get underwear on him.

Finally food appeared, and the priest's eyes lit up. The dishes and cutlery were placed on the table below the drip machine. A chair was brought in for the priest to sit on while eating. Looking at the food, Father Auger grabbed a knife and plunged it into his heart.

Chapter Thirty

The next morning I watched, horrified, in my room at a television scene of San Francisco police spraying tear gas on a crowd outside the Cathedral of Saint Mary of the Assumption. A police line was trying to hold back demonstrators waving signs that said, "US murders!" and "What Happened to Father Auger?" and "End the War—Stop Killing Priests." Using bullhorns, priests and nuns urged the protestors to follow them to the military-recruiting office on Market Street. The news switched to New York City, where injured demonstrators were trying to leave Times Square. In front of the Times Square recruiting station, helmeted police were lifting priests and nuns from where they were lying blocking the entrance. Television cameras panned on tourists with tears streaming down their faces as the area filled with tear gas.

The screen switched to Boston and showed a nun trying to beat police with a sign that said, "US Tortures Priests."

Stabbed in the eye by the sign, a policeman instinctually swung his baton. In the front of millions of viewers, the baton ripped through the nun's white coif, split her head open, and sent blood streaming down her habit. Realizing what he'd done, the policeman fell on his knees and prayed.

Later news reports gave the policeman's name as Liam Ryan, a loyal member of the Sons of Hibernia and devout Catholic.

"Did you see the news?" I asked, joining Grass and Tanner for breakfast. "I'm surprised we can see it. I thought the military would keep them from showing US news about antiwar demonstrations."

"From what I understand, they don't say much about it on the Armed Forces Network," answered Grass, shoveling pancakes into his mouth. "With all the Americans here, the hotel uses television feed from the United States. We are fighting to preserve the American right of free speech."

"And Father Auger's rights?" I worried.

"It was an error, and he was an enemy," shot back Tanner, spewing bits of egg. "I didn't think the methods would be that effective. It was too late with the Russian. He's useless—babbling and shaking and can't respond in Russian or Vietnamese. But we did break him."

"The info we got from the Vietcong generals proves it's all worthwhile," said Grass. "Headquarters claims it led to the capture of several villages and five hundred dead Vietcong. Too bad about the napalmed civilians."

"Napalm!" I gasped. "They bombed the location General Thảo pointed at?"

"Leveled the whole area," Grass proudly said.

"What about the villagers—you know, the women and kids?"

Professor Grass sat back and puzzled over whether or not civilian deaths should be considered economic losses. "You know, we haven't looked at the cost of collateral damage."

"Would the villagers be counted as enemies or friendly?" asked Tanner. "That would be important as to whether they are losses or gains in our spreadsheets."

"It could go either way." Grass paused, finishing his hash browns. "Since we have some ambiguity as to whether villagers are gains or losses, we should probably count the dead ones as benefits. That way our cost-benefit analysis supports our program."

"I think that's extreme." I sat up, almost spilling my coffee. "I can't work with an economic model that considers burning villagers alive a benefit."

"I don't want my methods tied to destroying villages,'" nodded Tanner in agreement. "I hope to get some journal articles out of this and put learned helplessness on the map as humane interrogation."

"I guess we can just ignore the destruction of villages as a cost or benefit," Grass suggested. He didn't look too happy about this. "It helps to convince others of the value of your work. After the Russian went crazy, General McCarty phoned me about constructing more deprivation rooms. We could get a sizable government contract out of this. I hope you patented the design."

Professor Grass looked at his watch and said, "The car should be here. Maybe we can get more out of the Vietcong generals."

"One more question before we go," I said. I was to be dropped off at a shack housing a new IBM computer while they went to the deprivation centers. "Should I include the costs of the protests over Father Auger's death?"

Grass looked exasperated at the question. "Billy, just include the immediate costs of getting info and don't consider the villages and demonstrations as overhead costs."

"What about the priest? Should I give him value? Should the crazy Russian be a cost or benefit?"

Tanner looked worried. I knew he wanted an outcome that benefited his career. I'd heard Tanner laughingly say to Grass one morning, "If we can prove this cost effective, we'll both benefit. I'll get more lecture income and government support."

"Make them both economic benefits." Grass stood up, ready to get to the waiting car. "The priest was a spy, and the Russian an undercover agent."

"How do I price them?"

"That's an interesting problem," said Grass as we headed out the hotel door to the waiting military car. "Use what it takes to educate a priest and make that the dollar benefit. Contact the CIA and see if they have any figures on what Russian spies are paid. I know we have income figures for American spies."

The car dropped me off outside a recently construct building containing the new data equipment. Inside, punch cards were whirling through machines and tallying the American kill count and cost. The staff was waiting for magnetic tapes to replace the punch cards to speed up reports. Generals were demanding quick battlefield numbers about enemy dead and our losses for the US evening news.

I went to my desk in a back room to work on the cost-benefit of humane interrogation. Sitting down at a desk strewn with notebooks and scraps of paper, I wondered how I should proceed after the breakfast discussion. Secretly I missed seeing the deprivation rooms. Images of Father Auger stabbing himself and the salivating Russian kept interfering with my concentration.

I decided to create two models, one to satisfy Professors Grass and Tanner and the other for my own use. Pulling everything together was the difficult part of the task. I had already started a list of costs and benefits. What was a US soldier or sailor worth dead or alive? I'd requested numbers from the army, air force, and navy. They supplied costs aligned with rank.

The cost of a general or admiral was considerably higher than that of a private or seaman based on training costs, experience, and salaries. What was an arm worth if blown off in battle? Was it worth more for an enlisted person or an officer? Were battlefield medical costs to be calculated differently based on the worth of the fighter?

Then there were equipment losses with major variations between the costs of a fighter plane or bomber, tanks, artillery, infantry rifles, and other handheld items of destruction. There were transportation costs of staff and equipment from the United States and from bases in Vietnam to the battlefield. The use of helicopters added fuel costs. I created a miscellaneous category for other expenses.

Over the previous week, I'd started designing a model to include these expenses. Now I needed to add the cost of our humane torture methods and any loss of life associated with them. When Tanner's methods yielded information leading to battlefield success or failure, the results were supposed to be easily calculated, if my model worked, by simply plugging in enemy and US casualties along with equipment, fuel, and other overhead costs.

I felt weary. Glancing at the clock, I saw that I'd been focused for five hours on the model and felt hungry. It was two o'clock when I stepped out into the eighty-degree February sun and walked a short distance to a military canteen for a sandwich.

Sitting at an outside table and eating, I pulled from my pocket a recent letter from Alice. It contained statements of endearment and missing me. Finishing my sandwich, I crumbled up the letter and, with my lunch trash, tossed it in a garbage can.

I spent the rest of the afternoon working on my own cost-benefit model to include the cost of controlling US antiwar demonstrations and deaths caused by Tanner's humane interrogation methods. Police expenses could be acquired from local governments. But how did you calculate the cost of a nun's head being split open or other hurt demonstrators? Should I include the loss income for demonstrators when they were thrown in jail?

Lost in thought, I decided to walk back to the hotel. The route was simple and short. I left the main gate and walked along the Saigon River and turned on to Dong Khoi, which led directly to our hotel. I looked down a teeming side street and decided to turn into it. The area was filled with bars and American soldiers.

"Honey, you want quick pussy?" shouted a cute little Vietnamese woman. Catcalls from GIs drinking outside drowned out the woman. "You take her and penicillin. She's fucked the fleet!" Alarm bells went off in my brain about incurable gonorrhea. From one bar blasted country and western music. Tempted, I walked into the cool dark interior. Through the dim light, I could see two naked women dancing on a small stage.

I sat on a barstool and ordered a beer. Within seconds, I felt a hand slide into my crotch.

"Want fun? Got pot, coke, smack. Hundred dollars all night, all drugs."

"Hundred?" I was taken aback at the price.

"Fifty, OK. You good-looking guy. Give you much fun."

Even with the dim light, she looked OK to me—young and not fat.

"Ten dollars," I offered, knowing living costs in Saigon.

"Twenty. Good price. All drugs. Do good things to you."

Her hand was now massaging me. I was horny and agreed.

"Do you have a condom? I don't," I asked, getting off the stool and still worried about diseases.

"Rubber! All sizes. Trojans. I'm clean girl. Call me 'Beautiful.'"

I followed her out of the bar. We went a short distance and stopped in front of a two-story, rickety-looking, wooden building. She led me up wobbly stairs, past women and children who eyed me and said things in Vietnamese that were probably not complimentary. We entered a room where an old woman was cooking rice. Beautiful pointed at a curtain leading to a back room.

There was a mattress on the floor covered by a dirty sheet. A table displayed bongs, needles, and jars full of what I guessed were drugs. She put her hand out, "Twenty bucks. Good price. Show you good time. You want?" She pointed at the table.

I stared at the table as I handed over a twenty-dollar bill. I'd heard that the pot here was powerful, and I'd never used a bong. I was tempted to try the cocaine and heroin. A soldier at the base had told me that coke was dynamite with sex.

"Coke," I said, pointing at the table.

She went to the table and, from a jar of white powder, made four narrow lines on a small mirror. Handing me a brass tube, she nodded for me to go ahead.

Never having used cocaine, I didn't know what to do. Also I was suspicious. The white stuff might be poison or designed to knock me out for several days. I handed the tube back, indicating that she should go first.

Bending over the mirror, she stuck the tube in her nose, quickly sniffed up two lines, and handed it back to me.

My paranoiac concern was the tube being in her nose. Could I get a rare nasal infection or parasite? I used the other end and snorted up the two remaining lines.

I felt a sudden rush of euphoria and sexual excitement. Trying to quickly remove my pants, I tripped and fell on the mattress and wondered if all the stains were from previous customers. She bounced on top. The feeling was incredible. My heart was pounding as I came several times.

Half an hour later as the high started wearing off, I wanted more. This went on for several hours until, feeling raw, I wanted something to drink. After taking some hits from the bong, we headed out to a bar, where I drank beer after beer. Stumbling out of the bar, we walked to the Mekong River where it emptied into the Saigon River.

My penis was raw, and it hurt as it rubbed against my pants. When we reached the river, I was gripped by fears of dying from some unnamed Asian venereal disease. I'd forgotten to wear a rubber.

Leaning over a wall and looking at the river, she rubbed against me. "Good time. Maybe big tip," she suggested, squeezing my cock.

The pain shot through my brain and mixed with the dread of my diseased member falling off and the effects of the beer, pot, and coke. I saw an apparition of Father Auger rising from the river and wagging a finger as if scolding me. The nun beaten on the news appeared at his side wearing only her bloody hood. She looked like Toots.

Their bodies entwined. The nun unzipped the father's pants and revealed a monstrous erection. He pushed her off and squeezed her throat until the she went limp. I watched the naked nun float down the river as the apparition sank into the muddy river water.

I blacked out. Returning to consciousness, I saw my evening's partner drifting lifeless down the river with the other rubbish.

Chapter Thirty-One

The area near the river was deserted. I saw a couple walking in the distance. My mind tried to push back against the numbing effect of the drugs as I worried about being caught. My watch indicated that it was two in the morning. The people on the stairs and the older woman who was cooking as we went to the girl's room, all of them knew I was with the girl. I still didn't know her name. She said to call her Beautiful. I couldn't remember the exact location of the building.

Leaning against the river wall for support, I worked out a plan. Taking my wallet out, I tossed it in the river. In my pocket was my ID attached to a lanyard for wearing around my neck. I started walking along a street paralleling the Saigon River to Dong Khoi. A couple scooters passed me, but otherwise the street was empty.

Turning into Dong Khoi, I spotted a military-police jeep headed in my direction. Waving it down, I showed them my ID.

"I was with this girl." I tried to look embarrassed about the situation. "When I suddenly blanked out. Too many drugs. When I came to, she was gone, and so was my wallet."

A sandy-haired sergeant smiled and looked closely at my ID. "You gotta be careful. You're not the only one given a drugged drink and robbed."

"You're a civilian," he said, handing back the badge. "All military are warned of this. I hope you used a rubber."

"I didn't."

"Hop in; we'll take you to the all-night base clinic. They'll give you a high-powered antibiotic shot and pills. Where are you staying?"

I got into the back of the jeep as the corporal who was driving and the sergeant laughed. "I'm at the Colonial."

"Fancy digs," commented the corporal.

"What was her name? Do you know where she lived?" asked the sergeant. "We try to track them. Not likely you'll get your wallet back."

"She never gave a name. I don't remember where we went; I was drunk," I lied, worried they would ask me to find the place.

"Probably a village girl brought here by a local gang. They arrive and disappear. It happens all the time."

It was four by the time I got back to the hotel with my bottle of pills and a powder to use in case of crabs. At the desk, I scribbled a note to Grass and Tanner telling them I was sick and couldn't meet them.

Collapsing on the bed, letting the drugs take over, I remembered hitting her with a loose pavement stone as Father Auger laughed from the river. Wrapped around him, the nun's face changed to hers as the Father and I throttled our victims. There was a vague memory of straining to dump her in the river.

In the afternoon, the phone rang with Professor Grass on the other end.

"You OK? Lot of tropical diseases here. You should get checked."

"I did; they gave me a shot and pills," I mumbled into the receiver as I tried to clear my head.

"They know what it is?"

Sitting up, I glanced at the container of powder next to the bed. "Probably nothing, but they didn't want to take chances. Just need more sleep. Everything OK?"

I grabbed the can of powder and searched my crotch for any signs of bites or red marks.

"General McCarty loves our work even without our cost-benefit analysis. Tanner and I just signed a training contract for operation of the rooms. The two Vietcong generals gave all the information the general wanted before losing it completely."

"Losing it completely?" I was barely listening as I looked through my pubic hair for bites.

"We thought the dripping water would be the key. But it turned out to be the music. They both huddled in corners and begged us to stop it.

We strapped them back on the table, started the floor and ceiling revolving, and turned on the music adding high-pitched screams of burning people."

I started dusting and made sure that the powder reached all parts of the hair. "Burning people. How'd you get that?"

"We found some footage by a reporter; they won't let it on TV. He recorded burning women and children as they ran to him; their screams are in the video. Very effective mixed with the pulsating music."

"I've gotta get back in bed. My head is killing me. What about the cost-benefit model?"

"General doesn't need it. He doesn't trust data and mathematical models. He saw the results when he visited. Both Vietcong generals were kneeling and begging us to turn off the sound."

"What should I do with the model?" I fell back in bed feeling a wave of guilt. I just wanted out. The whole war was sickening me.

"Tanner doesn't need it. He's already booked for a speech on humane interrogation at this year's meeting of the American Psychology Association. Frankly I don't like this stuff. Those rooms give me the creeps. Too much emotion for an economist. I'll leave it to the psychologists."

"What'll I do?"

"We're booked out of Da Nang to Osan next Monday. We'll wait there for a flight back to the United States. Get your papers together. Take any work on the cost-benefit of humane interrogation I might be able to use."

By Friday I'd recovered enough to make it to pack up my office. The antibiotics were causing indigestion and making me feel weak. At least no bites appeared around my groin.

I took classified material on the interrogation project for my future dissertation, but I saw it as an opportunity to develop it as a thesis. I wanted to prove that torture was not cost effective. I kept this goal to myself.

On Monday, the three of us boarded a troop plane to Osan.

"I'm not looking forward to that Chicago cold," said Grass as we put on safety belts. "Billy, you should take a week off when we get back. I'm recommending you to enter the PhD program next fall. Great work."

I wondered if I could continue working with Grass. My goal was to prove that torture was not cost effective. In the air, I said good-bye to Beautiful floating in the river.

After several days of delay at Osan, we finally landed in Chicago on February 10, 1965, a blustery twenty-degree day. Anxious to get home, we took separate cabs. Opening windows to chase the stale air out of my apartment, I watched snow squalls move across the lake as the sun slowly set.

Hungry, horny, and jet-lagged, I first stopped at Valois for an omelet and then headed to the Green Door and the Ayn Rand group. Ordering a cappuccino as I looked around at the antiwar posters, my eyes rested on a photo of Father Auger, which sent shivers through my body. He was wearing a crown of thorns, and the photo had the caption "United States Murders Priests—War is Sin."

I was relieved to see that Alice wasn't there. In the discussion group were some new female faces. I ignored them as I had difficulty taking my eyes off the Father Auger poster and couldn't forget Beautiful floating in the river garbage. I was free of crabs but still worried that despite the shot and pills, I might have an incurable venereal disease.

"Billy, we haven't seen you in a while. Where were you?" asked Phil looking like a beatnik in transition to flower power with his hair growing long and his black turtleneck replaced with a Nehru shirt.

"Went to see my family," I lied. I was not allowed to discuss the classified Vietnam mission. "What's been going on here?"

"Debating whether or not war will always be with us," answered Phil. "Zeke Compton here," Phil said as he pointed at an overweight, triple-chinned man, "argues that war is the highest expression of individualism. It is another form of free-market competition."

I almost gagged on my cappuccino as I thought of the burned bodies of villagers and the torture rooms. My eyes guiltily wandered back to the poster of Father Auger.

"War is collective, not individual." I tried to control my emotional outrage. "Troops follow orders. It is not an expression of Randian individualism."

"Come on," said Zeke, running his hand through his long blond, hair. Husky looking with a florid and pockmarked face, he wore a T-shirt with the words "The times they are a-changing" and a photo of Bob Dylan. "Historically warriors are heroes—look at Alexander the Great or Genghis Khan."

"They were horrible," said Phil. "Mass murderers better known for the riches they stole and lives they destroyed. War is hardly a free market."

"Isn't that what free-market competition promotes?" said a brunette with a cute little turned-up nose named Claudia Belcher. "Isn't every one fighting for market shares? Sounds like war to me."

I looked at her and wondered if I could entice her back to my apartment. I said, "But war is between nation states, not individuals. If individuals pursued their own self-interest, they wouldn't want to die. War puts the generals in charge of everyone's life. They kill at will."

"You're right!" I heard Alice's voice behind me and felt her hand on the back of my neck. "Down with the state; up with freedom." I could feel her lips on my ear.

"Freedom can mean death," Claudia said. She glared at Alice, who was pulling a chair up next to mine. "It is an acceptance of death that makes competition real and allows for the existence of the authentic individual. That's Rand's message."

"That's not Bob Dylan's take," Phil joined in. "He hopes war will end. Just listen to 'Blowin' in the Wind.'"

"Since when is Dylan a Randian?" snapped Alice.

"He gives an existential twist to things." Claudia was now sitting forward, her eyes darting between me and Alice. "Just listen to the song's lyrics about how many roads people must walk down until they are complete humans—it is a plea for freedom to determine one's life, define one's existence."

"War is the nation state defining its existence," I said. I avoided mentioning the flaming bodies and torture I'd just left.

Alice started stroking my leg. I didn't want to continue our relationship and began thinking of Claudia as a way out.

"Claudia is right." I smiled at Claudia and felt Alice's hand quickly leave my leg. "War could be the way individuals learn their mortality and build an existentialist self."

"That's total bullshit," Alice almost screamed, looking like she was going to smack Claudia. "It's fascism, defining oneself through the actions of the state."

"I'm tired," I suddenly announced, standing up. "Need to get some sleep. Good night."

Alice rose with me. I looked at her and wondered if she understood that I didn't want to see her anymore. I decided to make it well-known to her and everyone else.

"Claudia," I said, "could we talk for a minute outside."

Claudia stood up as Alice slugged me, causing me to trip on a chair leg and land on the floor.

"You take the fucker," Alice angrily said to Claudia. "He'll dump you the way he does every girl."

I picked myself up from the floor. Hearing the word "dump" I thought of Beautiful.

"I don't even know him," Claudia protested. "You're a real bitch shoving people around."

This was not what I wanted. I just wanted sleep, not fighting women. Still worried about how to get rid of her, I glared at Alice.

"Claudia," I said, "I owe you an explanation. We don't know each other, and Alice is a thorn for any man. She keeps pestering me."

I flinched, anticipating another punch, but Alice collapsed back in her chair crying.

Hurrying out, I noticed Claudia following me as others rushed to comfort Alice.

"Those were harsh words," she said in front of the coffeehouse.

"She deserved it," I grimaced. "Slept with everyone on campus. I think she's got a disease or crabs. A lot of men complaining."

"I know the type," Claudia agreed. "They'll fuck anyone in sight. We were warned about diseased bitches at orientation ruining men."

"You interested in something to eat? I know a good place, Valois, near my apartment."

"You have an apartment?"

"View of the lake. You want to see it? Fun to watch storms and waves from my windows."

Claudia turned out to be good in bed. She was also quite the gossip.

A week later I heard about Alice's suicide. It appeared that someone wrote to her parents about her having venereal disease and sleeping with most of the campus. The gossip reached her dorm mother, who told Alice to cover her toilet seat before using it so that others wouldn't get crabs. She was out of my life. Claudia lasted a month.

Chapter Thirty-Two

It felt good to leave Chicago in the fall of 1969 and return to San Diego to head the World Federation of Objectivists. I was tired of the extreme hot and cold of Chicago's seasons. I was haunted by too many ghosts. My apartment never felt comfortable after Alice's suicide, and I even had trouble taking the IC downtown—on the platform, I swore I kept seeing the man I had pushed onto the tracks.

I hoped the move would give me a fresh start, free me of my demons. But there were two demons in California, Toots and my brother. I hadn't contacted Toots since she had hung up on me when I had called about my Alaskan trip. I'd heard Sonny was married with a couple kids and worked in the defense industry.

My dissertation on the negative costs of wartime torture received world recognition. I presented the findings to the annual meeting of the American Economic Association. I worried that Professor Grass wouldn't accompany me to my graduation, since my work contradicted his Vietnam publications on the economic value of humane interrogation.

During the graduation ceremony at Orchestra Hall, Grass secretly confided to me his misgivings about torture. "You're entering the academic game searching for grants. The secret is to find a topic that'll get you government money and put you on the lecture circuit. I've made plenty lecturing about interrogation methods.

Phil Anderson got me the job at the World Federation of Objectivists. Writing about Ayn Rand's ideas, he'd graduated in philosophy the year before me. This had landed him a job at the Ayn Rand Freedom Institute in California. A group of institute donors wanted to explore the idea of a creating a research center focused on proving Rand's economic ideas.

They didn't want to invest too much money until the project looked worthwhile. Phil recommended me. The pay wasn't high, but the donors promised to expand the organization if I could attract economic scholars to work on Randian ideas. They wanted to influence politicians about the importance of individualism and free markets.

I liked my office near Torres Pines looking out over the Pacific Ocean. It was a short drive from my new apartment on Prospect Place in La Jolla. This gave me a new perspective on San Diego after the horrors of my childhood. I was now living in an upscale community and holding a high-status job with "doctor" attached to my name. What more could I want? Maybe higher pay?

Finally I contacted Toots to let her know I was back. She was still living in the same studio apartment near Mission Bay. With a great deal of anxiety, I called.

"Toots, I'm back. Got a job in Torrey Pines and rented an apartment in La Jolla."

"I suppose you want to meet," she gruffly replied.

"That'd be nice. What time or place?"

There was a long silence before she answered, "I get out at five. We could meet after I stop at my apartment. There's a Big Boy on Mission Boulevard near Emerald. See you at six tomorrow." She abruptly hung up.

I saw her immediately, sitting alone. In her late fifties, she still looked attractive.

"You look good." I bent over and tried to hug her, but she moved away from my reach. I couldn't remember her ever kissing me or me kissing her.

"Another fucking year—wish you'd let me die. Hate getting old."

A waitress appeared, and we ordered, giving me time to compose myself after her remarks.

"You're a success, I see." Toots looked at the new suit I was wearing for the occasion.

"I'm now Dr. Billy Durant," I proudly announced. "Not medical but economics."

"Whatever the fuck that means, economics." She laughed. "Here I thought you could treat my heart."

"What's wrong with your heart?"

"Last year I went to a Roller Derby in LA. Got so excited my heart stopped. Doctors warned it was smoking." She paused and lit up.

"Why didn't you tell me?"

"I don't want no fuss. Can take care of myself. Couldn't imagine you in a hospital room with me. They did some kind of bypass surgery. Called it a triple."

"You had triple bypass surgery and didn't call."

"Sonny said he'd call, but I told him not to bother."

"You told him not to bother calling me!" I was hurt. "He was there, I suppose."

"Sonny and kids visited. I was in the hospital over a week."

"How's he doing?"

The waitress set down Big Boy's classic double-decker hamburger in front of me and a salad for Toots.

"Go up there whenever I can. Grandkids are cute. You should go see them."

Pointing at her salad, I wondered, "Are you still worried about your weight? Kind of old to be sleeping around." I was getting angry.

Ignoring my snide remark, she announced, "Flying to Bangkok next week to meet my sailor boy. We been goin' together until his sea duty. Now we meet when he gets leave. He looks like you."

I set my burger back down, sat back, and stared at Toots. "He looks like me. How old?"

"Twenty-six."

I didn't know what to make of this revelation. I felt like a sledgehammer had hit me. "Planning to marry?" I spat out the words.

"Come on, Billy. There's a big age gap. We're just having fun."

I hurried out after paying the bill and left Toots sipping coffee. It would take me a long time to digest this conversation. I had difficulty thinking about it as I drove back to my office.

Still feeling confused, I tried to lose myself in work. I needed to raise cash. I'd heard of two free-spending Oklahoma brothers, John and Arnold Smith, who had made their fortunes in oil and were pure libertarian ideologues. At Harvard, they'd organized an objectivist group and funded an Ayn Rand scholarship for "individualism and freedom." Competitors wrote essays on how individualism and freedom built America.

Hearing about the prize in Chicago, I had wondered how slavery and Native American genocide fit into the topic. While finishing my PhD, I had written the brothers about these issues.

Arnold Smith had responded that the slave trade took place in a free market and that the conquest of Native Americans was for their own good by introducing them to market economies.

When I phoned Smith Enterprises in Tulsa, Oklahoma, I wondered if they remembered my question. Of course I didn't speak to either brother but left a message asking them to call me at the World Federation of Objectivists. The next day I got a call from—and I'd never heard of this title before—the director of academic investment, David Kronbach.

"Billy, you might not remember meeting at last year's economic conference," David started the conversation. "We briefly talked about the Ayn Rand group in Chicago. We're glad to hear someone is trying to spread the word."

"I remember." An image of David dressed in a pinstripe suit came to mind. "We're doing economic research on Rand's ideas. Also want to influence politicians."

"Read your Rand essay in the *Libertarian Journal*. Just brilliant."

"You probably know why I'm calling," I said, feeling hopeful after David's comments.

"I'm used to it. Never thought I'd have a title like academic investment. The Smith brothers want to get libertarian ideas out there. Thinking of forming a group in the Republican Party called something like Paul Revere Riders or the Tea Party."

"Wow," I exclaimed, "we're thinking along the same lines."

"The goal is to have all people believe they will benefit from cutting taxes and government. The Smith brothers want a media campaign enlisting Hollywood actors and academics."

"I'm supposed to focus on economists, which would fit your academic-investment strategy."

"We should talk," responded David. "Could I convince you to come to San Francisco next week? I'm checking out a group that wants a center to honor freedom and liberty. They may be too much into flower power for the Smith brothers."

"Sure, I can meet." I tried to not sound too excited.

"Of course we'll pay your way and expenses unless you've got a lot of funding. The Smiths need to spend money from their Hope for Freedom Foundation to meet tax requirements."

"That'll help. I'm just starting out."

"I'll be staying at the Fairmont. If that's OK, I'll book a room for you. Do you know the hotel?"

"I delivered newspapers there," I gulped, as a rush of unpleasant memories flooded my mind.

I was surprised to see Charley Krupp still at the bell captain's post. It'd been sixteen years since I had first entered the Fairmont. Krupp was now in his midfifties.

"Billy, my God, you've grown," said Charley after I told him my name. Looking me up and down, he said, "I didn't recognize you. You came a long way in life; now you can stay here."

"Got an education. My room's being paid for by Oklahoma oil money. I'm now Dr. Durant."

"Jesus, you remember that shit McCormick."

"Yes, he liked boys." How could I forget stabbing him and running out of the penthouse with Jerry?

"Fucker's doing twenty years in Folsom. Someone finally reported him. Police found all sorts of S and M stuff. Always wondered how he got it up there. Didn't see it pass my desk. One was a medieval rack; he must have brought it in pieces. He'd pay kids to get on it nude. A sixteen year old had his shoulders pulled out of their sockets. He had to tell his parents. Good-bye to McCormick."

David wanted to meet at seven in the Tonga Room for dinner. Never in my wildest imagination as a kid did I think I'd ever eat there. Designed in the 1940s by a Metro-Goldwyn-Mayer set director, the original swimming pool became a lagoon with a floating orchestra stage.

Arriving first, I was seated by the lagoon. A cute waitress with raven-black hair asked if I wanted a drink. Glancing through the drink menu, I ordered a lychee martini, which Shirley—I quickly learned her name—recommended as a house special. When she brought it, she was smiling and making eye contact. I mentioned I was staying at the hotel and wondered what she might be doing after work.

Before she could answer, David appeared. I winked and passed her my newly printed business card, writing my room number on back.

David sat down, asking, "Have you eaten here before?"

"No."

"Do you mind if I order for both of us? You eat fish and pork? I'm going to have their classic mai tai."

"Please order. I eat anything."

Shirley—we kept sending vibes back and forth—brought a feast of steamed pork and shrimp dumplings, tuna with toasted macadamia nuts and taro chips, Dungeness crab tacos with yellow curry, red-curry pork loin with black garlic and coconut milk along with a Tonga hot pot of spicy shellfish.

"This is great," I said, digging into the food.

"Tomorrow we're meeting this libertarian group at a warehouse near Fisherman's Wharf. They're thinking of turning it into a freedom center for tourists. The Smiths like the idea and want to spend money. I have my doubts. When I talked to leader—can you believe it, he calls himself Ben Franklin? He sounded flaky. We'll find out. Do you want to meet in the lobby around ten? They don't get up early."

When I got to my room, there was a phone message from Shirley wondering if I'd like to stop by the Tonga Room at ten when she got off work. I was at the Tonga's Hurricane Bar a little before ten and ordered a zombie from the menu.

"Hi," said Shirley, sitting down next to me. "Your card says Billy Durant. My name is Shirley Laski. Do you stay here often?"

"The hotel has memories for me," Billy explained. "In junior high, I delivered newspapers to the Fairmont, lived over on Clay Street. Then we moved."

"I came last month from Des Moines. I'm living in a boardinghouse on Pine."

Saying hello to the bartender, she ordered sambuca.

"Boardinghouse? Sounds like something from a novel."

"Get a room and breakfast, inexpensive for San Francisco. I'm here to study painting at the Art Institute. Your card said you headed the World Federation of Objectivists. What's that?"

"Ever read Ayn Rand? That's what objectivists are about—practicing her ideas."

"I don't want you to think," Shirley said as she took a sip of sambuca, "I just pick up guys in the Tonga Room. This is the first time I've ever done anything like this."

"Don't worry. I'm just happy to find someone to talk to. It's lonely traveling by yourself. The guy I'm with is from Oklahoma. I'm trying to get funding. And you, did you paint in Des Moines?"

"In high school and some at a local art school. When I turned twenty-one, I decided to see the world and learn to paint. It must have been great living here as a kid. You actually delivered newspapers to the Fairmont?"

"Yes, and I kissed my first girl over on Clay and Taylor."

She looked me in the eyes. "Can I be bold with you?"

"Sure."

"I'd like to see what a Fairmont room looks like."

Chapter Thirty-Three

I was in the lobby early feeling good about Shirley. Kissing me that morning, she had whispered, "I never had all those feelings. You coming to the Tonga tonight?"

"Yes," I answered, trying to look romantic. Shirley was fun but not very experienced.

"I called Ben Franklin. It's hard to say his name without laughing," said David when we met in the lobby. We're going to a building near Jones and Beach, a couple blocks from the wharf, close to the tourist area."

We took a cab down Columbus Avenue to Beach Street. There was Ben Franklin standing outside an old wooden warehouse.

"We've got some Hollywood set designers interested," explained Ben after I was introduced. "Thinking of calling it the Museum of Liberty and Independence. Got some big-name actors interested."

"Which actors?" I asked, thinking of my own need to advertise the federation.

"Ronald Reagan and John Wayne say they may be willing to attend the opening. I think Reagan wants to enter politics. It would be a big tourist draw."

Personally I didn't like Wayne with his macho acting and cowboy movies. All I could remember about Reagan was his supporting role to a chimpanzee in *Bedtime for Bonzo*. I was only eleven when I saw the film. As I recalled, Reagan played a psychology professor trying to teach human morality to the chimp Bonzo.

"I vaguely remember *Bedtime for Bonzo*," I said. "I'm not sure Reagan could add anything to the cause."

"Yeah, I remember. Stupid movie," added David.

"You both missed the point of the movie." Ben unlocked the building's front door and waved us in. "The Reagan character wanted an answer to the nature-versus-nurture problem. I think the movie shows the importance of education."

"How?" I asked, curious about getting a famous actor to support the World Federation of Objectivists.

"We're planning a special Reagan corner." Ben pointed to a dark space at the end of the empty warehouse. "We'll show his movies and highlight his work fighting commies in Hollywood."

"Could be a little shallow next to Rand's work," commented David.

"Maybe but not for tourists," I offered. "Most probably they don't know who Ayn Rand is. They do know Reagan."

"And if he wins a political office, we'll be famous for featuring him as a fighter for freedom," said Ben, pulling a notebook from a bag he was carrying.

"We thought this Reagan quote could be put in flashing lights on the front of the building." He read from the notebook, "Freedom is never more than one generation away from extinction."

"That sounds good. The Smith brothers will love the quote; they would agree," said David, starting to walk the length of the warehouse. "Are you actually thinking of a John Wayne corner?"

"It'll be educational."

"Educational? How?" I asked, following David and looking at the work that would have to be done to turn the wooden hulk of a building into a museum.

"You missed the point of *Bedtime for Bonzo*: nurture won out over nature."

Ben quoted the rest of the Reagan's freedom declaration: "We didn't pass it to our children in the bloodstream. It must be fought for, protected, and handed on for them to do the same."

"So that's where John Wayne fits—fighting for freedom," commented David, looking at the ceiling. "There's a lot of work to be done in here."

"We're going to have a continual showing of the *Green Berets*, Wayne's best film. Kids love it, and it'll teach them to fight for freedom."

I didn't want to discuss the war. I was biased by my experience with humane interrogation and didn't know where David or the Smith brothers stood on the issue. Vietnam discussions were emotional, dividing families and sending some to Canada.

"What about Jane Fonda? She's advocating freedom," I wondered, remembering her beautiful nude body in *Barbarella*.

"Antiwar peacenik. Smiths hate her," shot back David.

I quickly dropped the subject as Ben explained the proposed layout of the museum.

"We want to be educational, particularly for kids. So we're planning to include rides and carnival-like games. We're putting a replica of the Liberty Bell near the entrance. The front of the building will be covered with neon signs of famous freedom and liberty quotes."

"So Reagan's quote will be in neon," observed David. "Any from Wayne?"

"We've got this educational one: 'Life is tough, but it's tougher when you're stupid.'"

"What about the rides and games?" I asked, thinking of Reagan as someone I might use to influence politicians.

"We checked on zoning, and we can put a Paul Revere horse ride outside. It'll be small ponies for little kids. Have to start educating them early for freedom. Inside, we'll have a small helicopter ride through a make-believe Vietnam jungle, hopefully narrated by John Wayne."

"Ayn Rand?"

"We'll have continuous showings of *The Fountainhead* in a small theater. In the middle of the room, a large exhibit will highlight her ideas. Of course, her thinking will be simplified for tourists. There will be an individualist game, where participants win awards by throwing darts at great quotes like Mill's 'All good things which exist are the fruits of originality' and Rand's 'The word "we" is as lime poured over men, which sets and hardens to stone, and crushes all beneath it.'"

"Do you think tourists will understand?" I wondered.

"Learning by doing," retorted Ben. "Best education method. Whenever they win, they'll be given an explanatory coloring book and a box of crayons. Even if the adults don't color in the pictures of Ayn Rand and people like Mill, their kids will."

This is dumb, I thought.

"Then there will be the Give Me Liberty or Give Me Death game. Kids will love it. They'll wear revolutionary soldier hats and try to see how fast they can run around hurdles named after famous battles like Bunker Hill and Yorktown. All kids will meet an actor dressed like Patrick Henry. We'll have a Give Me Liberty or Give Me Death tattoo parlor for adults."

David seemed more impressed than me. In fact he rolled up his shirt sleeve to reveal a tattoo of small birds and the words "Have courage to be free. Anyone can die."

I grimaced at the multicolored tattoo, while Ben said, "Cool."

"Well, this is the beginning of our plans," Ben sounded the end of the tour. "I sent you the cost estimates."

"Got them here," replied David, pointing at his briefcase. "Any free-market games?"

"We're planning one for families. People begin with some fake money. They can earn more answering questions on liberty and freedom. They'll have to spend on food and shelter—we've got to work that one out. Some will end up in a poorhouse and some in a penthouse. We are having trouble with this. In our last attempt, over fifty percent ended up homeless."

"What'd you think?" asked David, hailing a cab.

"Honestly I thought it was stupid, a fun center for liberty and freedom. Will tourists really be attracted?"

"I agree. But the Smiths love the idea. They envision these all over the country spreading the word about free markets."

"What about Reagan? Do you think he'll make it as a politician? I think *Bedtime for Bonzo* is as stupid as Ben's museum and fun center."

Looking thoughtfully out the window as we went through North Beach, David sighed. "I think you're going to have to leave your ivory tower if you're planning to influence politicians. Most people are gullible. The Smith brothers and other right-thinking money people know that. The crowd is easily persuaded. They'll love Reagan; he doesn't act smart, and he's handsome."

"So what is their goal?" In asking, I was trying to figure out how to get money from the Smiths.

"Arnold Smith told me he wants all people when they hear the words 'America' or 'United States of America' to think of free markets and individualism. Then these words are to be linked to cutting taxes and reducing government spending."

"So," I interpreted his words, "Americanism will mean low taxes and minimum government."

"They're funding education groups to get this into school textbooks. A group of psychologists is training high school kids to respond to images of the US flag with the words 'Cut taxes and government.'"

"I wonder what Ayn Rand would say about mind control."

"Smiths don't see it as mind control but as teaching truth. They've hired some writers to change the Pledge of Allegiance."

"Change the pledge? I thought Congress just added 'God' to it?" I was hungry and thinking of the Tonga Room and Shirley.

"They want something like, 'I pledge allegiance to the flag of the United States and to the republic for which it stands, low taxes, no government regulation.' They want every school kid to say it to stop the spread of collectivist thinking."

I sat at the Hurricane Bar and mulled over the day's events. If I wanted the Smith brothers' funding, I needed to write my request as a plan to put Randian ideas in the public mind. Maybe they'd fund Randian-loving economists to contribute to school textbooks, advertising, and media.

As I was wondering about featuring Reagan or Wayne advertising free markets and individualism, Shirley sat down. I could tell from her eyes and smiles that I'd made her hungry for passion. I wanted only a casual affair.

"How'd it go at the warehouse?" she asked, putting her hand on my leg.

Moving my leg away from her hand, I asked, "Know anything about Ronald Reagan or John Wayne?"

She looked hurt and confused by my reaction. "Never liked their movies. Wayne is too macho, and it's hard to take Reagan seriously after *Bedtime for Bonzo*."

"They'll be featured at the Museum of Liberty and Independence being planned near Fisherman's Wharf. I don't think we should get too close. I'm not the kind of guy you'll want to be around much."

"Didn't you like last night? I did."

"I'm going back to San Diego tomorrow. You're a good midwestern girl. I'm a little older than you, and my advice is to avoid one-night stands."

"Tonight?" she asked a little too eagerly for me.

"Sure, but remember my warning," I relented, unable to control myself.

Chapter Thirty-Four

When I got back to my Torres Pines office, there were several phone messages shoved under my door by the building supervisor. I hoped to get funding for a secretary. One from David asked me to immediately call him. There were several calls from Liz Appleton, head of the Ayn Rand Freedom Institute. They wanted to know what I was doing. The most unsettling were a pile of messages from Shirley Laski. I had thought that when I had unceremoniously pushed her out of bed the next morning telling her to scat, she'd got the idea. I threw her messages in the trash.

First I phoned David.

"David, you got back fast."

"This morning I phoned the Smiths from the San Francisco Airport. By the time I arrived this morning, Smiths agreed to fund your federation. There is one catch. They hate the name, and they want you to popularize her ideas."

"I'll have to check with the Freedom Institute about a name change. Any thoughts about a new name?"

"They want something warm and inviting. They don't like John Wayne in the museum. They think he'll turn many off. They love Reagan's ads, particularly the ones for Chesterfield cigarettes. You might want to look at them."

"Any particular ad?"

"Arnold Smith liked the Christmas ad with Reagan smoking a Chesterfield and saying, 'I'm sending Chesterfields to all my friends. That's the merriest Christmas any smoker can have—mildness plus no unpleasant aftertaste.' He thought that tying low taxes and less government to Christmas would be a good idea. He wants to hire Reagan for an ad like that."

Linking Christmas with low taxes seemed a little too much for me. "Any others?"

"John Smith favors cartoon ads like the one Reagan did for V8 juice called 'How Ronald Reagan discovered V8'. He thought that one showing Reagan discovering free markets would be good. Reagan already did one showing him looking serious with the caption 'Ronald Reagan speaks out against Socialized Medicine.'"

"Smith brothers seem like big Reagan fans. Who's proposing socialized medicine?"

"They'd like to make him president. Arnold believes he has wide appeal among women, particularly after a fan magazine article 'New Answer to Maidens' Prayers.' It shows him in a swimsuit with the byline 'Girls love to be rescued by Ronald Reagan as a lifeguard. They could not resist his voice as radio announcer. Now he's thrilling them as a movie star.'"

Thought I'd be dealing with lofty ideas and not advertising script. I took a yellow legal pad from my drawer and started jotting down ideas.

It was a couple months before Christmas, so I thought of linking it to cutting taxes. Santa could be standing at a fireplace and dropping packages labeled "tax cut" in each sock. Maybe add a caption, "A Christmas gift to cherish from a limited government."

Or a dark, shadowy figure labeled "Big Government" wrapping its arms around a house where a family could be seen through the windows sitting down to a Christmas meal: "Don't let Big Government steal your home or happiness."

In the cab to meet Ben Franklin, David mentioned that the Smith brothers wanted to support the Second Amendment and protect gun rights. "They think," David said, "we should be able to protect ourselves against the government." He mentioned the National Rifle Association.

Trying to think of a new name for my organization, I drove from Torres Pines to the La Jolla Library to find information on the National Rifle Association, or NRA. I'd never heard of it and wanted to please the Smith brothers.

Taking my yellow pad into the library, I found that the organization's early goals were the opposite of the Smith brothers'. It was founded in

1871 by two Union Army vets who had been dismayed during the Civil War at the poor marksmanship of the troops. So their goal was to sponsor shooting matches to ensure good marksmanship for future wars. This was guns in service to the government, not guns for protection from the government.

I thought of Santa sporting a NRA logo on his cap and dropping pistols into Christmas socks. But that seemed weird. I remembered that the Smith Brothers wanted to appeal to women. So I thought of a home scenario with a mother standing in the doorway and pointing a rifle at a figure labeled "Big Government." Little kids are shown holding onto her apron. The caption would read, "Protecting her home and children: Let's arm America."

Wondering how I could combine the gun image with tax cutting, I sketched two men wearing side arms, like something from a western movie, confronting a robber wearing a hat marked "Internal Revenue Service." I wrote the caption: "Open carry to stop government robbery."

I wanted to get the sketches and ad ideas to David as soon as possible. I went to the La Jolla Post Office, bought a large special-delivery envelope, and sent them off.

Back in my office, I called Liz Appleton at the Ayn Rand Freedom Institute.

"Liz, the Smith brothers want to change our name; they don't like it. We need their money. They think the name World Federation of Objectivists will not capture the public imagination. They want something snappier to use in advertising."

"Advertising. What do they have in mind?" Liz replied.

I described the ads I'd sent to David promoting tax cuts, limited government, and guns. "I told them I'd contact you about the name change."

"Guns?" Liz wondered over the phone. "How'd that get in the equation? I don't remember Rand saying anything about guns. What happened to Randian individualism?"

"Do I take their money? I think they're trying to hijack Rand to promote some blend of conservative values. I should find out whether they support cultural freedom like free sex and drugs. Or do they want the government to stop it?"

"Are you willing to agree?" asked Liz.

"I did those Christmas ads on tax cuts and guns. I didn't agree with them, but we need the money. They have some kind of love affair with this actor Ronald Reagan. I'd please them if I used his name often."

"How?"

"I thought of contacting Reagan and asking if we could change our name to the Ronald Reagan Center for Tax Cuts and Limited Government. Smith brothers might like it."

Liz sighed. "I don't think Reagan represents Ayn Rand. Though I could see him playing Howard Roark in *The Fountainhead*."

"So it's OK to propose the new name?"

"Do what you have to do. They've got the money."

As I left the office for my apartment, I thought about the compromises I was making. The Ronald Reagan Center for Tax Cuts and Limited Government made me nauseated.

Trying to find a parking space near my apartment, I noticed a woman sitting on a suitcase in front of the building. It was Shirley.

How could I get rid of her? All I wanted was a stiff drink to forget the Smith brothers.

"What are doing here?" I snapped, showing my displeasure at seeing her.

"I wanted to be with you. Got fired from the Tonga Room. I tripped and dropped a tray of food and fell into the lagoon. The Art Institute rejected my application. You're all I have."

"Jesus, we were together only two nights. Why don't you go home to Iowa? How'd you find me?"

"Can't go home; dad beats me. I love you. I called the number on your card. The super gave me your address."

"This is sick. You can't be in love after only two nights."

"You're the man I always dreamed of—you can't throw me in the street. I'll kill myself."

"What do you want?"

"Can I stay for the night? Only had enough money to get down here. I took the bus."

"No!"

She broke down crying just as a man started up the sidewalk to my apartment building. Turning, he glared at me and asked her, "Is this guy bothering you?"

She sat on her suitcase and refused to budge.

"No," she answered the stranger, "but thanks. He won't let me stay with him. I'm homeless. He ripped me off in San Francisco."

The stranger looked questioningly at me.

"I don't know what you did up there, but you can't leave a pretty young girl like this homeless. What'd he do to you? You can stay with me. Or should I call the cops?"

The situation was now untenable. I relented. The stranger asked if she really wanted to go with me and said, "You're a cute young thing. I've got room."

This was not the evening I wanted as I sat with Shirley at my little dining table and looked out over La Jolla Cove. "You say you're an artist," I said as I knocked back my third shot of tequila. "Drink up!"

"That was my excuse for leaving," said Shirley. "I had to get away from Dad. Did art and some acting my one year in college. They said I had acting talent. Dad cut off the money and put me in a waitress job in downtown Des Moines."

"How could he 'put' you in a job? You're an adult."

I looked down at the La Jolla Cove and remembered the school of black jellyfish I'd seen there the other day.

"Don't fall into them," I had been warned by someone seeing me scramble around on the rocks.

"Enough stings," cautioned an abalone diver who was wearing a shorty wetsuit and sitting on a rock, "and you'll never come out. They can get to ten feet. Last year an abalone hunter died from those stings."

"You like to see the cove?" I smiled at Shirley. "It's dark, but they've got lights around. We could go on the rocks."

"I'm too tired. Don't want to move." She mixed some tequila with a little orange juice from a container in my fridge. "I could shop and clean for you. You don't have much to eat or drink."

"Shit, you're moving in. Sounds like marriage." Feeling drunk, I poured another shot. "This can't work."

We were so drunk after finishing off half a bottle of tequila that we didn't even make love after falling into bed.

Then my demons took over. I was holding Shirley's hand and looking down at the surge between the rocks. Dark-purple jellyfish gave off an iridescent glow as they bobbed in the gentle waves of the cove. I pulled her over a rock ledge and into the ocean. I watched her thrashing around, trying to swat the jellyfish away.

Ronald Reagan appeared hovering over the water. He reached down, grabbed Shirley's arm, and yanked her free of the deadly stings. He put her down on the grassy area above the cove.

Shirley awoke and headed for the bathroom. I worked to push myself through the tangled web of the nightmare. She kissed me on returning and cuddled against my body. "You'll like me being here," she whispered.

I panicked. She couldn't stay. I struggled to get back to sleep. Just as sleep washed over me, I saw Shirley and Reagan walking from the cove holding hands.

I knew what I would do. I didn't want any more blood on my hands.

Chapter Thirty-Five

"David, did you get my ads?" I called two days after my special delivery was to arrive at Smith Enterprises in Tulsa.

"They loved them, Santa Claus putting tax cuts and guns in Christmas stockings. We're creating the Smith Brothers Foundation to handle their philanthropic work."

"I asked Liz at the Rand Institute about the name change. Do you think the Ronald Reagan Center for Tax Cuts works?"

"I don't know." David paused. I could hear him talking to someone. "Sorry, I had to sign some papers. The Smith Brothers Foundation is setting up a special unit to provide political policy papers to support candidates. One may be Ronald Reagan."

"So the name works?"

"From my dealings with the Reagans, I think Nancy Reagan will just say no. I've got a better name if you want funding."

"What's that?"

"The Smith Brothers Center for Tax Cuts and Limited Government. After their comments about your ads, I can almost guarantee they'll give you a big junk of change if you use their names."

"I need funding to get these ads together and hire staff."

"Arnold Smith loves the ads. We're sending you fifty thousand dollars as seed money. John wants to hold off sending more until he sees more samples."

I gulped. Fifty thousand was a lot of money in 1969. "I have someone who can help in the office and has acting experience."

"Do you have a bookkeeper? The Smiths will want an account of how their money is spent."

"The Rand Institute works with a local accountant to fund my office and salary. We can use him."

"Have him contact me. We'll get the funds to your account under the name of the Smith Brothers Center for Tax Cuts and Limited Government."

Hanging up, I sat back and relished my good luck. I planned to use the $50,000 to give myself a salary increase, hire Shirley, and get her a separate apartment. I felt relief that I wouldn't need to do anything drastic to her.

"Got you a job," I said cheerily upon entering the apartment. Shirley was busy cleaning the kitchen. Thick prime steaks were on the counter for the evening meal.

"A job!" exclaimed Shirley. "What'll I be doing?"

"You'll be acting and doing a little office work. Salary will be five thousand dollar a year and maybe more."

"Five thousand!" she gasped.

"Tomorrow we'll find you an apartment."

"You're moving me out?"

"It's for your own good. You know nothing about me. I do like you. But you're too young. I need to live alone," I said, trying to look stern.

I thought she was going to cry but instead she gleefully shouted, "My own apartment! I've always wanted one. And pay! And I'll be acting. I want to kiss and love you."

Shirley wasn't seeking a long-term relationship; she was desperate, with little money, running from an abusive father.

She loved her new apartment and liked the cash in her pocket. After getting started at work, she quickly found a partner closer in age and less dangerous. She never realized how close she had come to death.

Shirley was a natural at doing ads. She had a cute, midwestern-looking face that would appeal to most white Americans. Her face became an iconic image for tax cuts and cutting government spending.

When Shirley started traveling, fans asked for her autograph and thanked God that she was saving America from high taxes and a caretaker government. Men hugged her for protecting their guns.

I took her to a local photographer on Ivanhoe Avenue near my apartment. The photographer, an ex–beach boy named Jim Kelly, winked and gave me a knowing smile when I entered his studio. I wondered about the greeting as we negotiated a price for Shirley's portfolio. He agreed to do ad mock-ups.

We spent time in my office going through the sketches I'd sent to David. None of them featured a woman.

"How about a homey scene of you wearing a Santa Claus hat next to a Christmas tree piled with presents underneath? We could do some variations to get in tax cut and gun ideas."

"I don't know much about taxes," Shirley admitted. "I did some target practice back in Iowa."

I started checking the yellow pages for San Diego costume stores.

"The Smiths want people to believe that cutting taxes will cause economic growth—you know, make everyone richer."

"I'll look cute in a Santa hat," she said, admiring herself in the full-length mirror I had requested from the super. "More money in the pocket after tax cuts."

"In the Smith brothers' pockets," I cynically replied. "There's no proof that cutting taxes will grow state or the national economies. Could hurt with government job cuts and no money going into government projects."

"Hi," I said into the phone. "Do you have a Santa outfit for rent and maybe some Santa hats and fake guns?"

Receiving an affirmative, I asked about filming studios in the area. I jotted down phone numbers, made a couple calls, and had a studio lined up for our Christmas scene.

I hired someone at the studio to create a living-room scene with fireplace, couches, chairs, and a decorated tree. I wondered if we'd have to go to LA for more professional help if they like these initial shots.

"Why do they want tax cuts if it's going to hurt?" Shirley continued, adopting different poses in front of the mirror.

"It'll make them richer; probably government cut backs won't help the poor."

The phone rang with David on the other end. "Got the photos. She's great. Looks so innocent. You say she's right off the farm."

"Not quite, but from Des Moines. We're getting a studio and costumes for initial shots. Our photographer will put in text. If the mock-ups are OK, we'll look for more professional help in LA."

"Can't wait to see them. I've got your bookkeeper's number. He'll keep us informed on expenses."

The first ads were great!

One showed Shirley in a white, tidy, and modest-looking polyester blouse and flared red pants wearing an apron with reindeer and snowflake prints and Santa hat. On the coffee table next to the fireplace lined with Christmas socks were a plate of cookies and a glass of milk.

A speech balloon from Shirley's mouth read, "Help Santa give more. Cut taxes." We tried several other tax-cutting texts. The one the Smith brothers liked was "More tax cuts mean more merry holidays."

For the gun promotion, we hired some kids and dressed them in pajamas. Shirley wore a modest green pantsuit and was sitting on the floor surrounded by joyful kids opening presents. She beamed taking a pistol out of its gift-wrapped box.

In the background could be seen a shadowy male figure dressed in black with a sinister smile climbing through a window. We tried a variety of captions: "Keep your Christmas merry. Protect yourself"; "Every Christmas needs protection"; and "Arm your family for many more merry Christmases."

We tried some shots with a fat actor playing Santa wearing a sidearm. Ideally the weapon-carrying Santa would be shown stepping onto a rooftop from a sleigh harnessed to reindeer. "Santa likes protection when carrying gifts to boys and girls."

Instead we used my original idea of putting pistols in every Christmas sock. We did one of Santa emerging from the fireplace holding a rifle: "For the man to protect his family"; "Let's arm our families for safer Christmases"; and "Be a man. Carry a gun for the holidays."

The next day, the fog made it difficult to drive back from the office. Shirley and I had been planning new ads. I dropped her off at her apartment a couple blocks from mine and then searched for parking. The phone was ringing when I entered my apartment.

It was Jim saying he'd completed the mock-ups and wanted to come over with them.

Sitting on my couch, looking, and examining the ads, I felt his hand on my leg. He'd kept giving me inviting smiles during the photo shoots. I didn't resist and felt excited as my hand drifted to his. We set the photos neatly on the coffee table and headed to my bedroom.

I felt terrible and angry afterward. I fought back childhood demons.

"Want to go for a walk?" I suggested. "We could get a drink near the cove."

"A little foggy out there," he said, pulling on his pants. "But I'd like a drink; we should celebrate our night."

I tried controlling my hands from clenching and unclenching. I could feel my heart racing as my head pounded, making it hard to think clearly.

I suggested that we walk out on the rocks.

"Isn't it dangerous with the fog?" he said.

"Don't worry; hold my hand. I come here every night and know these rocks well. No one will see us. Besides the fog blocks anyone's view. I want to kiss you near the water. I have a favorite spot."

I could tell from the squeeze he gave my hand that he was excited about the kiss.

"Easy on this rock. Step down, and we'll be in my favorite place," I said when we got there.

"We won't slip?"

I could feel his uneasiness as he gripped my hand. I guided him to the water's edge and hoped that the jellyfish were there.

Putting my arms around him as if to kiss, I pushed Jim over the side. I heard his thrashing and calls for help. I could tell that the jellyfish were doing their work.

I felt a great weight lift from me when his shouting stopped.

Chapter Thirty-Six

For a moment, I stood and heard only the waves lapping against the rocks. Should I run for help? I could act innocent and say, "He just slipped, and I couldn't see."

I concluded that it would be easier to go back to my apartment. If anyone asked, I could say that he dropped off the ads and mentioned taking a walk. But no one ever asked.

"Did you see the news?" asked Shirley, looking upset as she got into the car. "What'll we do?"

"What news?" I looked intently at the road and avoided Shirley's eyes.

"Jim, he's dead. Found floating in the cove."

"Dead!" I acted surprised. "Did someone kill him?"

"TV said he slipped on the rocks. Arms and face covered with jellyfish stings, some kind of rare black type. I didn't know they could paralyze you."

"I was stung by a jellyfish in Hawaii, and it hurt. If it had been a school, I'm sure I'd have drowned."

"What about the ads?" Shirley wondered. I was happy to hear that she was more concerned about work than Jim's death.

"He'd slipped copies under my door. Found them after I dropped you off. They're in back." I nodded toward my briefcase on the back seat.

"Can't wait to see them. Do I look OK? Too bad about Jim. Who'll we use?"

Shirley grabbed my briefcase from the car and hurried up the stairs to our office.

"I could be smiling more. Need a different hairstyle; might get a different colored pantsuit." She talked nonstop, racing through mock-ups. "Do I look OK? Wish my nose looked better. Do you think they'll see me in Iowa? Can't wait to hear from my friends."

"First we'll get David's opinion and then check on a Hollywood studio."

Ruling Jim's death an accident, newspapers reported that Jim had no enemies, and a temporary barrier was put up with warnings of black jellyfish. They called them "giant black sea nettles" and showed photos of Jim's lacerated and swollen arms and face. One headline read, "Tragedy Hits La Jolla Cove, Swimmers Warned." There was no suggestion of foul play.

Tossing and turning, I spent sleepless nights afraid of being caught. I vowed to stay away from relationships that could lead to a similar outcome.

"These are great," David was shouting into the phone. "She's a marvel. What a find. The Smith brothers hired a Hollywood set for making the final ones. They want them on TV. I'm working on a contract for ads to appear during *The Ed Sullivan Show*."

I handed the phone to Shirley, who was standing anxiously by my desk.

"Oh my God," she said, handing the phone back. "*The Ed Sullivan Show*. We're to meet Arnold Smith in Hollywood."

"Billy," instructed David, "Arnold and I will meet you next week. I booked rooms for you and Shirley at the Beverly Hills Hotel and made an appointment for Shirley at a Rodeo Drive fashion salon. They deal with big stars and will do her hair and face."

I thought that Shirley would faint when she heard the plans.

A year later she was the poster girl for the newly formed Paul Revere Riders. Supported by the Smith Brothers, they became a powerful force in the Republican Party.

One photo showed a Shirley and a Paul Revere Rider together on a horse. Shirley was dressed in a colonial outfit with a sharp V-neck partially exposing her breasts. Her fellow rider was dressed as Paul Revere, armed with a musket and waving a tricornered hat.

The word balloon from Shirley's mouth read, "I love men who protect me. Vote Republican and keep our men armed." Another one showed a group of Paul Revere Riders on a dock next to a sailing vessel painted with the words "Remember the Tea Party—Make America great again. Cut taxes."

Shirley started appearing with varying types of side arms and high-powered rifles. In one, she is pointing an assault weapon at a target labeled "Abolish the IRS." The Smith brothers loved it putting it in all major US newspapers.

Through the 1970s, we worked on these ads and public relations for the Paul Revere Riders. In 1980, I moved to Washington after the Smith brothers got me appointed chief researcher for Reagan's Council of Economic Advisors. John Smith told me to "work your magic." The Smiths got me appointed to boards of big-name conservative think tanks and foundations.

Shirley, in love with herself, was now living in Tulsa. I always wondered if the ads secured President Reagan's election. Arnold Smith, who I suspected was sleeping with Shirley, built her a studio and a house. She continued to star in right-wing ads and posters. Everyone in the Republican Party loved her. She received a special invitation to the White House. Her meeting with Nancy Reagan was kept secret. I often wondered if Reagan would have been elected if I'd sent her to the jellyfish.

Renting a large apartment in Georgetown, I avoided all relationships. I hadn't slept with anyone since Jim Kelly and Shirley. I poured my feelings into my work.

The memo from Reagan's economic advisors wanted me to research the effect of doing away with welfare, social security, and the Department of Education. I focused on social security, since welfare and education were more complicated as they involved state and local governments. How would seniors be affected if social security disappeared?

I decided to start with variations of my Vietnam models. How many lives would be shortened? How would the savings improve the quality of life for others? What would the affect be on Florida and other senior-citizen-housing markets? How much would be saved on medical costs and long-term care? My list of questions kept growing as I imagined an interactive economic model.

Walking back to my Georgetown apartment from my office on Dumbarton, I saw three white senior citizens seating on a bench outside a grocery store. Worried that I'd make the same error of never visiting Vietnam villages before they were destroyed, I decided to stop and talk to them.

I sat on a bench next to them and stretched my legs.

"Nice afternoon," I commented to a gray-haired and dignified looking man sitting closest to me on the next bench.

"I can only hope for a few more," he replied.

"You look like you've many afternoons ahead."

"Got to fill up the time. The three of us sit here every afternoon unless it rains. I'm Winthrop, and next to me are Harriet and Sam."

"Hello, Harriet." I nodded at a thin, heavily wrinkled woman wearing a babushka and flowered dress. "I'm Billy."

"You look too young to join us retirees watching the world go by; you must have something better to do," smiled Sam. He wore a gray fedora and threadbare gray suit needing cleaning.

"Must be nice retired. I work too hard; can't wait to quit."

"Keep working," advised Harriet. "It's boring retired, particularly when you've got no money."

"I thought social security gave a good boost. I'm not gonna have much of a pension." I leaned forward smiling.

"It adds enough to my pension," retorted John, "so I can live by myself. Without it, I'd have to live with my kids in Ohio. To me, that'd be like death."

I made a mental note that an alternative to social security was kids taking care of their parents.

"At least you have kids," snapped Harriet. "I've got no family. Can barely pay for food and rent with social security and my little pension. With just my pension, I'd be homeless and eating out of garbage cans like a lot of people in Washington."

"They've got mental problems," countered Sam. "You could sleep at the Mission House. Your pension is enough for food. I've got no pension.

My company went bust. Social security is the only thing keeping me from killing myself or sleeping in the park."

"Why're you asking?" Harriet demanded. "You're not one of those government types trying to take away our money?"

"I'm working to make social security better," I lied. "This isn't an official survey. Just thought I'd talk to some average seniors to get an idea of what's going on."

"You should talk to the coloreds," suggested Winthrop. "In this town, welfare and social security are the only things keeping them afloat. Cut those, and there'll be riots."

"Good talking to you." I stood up. "I'll probably see you often. This is my way home."

"You make sure to see us; we like talking." Harriet waved good-bye.

I hurried on to my apartment, where I immediately sat down with a sheet of paper I titled "Survey on Reducing or Eliminating Social Security."

No one ever asked to see the raw data for my report, which was based on my conversation with three white senior citizens on a bench in Washington, DC.

I jotted down the following conclusions from my survey:

1. One-third of seniors could live with their relatives. This would improve the quality of American families, which traditionally assumed care of family elders.
2. One-third of seniors have both social security and a pension. With just a pension, seniors could rely on charity services for help with housing and food.
3. One-third of seniors would be left homeless and without food. They might engage in acts of civil protest.

Returning to my office the next day, I included the costs of any civil disruptions from cutting social security. I could use my model for the effect of Vietnam protests on calculations of the costs of humane interrogations. I wondered if the cost of early death and suicides from social-security cuts should be positive or a negative. The savings from long-term care, hospitalization, and charity costs could be factored in.

Should economic value be placed on a retiree? I determined that retired people were of no economic value in the workforce. They had possible emotional value to their loved ones, but this could not be given a dollar value.

Retirees did benefit the economy by spending their social-security checks. But this money was taken from workers' pockets. Why not let the workers spend it? Cutting social security would transfer spending power from seniors back to workers.

I stuck the possible suicide increase and the effect on poor and minorities in several complicated endnotes. As I hoped, few people read them. My conclusion was that ending social security would benefit families, reduce medical costs, and grow the economy.

"Major National Study Concludes Social Security Cut Benefits Economy," read newspaper headlines after I submitted my final report to the Council of Economic Advisors on June 3, 1983.

"Abolish social security and make America great again," echoed Paul Revere Riders appearing on local radio talk shows.

I started earning large speaking fees from business and political groups. The Smith brothers used donations to have me selected as commencement speaker at prestigious universities. I received requests to turn the study into a book. One publisher wanted a dramatic title like *How Social Security Destroyed Families and America*.

"Dr. Billy Durant," Joe Cotton, president of the Family Values Institute said at a ceremony giving me a Cross of Gold medal, "is saving traditional families and seniors. Real American families should take care of their seniors."

They Kill Kids for Profit, an antiabortion group, hosted me on their national TV special for, in their billing, "Keeping senior babysitters home—Ending social security will end abortions."

"With social security, I would have killed my baby," claimed a young woman in the group's skit of her seeking an abortion but finding God and her grandmother. "Now Granny must live with my parents and can baby-sit. Thank you, God, for saving me from sin by ending social security."

Of course I received tons of hate mail from Florida and Arizona. The American Institute of Senior Citizens started a national petition against my report and collected two million signatures. On investigation, I discovered that members of the organization were senior-care providers fearing a loss of revenue. I'd explained this possible problem in another endnote to my report.

Sonny called a week after the report's release to tell me that Toots had died. "No reason to come all the way out here for it. She's cremated, and I dumped her ashes in the ocean and cleaned out her apartment. I think the old man is going next. Bad lungs."

I didn't know what to say. I felt relief about not having to go back for a funeral. I started crying and looked out my apartment window at a couple standing on the sidewalk. A fantasy swept over me. I pointed a rifle out the window and killed the couple.

My nightmares returned with seniors trawling garbage cans, committing suicide, and dying. I was in bed with Toots, fighting off her efforts to make love. Sometimes, starving seniors were mixed in with memories of me carrying Toots's pistol, floating corpses, and mutilated bodies spread across train tracks.

In one horrible dream, Paul Revere Riders on horses wore T-shirts proclaiming, "End Social Security," and used long poles with hooks to harvest dead seniors from the Lincoln Memorial Reflecting Pool. Toots was among the bodies.

Chapter Thirty-Seven

The honors continued to flow in. By the end of Reagan's administration, I was head of the Free Enterprise Institute and the Moral Majority Foundation along with being on the corporate boards of several gun manufacturers.

"Defend your homes. Buy guns and security systems," proclaimed the Paul Revere Riders on a world tour sponsored by Doug and Horlick, global gun distributors. European, Russian, Australian, and Chinese governments banned the group. They were a hit throughout South American and Mexico.

When they returned to the United States, Doug and Horlick sent them touring gun shows. One popular photo showed Shirley in a skimpy bikini holding an assault rifle.

"Let's go natural. Stop greenhouse gases," read the words painted on a nude woman who threw off her trench coat running onto the stage of the 1988 New Orleans Republican Convention.

Save the Earth and Green World led protests outside the Convention Center against greenhouse gases by showing grizzly photos of denuded landscapes.

Inside, they were forcefully ejected when they charged the nominating stage throwing bodies of dead birds and fish. Green World managed to dye the convention center's water black and lobbed green paint at delegates.

The demonstrations at the Republican Convention made the Smiths and other oil tycoons nervous. They decided to organize counterdemonstrations at the Atlanta Democratic Convention.

An oil-industry-sponsored group, Build More Pipelines, hired the Broadway cast of *Oklahoma!* to wear yellow hard hats with oil-derrick replicas on top to sing "Oh, What a Beautiful Morning" as they unrolled a banner, "Oil And Coal Make America Great. Greenhouse Gases Keep Us Warm."

An Earth Is Fine contingent distributed pamphlets explaining that climate science was a hoax and so-called pollution helped plants grow.

Outside the Democratic Convention, Earth First and Green Peace members clashed with Earth Is Fine, antiabortion groups, and oil workers in hard hats. Earth First ignited a huge pile of coal, which caused black smoke to seep into the convention hall. Earth Firsters were charged by Paul Revere Riders, who waved banners proclaiming: "Guns and Gas for All."

After the conventions, I received a phone call from David.

"We've got to do something. This is crazy; it could ruin our energy supplies. Can you do anything at the Free Enterprise Institute?"

"I saw the climate-science reports," I replied, looking out from my new plush office at Pershing Park and the Willard Hotel. "They seem to be correct. High skin cancer rates in Australia."

"Don't give me that shit," screamed David into the phone. "Smith brothers say they're wrong, so they must be."

"I could put out some feelers for college scientists willing to disprove climate change findings." I felt sick saying these words as images of blackened earth and forests swept through my mind. "It might be difficult. On the other hand, college profs are always for sale."

"I realize the Smith brothers and the Paul Revere Riders aren't popular on college campuses," worried David. "Remember, I'm head of academic investment. It's harder and harder to get on campus. Fuckin' liberal establishment in control."

"I could create another think tank and hide funding from the oil industry. We could call it the Institute to Save the Planet, like our Institute for Gun Safety funded by gun manufacturers. They've hired researchers to issue reports and inundate the press with messages that the more people own guns, the more safe they are."

After hanging up, I called Murray Cooper, the head of the newly created Institute for Gun Safety. I needed help getting this new institute started.

"Murray, Billy here. How are things going?"

"Just great. We're making America stronger. Stopped states from passing gun laws banning assault weapons. Can you imagine, some wanted laws to stop stores from selling high-capacity magazines and military ammunition? How un-American can you be?"

I quickly dismissed a fantasy of pouring bullets into a crowd of tourists outside my window.

"Smith brothers love your work. An armed America is a great America," said Murray.

I cringed at my own words. I couldn't stop the mantra of killing running through my brain. I was selling death.

"Murray, I need your advice on problems funding the gun safety group. The Smith boys want to start an Institute to Save the Planet."

"They've become environmentalists?" Alarmed, he shot back a stream of questions, clearly surprised and concerned about the funding of his institute. "Aren't they into oil? Should I be worried? Are they becoming liberals? Should I back gun laws?"

"Nothing like that," I laughed, amused that Murray didn't care what side of the weapons issue he supported, just so he got paid. I'd met him a year ago at a lecture at the Moral Majority Institute. I could tell immediately he was just looking for a handout. The best type to enlist; they sell their souls to any cause.

The tourist group was moving from Pershing Park toward the Willard. I couldn't shake the killing fantasy. I looked away from the crowd to stop my violent thoughts.

"Murray, don't worry," I assured him. "It's like your group. They want me to find any criticism of climate science. I know you were able to get a lot of those college profs to write research reports proving arming people saved lives. You think your list will help on climate change?"

"Not difficult. I found a bunch, really not all that many, at a national sociology meeting. You could do the same at any science meeting. Do you want my help?"

Thinking about his offer, I decided, "Sure."

"I could recruit scholars for you. You want me to head the new organization?"

"How about putting you on the board? I think the Smiths would like someone with a 'doctor' before their name to lead the institute. I'm sure they'd pay well for you to recruit, maybe a scientist as head."

"We're holding an Arm America symposium in Tucson next week. Got some crackerjack talks on why every family needs an assault weapon. Some of these sociologists know scientists at their schools. We could start from there. You want to come?"

I was relieved to watch the unharmed tourists enter the Willard. I was slipping too easily between fantasy and reality.

"You think it'll be useful? The Smiths are in a panic over this environmental stuff. They'll be big spenders on this project."

Arriving in Tucson the next week, I was greeted at the convention's location in the exclusive Golden Honey Resort with the banner, "The Institute for Gun Safety Welcomes the National Rifle Association, the National African American Gun Association, the Guns for Christ Club, the American Indian Tomahawks, and the Associated Gun Clubs of America." The banner was emblazoned with images of assault rifles, long guns, and pistols.

The lobby was filled with men and women wearing cowboy hats and carrying arms. Some side arms were in beautifully tooled holsters and belts. African Americans wore ones with engravings of Malcolm X and John Brown.

Across the lobby was a large group of white women, grossly overweight, wearing T-shirts emblazoned with the Celtic symbol for white power. Assault weapons were slung over their shoulders.

Native Americans wore shirts identifying their tribes on the front. The backs showed armed Apaches and the words, "Homeland Security: Fighting Terrorism Since 1492." They carried high-powered rifles with scopes.

The most heavily armed group was sitting around the lobby fountain wearing T-shirts with the fronts showing Christ lovingly cradling an AR-15 and on the back a seated Christ holding a toddler in one arm and pointing a pistol with the other and the slogan "The Good Lord Gave Us Guns."

Murray was standing at the hotel registration desk. I'd called him from the airport.

"Quite a bunch," I said as I gestured at the lobby's gun crowd. "Aren't you afraid they'll attack each other?"

"Got an agreement with hotel management and local police that they could openly carry but no ammunition. I hope they're complying."

The desk clerk handed me a key chain indicating the Santa Rosa Casita.

"Take the paved trail marked 'Camino Real' to a cross path marked 'Pistola Way.' Turn right, and your casita is the fourth on the left. Your luggage will be there before you."

During the registration, a number of people flocked around Murray and asked questions. When I received my room key, Murray whispered to me, "Follow me. I have a place reserved in the restaurant. Hope you like Mexican food. We'll be able to talk."

I followed him down a long hallway to the Aztec Chronic Tacos Café decorated with murals of smiling conquistadors watching happy Indians gather corn.

Along the hallway were session posters with intriguing titles like "Why Guns Make You More Compassionate, an International Study by Famed University of Michigan Psychologist Nat Turner"; "Yale University Historian, Dr. Cornell Wild, Lectures on the Importance of Guns for American Economic Development"; "Guns and the Heartland: Dr. Hunter Thompson, University of Las Vegas, Speaks About the Importance of Carrying Guns Through America's Turbulent Midwest"; and "Poet William Burroughs Reads About the Importance of Guns for Everyday Living."

"Those are great talks," I said, as the host seated us at a small table in back covered with plates of smoked chorizo, tortilla chips, guacamole, and green and red sauces. Murray quickly ordered two glasses of Barrique de Ponciano Porfidio tequila.

"Hope you like tequila." Murray passed me a plate of chorizos.

"Love it. Isn't that pretty expensive tequila?"

"Two thousand a bottle. Smith boys want me to spend money, so I'm spending away. I can help you get similar anti-climate-change speakers."

"That'd be great. The institute will have offices across the streets from the Environmental Protection Agency. The Smiths rented a floor, and I'm having it renovated and decorated with photos and paintings of coal mines and oil wells. They found someone who paints like Norman Rockwell to do the ceiling and walls with murals of happy Americans embracing derricks and cars along with homey scenes of families clustered around oil-burning stoves."

"Of the group I've recruited," added Murray, "Thompson and Burroughs are writers always looking for work. But I must warn you about their drugs; they're the reason the two always need a cash flow."

The tequila arrived in gold ornate shot glasses. I glanced at the unusual taco menu and, because I always tasted food I'd never had, ordered crispy grasshoppers mixed with corn smut and Oaxaca flying ants cooked in their own larvae.

"I've read some of their stuff," I admitted. "Give them the right hallucinogens, and they can produce weird green landscapes with smog-filled skies and flying oil cans. I might have them do public-school comic books to attack climate-change findings. I know some illustrators to help."

"The most important thing is getting speakers with credentials liked by the Smiths. They rejected many of mine for having the wrong political backgrounds."

"How'd Burroughs and Thompson get through the screening?" I sipped my lovely tequila followed by sangria. "Smiths were never keen on hippies."

"From what I understand, no one in Tulsa had heard of them, and they couldn't read them," laughed Murray ordering another round. "Sent me a note. They found them incomprehensible and mystical but thought they could fight the gun control lobby. Don't ask me. I think the two are pretty weird. They're sharing a large casita with loud tom-tom music coming out. I think they found some Indians to share drugs."

"Think I can use evangelicals?" I looked down at the tacos placed in front of me and wondered if one of the grasshoppers was kicking its legs.

"Creepy group. Look out," warned Murray, taking a bite from his enchilada made with Rocky Mountain oysters of the pig variety and cotija cheese.

"They're buying a billboard sign outside LA that will read, 'Gun control = Antichrist. He that hath no sword, let him sell his garment and buy one.' They said it was from Luke chapter twenty-two, verse thirty-six. I don't know. I never read the Bible. They are adding to the sign the words 'It's better to be naked than not have a gun.'"

"Will a naked figure be erect and pointing its rifle?" The tequila was taking over my mind. "What about them and the environment?"

"Saw a figure that fifty-four percent of evangelicals reject environmental arguments. Sometimes the message is mixed with antiabortion—you know, God's way is to flood us with babies who'll die from air pollution."

"Do they really say it's God's way?" I was now on my, I think, tenth tequila.

My next bite of taco felt like ants were crawling around in my mouth.

"I should get to my casita," I slurred. "You know, long trip, jet lag, tequila, and need for a nap."

I staggered from the table and tried to remember directions to my casita. Noting my distress, Murray waved a waiter over and asked him to order me a golf cart.

Collapsing in bed, I stared at the ceiling with ever-changing images of dancing tacos held up by swarming ants and caterpillars, naked Christs pointing dicks and guns, and evangelicals waving signs proclaiming air pollution as the Second Coming.

Chapter Thirty-Eight

The snow-covered mountains surrounded me as I walked down the promenade from the Hotel Seehof to the ice-covered Lake Davos. There were few people out in the freezing early morning hours.

It was David who had urged me to go to Davos. "You'll like the 1990 conference, and you'll have more time with the Smith brothers."

I had hesitated, thinking of all the work I had to do on the gun issue.

"A little cold in January," admitted David. "But this is where globalization is occurring with the Berlin Wall coming down. There will be a new world order with the collapse of the Soviet system."

"This is where we can stop this climate-warming shit," John Smith had told me on his private plane while traveling to Davos. I was handed a bloody mary by an attendant.

"Why don't you fuckers do more to stop this crap?" Smith continued. "We've given you enough money."

"It's hard; most scientists think it's happening. We got a couple lined up to refute them." I sipped my drink and tried to hide my discomfort at the idea. David had never told me how foulmouthed the Smiths were.

"Arnold's coming tomorrow. You better have answers for him. Even got some of those Jesus worshippers jumping on the climate bandwagon. Shit, as a kid, I hated those snake healers and Bible thumpers. You should've taken care of them."

I took a cab from the airport to the Seehof as John Smith headed to a large, rented villa.

Somewhere in Davos, German chancellor Helmut Kohl was plotting with industrial leaders to make German reunification profitable.

I hoped to get a quick look at the lake before the meetings started. Walking was easy with the sidewalk free of ice and snow. I was bundled in winter clothing ordered just for the trip.

Approaching me was a woman wearing sunglasses and various furry animal skins. She said something to me in German. Noticing my reaction, she rapidly switched to French and then to English.

"Have you seen any cabs? I need to get to Berghotel Schatzalp," she said.

"There are a couple in front of my hotel." I gestured behind me in the direction of the Seehof. "Just a short distance."

"Can you help me?"

"How? This is my first day here," I hesitantly replied, worrying about the strangeness of the situation. "You want the police? This is supposed to be a low-crime place."

"No police. I'm feeling dizzy. Not serious. Just my medication. Need to get back and lie down. Help me to the cabs."

Putting her arm through mine, I could feel her unsteadiness as we walked back to my hotel.

"You are an American? I'm Rosa Honecker, and you?"

"Billy Durant from California."

"You Americans always name your states. I'm from East Berlin or, as they say now, the former German Democratic Republic. It's all over."

My arms wrapped around her as she stumbled.

"Do you think you can make it? I can run ahead for help."

"Stop a minute. I need some more." Holding on to me, she reached in her purse, uncapped a small vial, and quickly sniffed its contents.

"Please come with me," she insisted, after reaching the hotel cab-stand. "Just help me to my room."

"Can't people help where you're going—what is it—the Berghotel Schatzalp," I stumbled through the last words, not sure how they were pronounced.

"I don't want them to see my condition. You don't know who I am?"

Pulling me into the cab, she whispered into my ear, "I'm the daughter of Erich Honecker—you know, head of the former East German government."

Good God, I thought, *I'm riding with a commie to someplace I don't know—I'm being abducted.*

"Don't worry," she said, seeing my reaction. "Those days are gone—capitalist Germany won. Profiteers and careerist are taking over."

"What is the Berghotel Schatzalp?" I asked, thinking it was a secret-police headquarters.

"You don't know? Thomas Mann's novel *Magic Mountain* was set there. Once it was a tuberculosis sanatorium. Now a hotel."

The cab climbed the mountain arriving in front of a four-story building with the top three floors with balconies overlooking the mountains and valley. Early risers, many probably attending the forum, were walking around the grounds.

A porter came running to open the cab door and said something in German to Rosa.

"He said Father is up waiting in the breakfast room. Please come and meet him. He'll be happy you helped me."

Wearing horn-rimmed glasses over his sharp facial features, Erich Honecker sat at a large table hovered over by his personal staff pouring coffee and arranging a large stack of newspapers. Rosa introduced me and mentioned that I only spoke English. Two chairs were immediately placed at the table, and Rosa motioned for me to sit. Place settings, coffee, croissants, cheeses, and cold cuts appeared.

"Daddy, how do you feel?" asked Rosa in English.

"My only hope is going to Chile. They've offered to take me. I'm not feeling good. And you?"

"This kind man helped me. The hotel car took me to the promenade for a walk. I got dizzy."

"I told you to stop sniffing that stuff. Opium never helped anyone. You'll need a sanatorium like this use to be, but now for the modern affliction of drugs."

"What do you do, Mr. Durant?" Honecker turned to me.

"I'm an economist, here for the forum."

"Capitalist? Out to get the workers, kill them with overwork?"

"Capitalist, yes—free marketer. Trying to save workers." I regretted the words as soon as they were out of my mouth.

"You really believe that?" gasped Rosa, waving over a tall, disheveled man. A chair and place setting appeared for him.

"This is Johannes Heisig," Rosa introduced us. "He is a famous East German painter. You capitalists probably don't know him—Westerners never saw our great socialist-realist art. You capitalist are trapped by abstract art—meaningless lines and confusion."

"You're a capitalist," smirked Johannes. "Now leading the world to ruin."

He ordered a beer, reached across the table, and grabbed with his bare hands a pile of cheese and cold cuts. Smearing mustard on a roll, he shoved the meat and cheese inside his mouth and started loudly chewing, belching, and swilling beer.

"You splattered canvases and drew some lines, while I painted workers and real life." Mustard covered his hand as Johannes wiped it through his hair, leaving a yellow streak. "Your abstract artists never cared about people; that's why you'll kill everyone. Western art portends death." He sneezed, spraying bread and cheese across the table.

"Mr. Durant," asked Erich Honecker, "are you cooking up a plan for world domination and exploitation?"

"I'm here with some oil people worried about climate change."

"I painted smokestacks belching people-killing smoke." Johannes waved for another beer. "Haven't seen any capitalist art on pollution."

"So you're here to save the world from capitalist pollution," said Rosa, sniffing out of her vial.

"Rosa, stop it," snapped her father. "You'll be in a drug clinic when we get to Chile."

"I've been asked to show how pollution and climate change helps people," I answered sheepishly, trapped by my own lies.

"So that's what they want," Erich spat back angrily. "Replace building a worker's paradise with industrial capitalism that kills. War machines and pollution. You Americans know the path to hell."

"What will your art be?" asked Johannes. "Symphonies of death and poems praising dirty air."

"We were building a new world order for workers," said Rosa, looking brighter after sniffing from her vial. "The world order being built at this forum will be based on greed and destruction."

"People will revolt!" Johannes managed to smear mustard on his shirt as he spat chunks of cold cuts onto his plate. "They always do."

"Capitalist governments will stop them," laughed Rosa.

"Then it will be terrorism against the state. Anarchism, terrorism, pollution, and death are the future of this new world order," predicted Johannes.

Erich Honecker suddenly looked pale and started coughing. Two men rushed over helping him to his feet.

"I'm not feeling well. Good meeting you, Mr. Durant," said Erich as he was helped from the room.

"You really think a philosophy based on greed will save the world?" laughed Rosa, taking a sip of coffee.

"Maybe self-interest will keep people interested in protecting each other," I answered, doubting my own statement.

"I've got to go." Johannes jumped up. "I'm finishing a painting of the new world order with jackboots trampling the masses. Kill people and the planet. What good is it all?"

"Can you help me to my room?" Rosa asked me.

After we undressed, I looked out of her window at the mountains and wondered out loud, "What was Mann's *Magic Mountain* about?"

Laughing, nude, spread-eagled across the bed, Rosa recounted, "It was about how early twentieth-century bourgeois society was destroying the world."

"Shit," I said, turning to her. "That's what we're doing here."

"The end of the socialist order heralds the rise of bourgeois values." Rosa grabbed my prick with one hand and with the other hand gave me her vial.

"Sniff this, and I'll suck you into the oblivion of the new world order."

I snorted from the vial; it send my mind reeling down a path and stepping over dead bodies.

"Freud was right, you know," she said, sticking my cock into her mouth. "It's a battle between love and aggression, Eros and Thanatos."

I saw stars as I came, fell down next to her, and snorted more opium. I missed the first meeting for German reunification and the new world order for dreams of bodies blown apart by terrorists, oceans sweeping over cities, and an earth with gnarled, leafless tree branches and barren wastelands.

Chapter Thirty-Nine

"I want you to fight for global free markets," ordered Arnold Smith after returning from the 1990 forum meeting.

The Smiths, their wealth guaranteeing their membership in the World Economic Forum, made me their liaison. I started flying back and forth from San Diego to Davos. After the 1992 election of Democrat Bill Clinton, my work with the President's Council on Economic Advisors ended. I moved back to La Jolla.

"This is a great view," said Rosa Honecker after flying up from Chile to spend time with me. I showed her around my new ocean-cliff house on La Jolla's Spindrift Drive. While her father's travel was restricted by war-crime charges, she traveled freely. It was 1992. She was fifty, and I was fifty-two.

"Just bought it." I kissed her in front of the panoramic window as we watched seals frolic in the waves.

"I'll take you tomorrow to see my office in Torres Pines. I'm going to Davos next week; we could stop in Paris."

"Still working for the capitalist pigs," she commented, slowly taking off her clothes. "I want the seals to see me."

"Hope you don't mind San Diego over Washington. I loved our time there."

"Can't believe I'm following you around America," she answered, tweaking her nipples and pushing her breasts against the glass. "It is improving my English."

"You really think the seals are interested?"

"You were—still can't believe I followed you back to Washington."

"You don't know how much it changed me. Never thought I'd be in a relationship, particularly with a communist."

"Maybe," she said, now pressing her body against me, "you're not a capitalist but a closet communist."

"Sex is my political ideology," I answered.

"You mean pleasure, a world filled with pleasure." She began unzipping my pants.

"I vowed not to be in any kind of relationship. Ayn Rand must be rolling over in her grave because my first serious lover is the daughter of the former head of communist Germany."

"I guess we scared away the seals," I said afterward as we lay in my second-floor bedroom with more stunning ocean views.

"You know, I almost didn't follow you back from Davos. Couldn't imagine being with a capitalist propagandist."

"Capitalist propagandist? What do you mean? I'm just working my way to the top of the food chain."

"You're a war criminal like father, only he had a more humane ideology."

"War criminal? How's that?" I rolled over, touching her favorite pleasure spots and feeling my desire returning.

"Admit it," she sat up, moving my hand away. "You and the Smith brothers are merchants of death—destroying the planet, arming the world, and making the rich richer and the poor poorer."

"I'm just an economist!"

"Economist working for self-serving capitalists—you're their whore."

"Please," I said, pointing at the seals that had returned. "I thought we'd got beyond this discussion back in Washington."

"This is a better view than Washington. The seals look happy. Love the ocean, but this discussion may never end."

"I didn't want love. I ran from it. Then you flew to Washington. I don't know what to do." I couldn't hold back the tears. "I'm awful. My mother was right; I should never have been born."

"Your mother told you that you should never have been born? Why the tears?" She grabbed tissue from a box on the nightstand. "Have you told me everything besides promoting world conflict and starvation?"

"I am a criminal. I've killed people."

"You mean your work for the Smiths has killed people."

"No, I've actually murdered many people, starting when I was ten." I told her my history.

"My God!" she exclaimed when I finished describing pushing Jim Kelly into the jellyfish.

"I thought there was something else," she whispered, gently rubbing my back.

"I'm evil. Plain and simple truth," I moaned as her hand caressed my body.

"It's never simple," she analyzed. "We are all a mix. I wish you spoke German. I could explain it better."

"Sometimes I have bursts of goodness," I almost shouted. "But I work for scumbags. I murder and kill others."

"Maybe that is why I'm attracted to you; you've got evil in your soul," said Rosa, smiling lovingly at me.

"Do you?"

"I tried being a good communist," she began her story. "Leader in Young Pioneers and Young Communist League."

"Shit, you really are a commie."

"Father was proud when I volunteered for the Stasi, the secret police. He promoted women's equality. In speeches, he often referred to my sacrifice fighting enemies of the state."

"You were in the secret police?" I wondered out loud.

"I was trained as an interrogator," she sighed. "I did awful things and liked it."

Whoa, I thought, *are we really that alike?*

"I could break a person in a couple days. We had to deal with all sorts of American spies and subversives."

"You tortured Americans," I gasped.

"I liked interrogating females the best. Used mainly physical methods— you know, cutting, pincers, and instruments used in the Spanish Inquisition."

I thought of our interrogation rooms in Vietnam. Her description of torture was more brutal.

"Catholic priests were into female torture; they were their main victims. They developed all sorts of instruments to shove up the ass and cunt. Many expanded slowly with nails and pins sticking out."

"You used those interrogating women?"

"Also shoved some up men. After a little expansion with nails cutting into their bowels, they talked. Often just the idea brought them to their knees."

"How many died?"

"Countless. I interrogated for ten years from my mid-twenties into my thirties. After a while, I smelled death everyplace I went."

"You quit?"

"No, I was promoted." Rosa went into the bathroom to pee.

"I taught others how to interrogate," she yelled from the bathroom. "I was given Patriotic Order of Merit medal in 1975 for special service to the state. It was considered a great honor since I was only thirty-five. The medal was usually given to the retired or those close to death."

"Did your father have anything to do with you getting it?"

"Maybe, but I wore it proudly. I was a good communist and proud of protecting against enemies of the state."

"Did it ever bother you? I keep having nightmares."

"It started in the 1980s. First I awakened from dreams of death and hearing screams. I began wondering if I was doing it for the state or my own needs."

"Did you get more awards for torture?" I headed for the bathroom when she returned.

"In 1980, I received a medal for the Karl Marx Order for my work supporting ideology and culture. In 1982, I was given the highest award, Hero of the German Democratic Order."

"Did you wear them?"

"Things changed when a 1983 May Day photo of me standing next to father reviewing troops appeared in the party newspaper. My Stasi uniform was weighted down by the medals. I kept looking at the photo, doubting the worth of what I was doing. I couldn't sleep fearing my dreams."

"I've often faced that problem," I said, getting back in bed.

"Then someone gave me some opium to sleep. At first I took it orally to hide my usage—smoking and injecting were more detectable. After a while, I wanted it to reach my brain sooner. That's when I started sniffing it. When we met in 1990, I was addicted."

"I know," I replied, deciding to get out of bed. "Why don't we shower and get something to eat, and then I'll take you out to my office. I'm glad the clinics in Switzerland and Washington worked."

"Still hard to sleep. I keep seeing my victims. Now I have you," she whispered softly in my ear.

"I remember the first time we both awoke screaming. I didn't realize we were plagued by the same demons. Now I know. We can help each other." I kissed her.

We took a slow shower carefully washing each other until we both came. After fruit and yogurt, we drove to the Smith Brothers Center for Tax Cuts and Limited Government.

"You could have done better as an economist in the Soviet system of central planning. It was easy to make life-shortening decisions. You could plan to produce more vodka and less healthy foods, driving up cancer rates and deaths from alcoholism."

"I guess it would be more direct. Now it's all hidden in free markets and cutting government benefits," I responded, pulling into my reserved parking space in front of a modernist two-story brick and glass building with a veranda in back for sitting and contemplating the trees and ocean. "But I would have made less money. Now the cash rolls in."

"You are still thinking like a capitalist." She slammed the car door. "Money isn't everything. Your dreams and guilt should have taught you that. Why not figure out how to be happy? I'd like to try that."

The center's offices had expanded through the years. There was now a full-time secretary, Molly McGuire, and an assistant to monitor projects, Chelsea Connelly. I introduced Rosa to both of them. They were surprised. Later I heard them whispering, "I thought he was gay. Never any girlfriends."

"So what are you doing?" asked Rosa, glancing around my office.

"Still trying to get more guns and tax cuts." I laughed as Chelsea brought in a report on the latest project to organize university research centers devoted to proving the benefits of tax cuts and an armed population.

"How many profs have expressed an interest in working in these centers?" I asked Chelsea.

"Almost a hundred now that we offer stipends to be added to their regular salaries. University presidents jumped at the chance of extra funding for their campuses."

"Any campus protests, like last year when we tried opening a center at Notre Dame?"

"You have protests about your little project to arm and kill?" laughed Rosa.

Clearly shocked by the statement, Chelsea defended the centers, saying, "Business people on trustee boards are getting on the bandwagon. We're keeping a low profile with students and radical professors."

"How do you know who is radical?" asked Rosa. "We used informers to find out."

"We use computers and a database," I answered for Chelsea.

"Do you have campus spies?"

Not understanding the references to informers and spies, Chelsea answered Rosa, "Last year a work-study student combed through articles in major academic journals using a political scale to identify campus radicals. We steer clear of them."

"That was an important project," I added, "which unfortunately the Smith brothers wanted to use to block any radical from getting tenure. I rejected the idea. If word got out, we would never be able to set foot on any campus."

"My father did that," Rosa laughed. "He fired or imprisoned any faculty not following the party line. I interrogated some of them. You could learn a lot from father about controlling ideas."

"But he failed," I observed.

Clearly confused by the conversation and not understanding the references to Rosa's father, Chelsea wondered, "Do you still want me to do this?"

"Yes," I answered. "Don't pay any attention to Rosa; she comes from a different world. Just continue; you're doing a fine job. The Smiths will love you."

After Chelsea left the office, Rosa bent over, licked my ear, and said, "Why don't you fuck the Smiths?"

"Not appealing. Have you seen them?"

"I don't mean fuck them physically but fuck up their projects."

"How?" I asked, stroking her leg.

"Let's think of this place as the Center for Promoting Human Pleasure and Happiness. Use their money for research into the topics. Never tell them."

"I could lose my income if they found out," I worried.

"Hoard some of the project money. My father stuck a lot in Swiss banks. I'm rich from the government money he stole. Give yourself a higher salary, more bonuses. There are a lot of tricks."

"I've got plenty already invested," I said, excited at the idea. I could undermine the things I'd learned to hate. "Would you help? I'm not sure how to promote pleasure and happiness."

"I don't have much experience. Father never thought like that, and the Stasi never promoted happiness."

"Did Stalin or your father include those goals in any five-year plans?"

"The only goal was economic growth, never people living a life of pleasure. Planned vacations and resorts were tied to productivity. You know, 'A rested worker is a good worker' was a vacation slogan."

"Stalin and the Smith brothers have a lot in common."

Chapter Forty

"No! No!" Rosa woke up screaming that night. She started talking German, raising her hands as if defending from an attack.

"What happened?" I sat up and hugged her.

"She came back; she always comes back."

"Who?"

"She was sixteen, protesting the government. We thought she was part of a wider movement. She died when I inserted a metal cylinder with needles in her vagina and slowly expanded it. Usually it only took a couple turns for women to talk."

"She didn't," I guessed.

"Sweet little thing. She bled to death denouncing my father. Then she wouldn't let me alone appearing every night, blood streaming down her legs, wanting vengeance. I can't forget her."

"Jesus," I said, trying to calm her. "I've had those kinds of nightmares."

"I need my opium. I need to escape my personal hell."

She started shaking and experiencing chills. I went to my medicine cabinet for a Valium.

"No opium." I handed her the pill and a glass of water. "This will calm you."

"What is it?"

"Valium. My doctor prescribed it for my nightmares. It takes away anxiety—my problem. See if it works."

She swallowed the pill and collapsed into my arms crying.

"The pill takes a while to work. But you'll feel more relaxed. You woke me as I was being raped and killing the black man. Jesus, we've got some pasts.

"I'll never escape," she wept. "They'll keep coming after me. I thought I was doing good; it was all evil."

"At least you thought it was OK." I decided to take a Valium.

I could feel her slowly relaxing in my arms.

The next morning we stared at each other over our coffees.

"Rough night," I observed, pointing at gulls circling over a large school of fish feeding near the surface.

"Valium helped, but if opium had been close, I would have run for it." Rosa dreamily looked out over the water.

"Do you want to go to the office with me? I'll be there only a few hours. I need to get ready to go to Davos. Do you still want to stop in Paris?"

"I don't know," she stared at me. "I need some time alone. Could I stay here while you're in Davos?"

"Is that good—I mean, being alone?"

"Just need space. Like you, I never thought of a close relationship. Chose only brutal guys—ones easy to get rid of. Ones I didn't want to connect to."

"I understand. Oddly I want to be with you all the time. That never happened before."

"Can you make it to Davos without me?" she laughed. "There wouldn't be anything for me to do anyway while you're managing the universe."

"Hardly the universe." I poured us more coffee. "Just world economics."

"What about pleasure and happiness? Are you putting them in your global plans?"

"That's a thought. I could practice sneaking the ideas in. If it works, we can talk about the research agenda for the Smith boys' university centers."

"I'm worried about you being alone. Will you be OK?" I asked, heading to the stairs to go up and dress. "I'll be gone a week."

"I'm touched that you're worried. I'm a big girl. Remember, I was a leader in the Stasi and Hero of the German Democratic Order."

"You won't hurt yourself?" I looked back. "I was worried last night."

"I haven't killed myself yet. Plenty of chances and reasons. I want to live even after killing so many."

I drove to my office and left Rosa behind. She was the first person I'd ever wanted to protect.

But we're both monsters, I thought, pulling into my parking space.

I gave instructions to Molly and Chelsea about where to contact me in Davos and about continuing work developing the university research centers. Pulling together my material on the World Economic Forum along with the Smith brothers' instructions, I sat down to organize my visit. The idea of pushing global goals of pleasure and happiness was appealing.

"Please call my house while I'm gone," I asked Molly as I left. "Check on Rosa to see if she has any needs. Remember, this is a foreign country for her and she's never stayed in La Jolla."

"And if there are problems?" Molly looked startled by my request. "I can't go over there."

Remembering that Molly was a secretary with a clearly defined job description that didn't include looking after my girlfriends, I rephrased my request. "Would it be all right if I asked you to check on her and if there are issues with the house, call repair people and have food delivered if Rosa needs any? She is a stranger and would appreciate any help."

"Sure," smiled Molly at my reworded request.

I drove quickly back to the house. I didn't know if I was hurrying because I missed Rosa or if I was worried about what she might do in my absence.

"I'm back!" I yelled entering the house.

I panicked when there was no response. I called again. No response. I ran up to the second floor and checked each room expecting to find her body.

Oh God, I thought. *I don't want to find her in a bathtub with slit wrists.*

Looking out the window, I could see her climbing over rocks on the beach below. Deciding it was best if I didn't disturb her, I began preparing lunch and setting the table.

"Hope you liked the walk," I greeted her. "Made a little lunch for us and arranged for Molly to check in on you."

"Beautiful," she replied. "I'll enjoy staying here while you're gone."

"You can still come. I'll miss you."

"I'll miss you." She kissed me gently. "I've a lot to think about after telling our stories. Am I, or will I ever be, prepared this type of relationship? All I want to do is hide from thoughts of what I've done."

"I know the feeling," I sympathized, pouring hot chowder in our bowls. "Can't get involved because you might not be able to focus on pushing away the bad thoughts—your demons might take over."

"You're so sweet to me," she said, sitting down and sniffing the chowder. "This smells great."

I flew to Davos the next day carrying with me worries about how Rosa would be while I was gone and whether or not she would be there when I returned. I couldn't remember any other time when I missed being with someone.

In Davos, I first met with the founder and executive chairman Klaus Schwab before attending the official meeting of the Executive Council of the Forum. I explained the Smith brothers' agenda.

I skipped the gun part of the agenda, since, as I had discovered in the past that not many world leaders were interested in arming their populations. They considered it a crazy American idea.

"I think we should be concerned about workers' enjoying life," I stated after Schwab opened the floor the Executive Council for discussion.

"How's that?" responded Nancy Drew, a tough-minded economist dealing with African development projects. "I'm more concerned that they have a job and are not starving. Eating must come before they can, as you say, enjoy life."

"What do you mean 'enjoying life'?" Schwab asked. "That's psychology; we're trained in economics. I agree with Nancy; you can't enjoy life on an empty stomach."

"Is working for economic growth enough?" I responded. "At every one of these meetings, we talk about global economic growth as salvation, but economic growth for what?"

"Economic growth feeds people," said Xi Jinping, head of the East Asian Trade Office. "People are happy if they can buy things. In China, we're on the road to a socialist paradise. Economic growth will fulfill Mao's dream."

"Economic growth will mean more shopping malls, longer and poorer working conditions, and pollution. Is it a workers' paradise if they one only breathe cancer-causing air?" I said.

"Last month you were calling for arming everyone and not worrying about pollution," said Ben Tucker, leader of the forum's agricultural efforts. "Now you're concerned with working conditions and bad air. What's changed your tune?"

"I realized," I responded, trying to sound humble in giving my proposal to this august group representing global corporate concerns, "that economic growth is not really a goal unless we define its purpose."

"Isn't eating enough?" snapped Nancy Drew.

"Ending global hunger is important," I agreed, "but afterward, what?"

"What do you think we should do?" asked Schwab.

"What about considering economic growth as a means of enhancing human pleasure and happiness? If we think this way, maybe we will create plans for better working conditions, shorter hours, protecting our health and the environment, and maintaining close and important human relations."

"Don't all those things result from economic growth?" asked Xi Jinping with a tone that suggested he was justifying China's socialist path. "Many are leaving poor rural villages and coming to our beautiful new cities. They find work. Their families may follow them. They live in new, tall apartment buildings. What more could they want?"

As I flew back, I thought of the tenor of the discussion. It seemed hard for most of them to see beyond economic growth to what type of society it might create.

What more, I thought, *can you expect from representatives of global corporate companies wanting to maximize profits?*

I called Rosa from the San Diego airport before going home. I didn't want any surprises.

"Billy, I missed you," whimpered Rosa into the phone. "I did something awful. Couldn't stop myself."

"We'll talk; don't worry."

Apprehensive about what was waiting for me, I drove rapidly out of the airport parking lot. I pulled into my driveway where Rosa stood shaking.

"What happened?" I took her into my arms.

"I didn't mean to do it," she wept. "I couldn't control myself."

She led me into the house and into the storage room off the kitchen.

On the floor was a nude girl, her throat slit and stomach swollen. From the smell, she had been dead a number of days.

"I cleaned up all the blood and shit, but I didn't know what to do with the body."

"What happened?"

"Met her walking on the beach. She reminded me of the girl in my dreams. I just wanted to talk and invited her up here."

"Does anyone know she's missing?" My mind started racing, wondering how to get rid of the body.

"All over the news. Parents are distraught; police banged on your door wanting to know if I'd seen her. She's seventeen, a local high school girl. The police combed the area. Neighbors looked all over the beach and even as far as Torre Pines."

"We've got to figure out how to get rid of the body," I said, squatting and looking at the wounds. "You cut her all over the place. What's that on her thighs?"

I stood up. The smell was dragging up memories.

"Cute little thing," Rosa said. "We started talking. I asked if she wanted something to eat or drink. She came up. I couldn't resist and tried kissing her. I never told you everything about the girl I tortured."

"What else?"

"After she was arrested, I fell in love with her. I went to her cell often at night to make love. Then I tortured her, thinking she'd confess and be OK and we could continue after she was released. You know the rest."

"So that's why she keeps haunting your sleep."

"The girl started struggling when I tried to kiss her. I just wanted to hold and kiss her breasts. My Stasi training came back. Without thinking,

I flipped her to the floor. I just wanted to see her young body and kiss it. She didn't understand."

"Didn't understand what?"

"I wanted to love her, hold her, kiss her, just like I did in the jail cell. She resisted and kicked me. Stasi taught me well. I grabbed a knife from the counter and cut her throat."

Chapter Forty-One

We rolled the girl up in a sheet of plastic. There was no blood. Everything had drained from her. Rosa had already shoved all the towels she'd used to clean up the blood and bodily discharges in a large cloth bag for burning.

"How'd you get rid of them in the Stasi?"

"We had a large crematorium. Father loved the enemies of the state just disappearing from sight."

"We don't have a crematorium, and burning is not practical. Can't just bury her; any animal could dig her up. There is the ocean."

We both stood staring out the window.

"Do you have any regrets about killing her?" I asked, thinking about how I'd get the body offshore.

"It came so easily, too easily. I'm trained to kill. I've got so much on my conscience that this will be minor. But I want to stop." Rosa broke into tears. I hugged her, trying to kiss them away.

"I know from years of struggling with the same thing," I tried to reassure her. "Maybe we can help each other."

I thought of Big Fish when I went to the San Diego Harbor and rented a twenty-foot powerboat with a big engine.

"Can this get us out to the kelp beds?" I asked at the rental dock. "My girlfriend and I want to fish for yellowtail."

"No problem, unless it's rough. Should be OK today and tomorrow."

I signed to take it out the next day and rented fishing tackle.

"What kind of bait do you recommend?"

"Squid. They love it. I'll put it in the boat tomorrow when you come down to the docks."

"Are there places to tie up if we want to come back for a drink or snack?"

"The Point Loma Yacht Club has a dock for their restaurant. Good place to snack."

On the way back to the house, I stopped at a hardware store for a power saw and five large metal coolers. I figured that the girl weighed about 125 pounds. We could distribute about twenty-five pounds of her to each cooler. I didn't want them to look too heavy as we carried them down to the dock.

Rosa was more efficient at dismembering the girl's body than I could ever be. She said it was her Stasi training. The real problem was the smell. We put each body part in a tight, plastic bag and sealed all of them with heavy waterproof tape. We cut the insulation out of each cooler to reduce buoyance.

Deciding to carry two coolers to the boat at the rental dock and then load the others at the yacht-club dock, I called car rental agencies until I found one that would drop a car off at the house in the morning.

The next morning we put two coolers in the trunk of my car. After taking the rent-a-car driver back, we put the other three in the rental car. As I drove the rental to the Point Loma Yacht Club parking lot, I hoped we'd contained the smell. A taxi brought me back to the house.

"Getting a late start," observed the boat handler who was bringing a pail of squid over after I put two coolers in the boat.

"Hard time getting out of bed, if you know what I mean. She kept me busy." I nodded at Rosa.

I drove the boat away from the dock. Passing the "No Wake" sign, I planed the boat, heading toward the tip of Point Loma. As we neared the yacht club, I slowed and found a spot near the dock's ramp. We quickly carried down the other coolers from the rental car. And to remove suspicion, we stopped at the club's bar.

"What've got on tap?" I asked.

"Bud and Miller," the bartender answered.

"Give us two Buds. Going out for a big day of fishing."

We tried not to look anxious as we sipped our beers. I must admit that Rosa, with her Stasi training, was better at looking cool than me.

Reaching the kelp beds, I looked around for other boats. Seeing only a few in the distance, we got to work filling each cooler with salt water and the few weights we'd brought in our backpacks. We tied the coolers shut with heavy rope.

"I don't think these'll float," I commented as we tossed the first one over the side. We watched as it slowly sank. With the cooler's insulation gone and the body parts drained of blood and filled with salt water, the cooler's metal casing was enough to make it sink.

"Do you fish?" I asked, taking a pole off the rack. "We should try to bring something back."

"Are you kidding?"

I put a squid on the hook and showed her how to lower it over the side. Almost instantly there was a tug on the line. Rosa had caught a fish.

"What do I do?" she yelled.

"Turn the reel; it doesn't look that big from the bend in the pole."

Rosa danced around her catch, afraid of the small flopping rockfish.

"Take the hook out of its mouth. It's eatable, and we have to return with something."

"I can't do it. Looks—what do you Americans say?—icky."

We wandered around the kelp bed and kept our distance from other boats as we unloaded the coolers. At each spot, we put in our lines and caught mainly small rockfish. Finally we were down to one cooler.

I ran the boat to the edge of the kelp bed, and we dumped the last cooler.

"Can we go back?" Rosa asked, looking at our catch flopping around in the stern. "The fish blood is getting to me. I can't stand looking at them dying."

"One more time. Then we should be good." I baited two hooks. "Can't just throw things in; we've got to look like we're out here fishing."

Of course Rosa's pole bent, and the line began spinning out. She had caught something big.

"I can't do this!" she screamed, handing the pole to me.

I played with it for a while, tightening and untightening the drag. Finally the fish was exhausted, and I pulled it alongside.

"It's beautiful," Rosa exclaimed, looking down at the fish. "What is it?"

"It's a yellowtail. Pretty big for these parts."

There was a gaff hook among the tackle put in the boat. I leaned over and hooked it through the fish's gills and pulled it on board.

The yellowtail flopped around, spraying blood on Rosa's pants.

"This is awful. I'll never fish again." She vomited partly in the water, leaving some in the boat. Between the fish and puke, things were getting slippery. "I'm covered with fish blood."

People gathered around the boat when we got back.

"Haven't seen one that size for years," exclaimed the boat attendant. "Must be over forty pounds. You could win the yellowtail derby with a fish that size. Who caught it? Got to have a photo."

Good, I thought. *A different boat attendant than this morning. He won't know about the two coolers we went out with.*

The dockhand hooked the fish onto a weighing scale and made Rosa stand next to it. She looked sick. I'd whispered in her ear that she should go along with it since it was our alibi. The Polaroid photo was posted in dock shack for all to see. He took two so that we could have one. The photo highlighted the fish blood on Rosa's pants.

"I've got to shower off this fish slime and blood," announced Rosa when we got back to the house. "I thought I would vomit standing next to that fish."

I watched her rapidly strip, leaving a trail of clothes and shoes to the bedroom shower. I could hear her mumbling something in German before the words were drowned out by the running water.

Stripping, I joined her.

"Please scrub my back." She turned her shapely butt toward me. I stood a minute and thought about how young her body still looked. All that Stasi exercise, I thought, kept her trim.

Putting body wash on her back, I took a washcloth and began scrubbing.

"Harder! I must have scales and blood all over. This was the dirtiest thing I've ever done. I'll never go fishing again."

"Stop killing young girls," I laughed, scrubbing harder.

"There were fish scales and slime in my hair."

"I doubt it. Must be your imagination. I don't remember fish being anywhere near your head."

"When you made me stand by the scale for that stupid photo." She turned, embracing me. "That was awful. Never again going after yellowtail."

"I didn't have time to tell you what happened at Davos when I brought up the issue of helping people have happy lives."

She wrapped a leg around my hips and put me in her.

"Is this a position you learned in training?" I tried to steady myself. "I'm not sure I can do it this way. Why don't we try the bed?"

She forced me to the shower wall. Excited, I tried to oblige while I worried about slipping on the wet and soapy floor.

"I bet those capitalist stooges didn't want people to be happy," she panted in my ear. "They only see dollar signs."

"Shit!" I yelled, falling and hitting my head on the shower faucet.

"Billy, you OK?" Rosa bent over to help me to my feet. "Did you come?"

"What kind of question is that? I'm bleeding." Blood trickled from my forehead down my nose and onto the shower floor. "Did you?"

"I don't know." Rosa started crying. "Blood everywhere—that sweet girl, the fish, your head."

After drying myself, I threw myself on the bed, held a towel to stanch the bleeding, and told Rosa where to find bandages.

"Your poor forehead," she said, applying antibiotic ointment and a bandage. "It isn't large, only a small cut. You'll live."

As she leaned over me, I stared at her breasts and pulled her down.

"So they won't listen to our idea," commented Rosa as we dressed after lovemaking. "Maybe we need another approach. Can I go to Davos with you next time?"

"Sure, come with me. I think I need to fund some economists—those approved by the Smith brothers—to explore the issue."

"Your economists might show that human happiness causes growth or some form of it. I don't think free markets promote happiness," she concluded, slipping on an expensive pair of designer jeans and a Chanel blouse.

"Do you think we can really change?" I worried. "Will we always kill? Is the girl we dumped the last one?"

"I hope it's the last one for me." She put her feet into a pair of Jimmy Choo sandals. "I can't stand the memories."

"You look great! You're wearing the fruits of communism. How much did your father steal?"

"The family calls it 'liberated money' saved from the capitalist exploiters who took over."

"Really," I giggled, "theft by another name."

Dressed, we went down to the kitchen to make dinner.

"We've got yellowtail. I can grill it," I offered.

"I can't look at it; let's go out." Rosa looked disgusted at the idea of eating fish.

Ordering steaks at the Grant Hotel Grill—we had decided to go into San Diego—we sat back and looked at each other sipping a California merlot.

"We used to have a debate at an old coffeehouse near the University of Chicago about whether or not free markets promoted morality," I related.

"That's stupid; free markets promote hurting others. Isn't that what competition is about?"

"How's that?"

"There are no ethics in free markets except winning. Communism and socialism protect."

I almost spit out my wine. "That's what you did in the Stasi, protect lives?"

"I thought we were protecting communism and stopping worker exploitation."

Filets with hot juices oozing out were put down in front of us along with garlic mashed potatoes and broccoli.

"And now?"

"I liked the interrogation and the killing." Rosa cut into the rare meat. "I admit that, but I want to change. Can I work with you?"

"The Smith boys would never approve hiring the daughter of Erich Honecker."

"I don't mean being a paid employee. Just work with you."

"To end free markets for communism," I laughed, putting more salt and pepper on the steak.

"No, to find a better way. There has to be something else. I'm tired of all the human meanness and killing. I want to sleep at night and not be visited by my victims."

Chapter Forty-Two

"I've decided to be a vegetarian," Rosa informed me in the cab from Berghotel Schatzalp to the 1997 meeting of the World Economic Forum.

"Why?" I asked, staring at the mountains surrounding Davos. "Next you'll be a vegan, which will seriously restrict our dining options."

"I don't want to be associated with any killing, even animals. My demons are slowing down."

"Could fit this year's theme," I suggested, "'Committed to Improving the State of the World.' But I wonder how many members will stop eating animals. They seem committed to worrying about humans."

"I didn't tell you, but I threw away all my fur jackets," smiled Rosa, moving her hand to my leg. "Animals have souls. The problem is that most religions only give humans souls."

The taxi suddenly veered to avoid a deer and threw us against each other as we finished the descent from the hotel and entered Davos proper.

"That was close," Rosa shouted, straightening out her matching Versace pants and blouse. "The forum should be concerned with animal welfare."

"What is this kick about animals and vegetarians? Throw away your furs! What about not buying all these expensive clothes and giving your money to the poor?"

"You know money doesn't buy happiness," said Rosa, stepping out of the cab. "The behavioral economists you paid proved that. Besides, look at you; you're dressed in the best, the new Davos Man."

"Didn't ask to be featured on the cover of *Esquire*. Why me the Davos Man?"

"Because you're so handsome," whispered Rosa in my ear as we entered the conference.

The lobby was jammed with delegates. I spotted Lin Fu in the corner holding forth on Confucianism and world trade. She supported my calls for more research on the effects of free trade on happiness. As a representative from the People's Republic of China, Lin advocated the revival of Confucianism as the new communist ethic. She rejected free trade because it undermined social harmony.

"Lin, I'm glad you are here," I said, as Rosa indicated she was going over to talk to the author Moacyr Scliar, chronicler of the lives of Brazilian Jews. Always laden with guilt, Rosa was still struggling, even at this late date, with the German persecution of Jews. She had told me before we left the hotel that she wanted to talk to him about those Brazilians who escaped the Holocaust.

"Billy Durant," said Lin in perfect English with an American accent. She had attended the University of Wisconsin and still wore a little Badger brooch below her communist-party pin. "Still chasing happiness?"

Lin had been present at the last two forum meetings when I had argued for focusing on the work of behavioral economists.

"Still working on it. And you are still saying free trade will disrupt Confucian harmony."

"It's a no-brainer," replied Lin putting down her teacup. "Of course competition destroys harmony by pitting human against human."

"What about animals?" I asked. "Rosa just announced she was a vegetarian and animals have souls."

Putting her arm around my shoulder, Lin guided me to a corner of the lobby.

"Are you interested in a foursome?" she asked when no one could hear us. "You and Rosa are a good-looking couple."

"What!" I exclaimed. "Are you kidding? Is this part of harmony?"

"I've had my eye on you two at the last meeting. My boyfriend, Deng Xiaoping, has the hots for Rosa. I like you. We're all in our fifties. It'd work."

"We've never been swingers. I don't know how Rosa would feel."

"I saw you in the Schatzalp lobby. We're staying there also. Could use your room or ours. Got the latest in Chinese sex toys."

"Chinese sex toys? What are those? Anything like the Chinese water torture?"

"We make a lot for American sex shops. When my boyfriend introduced free trade ideas in China, American sex people rushed over for the cheap labor. Got everything—vibrators, butt plugs, dildos, you name it."

"I'll have to talk to Rosa," I said. I was tempted. Lin was a good-looking woman whom I occasionally fantasied about.

"Tell Rosa about our new dildo with a Mao head that rotates as it vibrates. I came four times in half an hour."

"Jesus," I said, feeling embarrassed and looking around to make sure no one was overhearing us. "It could help trade relations. Hooking up with Deng would make the US State Department happy."

"Deng and I agree with you that we need a new policy promoting harmony and happiness. We could work together on it. Maybe all of us in bed could help us plan."

"Did Deng worry about this when he opened China to free trade and consumerism?"

"Yes, but at the time he was focused on overcoming the Cultural Revolution," answered Lin, searching in her large purse. "The Mao dildo is an important answer to the trouble caused by the Cultural Revolution and free trade."

"How's that?"

"It gives pleasure, happiness." Lin pulled from her purse a long, narrow box with gold-gilded edges emblazoned with the symbol for the Chinese communist party. "Here it is. Give it to Rosa."

"What is it?"

"It is the commemorative edition of the Mao dildo with revolutionary symbols carved into its shaft. It feels better than the plain ones, and it sings."

"Sings?"

"The 'March of the Volunteers'—Chinese national anthem, you know. 'Arise ye who refuse to be slaves. With our very flesh and blood, let us build our new Great Wall.'"

"Doesn't sound exciting. I can't imagine doing it to the 'Star Spangled Banner.'"

"It gets louder the faster you move it. Stanza good for males is 'Arise! Arise! Arise!'"

"Are you serious?"

"Very serious. China and the United States are biggest economies. We could bring happiness to all."

"Through free trade in Mao dildos." I laughed. "Is the world going to rally around the 'March of the Volunteers'?"

"We could have different national songs and leaders. World's people would be united around pleasure."

Putting the box in my hand, Lin instructed, "Show this to Rosa. I know she'll jump at the chance as a real woman. She'll like the action from Mao's head."

Our conversation was interrupted by a loudspeaker announcing the beginning of sessions.

"We can meet for dinner in the hotel lobby at six," suggested Lin. "Deng always wanted to get close to Erich Honecker; he loved German communism. Thought it could be a model for China. I guess Rosa will be the closest he'll get."

"I've gotta ask Rosa. I don't know how she'll feel about it."

I put the Mao box in the bag supplied by the meeting organizers and retrieved the program to find out my room number.

"What committee are you on?" asked Lin. "I'm on world health."

"World hunger," I answered, finding the room number. "See you at six in the lobby. We might not do the Mao thing, but we could have dinner. That'd be fun."

I hurried off to hear three hours of droning talk filled with incomprehensible statistics about calories, food values, climate issues, and new genetically modified crops. In the afternoon, a Monsanto representative explained their modified seeds for alfalfa, canola, corn, cotton, sorghum, soybeans, sugar beets, and wheat.

"These seeds will save the world," the Monsanto man, sweating with a slight pee stain on his pants, ended his presentation to a mostly empty room. Many had left when he'd got to the discussion of genetically modified canola. He died the next year of bladder cancer. There were rumors that it was caused by eating too many genetically modified sunflower seeds.

"They're all talking about you," greeted Rosa after our sessions ended. "My session on world peace was all about weapons and defense. There's no hope."

"Why are they talking about me?"

"You're the Davos Man after the *Esquire* cover. They kept mentioning an article in the *Economist*."

"Don't know anything about it."

Holding a copy of the article, Rosa read, "'Some people find Davos Man hard to take: there is something uncultured about all the money-grubbing and managerialism.'"

"That's not me," I reacted.

"'If an idea works or a market rises,'" continued Rosa, "'he will grab it. Like it or loathe it, that is an approach more likely to bring peoples together than to force them apart.'"

"Shit, is that how you think of me?"

"I think of you bringing people together." Rosa kissed my cheek. "We could hurry back and get together."

"Speaking of getting together, this is a present from Lin Fu. You might not want to open it here."

Ignoring my advice, she pulled out the Mao dildo and started waving it over her head, giggling, and shouting, "Look at the real fruit of communist revolutions!"

"Everyone's looking," I snapped, feeling embarrassed. "Put it back. Lin wants us to meet for a foursome. Deng Xiaoping wants to get close to an East German communist."

"Look at this," she said, flipping the switch on the bottom. "Its head turns and vibrates. It's a new meaning to giving head."

"Let's go," I hissed, pulling us out of the meeting site. "I thought you didn't like public displays."

"It's just so funny. You wouldn't appreciate it as a capitalist. If we'd had this vibrator, I don't think communist Germany would have failed."

"How's that?"

"Revolutionary people would have worked harder and supported us if we promised everyone a pleasure machine like this."

"What about Mao's head?" I wondered.

"Couldn't use my father's. He was too stern looking. In a book published after Lenin's death, there's a wonderful collection of photos some with Lenin laughing. Those could be models for dildos."

"You think," I said as I opened the taxi door, "German communism would have survived if you manufactured dildos with Lenin's head."

"His fist raised in revolutionary salute would've given added stimulation." Rosa couldn't stop laughing as the taxi turned on to the road to the hotel. "With a Lenin dildo, West Germany would have fallen. 'Communism makes better and more stimulating products' could have been our slogan."

Just before reaching the hotel, I asked, "What do you think of a foursome? I've never done it. Could barely handle one person. Avoided swinger clubs when I was younger. You never suggested swinging."

"Did some in the Stasi with prisoners—once with the girl I mentioned and two other inmates. I loved the girl." Rosa started sobbing with tears running down her face. "Will she ever forgive me?"

I hugged Rosa and wiped away the tears as the doorman opened the taxi to let us out.

Standing near the hotel entrance were Lin Fu and Deng Xiaoping, both clutching boxes similar to the one I had given Rosa.

Chapter Forty-Three

"Have you tried velvet deer antlers?" Lin translated Deng's question as we took turns dipping pieces of sourdough bread in a spicy fondue of cheddar and pepper jack cheeses with jalapeños and hot paprika. In the hotel's Panorama Restaurant, the maître d' had seated us next to the window with its beautiful mountain views.

When we had been introduced outside at the hotel entrance, Lin had explained, "Deng wants me to translate for him. He feels that a foursome with German and Chinese communists and a Western capitalist is too important for him to be misunderstood."

"Velvet deer antlers," I repeated. "You mean for dipping bread in fondue?"

"He means for staying hard," translated Lin. "Ancient Chinese sex stimulant. Sliced and pulverized, best mixed with virgin boy eggs."

"I've never had virgin boy eggs," commented Rosa as a piece of bread fell off her fondue fork into the pot. Trying to retrieve it, she continued, "Had some virgin boys in Stasi. We called it the fruits of German communism—nice little balls."

"Not that," laughed Lin. "The fruits of Chinese communism include healthy food. Virgin boys eggs good for blood circulation and with deer antlers keep you hard for hours."

"Are virgin boy eggs their testicles?" I asked, starting to have a weird fantasy about our foursome including young boys. "Do you harvest them as population control? Communism can have a one child policy, but free markets support population growth, more shoppers."

Deng started laughing as Lin translated the conversation.

"Ancient Chinese medicine calls for soaking eggs in young boys' urine and then cracking them open and cooking in the urine. Gives the eggs a salty taste," Lin interpreted Deng's explanation. "Blend mixture with deer antler, and you'll pop right up. Mao used it daily during the Great Leap Forward."

Our spicy cheese fondue and bread were replaced with a chocolate fondue and a plate of caramel and banana bread cut into squares.

"Why the Great Leap Forward?" I asked, spearing one of the bread pieces and dipping it in the chocolate. I thought of Mao's attempt in the late 1950s at rapid industrialization. The Great Leap Forward had ended in famine as Young Pioneers tried killing all birds that ate grain and left insects free to destroy the crops.

"He believed that sexual stimulation increases worker productivity. Sex is key to making people love communism and produce more goods," answered Lin, translating the conversation for Deng, who broke out in uproarious laughing.

"Capitalism is similar," I replied, savoring the Swiss chocolate. "We use sexual stimulation to drive shopping—you know, with sexy ads. Sex keeps the free market running."

"I'm still interested in the virgin boy eggs," said Rosa, looking intently at Deng and Lin. "How do you do it?"

"Deng says officials put buckets in hallways of elementary schools for boys under ten to pee in," Lin translated Deng's explanation. "After soaking and cooking eggs in boys' urine, whites have a pale golden hue, and the yolks turn green. You sprinkle deer antler on top. He says it is better than ox and goat penis. They can be hard to chew."

"Shit," I said. "Under capitalism, we could package and sell millions, turning them into TV dinners for microwaving. Package designs could appeal to local cultures and create a truly multicultural global economy."

Deng laughed so hard that chocolate sprayed off his fork onto his suit. He spoke rapidly to Lin.

"What's he saying?" asked Rosa. "I'm wondering what young boys' urine tastes like. Some of our prisoners drank their own urine when we cut off the water to force them to confess."

"When he introduced market economies," interpreted Lin, "there sprang up many new companies selling virgin boy eggs mixed with deer antler. The big one was the Dongyang Pleasure Company. Big sales in China until the scandal."

"Sounds like capitalism." I savored a piece of chocolate soaked bread. "What's the difference? What scandal?"

Lin spoke to Deng before turning to us to explain, "Some companies didn't have enough young boys' urine, so they found a source in men's public bathrooms by tapping into waste pipes from urinals. Some said adult urine gave eggs a hint of tarragon."

"Free markets have a way of finding scarce materials." I recalled my free market economic courses. "Also free-market behavioral economists say that consumers adapt easily to changing market tastes."

"Some factories undercooked the eggs," continued Lin, interpreting Deng's story. "This led to a rapid spread of exotic venereal diseases eventually traced to a public toilet near Shanghai's busiest whorehouses."

"What happened?" asked Rosa, pushing back her plate and indicating she was finished.

"After months of investigation, the government forced the companies to close. Only those with certified young boys' urine were allowed to stay open. Communism looks after the welfare of its people."

"It takes years to close negligent US factories." I felt bloated from the combination of chocolate and cheese. "Capitalism operates under the rule of law, which means that protection of human welfare is a long process."

"That's right," Rosa interjected. "When my father found something wrong, he acted. Communist parties look and act for the good of all. In capitalism, law protects the rich."

"Are we finished?" smiled Lin. "Want to come to our room? All sorts of toys."

Deng stood up and gestured for Lin to stand beside him. He started speaking loudly with Lin translating. Surrounding diners stopped eating and listened.

"There are no fundamental contradictions between a socialist system and a market economy," declared Deng his fist raised in the air. "It doesn't matter if a cat is black or white so long as it catches mice. Under capitalism, markets serve the rich; under people's communism, markets serve all. Something wrong, the party fixes it. Something wrong in capitalism, the rule of law insures that remedies protect the rich."

"We should go to our room," whispered Lin into Deng's ear.

"China's communist party," Lin continued, translating, unable to stop Deng, "now ensures the purity of young boys' urine. Under capitalism, the public toilet would be privatized—charge a fee and sell urine. The rule of law would protect the owners, and there would be a steady stream of infected young boy eggs. Communist markets work for all."

We followed them from the dining room. I was still hesitant about swinging as I had the usual male concerns: Would I look small next to Deng? Would I be able to get it up?

I was gripped by performance anxieties as we entered a room filled with sex toys. In chairs and leaning against the walls were full-size male and female nude dolls with accentuated genitalia. There was a silicone Leonardo DiCaprio doll sporting a red-tipped erect member that I judged to be more than two feet long. I immediately felt inadequate.

"I see you staring at our most popular Leonardo model," said Lin. "Rosa might want to try him. Billy, you might like this Warmdoll made by China's top producer, Shenzhen, with its pulsating and self-lubricating vagina. Deng uses Warmdoll when he's depressed about China's economy."

"Most of the time it's doing well," I laughed. "Bigger percentage growth than the United States."

"When the economy shows good growth, he likes Lanfang's masturbator model." Lin pointed at a brunette with huge tits next to the bed. "Uses her so much he has to keep replacing her privates. Easy to do with new slide-in vaginas."

I was stunned, not only by the array of dolls but also by the number and variety of dildos and silicone vaginas displayed on tabletops. Next to the bed was a large bottle of lubricant.

Deng said something as he picked up a huge butt plug. I couldn't imagine it being shoved up me.

"Deng said he'd like to see your penis," translated Lin. "Also I'd like to see Rosa."

Lin and Deng took off their clothes, revealing Deng's massive member, which could favorably be compared to the one ornamenting the Leonardo DiCaprio doll.

"Holy Lenin," exclaimed Rosa. "I can't get that in me. It'd hurt."

"I don't want to do this," I said, overcome with feelings of inadequacy after seeing Deng's erection.

Saying something in Mandarin, Deng pushed his member against Rosa's crotch.

"He wants to see and measure you," Lin said to Rosa.

"Measure me? You mean my vagina?" asked Rosa, looking confused. "I need more time to get into this."

"He believes," Lin tried to clarify the situation, "that East German communism will provide a good fit. He sees his penis as a perfect extension of Chinese communism."

Deng began rubbing against Rosa, speaking in Mandarin, and singing "The East is Red."

"What's he singing?" I asked, suddenly feeling jealous. Would Rosa like his bigger member over mine? Would communism win over capitalism?

Lin joined Deng and sang the English version. "The east is red. The sun is rising. China has brought forth Mao Zedong...He is the people's great savior."

The singing ended with Deng trying to take off Rosa's pants. Lin started unzipping my fly.

"Deng says capitalists have small pricks," translated Ling, trying to get her hand inside my pants. "That's why they want more money to compensate for their inadequacies."

"Ouch," I yelled as she squeezed.

"Deng is right." Lin removed her hand. "Communism always provides people with more. You're too little for me. I need big communist members."

Rosa pushed Deng away. He still came at her, mumbling in Chinese, which Lin translated as, "We make good communist babies. Look like Mao and Lenin."

Rosa grabbed a silicone vagina and shoved it over Deng's communist member, causing it to spurt.

Well, I thought, *he's got a premature-ejaculation problem.*

"Billy, let's get out of here." Rosa grabbed my hand. "I'm not interested in East meets Western communism."

"They're big but come easily." I giggled as we left. "Capitalists are small but have control.

Chapter Forty-Four

We were exhausted when we got back to La Jolla from the 1997 forum meeting.

"Do you think they were serious?" I asked, opening the door and looking forward to sleeping in my own bed. "All those sex dolls. My mind keeps trying to imagine the sexual merger of socialism and capitalism."

"Not difficult to do," answered Rosa, running down the hallway to the first-floor toilet. "I have to go badly; must be the airplane food."

"How so?" I asked through the closed door.

"You need the dictatorship of the workers," shouted Rosa over her grunting sounds. "You still cling to the idea of democracy. Do you really trust the people? They've turned it over to the rich."

"Democracy allows people some control," I answered as Rosa emerged from the bathroom looking pallid. "Maybe it was all the fondue. Cheese can do that."

"Masses don't know their own interests. Easily swayed. See how their votes protect the rich." Rosa lurched toward the stairs and headed for bed.

"Communist-party dictatorship only serves the interests of party members. Classic economic example of how self-interest determines political outcomes." I helped her up the stairs.

"Party dictatorship ensures government works in the interests of the people." She moaned as I helped her undress and get in bed.

"Can I bring anything?"

"A bucket or something to vomit in. I need to sleep; lower the blinds."

I ran downstairs to the garage and brought back a plastic bucket. Placing it next to the bed, I kissed Rosa on the cheek. Lowering the blinds, I brought a glass of water from the bathroom and placed it on the nightstand next to Rosa. She was fast asleep as I headed downstairs to my home office.

"The Davos meeting went well. I'm now closer to the Chinese leaders," I informed David Kronbach on my speakerphone. "Got close to Deng Xiaoping, but I don't trust communist party members."

"That's great," replied David. "The Smith Brothers Foundation is looking for opportunities to convince China about free trade. Deng Xiaoping spearheaded the effort. They think the coming handover will help."

"Handover?"

"Next month, July first, the Brits will return Hong Kong to China," explained David. "The Smiths and many others have a lot of money in Hong Kong banks. They think it'll be easier to invest in mainland companies."

"Don't they have a moral or ethical problem with investing in a communist country?"

"No problem if they make money," laughed David. "The moral value of actions is determined by economic return."

"Fuck," I shouted into the phone, "is that what they really believe? Killing is OK if I make money?"

"They want you to go to Hong Kong," David changed the subject, "and start a think tank to influence Chinese thinking to protect the Smith Brothers' investments. I checked, and many faculty at the University of Hong Kong can be bought."

"How do you know that?"

"We hired a professor who brought up the subject at faculty meetings. She reports that they're all scared of losing their jobs with the handover. Many Brits and other foreigners are packing their bags."

"Why me? Have I become the guru for planning foundations and think tanks?"

"Actually you are," answered David. "This is your calling in life, using other people to make money for others. I have many contacts in the foundation networks, and everyone thinks you're a genius at this game."

"Shit, that is so cynical—my only purpose is to influence the thinking of others for the benefit of people like the Smith brothers."

"Ha, you've made plenty of money at it, like me," laughed David. "Do you think you're somehow pure? Could you do anything else?"

David is right, I thought. *I only have blood on my hands. I'm evil, so I might as well follow an evil vocation.*

"I don't know about living in Hong Kong," I said into the phone, thinking about my effort with Rosa to work through our former lives and do some good. "I have no idea what it's like there."

"You'll like it," explained David. "Warm weather, beaches, luxury apartment buildings, international crowd, plus easy travel to other Asian places. You could visit Australia."

"I've got to think about this," I responded. "Remember I'm now in a relationship with Rosa Honecker. She could have visa problems traveling on a Chilean passport."

"No problem. Chinese loved East German communism; she'll easily get a visa. We can get you a two-story apartment or town house with maid quarters. You'll have a Filipino maid and Chinese cook. Hired help is dirt cheap."

"Rosa's sick right now from airline food. When she gets better, we'll talk."

Rosa liked the idea of living in Hong Kong. I called David back and confirmed the move. David said that it would take time to arrange an office and housing for us in Hong Kong. Plus I needed to complete my other work for the Smith brothers before leaving.

Two years later, on January 14, 1999, Rosa and I were greeted at the Hong Kong International Airport by a representative from the Island Shangri-La Hotel, who put us in a luxury car that whisked us into the heart of city. We were ushered from the car to the hotel elevator and escorted to our harbor-view suite.

"Holy Lenin," gasped Rosa, looking out of the glass elevator at a tapestry hanging down twenty floors in the hotel atrium. "I've never seen a hanging that large."

"Called *The Great Motherland of China*," explained our hotel escort. "It took forty artists and six months to complete. We are proud of our art collection."

"Look at that view," I said as the room's lighting and cooling systems were explained. "Is that Victoria Harbor and Kowloon on the other side?"

"Yes, your breakfast will be served in the Restaurant Petrus on the top floor."

The next day, a Friday, I headed for the offices David had rented in the Central District on Chater Road near multinational investment and banking firms. David named the think tank West-Meets-East. It was an unfortunate name, being often confused with dating and matchmaking sites.

"Good morning, sir," a sweet-looking, twenty-something Eurasian man greeted me in a strong British accent. "My name is Lawrence Chen. I was hired by David Kronbach as your office manager to guide you through Hong Kong's laws and regulations to get started. He also sent a list of University of Hong Kong faculty you might use."

"You sound British, but I guess you would since the Brits owned this place. Were you born here?"

"Yes, my father was Chinese, and my mother was British. I went to St. Paul's here in Hong Kong and then to Cambridge. I was hired by Mr. Kronbach because of my parents' contacts."

"Will they help hire people to write policy statements advancing the Smiths' investment agenda?"

"My father is president of China National Bank, and my mother is in Hong Kong's elite social circles. She'll help you get started. I understand that your partner is the daughter of the former head of the East German government. That will help!"

"What kind of social elites?"

"Before the handover, British and wealthy expats dominated social life. Even horse racing was segregated, with the Hong Kong Jockey Club having separate facilities at the Happy Valley racetrack. Now communist party leaders are part of the elite, sometimes socializing in expat circles but mostly remaining with their own."

"Am I in the expat group? Who makes up this group?"

"With Ms. Honecker by your side, you are in both. Not this weekend, but the following Saturday, I have got you an invitation for the winter dance at the Hong Kong Club, one of our oldest and most elite. There is, of course, a dress code. The dance will be black tie."

"I don't own formal clothes, and Rosa's going to need something."

"Don't worry," smiled Lawrence. "Hong Kong tailors are famous. I'll arrange for you to be fitted at Sam's Tailor over in Kowloon. They've done suits for your American presidents George Bush and Bill Clinton. Mayeelok, here in Central, will make Ms. Honecker's gowns."

"She'll love that, only wears designer stuff. What should I do besides worry about circulating among the social elite?"

"On Sunday, I have an invitation for you to attend a cocktail party at the China Club. Sam and Mayeelok will make you clothes for the party. Ms. Honecker might be asked to join. Good contacts with Hong Kong and mainland Chinese elites."

"What about the University of Hong Kong faculty? I need them to write policy statements."

"I've arranged for you to speak to a general faculty meeting next Wednesday. They want to hear about alternatives since many may lose their jobs with the handover."

"So my work begins next Wednesday and the following weekend. Any suggestions on entertaining ourselves this weekend? We'll be moving from the hotel to an apartment next week."

"Yes, I arranged it all. Actually you'll be moving into a town house in the Peak, the most exclusive residential area."

"And this weekend?"

"I can book you tours."

"Ugh, hate organized tours. I'll check at the hotel."

I returned to the Island Shangri-La and shoved a wad of Hong Kong dollars into the doorman's hand before meeting Rosa in the lobby. "My girlfriend and I want to visit some hot spots here—you know, drugs, sex shows, low life."

The doorman nodded and wrote some Chinese characters on a hotel card. "You'll want to go to the Wan Chai area and the Kit Kat Klub. Knock on the door in back and show them this card. They'll let you in. Just ask a taxi driver. They all know the place. Famous for special shows."

I met Rosa in the Lobby Lounge, where she was having tea and reading a book on the life of Mao.

"I've got a lot to tell you," I said, sitting down. I explained the events for the following weekend and the tailors.

"Mayeelok. I've heard of them. World-famous fashion designer. I hope you have the money for this," said Rosa, overjoyed at the prospect. "These Asians know how to spend."

"Fortunately David set up a special fund to dress us for the island elite. Also I found out where we can go this weekend for some fun. We'll need to dress down."

That evening the taxi driver pulled up to a dirty alley off Wan Chai Road and pointed at the dimly lit sign for the Kit Kat Klub. "Be careful," he said. "Dangerous."

I never worried being with Rosa, who could take down any man in minutes. Dressed in jeans with Rosa in a dark Dior blouse and me in an Old Navy black sweatshirt, we entered the Kit Kat Klub and were immediately surrounded by young men and women seeming to represent every nation. They greeted us with invitations. "You want boy-girl?" "Can do it any way you want." "You like ass job?" "Want to eat shit? I ate spicy food."

We made our way through the hustlers to a red door in back and showed the doorman's card to the guard. Behind the door was a garden of Asian delights.

Lying on a waist-high table, a Filipino woman was shooting darts from her vagina at a circle target with differing numbers of penises. It turned out to be a betting game with a bull's-eye of ten penises. A group of men waving dollar bills stood around betting as young boys jerked them off into beer glasses.

"I did similar stuff in Paris," I confided to Rosa. "I participated in a snuff show."

"You did a snuff show? We did something like that in the Stasi. Screwed them to death," she laughed, pointing at another large table where a woman was engaged with a live octopus. One tentacle in was her vagina and another in her ass.

"Wow," Rosa exclaimed. "I heard about that, but I've never seen it. Popular in Japan. I've seen etchings of women in different postures with octopuses and squids."

"You want some smoke—opium, crack, whatever?" Asked a tall topless woman with Disney characters on her breasts. A Mickey Mouse tattoo was on her lower belly with its finger pointing down. On her arms, Snow White was having sex with a variety of characters including Dumbo.

"Opium," Rosa brightened. "I haven't had any for years. Probably pretty good here."

"You were addicted," I reminded her. "We should try something else."

"Have you had Yah Dong?" asked the Disney woman. "We got new batch from Thailand. Smoke crack and drink Yah Dong and see the gods."

"Never heard of Yah Dong," I replied, trying to name in my head the Disney characters on her body.

"Made with cobra blood; works on men and women. We have special room for you. Crack and Yah Dong, fifteen hundred Hong Kong dollars—you can stay all night. Also can order transgender, multiple organ, and deformed companions, along with the usual boys and girls."

"Deformed?" Rosa wondered. "I did some after we crippled them."

"Some people like legless boys and girls; a legless and armless she-male costs more."

"She-male?" Rosa asked. "You mean with breasts and penis."

"Or male top, female bottom, your choice," explained the Disney-covered woman. "Or you can have both."

I looked questioningly at Rosa, wondering what she'd decide or if she wanted to leave.

"I'd like to try this," Rosa consulted with me. "We've never done this type of thing. Almost with Deng Xiaoping, but this sounds better."

"You want the dart shooter and octopus woman or spicy turds," I laughed.

"I'm tempted by the legless and armless she-male," she said seriously.

"Two thousand Hong Kong dollars—get you all—room, crack, yah dong, and she-male."

"What about the other type—male top and female bottom? I'd like both." I was feeling excited.

"Only two hundred more—give you bargain—you're nice. Only give bargain to special people."

We were led out back to a little apartment with toilet, sink, and several large futons on the floor. The wallpaper was done with the latest Japanese anime porn. The Disney woman brought in crack and a pipe along with a jar of brown-looking liquid and a couple glasses.

"You have smoke and drink Yah Dong," we were ordered. "I bring special companions in little time."

The crack and aphrodisiac took hold. We decided to try all the positions on the anime wallpaper until it felt like I'd seriously injured my back. I stretched out to take the pressure off my back. Panting, Rosa straddled me.

"Who is it?" I called out, hearing a knock at the door.

"Special companions, we bring in."

Two wheelbarrows were brought into the room and their contents dumped onto the futons. Two armless and legless young people, one with melon-shaped breasts and a full-size penis and the other with a vagina and beard, now lay next to us.

Chapter Forty-Five

Sunday morning we were groggy from fatigue as we ate breakfast in the Petrus and stared out at Victoria Harbor. We'd made it to the hotel just as the restaurant opened. We were starving from the thirty-six-hour orgy that left me with a bad back and both of us worrying about our hearts.

"I'm feeling my age," I admitted. "Approaching sixty is not a good time to be smoking crack. I've got to find a chiropractor for my back. I may never be able to stand straight again."

"You should try the hotel spa," suggested Rosa, wolfing down a stack of pancakes, which she rarely ate but hunger had driven her to ordering. "A good soak, a sauna, and massage will help."

My ravenous hunger had led me to order a plate of spicy noodles and eggs Benedict along with croissants and a bagel with cream cheese and lox. In the end, my stomach couldn't hold all the food, and I left the bagel untouched.

"I worry about my heart," said Rosa. "When we dozed at the Kit Kat Klub, I'd awake thinking my heart had stopped. I'm sore between the legs."

"Shouldn't have asked to try the octopus; the suction cups must have been rough."

Frowning, Rosa stared at the ferries crossing the harbor. "I feel bad about the whole thing. Don't get me wrong. I liked the pleasure, but now I feel weird about the legless and armless she-male fucking me. I can't believe I did it."

"I feel depressed," I sighed, wrapping noodles around my fork. "Actually more than depressed. I feel guilty."

"Guilty?" Rosa gestured for the waiter to bring more coffee. "You didn't kill or hurt anyone, except maybe when you threw the bearded tranny against the wall. Why'd you do that?"

"I was suddenly repulsed at doing it with an armless and legless person. It seemed 'evil,' for the lack of a better word."

Rosa sat back looking at me and then reached across the table to stroke my cheek.

"I think I love you," she confessed. "You make me want to care for others. The Kit Kat Klub gave me a bad feeling about myself. Now I feel guilty about the Stasi interrogations."

"I feel the way I did when I killed people, full of remorse." I started thinking about Rosa. I used to run from relationships. Now I wanted to care for her.

"I love you." The words came slowly and unexpectedly from my mouth. I had never thought I'd say that to anyone.

"It was evil, what we did," I said, agreeing with Rosa. "We took advantage of those disabled people. Can't believe I threw him against the wall. I was in a rage about myself."

"Free market," Rosa smiled at me. "People are free to sell themselves, and you're free to buy them."

"The free market is evil. We should be taking care of people, not using them for our own pleasure."

"Never thought I'd hear you say that." Rosa finished her pancakes and took some of my toast to mop up the remaining syrup and butter. "You'll be a good communist yet."

"Fuck communism. You didn't do much good in the Stasi."

"I thought I was protecting the people's interests," groaned Rosa. "I just hurt people."

"All I do is bad. Toots always said I shouldn't have been born. I'm sure the people I hurt feel the same way."

"But we're doing the same thing with this West-Meets-East think tank," reminded Rosa. "We'll be protecting and advancing the Smiths' interests. I think they're evil. All that oil money destroying the environment. All those mass killings from guns they promoted."

"You're right; they want to sell oil and buy up Chinese companies. Maybe they won't kill anyone. It could lead to world peace," I suggested halfheartedly.

"If China grows, so will world pollution. Communists aren't interested in the environment, only in economic growth," warned Rosa. "Cities will be enveloped in smog with more deaths."

"You think it'll be that bad?"

"Think of China's population if they all drive cars and use the Smiths' world oil supplies." Rosa pointed out the window. "I bet in a few years the smog will cloud this view of Victoria Harbor."

"You think our West-Meets-East Institute will kill," I worried.

"The world would have shortened lives, lung cancer, and weakened hearts." Rosa began listing possible spin-offs from our work. "Pollution could mean more disabled babies, like the two we used at the Kit Kat Klub. I think the one you threw has brain damage. Its eyes were dilated after its head hit the wall; didn't seem better when we left."

"I'm exhausted," I confessed, pushing back my chair. "What can I do about it? I'm killing people by promoting free markets and China's economy."

"You've always been killing with this free-market crap." Rosa put her napkin on the table. "We should do something about it."

"How?"

"Let's use West-Meets-East to help people and say fuck to the Smiths' interests." Rosa stood up, yawning. "I need a shower to wash off all the evil and then bed. I want happy dreams, not demons."

"I'll figure something out," I said, pushing my chair back and straining to stand straight. Rosa came around the table to help me. We wobbled walking to the elevators and eventually our bed.

The demons took over. Armless and legless trannies joined my parade of murder victims. Africans, starving from climate-change-induced drought, stood with emaciated bodies and cupped hands and pleaded for food from grocery trucks whizzing by bearing the Smith brothers' logo. Killed by terrorism and police violence, corpses riddled with bullets stood, their fingers pointing at me. Ayn Rand appeared holding over her head copies of *The Fountainhead* and *Atlas Shrugged* as her feet trampled the masses into a bloody pulp.

I kept waking up covered in perspiration and feeling my heart racing. After hours of tossing and turning, we both woke around seven in the evening, thirsty and still fatigued.

"Do you think we should get up?" asked Rosa. "Maybe we could order room service. A little food and drink will put me back to sleep. I'm still tired."

After staggering to the bathroom and trying to straighten my back, I ordered two club sandwiches and took a couple small vodka bottles and orange juices from the minibar. Putting on hotel bathrobes, we sat sipping screwdrivers and looking out at the harbor as we waited for room service.

"I can't take it," I admitted. "Dreams are worse than ever. My whole life is a failure. All I have is money and murder on my mind."

"You have me," replied Rosa. "I know what you mean. What can we do?"

"We could try working with the Chinese communist party to do some good. You've got experience with communism. It could be better than the free market."

"I think they're about equal in terror," observed Rosa. "I don't know about China. They seem to be trying to combine the two. This could double the harm."

Hearing a knock, Rosa got up and let the waiter in with our sandwiches.

"Have you read the Chinese constitution?" asked Rosa, bringing me my sandwich.

"Thank you. It is hard for me to stand. I wonder if I can get a masseur to come to our room."

"You might think of acupuncture; this is China," suggested Rosa. She called the concierge, who said he could have an acupuncturist to our room within an hour.

"The acupuncturist will help." Rosa sat down and started smearing mustard between the sandwich layers. "I read their constitution. It's not bad and probably better than anything written by Ayn Rand."

Laughing, I warned, "Don't attack my life's guide. I can imagine a debate between supporters of Ayn Rand and supporters of the Chinese constitution. Maybe truth would result. Or, even better, world peace."

"I have a copy," said Rosa, standing up and going to her bag in the closet.

"You just happen to be carrying around the Chinese constitution. That's weird."

"Got some Chinese stuff at a bookstore before we left. I read about Hong Kong before leaving. The book on Mao's life has the constitution in back. You saw me reading it in the lobby."

"Here's Article One," said Rosa, sitting down and taking a bite from her sandwich.

"The People's Republic of China," she said as she sat back and chewed her food, "is a socialist state under the people's democratic dictatorship led by the working class and based on the alliance of workers and peasants."

"What the fuck is a 'democratic dictatorship'?"

"Like Germany, it means the dictatorship of the communist party, which represents the interests of workers and peasants."

"I guess we can dictate happiness," I smiled, finishing the salad that came with the sandwich.

"You've got a piece of lettuce stuck between your teeth." Rosa handed me the wrapped toothpicks that came with the meal.

"But we're only meeting the party elite, not workers and peasants." I used the toothpick to remove food particles, including strange-looking hairs.

"Christ, where did these come from?" I spat the lettuce and hairs onto my plate.

"Could be from the Kit Kat Klub," laughed Rosa. "Theoretically the party elite are working in the interests of workers and peasants."

I gagged, looking at the short black hairs mixed into my spit with bread crumbs, chicken, and shreds of lettuce.

"Are these yours?"

"How would I know?" answered Rosa disgustedly. "It might be from the tranny. The one you threw against the wall."

"What should we ask for?" I wondered, feeling groggy from the screwdriver and food as fatigue again took over my body. "Could use the Smith money to invest in health companies and others that improve the welfare of Chinese workers."

"You think the Smiths will be OK with that?" responded Rosa, heading for the bed. "I'm wasted. Wonder if I'll ever get my strength back."

"Hope I didn't get something." I wearily got in bed as a knock announced the arrival of the acupuncturist.

Opening the door, Rosa ushered in a bearded acupuncturist.

"My husband strained his back," explained Rosa.

"No problem. I'm Bian Que. Specialize in back pain. Acupuncture works best for back problems."

Bian opened his bag of needles next to the bed where I lay sprawled on my stomach.

Putting needles in my back, Bain told me, "This will cause the release of pain-killing chemicals. They trigger the release of natural opioids. Your muscles will relax. You will feel sleepy."

I tried to fight back the drowsiness, but within minutes, I was fast asleep. I wasn't conscious of Rosa escorting Bain from the room and paying the bill.

Chapter Forty-Six

By April 1999, the West-Meets-East Institute was in full swing with English and Australian professors from the University of Hong Kong writing policy papers on the Chinese economy and methods of promoting people's happiness and well-being. We paid high salaries to Chinese scholars to translate and send them to party officials.

Rosa and I were in full swing in Hong Kong's elite social circles. I'd spent an hour having my body measured at Sam's Tailor and let them select fabrics and styles for every occasion including formal and sportswear. My bedroom closet was stuffed with the latest fashions.

Rosa spent several days visiting Mayeelok carefully selecting designs and materials. This was followed by many days for fittings and adjustments. We were a smart-looking couple in Hong Kong's high society.

By the spring of 2000, we were caught up in Hong Kong's social whirl. At the China Club, I met mainland business men always interested in extra cash for investing in their companies or for starting new enterprises. Upper-echelon communist leaders welcomed the idea of promoting well-being and happiness. At one evening function, we talked to Jing Qishan, a member of the Central Executive Committee of the Chinese communist party and Harvard graduate. He declared the goal of well-being and happiness "Confucian."

"We're losing our ethical direction," explained Jing. "Since the Cultural Revolution, people are only pursuing wealth. Greed is the new motivator. We are resurrecting Confucian values to provide moral guidance to the masses. Fighting over money should be replaced by harmony."

"Don't you teach Maoist-Marxist thought in schools?" asked Rosa. "Doesn't it provide a national ethic?"

"How'd that work in East German schools?" Jing smiled. "Didn't East German students help tear down the wall?"

"I don't think school indoctrination works," I said, reflecting on my own patriotic education in US schools. "It was just boring flag salutes, mind-numbing slanted history, and nationalist songs. Seems to have had some effect with all the chants of 'USA, USA, USA.'"

"We can hit the emotions," said Jing. "I think most school graduates love the Chinese motherland and feel patriotic hearing our national anthem. But their rational minds are plotting to make money. They all want to be rich."

"That's like American students," I added.

"I know from my time at Harvard," replied Jing, emphasizing his American accent. "A few talked about social justice, but most wanted high-paying jobs."

"Our West-Meets-East Institute is promoting well-being," I said, taking another drink from a passing tray. "We're trying to get material in the *People's Daily*. Any good Confucian scholars in Hong Kong we could consult?"

"Talk to Mou Zongsan. He's leading the new Confucian movement. He hangs out at a place called the Kit Kat Klub in Wan Chai."

I controlled my reaction at the mention of the Kit Kat Klub and calmly commented, "I'll check him out. Good talking, but I see Wang Jianlin. He can help get our messages out through his entertainment enterprises."

"Check out Mou at the Kit Kat Klub," said Jing, who started walking toward a group of local officials near the food table. "Send me some material, and I'll see about getting it in the *People's Daily*."

Pleased with my networking with Jing Qishan, I approached Wang Jianlin. He was deep in discussion with Hong Kong's wealthiest man, Li Ka-shing. Li, I knew from my contacts with the Smith Brothers, was heavily invested in North American oil.

"Billy Durant," Li greeted me. "I've heard about you from the Smiths. You should contact me." He handed me his card. "I know your work against those climate-change fanatics. Meet Wang Jianlin. He'll help get your message out in the mainland."

Rosa waved at me from across the room as I finished talking with Wang. As I approached Rosa, she pointed at the door opening onto a large balcony off an upper-floor apartment in the Mid-Levels of Hong Kong.

Leaning against the rail and looking at the sparkling harbor, Rosa whispered, "I was talking to some high-powered real-estate people when they noticed you talking to Wang Jianlin. He's a big developer in Shanghai."

"Yeah, I wanted to get our messages into his entertainment empire."

"We should go to Shanghai," urged Rosa. "We could hook up with one of Wang's associates. The men I was talking to think the Smiths would like to invest in Chinese businesses."

"You'll never believe it," I muttered, not wanting others to hear the name of our infamous club. "But I've been advised that the leading Hong Kong Confucian scholar hangs out at the Kit Kat Klub."

"You're kidding me," gasped Rosa.

"Jing Qishan is a member of the Central Committee and promotes Confucianism to fill a so-called 'ethical void' left by the Cultural Revolution. We're going to have to talk to the Confucian scholar."

"We can go to Shanghai in September," Rosa informed me. "The guys I talked to gave me a list of contacts including one for Wang Jianlin's advisor. Investments in pharmaceutical and food products would promote well-being."

"September?"

"Many on the list will be there for a big conference on Chinese health and nutrition," explained Rosa. "It ends in a couple days. I think we could do some good there."

On September 15, 2000, we boarded a Dragon Air flight to Shanghai. Met at the airport by representative of Chun King foods, we were taken to the Peace Hotel on the famous Bund along the Huangpu River. After registering and leaving our luggage, the Chun King representative took us to a trade center on Nanjing Road. Above the door, in English and Mandarin, a sign greeted us, "Welcome to Health and Prosperity in the Growing Food and Pharmaceutical industries—Leave Your Bad Feelings Behind."

Inside, entertainers dressed in costumes of foreign countries were dancing between exhibits. In the dairy section, Chinese dressed in lederhosen were yodeling and doing a Swiss folk dance. In the meat section, little Chinese girls wearing cowboy hats and boots were singing "Deep in the Heart of Texas." The poultry area was filled with Colonel Sanders imitators clucking and dancing around a one-story, plastic, chicken leg.

"KFC wants to expand in China," said our Chun King escort, who turned out to be a Korean American named Tony Lee, born in Queens, New York.

"Tony, what are you doing in China?" asked Rosa.

"Chun King has opportunities in China. American Chinese food is becoming popular here. You can see our exhibit in the canned- and frozen-food sections."

"American Chinese food is becoming popular here," I repeated in disbelief.

"Used to eat Chun King back in Queens," said Tony, smacking his lips. "I always thought it was tasty. Mom would say, 'No Kim Chi tonight; we eat Chinese.'"

"Why do they like it?" asked Rosa as we were led through a dance troupe dressed as food cans doing Rockettes-style leg kicks in front of the Chun King exhibit.

"Italian spices added by Jeno Francesco Paulucci back in the 1940s. He thought Chinese food was too bland. After Chun King, he did Jeno's Pizza Rolls. Both are popular here. They love Chun King's Chop Suey. Chop Suey is an American invention. When Chun King added Italian spices, it became an American staple."

I noticed a booth off to the side of the Chun King exhibit sporting a bilingual sign, "Eat Real American Chinese Food Here."

"We're looking for Chinese investment opportunities," I reminded Tony.

"I know. Your cute little assistant, Lawrence Chen, phoned me and arranged the escort."

"Cute?" Rosa wondered.

"We hooked up last time I was in Hong Kong."

Tony took us past the Chun King exhibit to a product-display section for powdered milk.

"This is the best investment. Hard to get enough cow's milk in China. A big push for parents to give their children more to strengthen bones. Best is baby formulas. Breast feeding is old-fashioned, and mothers work."

We stood in front of the exhibit for Guangzhou Milk and Baby Formula. Large bilingual banners read, "Our Milk Makes You Stronger than Mao" and "Better than Breast Milk. Life-saving Baby Formula."

"I'll introduce you to Zhang Gaoli," said Tony. "He wants money to expand operations. Don't mention the Baby Likes Nipple scandal."

"Baby Likes Nipple scandal?" I wondered.

"Name of formula made with water from Pearl River, lots of deaths. They offered canned milk back in the eighties called Mother's Dream sold to pregnant women to help fetuses grow. Many born without arms and legs and with mixed genitals."

"Shit," I said. "Any get to Hong Kong?"

"Popular in underground sex shows. Many recruited for Hong Kong and Bangkok clubs."

"I don't think we want to get mixed up in this," said Rosa. "We want products to improve lives."

"Don't worry," said Tony as he guided us to a fat Chinese man with a flowing white beard. "They stopped relying on the Pearl River. Zhang even bought glaciers for high-priced products. Big seller among the rich; they rush to buy exclusive things like Glacier Water Baby Formula."

"Good meet you," said Zhang in broken English as he stroked his beard. "I hear interest in money for milk and babies."

Rosa and I explained the Smiths' investment interests, pitching them toward improving human well-being.

"Products always good. Help mothers. Help children. You no go wrong giving me money," smiled Zhang.

Telling Zhang that we would explain the investment opportunity to the Smiths and send him material after returning to Hong Kong, we asked Tony to take us back to the hotel.

"I'm stuck here with the Chun King exhibit for another couple hours," responded Tony. "You can wait or take a taxi. I recommend walking down Nanjing Road and following signs to the Bund. Signs are bilingual in English. You'll see part of Shanghai that way."

We liked the idea of walking. Tony took us to the hall's exit onto Nanjing. Stores lined the road. There were many signs pointing down alleys off Nanjing that read "Learn the English Words Your Boss Wants to Hear."

Rosa stopped and pointed at a sign in written only in English for foreigners: "Learn Chinese Love Secrets." An arrow pointed down a narrow side street.

Chapter Forty-Seven

"I can't believe we fell for that scam," declared Rosa, opening the door to our Peace Hotel room overlooking the Huangpu River.

"Well, your lust for beauty cost us five hundred US dollars. Were you a communist secretly wishing to be an international fashion plate?" I laughed, putting our small shopping bag on the bed.

"It said, 'Learn Chinese Love Secrets.' Who would have imagined it meant foot-binding?" Rosa opened the bag and took out small soft shoes and binding cloth. "I paid five hundred for this stuff. I can't believe it."

"Look, I paid fifty dollars just to get us into the Tunnel of Chinese Sex. The guy whispered in my ear that we'd both get turned on. What a laugh!"

"I almost got sick," said Rosa, "looking at photos of bound feet and deformed little girls."

"He said real Chinese men get hard just looking at tiny feet."

"That was a century ago. Did you get hard?" asked Rosa as she decided to keep the slippers and binding material as souvenirs.

"What do you think? Why did you agree to pay five hundred dollars for, what did he call it, 'Lotus Feet' treatment?"

"I think my feet are too big. I wonder if they broke any bones trying to make my lotus feet."

"You screamed and had a little trouble walking. Do you think I should call a doctor?"

"You were suckered by that see-my-art routine," smiled Rosa.

"Nice young couple. I thought they were legit. They said it was a modern Chinese art movement."

"You couldn't refuse giving them all that money. What was it? Fifty dollars. Didn't you think it was weird when they asked for a loan just before entering the gallery pleading they were poor students?"

"No," I replied. "Toots always said Chinese were the most honest people in the world. I'd heard Chinese students struggled and loved learning.
How could I refuse?"

"That gallery owner had a good laugh when they took your money
and ran—modern Chinese art movement, my ass. Now we find out from
the front desk that it is a common scam against foreigners."

"I can see why Jing said that Chinese had lost their ethical values. We'll
need to contact that Confucian scholar when we get back tomorrow."

"I'm hungry," announced Rosa. "It's six, and we should find some
dinner."

"We could eat here," I suggested. "Or ask the concierge for restaurant
recommendations."

"I heard the night kitchens are a must to try. We passed a couple
streets near here where they were setting up."

"Night kitchens?" I was leery about eating street food.

"Many people eat out because they lack apartment kitchens or lodge
with others. They don't have much money. Stoves and grills are set up
in the street along with plastic tables and chairs. Supposed to be really
good and authentic. Mentioned in all the guidebooks."

We left the hotel, walked away from the Bund and the Huangpu River,
and looked down side streets. Finally we spied a narrow street lined with
cooking stalls and plastic chairs and tables.

Walking past several stalls, I noted people laughing and pointing at
us. We tried to read the menus, but they were filled with Chinese characters. We stopped and asked a woman wearing a filthy garment covered
with food stains what she was selling. I don't know why, but when she
answered in Chinese, the words "No speakee Chinesee" came rolling out
of my mouth. People at tables roared with laughter as they gestured at us
with their chopsticks.

"What's going on?" I whispered to Rosa.

"I read they make fun of foreigners and think if you don't speak
Chinese, you're stupid. They're very ethnocentric. Let's just point. It
should be good."

"I'm skipping the insects." I pointed at a neat display of various insects lined up in a row. "I can't eat skewered grasshoppers and scorpions or the snakes. What are those things crawling around in that basket?"

"I don't know. Maybe grubs," answered Rosa, stopping at a stall and pointing at various dishes they were serving others.

The stall owner nodded and filled two bowls with substances I couldn't name. They gave us chopsticks. We sat on some small, white, plastic chairs, balanced our bowls, and tried to manipulate our chopsticks.

"Look at that." I pointed at the stall's cook who was taking bowls and chopsticks to the street gutter and rinsing them with gray-looking water. "That doesn't look sanitary."

"I wonder if that is the reason why I see many people handing cooks their own bowls," said Rosa. "They also seem to have their own chopsticks."

"These people eat this every day. They don't look sick," continued Rosa. "You're just a finicky American; eat up."

The next day we boarded the Dragon Air flight back to Hong Kong after a night of tormented stomachs.

"I worried about the food," I said, helping Rosa sit down as she clutched her stomach. "You said all those people looked well and concluded the food wouldn't bother us."

"People have different gut flora; changes with national foods," moaned Rosa, looking out the airplane window at the disappearing Shanghai skyline. "We just need to adapt."

"Will you be OK to see the Confucian scholar tonight?"

"Why don't we wait to see how I feel," suggested Rosa, burying her face in an airplane pillow and waving away a plate of steamed dumplings brought by the attendant.

It took a couple days before Rosa felt well enough to visit the Confucian scholar, Mou Zongsan. I'd kept the card with Chinese characters allowing us access to the back room.

"I can't take any wild stuff," informed Rosa as our cab headed to the alley with the Kit Kat Klub.

"I don't even know what he looks like. Will he be in the front room or in back? I can't take any more crack and sex play," I confessed.

"We're looking for someone named Mou Zongsan," I told the guard at the front door. The guard erupted in peals of laughter.

"Why the laughing?" asked Rosa.

"Mou always tells good jokes," replied the guard. "How about, Confucius say, 'Virginity like bubble. One prick, all gone.' Or Confucius say, 'Man who do business in whorehouse get jerked around.'"

"Is he here?" I asked as the guard tried to stop laughing.

Stuck in a laughing mode, the guard's belly shook. "Confucius say, 'Man with hand in pocket feel cocky all day long.' Confucius say, 'Squirrel who runs up woman's leg not find nuts.'"

"Jesus, is Mou a jokester?" I wanted to know.

"Mou thinks the world should run on laughter. It will be a better place," replied the guard. "You'll find him at a table in back. Can't miss him with his big belly; many pay to rub it. He also makes money telling jokes. There is a little bowl in front of him. Remember to tip."

Entering the Kit Kat Klub, we had to press against a wall to pass a bestiality game that had replaced the vaginal dart shooting. A number of different animals, including a small pony, were in a pen next to a woman kneeling doggy fashion on the floor. As best as I could tell, the betting had something to do with the fit between the animal and woman. I couldn't figure it out. The pony had highest-posted odds.

"That must be him," said Rosa, pointing at a back table where a fat man dressed in tattered monk clothing sat. In front of him was a small, teak table with a golden-colored bowl.

"Are you Mou Zongsan?" I asked.

"Confucius say," giggled Mou, "'Man who fart in temple, sit in own pew.'"

I didn't think he'd stop laughing. When he finally did, he pointed at the bowl. "Twenty Hong Kong dollars for joke. You rub my belly, that's thirty."

"I was told to talk to you," I found myself shouting over the yells from bettors as the pony was put in place, "by a member of the Central

Committee. They want to revive Confucianism to provide people with ethical values lost in the Cultural Revolution."

"Confucius say, 'Man with ethics and no money starves.'" Mou pointed at his bowl.

"We're willing to pay you to help write Confucian essays to influence the Central Committee," said Rosa, covering her ears to protect them from the loud shouts as the pony mounted the woman.

"There is only one Confucian ethical principle you need to know," Mou smiled. "Communist party will never follow it."

"What's that?" shouted Rosa over the noise.

"What you do not want done to yourself, do not do to others," smiled Mou. "Simple idea, but few can practice it. Or try 'Learn to masturbate; come in handy.'"

"We're serious," I said, exasperated by the jokes and noise as the woman screamed in pain and the winners yelled for their earnings.

"So am I. I gave you best ethical principle and good jokes. How about, Confucius say, 'Man who get kicked in testicles, left holding the bag.'"

"I can't believe this is really the new Confucian scholarship," I wondered. "We can't get anywhere with this."

"Please put money in bowl for final laugh."

I put a bunch of bills in the bowl as Mou pointed at Rosa and said, "Confucius say, 'Woman who dance wearing jockstrap, have make-believe ballroom.'"

At that moment, the pony broke its restraints and started bucking its way around the room scattering customers. Avoiding its hooves, we rushed out.

"Well that was an eye-opener," I said to Rosa after we'd found a cab to take us back to our town house. "I don't think the neo-Confucian movement will be much help."

The next day I went to my office and arranged for future policy reports to be sent to Jing Qishan for possible publication in the *People's Daily*. I asked Lawrence to hire a lawyer to find out about investments in Guangzhou Milk and Baby Formula Company. Also I began writing a report for the Smith brothers on the value of investing in milk given the strong demand in China.

I spent the next six months issuing reports and worrying about doing more harm if the policy statements on free markets were actually published in the *People's Daily*. Rosa occasionally complained about her stomach. But she said there was nothing serious.

Then things rapidly changed. On June 5, 2001, Rosa phoned me at the office and said, "I feel terrible. I think I should see a doctor."

"I'll ask Lawrence to get a doctor's appointment for you."

Lawrence arranged an appointment for the next morning with a Dr. Wong. When he heard we'd recently returned from Shanghai, he recommended that Rosa go to Queen Mary Hospital for tests.

"Mainlanders have parasites that cause digestive problems," said Dr. Wong. "You probably don't have any. It could be just a passing digestive disorder. But best to check."

I went with Rosa to the Queen Mary Hospital and waited as they ran a series of tests.

After returning to our town house, Rosa ran for the toilet.

"Hope that doesn't keep up," said Rosa, emerging from the bathroom and going to bed.

She was only in bed a few minutes when she made another dash for the toilet.

"Oh my God!" she yelled from behind the closed door. "There's blood in my shit."

I immediately called Dr. Wong's office and left a message. He called back almost immediately.

"You say there's blood in her stool and she has diarrhea."

"Yes," I answered the doctor. "Is it serious?"

"Sounds like dysentery," answered Dr. Wong. "It could be a bacteria or parasite. We'll have to wait for the test results. This will take time. Tell her to rest and drink a lot of fluids."

"Is there anything I can do for her?"

"Nothing until we get test results. Probably not serious," Dr. Wong assured me. "I will call the hospital to tell them that Rosa is experiencing dysentery so that they can look for causes in the blood and stool tests. Did you eat anything strange in Shanghai?"

When I told him about the night kitchen, his first question was, "Did you bring your own eating utensils and dishes?"

Hearing my no, Dr. Wong said, "That could be the source. Sometimes night kitchens use contaminated water to clean their dishes."

The hospital called the next day and asked for Rosa to come in for more tests and to bring stool samples.

The day after the second series of tests, Dr. Wong called in the morning. "I've good and bad news. The good news is that the cause has been identified."

"What is it?" I asked, worried about what I would hear.

"I should talk to Rosa," replied Dr. Wong.

I handed the phone to Rosa.

"Oh my God," Rosa said into the phone. "How serious is it?"

"What'd he say?" I was having a hard time containing myself.

Rosa waved at me to be quiet as she listened intently.

Then in tears, she handed me the phone. "Dr. Wong wants to explain."

"What?" I said into the phone. "I can't spell that. I want to write it down."

Over the phone, Dr. Wong spelled out "e-n-t-o-m-o-e-b-a h-i-s-t-o-l-y-t-i-c-a" as I hastily wrote out the name.

"It's a parasite and can live in other organs. Besides dysentery, it can cause liver abscesses," informed Dr. Wong. "We should start treatment tomorrow."

"Will she be OK?"

"There are drugs that will kill it. I must warn that you the parasite can be fatal."

Chapter Forty-Eight

"Can be fatal" echoed through my mind. I asked Dr. Wong to recommend a nurse. I called Lawrence with the nurse's information and asked him to make arrangements.

"You'll be OK," I tried to comfort Rosa. "I'm getting a nurse. I've alerted our household staff. You must drink plenty of liquids."

"Is this how I end my days?" moaned Rosa. "A little bug crawling around in me. After all those people I killed."

"Don't be dramatic. The drugs will kill it. You'll be fine."

After the nurse arrived at noon, I went to my office in Central and called David in Tulsa.

"Rosa is seriously ill," I told David. "I want to get her back as soon as possible."

The line was silent for a minute. I knew David was thinking through the possibilities, including the reaction of the Smith brothers.

"You have to do what you have to do," David broke the silence. "I can get someone to take over your work. Will Lawrence be able to manage on his own until I get someone out there?"

"Yes, everything is operational. I've made contacts with Chinese Central Committee officials. We've got scholars churning out policy papers. Some will be discussed in the *People's Daily.* Also I arranged for possible investments in the Guangzhou Milk and Baby Formula Company. This is a big growth area in China."

"Milk and baby formula," exclaimed David. "The Smiths will never agree. They want to keep their fingers in energy. How about coal?"

"We have a scholar working on that. He claims China's coal use is causing an epidemic of respiratory diseases and lung cancer. He predicts they will stop using coal sometime in the immediate future."

"Shit," replied David. "You think the Smiths care about that?"

"There could be a couple million deaths in a few years. You have no idea how bad the pollution is getting."

"I'll send a replacement to follow up on coal investments," said David. "I don't think a couple million will hurt the Chinese population. They've got enough people. Forget about the milk and baby formula stuff."

I hung up feeling disturbed by David's callous response. "Why do I continue to work for these people?" I wondered. "From Vietnam to the present, I'm a calculator of death. It feeds my anger but destroys my well-being."

Worried and wanting to get Rosa back to our home in La Jolla, I crossed my fingers that parasite treatment would be available in the San Diego area. I called the medical school at the University of California in San Diego. After being transferred to a number of different offices, I finally received information on whom to contact from the dean's office.

"Best place in the area and one of the best in the world," said a helpful voice after I explained the situation, "is the naval hospital in Balboa Park. They treat sailors with parasites from all over the world."

I called the Naval Medical Center San Diego in Balboa, the very hospital where I had been born, and was immediately transferred to the Department of Infectious Diseases. I talked to the nurse, Julie Crane, who, when she heard the parasite's name, said they had the facilities and doctors to treat Rosa. "You should come in as soon as get back. This is not a bug you want to play around with. Early treatment can keep it under control."

Our Hong Kong town house and staff were to be taken over by my replacement, who arrived a week after my conversation with David. By July 1, 2001, we were on a plane to LA and then to San Diego.

Rosa and I were happy to be home. The drugs given in Hong Kong seemed to have brought the dysentery under control.

"I'm feeling better already," smiled Rosa as I carried our luggage to our upstairs bedroom. "Look for me on the deck. I want to say hello to the ocean and beach."

"Don't start looking for girls," I laughed. "I'm wondering how the last one is doing out in the kelp beds."

"Billy, don't remind me," yelled Rosa. "That's the past; now I want to be good."

After putting the bags in the bedroom, I joined her on the deck.

"I can see some seals over there," pointed Rosa. "It's so beautiful looking from here. Victoria Harbor seemed so artificial with all those skyscrapers. This is wild. I'll be OK."

"Great," I responded. "I'm happy to leave Hong Kong. Your medical issue gave me another reason. I was looking for an excuse. Frankly I hated the social life. They were all worried about appearances—dress, type of car, cost of home, amount of servants—the list goes on. Too status conscious for me."

"I liked the clothes," smiled Rosa. "But we couldn't do much with the Chinese communists. They're so greedy."

"You might miss the Kit Kat Klub?" I giggled. "Not sure we'll find anything like it in San Diego."

"Maybe Tijuana," suggested Rosa.

"Think you can sleep? It was a long flight."

"I'll take a sleeping pill. It shouldn't be a problem." Rosa yawned. "I'm still tired from the medicines and this little bug. I've named it."

"You've named your parasite," I said, surprised at the idea.

"I played with the names of the great killers of history—you know, Genghis Khan, Alexander the Great, and all the other butchers including the most recent, Hitler and Stalin."

"And you decided on what name?"

"Rasputin. He inspired the czar to kill," said Rosa, heading up to the bedroom. "I like that he was a mystic and saved the royal son who had hemophilia. His very name will kill this bug."

"Did he die?"

"You mean the son. Of course they all died. We can't escaped death. Rasputin was poisoned and his body thrown in St. Petersburg's Moika River."

It was too late to call my office, but I planned to stop by the next morning before taking Rosa. In Hong Kong, I'd arranged a one o'clock appointment with the parasitologist, Dr. Earl Bruner. I had checked with the American Society for Parasitologists. He was cited as one of the best in the country, having published a large number of research papers.

The next morning I looked askance at my office sign: "Smith Brothers Center for Tax Cuts and Limited Government."

"How could I have let my life get this low?" I asked myself.

"Welcome back," greeted Chelsea Connelly, the project manager. "Sorry about your partner's illness. I'd like to hear about Hong Kong. My husband and I are planning a China visit. High on our tourist list."

"I'm taking Rosa to the doctor this afternoon," I explained to Chelsea. "Anything I need to deal with right away?"

"The Ayn Rand Freedom Institute wants you to do a lecture next week in San Francisco on—they already selected a title." She looked down at her notes. "'How Free Markets and Individualism Saved China.'"

"You mean, killed millions," I immediately reacted and noted Chelsea's surprised look. "I'll let them know after Rosa gets checked out."

"Did they kill millions?" gasped Chelsea at the idea that free markets could harm others. "I read your articles while you were in Hong Kong. You argue that free markets save lives."

"You live and learn," I replied. "Any other pressing business?"

"David called and wants you to be available if your Hong Kong replacement needs help. He said to shred the studies showing that coal usage will kill millions of Chinese."

"Right," I responded angrily. "Smiths want a new version of the Bataan Death March with footprints in coal dust. Fuckers will kill the world with greed."

Chelsea's face became stony. I wondered if she secretly reported back to David and the Smith brothers.

"I'll call David and let him know I'm back, and then I'm going home to take Rosa to the hospital."

I bundled Rosa into the car, putting my briefcase full of her Hong Kong medical reports on the back seat.

"How are you feeling?" I asked, starting the car.

"OK, just a little discomfort in my belly. Hope this Dr. Bruner can get rid of it."

"*Entomoeba histolytica*," commented Dr. Bruner, looking through Rosa's files. "You got good care; they prescribed the right treatment. You still feel uncomfortable. Any blood in your stools?"

"I think some this morning," answered an anxious-looking Rosa, "but no diarrhea."

"I thought the blood had ended," I gasped.

"Just a little now and then. I didn't want to worry you."

"Ms. Honecker, the continued blood means the parasite is still there," informed Dr. Bruner as he wrote on a naval-hospital folder. "The drugs they gave in Hong Kong should have killed it."

"Will I die?"

"I doubt it," smiled Dr. Bruner. "I think you should stay overnight for a series of tests. Take this hospital folder down to the admission desk, and they will make arrangements."

Going back to an empty house, I worried about being alone. Without Rosa, I might slip back into having no relationships.

Not wanting to eat in an empty house, I went to the nearby Shores Restaurant, sat at the bar, and ordered, in memory of Rosa, firecracker yellowtail and a double shot of tequila. Eating, I thought about the yellowtail Rosa had caught. After more tequila, I stumbled out of the restaurant and decided to walk on the beach.

It was dark as I picked my way through the boulders to reach the beach. I passed a young couple covered in towels to hide their lovemaking. Reaching the beach, I acted like a kid throwing rocks at waves.

"Quiet down here," said a voice behind me.

Startled, I turned to see an Asian-looking man carrying a mesh bag filled with black snails.

"You've been collecting," I observed.

"Lot of good food for the picking," said the man, who I could now see was wearing shorts and a colorful Hawaiian shirt and looked about fifty. "I'm John Chin. I live near here. I've seen you around."

"Billy Durant," I introduced myself, "just out for an evening stroll. My partner is overnight at the hospital."

"I hope nothing serious."

"Parasite she picked up in Shanghai. We had to come back from Hong Kong for treatment."

"I used to live in Hong Kong," said John. "Made some money and decided to come back a couple years ago. My family was originally from Beijing. They moved to LA in the 1930s when it looked like war with Japan."

"That was smart. So they missed the revolution."

"My grandfather was a government official. He would have been killed in the communist takeover or most certainly during the Cultural Revolution."

"What have you got in the bag?" I asked.

"Periwinkles tonight—they're good out of the shell and dipped in a spicy sauce. Sometimes I get mussels. If I wear a wet suit, abalone. Have you ever tried periwinkles?"

"Never. They're just snails, aren't they? I'm a little leery with my partner getting a parasite."

"That's from bad water." John opened the bag for me to look in. "Many in my family left China with tapeworms. Pulled a five-footer out of my grandfather."

"That's disgusting," I said, peering into his bag. "I guess these are clean."

"Want to try some?" he offered. "My house is a couple doors down from yours. I couldn't help noticing that tough-looking woman of yours."

"She's tough, all right. I hope she's tough enough to get rid of this parasite."

"The path is over here." He pointed down the beach. "I've got the sauce made. My husband is in New York."

"Your husband?" I loudly repeated. "Sorry, just getting use to the rainbow issues. Can gay couples marry in California?"

"No, we went to Tijuana. Now we're officially married in Mexico. You can buy anything there with enough money. Follow me." He gestured up the beach.

I followed as the memory of pushing Jim Kelly into the jellyfish school flashed through my mind.

I've got be careful, I thought to myself. *I don't want to go down that road again.*

John stood at the sink and washed the periwinkles as I sat at his kitchen table and had more tequila. I admired the tight curve of his ass and muscled legs.

Dumping the periwinkles in a bowl, he brought them to the table with a sauce from the refrigerator and more tequila.

"Just stick the shell in the sauce and suck out the body," explained John. "You'll like the flavor."

They tasted salty, like the ocean water. John's sauce added sweetness to the flavor.

"Do you like?"

"Tastes like ocean, but your sauce could make it addictive," I replied, throwing back a shot of tequila.

I panicked when he rested his hand on my knee and lightly squeezed. I didn't want to kill.

"You're good-looking," said John, noting my lack of resistance to his hand. "Ever been with a man?"

"Yes, but not a good idea. I can't betray my partner in the hospital."

"You're married like me, but I have an open relationship."

"We're not married," I responded, feeling my heart race as his hand moved up my leg. "But I don't know what I'll do."

"What do you mean, you don't know what you'll do? I can see in your eyes you're excited."

Violent memories swept through my mind as I looked around for a knife.

"What are you looking for?" smiled John.

"I don't want to hurt." I started crying.

Startled to see a man in his sixties crying, John withdrew his hand.

"I'm sorry," said John. "I didn't mean to trigger that reaction."

"It isn't you." I reached over and took his hand. "I've had bad experiences that I don't want to repeat."

Pushing away childhood rage, I decided to honor Rosa and our vow to do good. *Maybe*, I thought, *if I go with John, I can sooth my violent feelings. This could be my answer to the demons. They could leave me.*

The next morning I awakened with a blood-soaked pillowcase next to a lifeless-looking John. I couldn't remember what had happened.

Chapter Forty-Nine

I lay there unable to move, worried that this was a murder I wouldn't be able to escape. My fingerprints were all over John's house and my sperm somewhere in his body. I thought of Rosa, whom, when I was arrested, I wouldn't be able to help. This was the penalty for betraying her. Images of dead bodies and rape crowded my mind as I thought about suicide.

"Damn it," John said and suddenly sat up. "I get these night nose-bleeds every so often. The doctor says I must pick my nose in my sleep."

Grabbing the bloody pillowcase, he headed to the bathroom to use a lubricating nasal spray.

My mind went blank for a moment as I felt a wave of relief. *I didn't kill,* I thought, *but I did betray Rosa.*

"That was fun," hollered John from the bathroom.

Returning to bed, he tried to kiss me. I rolled away, confused by child-hood memories and this new feeling of infidelity.

"What's this? You didn't act like that last night," said John with a slight touch of anger.

"I'm just confused," I admitted. "Rosa's in the hospital. I haven't done this with a man since childhood, and I'm violent."

"You weren't violent last night," responded John as he tried to arouse me.

"I've got to go," I said, hurrying out of bed and into my clothes. "I need to check on Rosa."

"Will I see you again?"

"I'm bringing her home today. So I don't think so."

"We could try a threesome," offered John. "That would be fun tonight. My husband gets home on Friday. We could do a foursome."

"Rosa won't be up for that," I said, putting on my shoes. "Remember, she's sick. We've been offered a foursome in the past." I thought of our encounter in Davos. "But it's always too complicated. But thanks."

Stretching, John climbed out of bed and, nude, followed me down the stairs.

"You need to loosen up," said John as we reached the bottom of the stairs. "You may be too prudish. Ever do sex acts? Know some places in Tijuana."

"We've done that," I smiled, noticing that he had an erection. "We could try Tijuana when Rosa gets better. Any particular place?"

"The Four Mules on Chiapas Street is famous for its shows. You can participate. We once saw a couple take on all four mules. The place is named after the mules."

Jesus, I thought, *I'm getting tired of this deviant crap. It's getting boring.*

"You and your husband tried the mules?" I asked, ready to head home.

"We shy away from bestiality. It's rough on the asshole. They have side rooms for gay couples. We like the bondage room. The mules are named, if you two want to try."

"Named! We're getting too old. We vowed to stick with straight sex."

"Too bad," said John, looking disappointed. "They named them after US presidents. You can be ridden by Jackson, Lincoln, Nixon, or Reagan."

I felt sick at the idea of a mule named Nixon mounting me. Or even worse, Reagan.

"I'll let Rosa know. She needs to get better. We probably won't. Crazy sex is no longer our cup of tea."

"She looks strong. I heard a slight accent one time when she called out to you as you got in your car."

"She was an interrogator for the Stasi. I feel safe knowing she can kill with her hands."

"Stasi?"

"Old East German secret police. No longer exists, and she's changed."

Stepping out of John's house, I walked to our house a half a block away. As soon as I was inside, I called her hospital room.

"Hello," answered Rosa, sounding weak.

"How are you doing?"

"Did the usual shit and blood stuff. Then an MRI."

"They didn't do an MRI in Hong Kong. Did they say why?"

"Drank these God-awful-tasting liquids. They want to see if the parasite is in other body parts."

"Other body parts?" I gasped. "Dr. Wong mentioned it could affect the liver."

"I hope Rasputin hasn't drifted. You can't trust Russians."

I'd forgotten she'd named the bug. Now Rosa spoke as if in direct communication with the parasite living off her body.

"When can you come home?"

"Dr. Bruner said sometime this afternoon. You can call later for an exact time."

"Will you know the test results?"

"He's made an appointment to see me this Friday to go over them. We'll find out about Rasputin then. I hope Rasputin isn't being a naughty boy."

"It's Tuesday. You mean we've got to wait until the end of the week to find out?"

"They're rushing the lab tests. All the reports, according to Bruner, won't be available until then."

I picked her up around three and drove home. John waved at us as we got out of the car.

"Who's that?" asked Rosa.

"John Chin, our neighbor. I met him yesterday. He's married to a guy. John offered to take us to the Four Mules in Tijuana. It sounds like the Kit Kat Klub with the mules named after American presidents. You want to be mounted by Ronald Reagan?"

"Sounds disgusting. I don't want to do that type of thing again. Rasputin is urging me to get to the toilet."

She rushed inside as I brought in her overnight bag.

"Can I get you anything?" I yelled through the bathroom door.

"I'm starving," she called back.

"What would you like?"

"Something mild, like yogurt and cereal, and some herbal tea. I can't seem to drink coffee; it makes my stomach sour."

Hearing that coffee made her stomach sour worried me. She was getting thinner every day. There was no sign of improvement.

I left her when I went to my office. There Chelsea greeted me with the news that the Ayn Rand Freedom Institute insisted that I do the lecture on September fifteenth.

"They insisted? Why?"

"They've booked a ballroom at the Palace Hotel and are expecting a couple hundred to attend. David called and said the Smith brothers are funding the event and are broadcasting it worldwide."

"Worldwide? How many are interested in a lecture on 'How Free Markets and Individualism Saved China'? Can't be many. How'd they get a couple hundred to sign up to hear me at the Palace?"

"You're famous. I'm sure you know that. Randians and libertarians are coming from all over the country. I hope you'll let me come."

"Famous." I dismissed Chelsea's description as I thought about the lecture. "I don't have anything prepared. Of course you can come. There is money in the budget."

"Oh, goody," exclaimed Chelsea, "I've always wanted to hear you. You're one of my free-market heroes. Should I book us rooms at the Palace?"

"My favorite is the Fairmont. We can take a cab to the Palace. I don't know if Rosa will be well enough to come. Anyway get us a suite and a good room for yourself."

"Fairmont. They have the Tonga Room, don't they? Read about it in a movie magazine. Supposedly designed by some famous Hollywood guy."

"Tell the Ayn Rand people and David that I'll be there. I'll work in my office on the lecture. I wonder what I'll say."

On Friday, we arrived early and waited outside Dr. Bruner's office.

"Rasputin is talking to God about me," whispered Rosa.

"Don't worry. Dr. Bruner said the treatments will kill Rasputin." I surprised myself by using Rosa's name for the bug.

"He can talk to God. He did for the czars. God is probably telling him to kill me."

"That's nonsense." I tried to comfort her by putting my arm around her shoulder. "God is dead, and so is Rasputin. Your bug will shortly join them."

"Come on in," invited Dr. Bruner, opening his door. "I was just going over the lab results."

We sat in chairs facing the doctor as he began writing out a prescription.

"The good news is that the MRI shows the parasite has not migrated from your colon," said Dr. Bruner. "But I'm recommending monthly tests. It could get out."

"So little Rasputin is still in the crib."

"What?" Dr. Bruner looked startled.

"She's named the parasite," I said, wondering what was happening with Rosa using the word "crib."

"OK. I never heard of naming one," commented the doctor.

"Can we kill Rasputin?" Rosa looked on the verge of crying.

"There is a more powerful drug that hasn't been tried. Here's the prescription, which you should take to the hospital pharmacy. Regular pharmacies will have problems getting it."

"Why is that?" I asked.

"Our medical system is all screwed up. A hedge fund bought a bunch of drugs used for rare conditions like this one. They jacked up the price to eight hundred dollars a pill. There is a Congressional investigation. But if you're going to live, you'll have to pay. Two pills a day is sixteen hundred dollars. Medical insurance won't touch it."

"Sixteen hundred a day!" I gasped. "How can they get away with it?"

"It's the free market," said Dr. Bruner, indicating our meeting was over. "You could have socialized medicine like the US Navy."

"How long will she be taking them?" I asked as Rosa disappeared into her own world.

"One month, and if it's not gone, we will have to try something else."

"Thirty days times sixteen hundred," I calculated as I pulled out of the hospital's parking lot, "is forty-eight thousand dollars."

I looked over at Rosa, who was still spaced out.

"Rosa, can you afford forty-eight thousand dollars a month for pills? Remember, you are not on my insurance plan."

I knew she had plenty of money stashed away, but I worried that I would get entangled in her medical bills, which could be considerable.

"A penny for your thoughts," I said loudly when she didn't respond.

"Rasputin is talking to God about me. He used to do that for the czar's family. God is calculating my sins."

"Rosa!" I almost yelled. "There is no God, and you're a communist atheist. What's this about sin?"

"You know what I did. It was all sin in the eyes of God."

"You're going over the edge with this Rasputin and sin crap. You're not a Christian or Jew or any other religion that talks about sin. You're just a human who killed and tortured and got away with it."

"Daddy always said good communists before they die should get religion as an insurance policy."

"Insurance policy?"

"In case there is a heaven."

"Your father, Erich Honecker, joined the Church before he died."

"Just before. There are a lot of Catholic churches in Chile. He took the last rites and had a church funeral."

"And you?" I asked as we pulled off the freeway and headed home.

"Rasputin wants me to join. I think God is telling him to kill me. I've sinned."

"Which church would you join?" I was concerned. Was she going mad?

"Russian Orthodox. That's Rasputin's church." Rosa made the sign of the cross, moving her hand in Orthodox fashion.

"Russian Orthodox," I exclaimed. "I don't know if there are any in San Diego."

"I asked at the hospital. There is a St. Basil Orthodox Church. Rasputin tells me to go there."

"Your parasite is giving you instructions?"

"Rasputin wants us to marry. I must do it before I die. I must be forgiven for my sins."

Chapter Fifty

As I prepared for my lecture, Rosa grew weaker and thinner. Her body was getting gaunt, and her face looked haggard.

Advertisements for the lecture were appearing in libertarian journals and newsletters: "Hear famous libertarian thinker Billy Durant on 'How Free Markets and Individualism Saved China,' Palace Hotel, San Francisco, September 15, 2001."

The pills were taking a toll. Rosa spent most of the day in bed and was in no condition to go to San Francisco.

In early September before I left for my lecture, I took Rosa to the hospital for more tests.

"Can't understand it," said Dr. Bruner. "None of the medicines worked. The parasite is still there but hasn't moved."

"Rasputin doesn't want to die," said Rosa. "He must punish me for my sins."

"I don't know about sin, but I'm calling colleagues at the Centers for Disease Control in Washington. They will be very interested in the lack of response to treatment. You'll be part of a study."

"Rasputin doesn't want to be studied; he wants to go to church."

Dr. Bruner glanced at me with a worried look. He then asked Rosa, "Are you experiencing any problems thinking or with your emotions? The drugs and the parasite can cause fatigue."

"I stay in bed dreaming," answered Rosa. "Rasputin directs me to God."

After the doctor's appointment, I had promised to take Rosa to meet Father Kirill at St. Basil Orthodox Church.

Rosa had called ahead and received directions to the priest's office in back of the church. Entering, we were engulfed in heavy incense and surrounded by panels covered with icons. I started sneezing as Rosa took me to the office.

I was still sneezing when Father Kirill let us into his office, crowded by cases of religious books. The priest was dressed in black robes and sporting a bushy beard.

"Incense getting you?" smiled Father Kirill.

"I have allergies," I laughed, wiping my nose. "Maybe I'm allergic to religion."

"Billy," snapped Rosa, "that was uncalled for. I'm here to repent."

"Repent," laughed the father. "What would a nice looking woman like you have to repent?"

"I've sinned, and I'm living in sin."

"We've all sinned. What do you mean by 'living in sin'?"

I was taken aback when Rosa responded, "We're not married; just living together."

"Hmm." The priest glanced back and forth between the two of us. "You're both members of the Church?"

"No," said Rose. "We want to join."

"What?" I exclaimed. "I'm just here for you."

"Rasputin wants us to join." Rosa started crying.

"Rasputin?" repeat Father Kirill.

"She picked up a parasite in China that she can't get rid of," I explained. "She calls it Rasputin and thinks it is killing her. She's been in treatment for months and is weak from fighting it."

"Why the Russian Orthodox Church?"

"Rasputin sent me." Rosa was now staring at an icon of the Virgin Mary and child above the bookcases. "He said God's ways are strange."

"They certainly are," agreed the priest. "Have you both been baptized in any Christian church?"

We both answered no.

"That is the first step, and then I can help you repent your sins. How about Monday the tenth at eleven? I can schedule you both."

"I lecture on the fifteenth."

"That doesn't have anything to do with this," barked Rosa. "We'll be here. You can marry us then?"

"After you are members of the Church, we can talk about marriage vows."

"How did you rope me into being baptized, plus baptized in the Russian Orthodox Church?" I screamed as we got back in the car.

"Don't you want me to be forgiven for my sins?" Rosa burst into tears.

"Do you really want to marry in that church?"

"Beautiful ceremony," said Rosa between sobs. "Saw one when I was with Daddy in Moscow. I can't repent if I'm living in sin. I've requested the choir for our baptisms."

"When did you do that? A chorus just for us. Are we paying?"

"I talked to Father Kirill on the phone yesterday. He said a small donation of one thousand dollars will get us the choir and a soloist for an hour."

"You didn't tell me that. Are you and Rasputin keeping secrets?"

Worried about my lecture, I stood at the church's altar with Rosa, who was dressed in what looked like an adult version of a christening gown. To the side was a chorus with a deep-bass male soloist doing traditional Russian church music. It was hard to focus on the ceremony as Father Kirill anointed our ankles and wrists with oils and cut small sections of hair in the sign of the cross.

At the end of the ceremony, Rosa fell on her knees, raised her arms in the air, and called out, "Rasputin, forgive me, for I have sinned."

Unsettled by the experience, I took Rosa back to the house and went to the office to put finishing touches on my lecture. At the office, Chelsea informed me that I would be speaking to a full house.

"Also," she told me, "there will be a special section for the press. There will be reporters from all the major TV networks and the *New York Times, Washington Post, Chicago Tribune*, and *San Francisco Examiner*. The *Journal of Libertarian Studies* wants to publish your entire lecture."

"I don't think they'll want to after they hear it."

"You're too modest," replied Chelsea. "We're also lining up talk shows for you around the country."

"You should wait until you hear the speech. They might want to tar and feather me. Will you be ready on Friday?"

Ignoring my warning, Chelsea said, "I'm all set; plane and hotel rooms are booked. Is Rosa coming?"

"No, and I need to arrange for a driver to take her to church on Sunday. Would you do that? Please have the car service pick her up on Sunday at my house at seven so she can make the eight o'clock morning service. She's become religious."

"Born again?" asked Chelsea asked. "Of course I'll do it. I came to Christ last year. Are you interested in salvation? Which church?"

"St. Basil Orthodox Church. You can look up the address."

"Is that an evangelical church? I never heard of it."

"Russian Orthodox," I replied. "Don't ask me why."

On Saturday, after a night full of childhood memories of exploring the Fairmont neighborhood and eating in the Tonga Room, I stood behind a lectern in the Palace Hotel's grand ballroom with its eighteen-foot ceilings and antique crystal chandeliers. Before me was a well-dressed audience, many of whom I knew from my many years moving in libertarian and Ayn Rand circles. A television camera from China's CCTV was to broadcast the lecture live to affiliates around the world.

I don't remember at what point my audience began to boo and walk out.

It might have been when I argued that Ayn Randian individualism created psychotic personalities alienated from fellow humans and bent on human destruction. Someone screamed and hurled a pen at me when I said, "Rand's novel *The Fountainhead* has contributed to mass murders as ideological, individualist freaks pursue their own ends."

Libertarian journalists started squirming and trying to interrupt when I argued, "Free markets promote greed and, driven by selfishness, create monopolies, exploitive corporations, and oligarchies." The CCTV camera went off when I stated that market economies in China were causing death and inequality. I presented figures on the numbers of people who would die in China from air pollution.

"Economic theories of individual self-interest, human capital, and free markets," I concluded the lecture, "will, in the end, do nothing about climate change, human violence, and mass destruction, which, consequently, will result in the end of human life as we know it."

Only a few people remained in the room as I finished, and Chelsea, looking teary eyed, passed me a note saying, "The Smith brothers will be formally withdrawing all funding for projects, your office, and your salary."

On Sunday, I returned to a house thick with burning incense and decorated with religious icons. Speakers blasted Russian choral music.

"I am praying for our souls," said Rosa when I found her on her knees on the outside deck.

Rosa had torn holes in her nightgowns. She smeared them with ashes she had collected in a pail from a fire pit on the beach. Kneeling, she put ashes from the pail on her head.

"What are you doing? Where did all those paintings come from?"

"I'm in sackcloth and ashes before our God," she sang out. "Rasputin wants us to repent."

"Can I turn down the speakers? I can hardly hear. Where did you get the music and paintings?"

Without waiting for an answer, I went in and turned off the sound system.

Rosa came crawling in from the deck, her arms bloodied by self-inflicted fingernail gouges. She squatted in a corner and chanted, "Repent, repent, all ye who have fallen."

Unable to get anything from Rosa, I called the car service that had taken her to church. They put me in contact with the driver.

"I waited outside for the end of the service," the driver told me. "When she didn't come out, I went looking for her. She was in the gift shop with this bearded priest."

"Churches have gift shops?" I wondered. "I guess even God is open to profiteers."

"The priest and I helped her carry paintings, sculptures, incense burners, and a large bag of CDs."

"Thank you," I said, hanging up.

I looked at Rosa huddled in the corner praying.

"I lost my job," I said, hoping for some kind of reply. "My lecture caused the Smith brothers to withdraw all funding. I have no more money but what I have saved."

Screaming, Rosa rose, clawing the wall and leaving streaks of blood.

I called Dr. Bruner's emergency number and described to him Rosa's condition.

"Do you have those sedatives I prescribed?" asked Dr. Bruner.

"Yes."

"Get her to take one. Stop all other medications; they may be making her delusional. Bring her in tomorrow. I can see you around two."

Hanging up, I went to the medicine closet and found the bottle of alprazolam labeled with the instructions, "Take one pill by mouth. For panic and anxiety disorder."

"Rosa," I ordered, bringing the bottle over to her, "take one of these. Dr. Bruner wants to see you tomorrow."

"Rasputin doesn't want pill," she babbled. "He wants me to feel the pain of sinning."

She collapsed on the floor, her tattered gown pulled up over her head and revealing a body covered with bleeding scratch marks.

The telephone rang. I left her on the floor to answer it.

"I'm calling from the *New Republic*. We'd like to arrange an interview. We read reports of your San Francisco lecture."

That was the beginning of a flood of calls from radio and television talk shows and other liberal journals like the *Nation* and *Mother Jones* wanting interviews.

On Monday, an article appeared in the *New York Times*, "Famed Libertarian Disowns Ideology."

Chapter Fifty-One

"The recent MRI shows abscesses on your liver," explained Dr. Bruner when we arrived on Monday. "We need you to stay for a while."

"Don't hurt Rasputin," wept Rosa as she was admitted to the hospital. "I need Father Kirill," she pleaded.

"We're keeping her sedated," explained Dr. Bruner. "She is upset from the treatment and her weakening condition. This new development, if I may speak frankly, doesn't look good. You should call her priest."

I went to the hospital's admission desk to check about the costs. Previously Rosa had arranged for the medical bills to be paid from her inheritance held in an investment account at Goldman Sachs, a New York investment bank. The admission's clerk said that all the bills were paid and that there was a line of credit to pay for future costs. "She must have a lot of money," commented the clerk.

Driving home, I started thinking about the clerk's reference to Rosa's money. I'd never paid much attention to her finances, and she'd occasionally given me money to cover household expenses. I was worried about house payments with the Smith brothers' income ending. I had invested well, but that was for my retirement. I needed another job.

When I got home, I started rummaging through Rosa's personal papers stored in an alcove desk. I found her account at Goldman Sachs, plus the name and number for her money manager, Felix Blankfein. I was shocked to see her statement balance of $25 million. It was two in the afternoon, too late to call her money manager on the East Coast.

They must have stolen a lot from the East Germans, I thought. *I wonder how much her father took out of the country.*

Since I'd been kicked out of my Torres Pines office, I began answering requests for interviews from my home. Most of the calls had to wait until the next day because of time-zone differences. I phoned the *San Francisco Examiner* and arranged a telephone interview for the next morning. Also there was a tantalizing letter from a New York literary agent to write a book on "How I loved and rejected Ayn Rand."

I was lonely without Rosa. I took a sleeping pill and a couple shots of tequila before falling asleep.

My first call the next day was to Rosa's money manager.

"Felix Blankfein's office," the voice on the other end greeted me.

"I want to talk to Mr. Blankfein about Rosa Honecker's account."

Shortly afterward I heard, "This is Felix Blankfein. Can I help you?"

"First you should know that Rosa—I'm her partner, Billy Durant—will be in the hospital for an extended period. I talked to the hospital's admission desk, and they informed me that a line of credit from her account to the hospital would cover expenses."

"I'm sorry. You're not listed on Rosa Honecker's account, and therefore I cannot talk to you about it."

"What? We've been living together for over a decade."

"That doesn't matter. She must list you on the account, or if she is that sick you need to get a power of attorney. Otherwise it is against the law for me to discuss her account with you."

"And if she dies?" I gulped. "She has no relatives that I know of."

"Again, Mr. Durant, I can't talk to you about her account. You need power of attorney—or you could marry her."

"Marry her. What would that do?"

"If she dies, you would have a claim on her money. Does she have a will?"

"I don't think so."

"If she doesn't have a will, then as her husband—I don't know the exact California laws—you would inherit her money."

"So there's nothing I can do at this time," I said into the phone.

"My advice is to hire a lawyer. I would appreciate you keeping me informed about Ms. Honecker's condition. There are no relatives or other contacts listed on her account."

I then called the hospital to find out how she was doing.

"Are you her husband?"

"No."

"We can't give you information unless you are her husband or next of kin."

"But I brought her to the hospital."

"Who is the doctor?"

"Bruner."

"You should contact him. Sorry, we can't help you. You can see her during visiting hours from nine to nine."

I called Rosa's hospital room. Her groggy voice answered.

"Are you OK?" I asked. "I'll visit you this afternoon."

She mumbled something and hung up.

I spent the rest of the morning answering interview requests and talking to a reporter at the *San Francisco Examiner*. I received a call from the program director for the American Economic Association asking if I would be available for a lecture on free markets and the individualist aspects of Ayn Rand's thought.

I was still worried about employment with the high mortgage payments on my very expensive house. I might have to put it on the market.

I decided to call the economics department at the University of California at San Diego and ask about teaching adjunct courses. While I had a PhD in economics, I had never taught. The secretary connected me with the department chair, Lloyd Keynes.

"Billy Durant, I've heard so much about you. I've read many of your articles. Very good, but of course I disagree."

"Thank you," I replied. "I'm calling about teaching. Since my speech last weekend, my funding has been withdrawn and the center closed."

"I've read about the speech." Keynes sounded enthusiastic. "Can you send me a copy? How about doing a seminar for the department? We'd love to talk to you."

"Sure, I can do a seminar. It would be based on my lecture."

"Good, everyone will want to talk to you. You've become a hero for many in our department. How about noon on Wednesday next week in our departmental seminar room?"

"OK. I'll be there. I'll send you the lecture and outline the arguments at the beginning of the seminar for those who haven't had a chance to read it."

"Great. I'll let the faculty know. Regarding teaching, we have position open in behavioral economics. Any interest?"

"That's my field," I responded. "Can I apply?"

"Bring your vita to the seminar. I'll mention your interest in the position. Your seminar will acquaint others with your work."

Hanging up, I glanced at the clock. It was time to see Rosa. Quickly dressing, I drove to the hospital.

Father Kirill was seated next to the bed and listening intently to Rosa, whose voice was barely audible.

"Can I be saved?" I heard Rosa whisper as I entered the room.

"Yes, you can repent," replied the priest as he rose to shake my hand. "Billy is here."

"Billy, I love you. Will you join me in repenting?"

I nodded yes, thinking that I couldn't say no given the circumstances even though I didn't believe in God.

"Rosa was talking about marriage," said Father Kirill. "She believes it is necessary for redemption."

"Marriage would be OK." I thought of my conversation with her money manager. Would I be taking advantage of her? I felt a wave of guilt.

At that moment, Dr. Bruner came in, said hello to me, and introduced himself to the priest. The doctor looked at her charts hanging on the end of the bed.

"Billy, could I talk to you outside?" requested Dr. Bruner. "We can leave Father Kirill to comfort Rosa."

"Billy, let me be frank," Dr. Bruner began once we were in the hallway. "Her condition does not look good. The drugs failed to kill the parasite and stop its spread. I've never seen this before."

"Does this mean she'll die?" I tried to suppress thoughts about her money.

"That could be the long-term result. Currently she's deteriorated so much that she needs twenty-four-hour attention. I would advise moving her to a nursing facility. You won't be able to take care of her at home."

"How long will she be there?"

"I don't know; it could be weeks, months, or even a year. She is dying."

Going back into Rosa's room, I announced, "Rosa, I agree to marry you. Father Kirill, how soon can we perform the service?"

"Will she be well enough to go to the church?" asked the priest.

"Rosa," I said to her, "you are being moved to a nursing facility. I'll talk to the good father about marriage."

Turning to the priest, I asked about a bedside service.

"Certainly," he replied. "It will be a simple service."

"Simple is good. Rosa would you agree?"

"Is Rasputin coming with me?" Tears streamed down her face. "I don't want to lose him. He'll save me."

"Yes, Rasputin will be coming and will be at the ceremony."

Rosa smiled blissfully closing her eyes.

Things sped up in my life. I was flown to New York City to appear on talk shows and do interviews for liberal journals. I was well prepared by the time of my seminar at the university.

After Professor Keynes introduced me, I started discussing my intellectual history from the first encounter with Ayn Rand's work and the stress on free markets at the University of Chicago. I explained my early doubts and the way that they had become more critical as I saw the actual results.

I was frequently interrupted by an enthusiastic faculty, whose questions reflected the liberal bias of the department. They almost broke into cheers when I called Ayn Rand's individualism pathological and free markets murderous.

During the questioning, Professor Keynes asked about my relationship with Rosa Honecker.

"We met at the World Economic Forum and fell in love," I answered. "At the time I was funded by the Smith brothers."

They all grimaced, and I thought some were on the verge of booing at the mention of the Smith brothers.

"Being a communist, did she persuade you of the errors of your ways?" asked Manchu Bower, a young assistant professor.

Not mentioning our mutual affinity for killing, I answered, "We acted out of love. It was China, not Rosa, that showed me the consequences."

"It would be wonderful if you could convince Rosa Honecker to do a seminar here," said Professor Keynes. "We could learn from her."

"I know she would enjoy giving one, but she is very sick right now from a parasite she got in Asia."

Professor Keynes escorted me from the seminar room to my car. "If you're interested in our faculty opening, let me know. I'll talk to the faculty for their impression of your work and the possibility of hiring you. Nothing is guaranteed."

"I'm interested," I responded. "Do you need any other documents?"

"Your vita and this presentation are enough to get the ball rolling. The faculty is very acquainted with your work. We've been having difficulty finding a qualified behavioral economist. Again I can't promise anything. But for sure, I'll be in touch."

When I got back to the house, there were calls from Father Kirill and Dr. Bruner.

Wanting to find out Rosa's condition, I phoned Dr. Bruner first.

"She's getting much worse," said Dr. Bruner. "The nursing home called me this morning to authorize returning her to the hospital. She is now in the critical-care unit. It could be a day or a week before she passes away. You should call her minister."

"Rosa's dying," I told Father Kirill when I reached him. "It could be anytime. She's back at the hospital in critical care."

"Do you want me to administer last rites?" he asked.

I was starting to panic that Rosa might die before we were married.

"Remember, she wants us to marry as part of repenting her sins. Would it be possible to marry us this evening?"

"Do you have a marriage license for me to sign after the ceremony?"

"No!" I hadn't thought about the license.

"You'll need to get one from city hall or the county to make it official."

Shit, I thought. *I should have got a license when Rosa first mentioned marriage.*

I called the law office I used for the Smith Brothers Center for Tax Cuts.

"Trump, Limbaugh, and Rush, how may I direct your call?"

"Either Trump or Limbaugh. They both handled my account."

"Billy," answered Mr. Limbaugh, "good to hear from you. Sorry that the Smith brothers closed your account. Can I help you with anything?"

"I need to get married, but she's dying in the hospital. How can I get a marriage certificate? I need one right away."

I must have sounded desperate, because the lawyer began to shower me with questions. Of course, he told me, we were now on the clock, and I would be charged for the time. "Why marry a dying woman? Can she talk? Can she sign documents? Who will marry you?"

"I think she can still sign. Will any mark count?" I was rattled, worried about expenses.

"What we need is for her to sign a document giving you power of attorney and a letter of consent for a marriage license and a statement from the hospital about her medical condition."

"Can you do that—maybe go to the hospital this evening for the power of attorney and the other paper work. Tomorrow could we take the documents and get the license?"

"You're in that big of a rush," said Limbaugh. "I can have one of our paralegals get the signature and license. You'll have to pay for their time and, of course, mine."

"I understand, but we need to do this as soon as possible."

"I'll call you back with a time to meet our paralegal at the hospital. You should be present to explain to your future wife. Don't worry; we'll get you married."

I then phoned Father Kirill and explained the situation.

"Do you want a small chorus or singer for the service? I will need to bring an altar boy to assist. With travel time, the altar boy, and other religious items, a donation of five hundred dollars should cover it. A chorus and singer would be another four hundred. Do you need a photographer? There is one who works with our church. Her charges are reasonable."

I thought to myself, *I hope this works. I'll need the inheritance just to pay the lawyer and church.*

Chapter Fifty-Two

"Rasputin loves me." Rosa could barely be heard over Father Kirill's chanting.

"I love you," I whispered in her ear, holding her hand.

I'd rushed to a local La Jolla jeweler for a wedding ring. The clerk had asked me how much I wanted to spend. I had replied, "As little as possible."

"Do you take Billy Durant to be your lawful husband?" the priest asked her.

"Yes, and so does Rasputin. Oh, God, forgive my sins, for I have killed many."

The priest's altar boy and the nurse looked aghast at Rosa's confession. Unable to control her surprise, the nurse exclaimed, "She killed! What about the police?"

Father Kirill looked confused.

"She's talking about when she lived under communism," I explained to the nurse, worrying she'd report Rosa and end the ceremony.

"Oh," responded the nurse as she adjusted Rosa's pillow. "Sorry, dear; it must have been tough living under commies."

"Rasputin knows. He killed and is killing me." Rosa squeezed my hand as I bent over to put the ring on her finger. "Rasputin says all those I killed are watching. They give us their blessings."

Whoa, I thought, *a wedding blessed by her maimed and bloody victims. I wonder if mine are attending. This is a marriage born in hell.*

"I pronounce you man and wife. Billy, you can kiss her," Father Kirill concluded the service.

As I bent over to kiss Rosa, I hesitated; her breath was putrid and smelled of sulfur. Were these the winds of hell? I held my breath as our lips briefly touched.

I hurried home after paying off the priest and altar boy. I now had power of attorney and a marriage certificate. I immediately called Felix Blankfein at Goldman Sachs.

"I have power of attorney, and we were just married," I almost shouted over the phone in my excitement.

"Have your lawyer send me certified copies, and we can talk."

"Shit," I said out loud. "More lawyer fees. I'm going broke just trying to get money to pay my mortgage. Fuckin' church and lawyers just steal."

I called Limbaugh's office and requested that a certified copy of the power of attorney be sent to Goldman Sachs. I'd send the marriage certificate.

"Mr. Limbaugh would like to talk to you," said his secretary.

Wondering if the conversation would be on the clock and cost me more money, I waited for Limbaugh.

"We'll send the power of attorney today," assured Limbaugh. "Did you marry?"

"Thank you. Just married. I'm a newlywed."

"Congratulations. First I want you to know that our conversation is confidential. I know she is dying. Is there a will? How much is the estate?"

"Is this on the clock?"

"Yes, but I think you need legal advice if there are large sums involved when a marriage takes place just before death. Is there a will?"

"Not that I know of. I went through her papers."

"How much at Goldman Sachs? I was just informed that you wanted to send the power of attorney there. I assume they hold her estate."

"More than twenty-five million in statements I found in the house."

"Does she have any relatives who might object to you inheriting her estate after a last-minute marriage? Someone could claim she was not mentally competent to marry and you were just after her money."

He knows what I'm doing, I thought, feeling guilt and remorse.

"I don't know of any relatives."

"Good. Do you want me to handle her estate?"

I hadn't even thought about the legal angles to getting my hands on her money.

"Sure," I responded. "How much do you charge?"

"Hourly rate. It will not be expensive unless a relative appears and challenges your claim."

"OK." I put down the phone and wondered what I was doing. On the same day that I married, I was planning for my wife's death.

Hanging up, I walked down the block to John Chin's house and rang the doorbell.

"Hello, stranger," John said as he opened the door. "Didn't think I'd see you back here. How's the woman? Thinking about the Four Mules?"

"She's dying."

"Oh God, I'm so sorry to hear. Come on in. My husband's away on another trip."

"You have anything strong?" I asked as I followed him into the living room.

"Liquor and some pot are about all. Dick, my husband, has some mescaline. But you've got to replace it if you use some."

We spent the evening making love and consuming a bottle of tequila, a number of joints, and some mescaline. By the time midnight rolled around, we were wrecks.

"How about a walk on the beach?" proposed John. "I need some fresh air. We could recoup for a little more sex."

My heart raced in anticipation. As we left John's house, I started thinking about an alibi. My prints were all over his house, but I might be able to go back to remove evidence from the evening. I could say that I had stopped briefly to tell John about my marriage. That would sound innocent.

I could hear my heart pounding when we reached the beach. I looked around for a rock or something heavy. I picked up a piece of driftwood. I wouldn't be able to control myself.

John stopped and turned to me for a kiss. My lips met his as my hand swung the driftwood into the side of his head. I started beating him. I couldn't stop. His nose collapsed as he fell to his knees pleading with me.

I could hear his arm break. Then his head split open. Looking, I started vomiting as John attempted to crawl away. Jumping on his back, gagging from my vomit, I broke his neck.

I dragged John's body toward the cliff and looked for a place to hide it. I knew that nothing on this popular beach could be hidden forever. Someone would eventually find it. I just wanted time before the police were alerted. Finding two large boulders, I shoved the body into a crevice between them.

Still feeling the effects of the liquor and drugs, I stumbled up the path from the beach to John's house. I'd taken his keys. My hope was that no one saw me enter the house or our trip to the beach. It was two in the morning when I reached his house. Looking around to see if anyone might be looking, I let myself in.

Finding a garbage bag in the kitchen, I hurriedly went through the house and disposed of the drug paraphernalia, emptied roaches from ashtrays, and neatly rinsed and stacked our glasses in the kitchen sink. I unlocked all the doors and, after wiping away my fingerprints, put John's keys in a basket that he kept them in near the front door. My hope was that an autopsy would reveal the amount of drugs in his system, which might lead the police to suspect that, drugged, he hadn't paid any attention to locking up when he had decided on a beach walk.

I went out the backdoor, wiped my fingerprints off the handle, looked around for anyone who might see me, and snuck home. My plan was to dump the garbage bag in one of the large Dumpsters on the fishing dock in San Diego. I hoped that no one would notice my garbage bag among the fish entrails from the nearby cleaning stand.

I took a Valium and collapsed into my bed. The phone woke me around nine. I had to have the caller repeat himself several times as I tried to wake up and clear my mind.

"Can you hear me now?" Dr. Bruner spoke loudly.

"Yes, sorry. I was is a deep sleep."

"Rosa has only a few hours to live. You should get over here right away. I called Father Kirill. He'll be here shortly to perform the last rites."

I dressed quickly, tossed the garbage bag in my car's trunk, and headed to the San Diego Harbor before driving to the Balboa Hospital. At the dock, there were a few early morning fishermen cleaning their catches and tossing the waste into a nearby Dumpster. My garbage bag joined the fish heads and guts.

I immediately started sneezing from the incense when I entered Rosa's room. Father Kirill was swinging an incense burner and using his fingers to form the sign of the cross on Rosa's forehead as I ran to the bed. A nurse stood near machines that monitored her life signs.

"Rosa, don't go," I wept. I suddenly felt the weight of my loss. The only person I could love was leaving my life.

"I'm going with Rasputin. My soul is clean. You are my eternal husband." She was barely audible.

Rosa coughed. The machines around the bed sounded alarms. The nurse called for Dr. Bruner, who declared her dead.

I was crushed. I truly loved her. In my grief, I tried to not think of the inheritance.

"I'm sorry for your loss," Father Kirill offered condolences. "She was a remarkable woman. She told me about her life during my visits. She said you were the only person she could love."

"Thank you."

"With a true Christian spirit, she left a large donation to the Church for the last rites."

"How?" Now I was seriously worried about money. "How in her weakened condition could she give a big amount to the church?"

"I'm so sorry for your loss. We have a preprinted form for last rites, knowing the beloved will be shortly going to heaven. She wasn't strong enough to sign her name, so she just made a mark with the nurse as a witness. Don't worry about it until the estate is settled."

Christ, I thought. *Let's chase the money changers out of the temple.*

"Rosa requested a full Russian Orthodox funeral service." Father Kirill handed me the church's funeral-planning pamphlet and made the sign of the cross on my forehead. "I can make all the arrangements. We work with an affiliated funeral parlor and cemetery."

I was relieved to be able to turn funeral arrangements over to the church. I just had too much to worry about to add funeral planning. I'd wait for Rosa's estate before paying.

"We got the power of attorney and a copy of your marriage certificate," said Blankfein when I called after getting back to the house. Despite my grief and loneliness, I tried to deal with practical matters.

"She died this morning."

"I'm so sorry to hear that. The whole family was amazing. I briefly worked with Erich Honecker's during his last years. I handled Rosa's account after her father died."

"Is there any way to get money out of her estate to pay funeral expenses?"

"We can't do anything until her estate is settled. You need to have your lawyer contact me."

I next phoned Limbaugh.

"As soon as you get the death certificate send a certified copy to me," requested Limbaugh. "I'll send it along to Goldman Sachs. I assume you want me to handle the estate."

"Yes," I answered, wondering about legal fees. "How much will it cost? I'm a little short now because my foundation income was cut."

"Don't worry; we'll take our money out of the estate. Without a will, we must publish a notice to see if others might have claims on the estate."

Next I turned on the television and radio to find out if John's body had been found. After listening and watching an entire news cycle, I was happy there was no mention of a found body.

It was now afternoon, and I felt waves of fatigue. I took another Valium, unplugged the phones, and, filled with sadness, went to bed. I slept until six the next morning.

It was Saturday. I felt frustrated that both Goldman Sachs and the lawyer's office were closed. There was a message on the answering machine from Father Kirill saying that Rosa's body was now at the Wood and

Stiff Funeral Home and that burial could take place any time next week. The church had bought a plot in the Bleeding Virgin Cemetery.

I made some coffee, took it out on the deck, and wondered if I could see the rocks where I had stuck John's body. The beach was empty of people, and despite looking carefully, I could not identify the boulders.

Turning on the early morning TV news, I was greeted with a photo of Rosa. An anchorwoman announced, "Yesterday another chapter of communism closed with the death of Rosa Honecker, the daughter of the former head of the East German government. She passed away at San Diego's Balboa Naval Hospital, succumbing to a deadly form of a parasite. She was given important medals by the East German government and hailed as a true daughter of the motherland. She renounced communism and lived with her partner, Billy Durant, an economist, in La Jolla. In other breaking news, a massive car pileup on Interstate Five left ten dead…"

I should get a front-door funeral wreath, I thought, *in case the police come by. A little sympathy helps if they ask questions.*

I was sitting glumly on the deck, watching the ocean, and wondering what to do with her clothes and personal effects when I heard the phone ring. It was Professor Keynes.

"Please accept my condolences for your loss. Will there be a service? I know some of my colleagues might like to attend. She was famous."

"The funeral service hasn't been scheduled. She will be buried at the Bleeding Virgin Cemetery. It will be a Russian Orthodox service."

"Russian Orthodox is appropriate, given her past history with the Soviet Union. Will you be having a dinner on her grave?"

"What?" I almost shouted into the phone.

"I understand that's a traditional part of the service," said Keynes.

"No!" I would have to contact Father Kirill to make sure it didn't take place. "There will be no dinner. I will let you know the time and day."

"I realize you're grieving, but I want you to know that the faculty met yesterday and voted to offer you the job. Your publishing record is astonishing."

Happy at the news about the job, I called Father Kirill about the grave-yard dinner.

"Yes, it is a tradition to serve *koliva* and vodka," the father said. "We work with a local restaurant to prepare it. I was going to contact you about the number of dishes and so on."

"*Koliva*. What's that?"

"Simple dish made with wheat berries, nuts, and sugar. The restaurant will cater it."

What, I thought, *the church wants every last penny out of me.*

"No, I don't want *koliva* or vodka at the grave. I could be the only one attending."

"We've been contacted by people from all over the world asking about the service," informed Father Kirill. "Have you thought about a reception and dinner afterward? We could fly in food from the Petrossian Restaurant in New York City. We do that at for our best services. Nothing is too good for a famous woman like Rosa."

"No dinner and reception, no graveside vodka," I told the priest.

Hanging up, I looked at the clock and decided that flower shops would now be open. I called La Jolla Florist, and they told me that I could pick up a front-door wreath in the afternoon.

I spent the rest of the morning packing away Rosa's clothes. I then drove to the florist and, returning, put the wreath on my front door.

Now all the neighbors knew that I was grieving. Soon they were knocking on my door, bringing food, and offering comforting words.

Feeling a pit of loneliness, I rattled around the house. I started drinking and taking more Valium. I passed out early and woke early Sunday morning.

I could hear an engine on the beach. I went out on the deck in the early morning light and saw a backhoe moving a boulder. Police and medical personnel stood around.

Chapter Fifty-Three

The Frisbee game was suddenly interrupted by a rainstorm blowing off the Pacific and sending students running for shelter. It was September 2, 2002 and I was moving into my new university office. I opened a box of academic awards and arranged them on a table near the window. Then I found the shoe box of photos from my early years. I stared at one showing Toots posed on the hood of a 1954 chartreuse and black Chevrolet Bel Air, wearing a black skirt and white blouse with a plunging neckline.

Not bad looking for forty-two, I thought, looking at Toots, a cigarette in her mouth and skirt suggestively pulled up to her knees. I felt a slight wave of desire.

With Rosa gone, I imagined a bleak and lonely year. All my money problems would be over by next January, promised my lawyer and the Goldman Sachs money manager. I was using money from my investments to pay the house mortgage and expenses. My new salary would help.

The police had started hounding me about John's death. They'd knocked on doors throughout the neighborhood after his body had been found. When they came to my house, they had expressed sympathy for Rosa's death before asking if I knew anything. I had told them that I'd gone to John's house early in the evening of his death to tell him about Rosa dying. I didn't see anything unusual in John's house and left early, worried about Rosa and wanting to lose myself in sleep.

Afterward the police had ignored me until, for reasons I don't know, they started coming back and asking me more questions. Last week they had told me that I was a "person of interest" in the murder and that I shouldn't leave the area without telling them.

Putting my Ayn Rand books away, I started thinking about of the consequences of working for the Smith brothers. Were my advertisement and policy propaganda on gun ownership leading to more violence? Last week two billionaire heads of tech companies had actually dueled in a San Francisco bar for control of each other's companies. They had both died, with five others injured from ricocheting bullets.

Failing mutual attempts at hostile takeovers, these two company heads had agreed to mimic the popular video game OK Corral, which required counting off twenty paces, turning, and shooting revolvers with one bullet in each cylinder. The duel had taken place at the famous Silicon Valley Bar. Many had believed that nothing would happen, given the shooters' vision problems and the use of only one bullet. Odds were posted in Las Vegas and online betting sites.

Lifelong cheaters, known for stealing patents and exploiting foreign workers, they had both hidden semiautomatic Beretta 9000s with twelve-bullet magazines under their shirts. After they had both missed with the single-shot pistols, they had unleashed a fusillade, with bullets bouncing off the bar and walls. To a cheering group of their workers, who had been drinking heavily at the bar and making bets, the corporate heads had been pronounced dead.

Those accidently wounded would later proudly show off their scars from the famous shootout. Inevitably T-shirts appeared on the market displaying two dead men straddled by a John Wayne gun shooter figure under the banner "Silicon Valley bar duel" and the words "Too much data leads to death."

Did I help create, I worried, *this violent America?*

I was relieved that the state legislature, because of the Silicon Valley bar duel, called an emergency session to restrict gun ownership. Few believed the National Rifle Association's claim that gun ownership would reduce violence.

I was surprised when my proposed Ayn Rand seminar was oversubscribed by students. I had wondered if anyone would be interested. The seminar attracted economics and American history students along with peaceniks and neoanarchists. In addition, Professor Keynes scheduled me for a series of campus lectures on the failure of communism, free markets, democracy, and world religions to provide human happiness.

When I met with the seminar the next day, I was reminded of discussions at the Green Door Coffeehouse back in the 1960s. One student, James Albright, who was like Phil Anderson, raised the basic question of whether or not individualism and pursuit of self-interest could create a just world.

"Remember the words from *The Fountainhead*," I said and quoted, "'Self-sacrifice? But it is precisely the self that cannot and must not be sacrificed.' Don't confuse helping others with self-interest."

"But for me to be free," Albright pressed the issue, "I need others to help."

Again quoting *The Fountainhead*, I replied, "Freedom is 'To ask nothing. To expect nothing. To depend on nothing.'"

After the seminar, I finished unpacking and found a special place for my old shoe box of photos. That evening I gave a lecture on the nature of evil in free markets.

Shortly after I arrived at my office the next morning, there was a sharp knock at my door.

"Professor Durant," a young co-ed, wearing tight shorts and a revealing blouse, introduced herself. "My name is Sally Bowles. Do you have time to talk? I was disturbed by your lecture on evil last night."

"What bothered you?" I pointed to a chair for her to sit in."

She sounded nervous and uncertain of herself. "I was upset by your definition of evil. It caused me nightmares."

Her young body, blond hair, and movie-quality face excited me.

"What about it?"

"I could see your point that human evil involves hurting other humans," she said, shifting in her chair. "Do you have any water? I'm nervous."

"Yes, that's what I said." I got up, took a bottle of mineral water from my office fridge, and gave it to her. "Why are you nervous?"

"Did you ever want to kill?"

"Yes," I hesitated, worried she might drag up something from my past. "I think most people at one time or another have those feelings; nothing to worry about."

"I dream of killing," she said, leaning forward and revealing more of her young breasts.

"Before you go any further, remember that this is not a lawyer or doctor's office. Our conversation is not confidential," I warned. "On the other hand, I'm not going to tell anyone about it."

"I know, but you're old and probably understand. I need to talk to someone."

"There is the wisdom of age," I chuckled. "But still be cautious about talking to people about killing. You never know."

"Are you laughing at me?" she almost shouted.

"No, I was thinking; it is a question I've been pondering my whole life. And now you have to deal with it."

"Have you ever killed?" she asked, fidgeting in her chair.

I paused, wondering how to answer. Should I tell the truth or a partial truth? Did it matter at my age?

"Yes," I finally said. "Many times. But I'm not going into details."

"Many times!" she gasped. "Is that why you said you are evil?"

"Yes, but what about you? Why are you plagued with worries about evil at your age?"

"You said that evil was always with us. It is hard to do something without hurting others."

"Yes, that's the lesson of the free market and Randian individualism. All religions are evil in the end, hurting others. You should come to my seminars on Ayn Rand, who basically was proposing a philosophy of evil."

"I killed my boyfriend." She suddenly burst out in tears. "What should I do?"

"What do you mean? Remember, this is not confidential. Did you kill him accidently or on purpose? My mother killed her boyfriend in a car crash. Maybe you should see a college counselor."

"Fuck, they're no good. I don't think any have killed. You don't know until you've done it yourself."

"That's probably true," I agreed. "You still didn't answer my question—was it an accident?"

"Can I trust you?"

"No, you can never trust anyone. But I've killed, and I'm old and, frankly, don't give a shit. Feel free to confess."

"Is there some place else we can talk? I'm worried about being heard in the hallway or someone coming in."

"We could go to my house and have a drink."

"Are you a dirty old man?" Sally looked at me intently. "I'm twenty, never been with a guy your age."

"That wasn't a proposition," I replied defensively. "I do have those feelings, but you're too young. Don't worry—no one to hear us at my place. My wife passed."

As I drove her to my house, I wondered what I was doing. Once inside the house, Sally looked at the many photos taken around the world of Rosa and Rosa and myself.

"What would you like to drink?" I asked, leading us into the kitchen.

"Juice of some sort would be fine." Sally stopped in front of a photo of Rosa on the kitchen wall and dropped her backpack on the floor. I poured two glasses of orange juice.

"What's that uniform she's wearing? It looks like something from an old movie."

"She was in the Stasi. Older than you but still in her twenties when the photo was taken."

"Stasi?"

"You're too young to know. The Stasi was the East German communist secret police."

"Wow, she was in the secret police." Sally stared admiringly. "What are all those medals?"

"She got many for her dedication to the motherland. Let's go on the deck and talk."

We took our drinks outside, sat around a table, and stared at each other.

"Did she kill in the secret police?"

"Yes, but I don't want to talk about Rosa; it's too painful. She's the only person I ever loved, including my parents."

"I hate my parents; my father is abusive. I should've gone to the police."

"What's this about killing your boyfriend?" I smiled, admiring her body.

Looking down at her feet, Sally mumbled, "Poisoned him with an overdose. Police didn't blame or suspect me. I'm haunted, worried I'll get caught."

"Why?"

"He started acting my like father. He hit me. We'd just used some heroin. It didn't mellow him out. He just got angry and started beating me. When he went to the bathroom, I dumped the whole bag into his drink along with some sleeping pills I had. He came stumbling back from the bathroom before finishing peeing. I'll always remember his piss spraying me. He drank the whole thing and grabbed at me."

"No one saw you leave or arrive with him?"

"I slipped out," she said, "as he began stumbling around holding on to the walls. His apartment is near campus. No one saw me."

"So you feel evil." I moved my chair around so that I could put my hand on her leg. "Did you report it to the police?"

"He was found dead a few days later. His parents told police he'd been depressed about grades. They had worried he'd do something. Investigators found notes on his computer about death and located Google searches on suicide. I was lucky."

"You didn't leave any evidence?"

She didn't resist as I stroked her leg.

"When he started staggering and losing control, I cleaned my glass and wiped anything I had touched. I went to class late and signed the attendance sheet in the back of the room. The prof never noticed I was late. That was my alibi—but no one asked."

She took my hand off her leg, kissed it, and hugged it against her cheek before putting it down on the tabletop. "I worry about getting caught and going to jail. Don't killers always get caught?"

"Not always; in fact, the smart ones get away with it." I looked at her. I was disappointed at being rejected but not surprised. "Look at all the corporate execs and politicians; they get away with murder, claiming their actions are for stockholders or in the national interest."

"Which is the greater evil, killing or not admitting to it? I have nightmares about both."

"Are you religious? That could explain your worries about confession and punishment." I stood up and went into the kitchen for more juice. When I returned, she was standing looking at the horizon.

"Shouldn't I be punished?" Sally turned, moving toward me.

"Punishment means hurting you. I would consider that evil. Should one evil lead to another?"

"But doesn't it keep people from being evil? I'm scared of prison."

"I don't think there's much proof in history." I groaned as she pressed her body against mine. "People keep being evil. Nations hurt others."

"So," whispered Sally in my ear, "I shouldn't feel guilty. I should kill my father."

"Guilt could be in the human psyche as part of evolutionary protection of the species. We're never able to get rid of it." I could feel myself getting hard. "I wanted to kill and fuck my mother all at the same time."

"My father raped and beat me," Sally coldly related.

"They say parental love," I smiled, "is unconditional. Mother-love keeps babies alive; it protects the species."

"We both know that's not true," Sally said, pressing harder.

"Maybe evil passes from generation to generation; evil parents produce evil kids." I stared down at her breasts nestled against my chest.

"Do you know the real reason I stopped by your office? You reminded me of my father." She put her lips on mine.

"You didn't kill your boyfriend? You're just interested in me?" I put my arms around her.

"I killed him. I liked it. I like evil. I liked your talk on evil. I want you."

"I'm too old." I started pushing her away, thinking that this might cost me my new job.

"Not for that. For this."

I felt a sharp pain as she shoved a knife into my heart. My mind was flooded with images of all those I'd killed.

Sally

"You're like all the other fuckers. Just like my father. I'll get away with this. I looked. No one saw us come in together. Who'd think of me as a killer? Everyone says what a good girl I am."

I bent down and pulled out the knife.

Looking down at his body, I concluded that it would be impossible for me to dispose of the corpse and clean up the blood. I decided to leave it for someone else.

"You fucker," I said, stepping away from the professor's body. "I did attend your Ayn Rand seminar; I hid in a corner. You never noticed me. I tried to ask about individualism and evil, but that guy, Albright, kept interrupting with individualism and social-justice crap."

I took the knife and the glasses into the kitchen. Taking my gloves from the backpack that I'd left on the kitchen floor, I methodically cleaned my glass, put it back in the cabinet, and left the professor's in the sink. I wiped down all surfaces, including doorknobs, I'd been near to remove any possible fingerprints. Cleaning the knife, I put it in my backpack; I planned to throw it in a college Dumpster.

Who'd know, if anyone found it, I thought, *what it was used for?*

I took a binder from my backpack and opened to the notes I'd taken in the Ayn Rand seminar and read, "I'm free to create my life. I'm free to be me and not someone molded by others. If I hurt others, that's evil. But everything I do hurts others; even eating takes food from the starving. I must be evil to exist. Therefore, I am."